THE QUEEN OF BLOOD

BOOK ONE OF THE QUEENS OF RENTHIA

SARAH BETH DURST

HARPER Voyager
An Imprint of HarperCollins Publishers

Excerpt from *The Reluctant Queen* copyright © 2017 by Sarah Beth Durst.

THE QUEEN OF BLOOD. Copyright © 2016 by Sarah Beth Durst. All rights reserved. Printed in the United States of America. No part of this book may be used or reproduced in any manner whatsoever without written permission except in the case of brief quotations embodied in critical articles and reviews. For information, address HarperCollins Publishers, 195 Broadway, New York, NY 10007.

First Harper Voyager mass market printing: May 2017
First Harper Voyager hardcover printing: September 2016

ISBN 978-0-06-247409-4

Cover art by Stephan Martiniere
Map illustration by Ashley P. Halsey

Harper Voyager and) are trademarks of HCP LLC.

22 23 24 25 26 LSC 10 9 8 7 6

By Sarah Beth Durst

THE QUEEN OF BLOOD

Coming July 2017
THE RELUCTANT QUEEN

FOR RICK KEULER

THE
QUEEN
OF
BLOOD

CHAPTER 1

> *Don't trust the fire, for it will burn you.*
> *Don't trust the ice, for it will freeze you.*
> *Don't trust the water, for it will drown you.*
> *Don't trust the air, for it will choke you.*
> *Don't trust the earth, for it will bury you.*
> *Don't trust the trees, for they will rip you,*
> *rend you, tear you, kill you dead.*

It's a child's chant. You jump over a rope, faster and faster, as you name the spirits. Trip on the rope, and that is the spirit that someday will kill you. Fire, ice, water, air, earth, or wood.

Clutching her rope, six-year-old Daleina slipped out her window and ran along the branches toward the grove, drawn to the torchlight. Her parents had said no, absolutely not, go to bed and stay there, but even then, even when she was still so young and eager to please, Daleina would not be kept from her fate. She'd run toward it, arms open, and kick fate in the face.

All the other children were already gathered on the forest floor, under the watch of the local hedgewitch. Dropping from the branches onto the moss, Daleina joined them. Her cheeks pink from her run and her hair wild from the wind, she swung her rope and began the chant. *"Don't trust the fire . . ."*

Ribbons fluttered around them, bright colors to represent each of the six spirits. Buried beneath the ribbon poles and dangling around them and between the torches were charms. The children's chant and the ribbons would tempt the spirits, but the charms would repel them. It was as safe as the hedgewitch knew how to make it, and she smiled at the children as she circled counterclockwise and spoke the words of protection as she'd been taught.

The children jumped faster, repeating the chant. At least two dozen girls and boys, the youngest six years old and the oldest twelve, had come to the grove to prophesy their future. Some were dressed in their finest, with lace in their hair and starch in their shirts, blessed with their parents' approval. Others, like Daleina, wore their nightshirts and dresses and had uncombed hair and bare feet.

As she skipped, Daleina saw the first tree spirit poke its sharp nose between the leaves. It scurried over the branches and hung upside down to watch them, its shadow large in the torchlight. *"Don't trust the water . . ."* Another wood spirit separated from the trunk of a tree, its bulbous body covered in a thick mat of moss and leaves. Teasing the edges of the charms, an earth spirit, hairless and brown, bared its rock-like teeth. *"Don't trust the air . . ."*

One child faltered.

Another fell.

Like Daleina, they'd seen the spirits emerge from the dark forest and encircle the grove. *"Don't trust the earth . . ."* Her bare feet squished on the soft ground. It had rained a few hours before, and mud stained her toes. She imagined an earth spirit reaching up through the muck to grab her ankle, and an air spirit swooping her into the air and dropping her from high above. Squeezing her eyes shut, she kept jumping. *"Don't trust the trees . . ."*

Because her eyes were closed, she didn't see when the tiny tree spirit launched itself off its branch and over the charms, or when the other children stumbled and fell, every one of them, tripping on their ropes. ". . . *rip you, rend you, tear you . . .*"

Hers was the only voice, until the screaming began.

She opened her eyes as the hedgewitch shouted and the children shrieked. Blood stained the woman's bodice, and the gnarled, leaf-coated creature clung to her shoulder. Daleina's foot stuck in the mud and she forgot to jump as the rope swung down.

Her parents ran toward her—her mother first, with a knife—and sliced the rope as it swung toward Daleina's motionless feet. The two halves of the rope fell on either side of her.

Other villagers poured into the grove. Swarming past Daleina and her parents, the others scooped up their own children. Several hurried to help the hedgewitch. Still clutching the ends of the limp rope, Daleina saw the spirit, blood on its shriveled, leafy face, flee up the trunk of an oak and then disappear into the night.

"Wood will not take you," her mother murmured into her hair. "Nor fire, nor ice, nor water, nor earth, nor air. You will live, my child. You *must* live."

"I'm fine, Mama," Daleina said.

"You were stupid." Lifting Daleina's chin, Mama forced her to meet her eyes. "Just because something is a tradition doesn't mean it's smart to do, or necessary. Promise me you won't ever endanger yourself again."

"I'll try," Daleina said, her cherubic face solemn, "but, Mama, I can't promise."

DALEINA WAS TEN YEARS OLD WHEN THE CHILDREN'S prophecies came true. She'd grown into a miniature of her mother: hair streaked with autumn-leaf colors—oranges, golds, reds, and browns—and calloused hands tan from the sun and roughened from days spent climbing through the village. She'd been charged with taking care of her younger sister, Arin, who was four.

On that afternoon, Daleina was leading her sister home from school. The sun filtered through the leaves and laid a patchwork of green and yellow shadows across the tree trunks and the huts and over Daleina's bare arms and legs as she clambered up the branches.

"Come on, Arin, keep up!" she called.

"When I'm older than you, I'm going to tell *you* what to do." Arin hooked her harness clips over a branch and scrambled her pudgy legs on top of it. Her cheeks puffed with the effort.

"You can't be older than me."

"Can too. Got a birthday and then another and another, and I'm going to catch up. And then I'll be bigger than you, Mama said so, because I eat my oatmeal."

Reaching down, Daleina helped her sister hook onto the next branch. All of the routes through the village were marked with anchors and hooks, to help the very young and the elderly travel between the trees. "You might get bigger, but I'll still be older. I'll always be older. That's how it works." She thought she sounded very reasonable.

"Not fair!"

Oh no, she thought, *tantrum coming*. Mama said that Arin had honed her tantrums to artistic perfection: First, she'd twist her lips into a perfect rainbowlike frown, then she'd pool tears on her lashes. Her face would flush pink, with darker rose staining her plump cheeks. As the pink deepened, she'd begin on the whimpers. She wouldn't scream, not outside—it wasn't safe—but she'd bleat, like a beaten lamb, until whatever neighbor was closest came out to see who was torturing the poor, innocent, angelic Arin. "If you cry, I'll feed you to the wood spirits," Daleina told her. It was the most terrible threat she could think of.

Arin's eyes grew round, her mouth dropped open, and her lower lip quivered.

Wonderful. I made it worse.

"I won't," Daleina said quickly. "I didn't mean it. But please don't cry, Arin."

She spotted the wood spirit then, above Arin, a few trees over. It was a small one, with pale leaves poking out of its skin and berries ripening in its hair. Its eyes looked like walnuts, and its long, twiglike fingers curled around the branch it perched upon. It was watching them.

"Come on, let's get home." She eyed the spirit—it didn't seem to be moving any closer, but she didn't like that it had noticed them. Mama always said to be careful never to catch their attention. When Daleina was five, her uncle had caught the eye of an unstable spirit and been torn apart in his own orchard. The rogue spirit had been caught and sent to the queen for punishment, but that didn't mean other spirits were to be trusted. This far from the capital, a lot of spirits liked to test the strength of the queen's do-no-harm command, or so people said whenever someone died unexpectedly. "I'll stay with you, but you have to try to climb a little faster, okay?"

She helped her sister shimmy up the trunk of a thick oak, boosting her so that she could wiggle onto the bridge. Backpack bouncing, Arin flopped onto it, and Daleina crawled up after her and stood. Almost home. Inhaling deeply, she breathed in the smell of pine, of mildewed leaves, of fresh laundry, and . . . ah, there it was: gingerbread! Mama had baked today, as she'd promised.

The laundry smell was from their neighbor. Near the base of the village tree, old Mistress Hamby straddled two branches as she hung out her wash. Her husband was on their roof, tucking new charms in between the shingles. He waved as Daleina and Arin passed. Daleina waved back, and Arin inexplicably wiggled her elbows.

"Don't be rude," Daleina told her.

"Don't be boring," Arin shot back.

Higher up in the tree, a few of Daleina's friends called to her to come play—Juju, Sarbin, and Mina. She waved at them and pointed toward her sister. She'd have to play later, after Arin was delivered safely home. Using the rope ladders, Daleina and Arin climbed up past Mr. Yillit, who was pounding nuts to make nut flour. The fine dust coated his arms and clung to his arm hairs. He smiled and nodded at them. Arin did wave back at him. Daleina knew her sister liked Mr. Yillit because he was missing a front tooth, like Arin herself. Higher and to the left, they saw their second cousin Rosasi, who was stretched out in the crook of a branch, her bare feet stuck in a patch of sunlight, high above their house. She had a pile of knitting on her lap, though she wasn't working on it. Mama often said that Rosasi was allergic to work. But she told excellent stories, about queens and heirs and their champions. When she tucked Arin in at night, as she did sometimes when Mama had late-night whittling to do, Daleina liked to listen in from her bed in the loft.

Like the other village houses, Daleina and Arin's house was woven into the branches. Its floors and walls were living parts of the tree itself. Village history said that two generations ago, a queen had commanded the spirits to grow their village from a handful of acorns. Daleina wished she could have seen that. The only power she'd ever seen up close was the local hedgewitch, and her skill was mostly with charms, not commands. To make a tree like theirs . . . Their tree housed twenty families, in homes that budded from thick branches above and below Daleina's family's, spiraling up the massive trunk. Ladders, pulleys, and bridges connected them. In the day, it was swarmed with people, going about their business and living their lives, and at night, jars full of firemoss were lit everywhere, making the tree look like it were covered in lightning bugs. Mama liked to say there was something to love about their tree during the day and night, as well as every season. In fall, the leaves changed to red and gold, and in winter, it was laced in ice. In spring, the villagers coaxed flowers to grow in buckets and troughs of earth, spilling out of every window and covering every roof. And in summer, now, it was fat and green and heavy with swelling, unripe fruit. Mama said there were hundreds of trees like theirs in the forests of Aratay, but Daleina had never left their village. *Someday,* she promised herself, *I'll leave and see other villages, maybe a city, maybe the capital, maybe even beyond.* Up north, near the mountains of Semo, the trees were said to stand like sentinels, with white limbs that stretched straight like raised arms. And in the west, where the forest touched the untamed lands, it was said that the trees were a wild tangle so thick that nothing grew on the floor below. There were even areas of Aratay that had been abandoned to the wolves, bears, and spirits, and were full of sights that no one had seen and sounds that no one had heard for years.

I want to see it all!

Mama waited for them on their front porch. Seeing her, Arin sped across the bridge and scurried up the ladder without any help at all. Daleina followed behind.

"Any trouble?" Mama asked.

Daleina glanced back, but she didn't see the small tree spirit, only the thick mat of leaves and the west bridge. "None, except Arin's teacher said that Arin didn't eat her lunch."

"Tattler." Arin stuck out her tongue at Daleina.

"Arin, that's not polite. Also, you'll catch flies on that

if you stick it out too long." Mama wiggled a finger, fly-like, toward Arin's tongue, and Arin quickly pulled it in. "I packed your favorite lunch. Why didn't you—"

A drop of red splatted on Arin's cheek. Her fingers touched it, and she pulled her hand away and stared at her bloodstained fingertips.

For a split second, all three of them stared at it, and then Mama said, "Inside. Now."

"Mama, I'm bleeding! I'm hurt! Mama!"

She wasn't. It wasn't her blood. It was from above. The tree was raining blood. Daleina ran for the house as Mama caught Arin in her arms and ran inside. "Where's Daddy?"

Mama didn't answer. She slammed the door behind them, drove the bolt across it, and then ran to each of the windows and locked them. "Daleina, the charms, quick!"

Daleina hurried to each window, shoving charms into the crevices. She pushed them in so hard that her fingers hurt.

"Mama, where's Daddy?" Arin was crying, full out sobs.

"Hush," Mama ordered. "I don't know. He's fine. He's hiding. We have to stay inside too. Quietly." She dropped to her knees. "Please, baby, be a good, strong girl for me." Arin gulped, trying to swallow her sobs, but they burst out of her. Mama crushed her close to her breast, stroking her hair. "Shh, shh . . . Calm down, baby, calm down."

Daleina shoved charms under the door and into the fireplace, filling it, until she ran out of them; then she ran back to her mother, who wrapped her arm around Daleina too. The house began to rattle and shake.

"Your papa is hiding. Don't worry. It will all be fine," Mama said. "The spirits won't hurt us. They won't dare. The queen won't let them. 'Do no harm,' remember? It's her command. Her promise. Her duty. Trust in her. Believe in her." She rocked back and forth as Daleina and Arin clung to her. Arin sniffled against her blouse, and Daleina buried her face in her mother's hair. Outside, the screams sounded like the cries of a wounded hawk that Daleina had once heard, but louder and multiplied by a dozen. The leaves in the walls shook, and the wood in the floor cracked.

Mama held them tighter.

Daleina watched the cracks appear in the wood, chasing one another up the walls, fracturing like an eggshell as the house shuddered. The windows rattled, and Daleina saw shadows pass in front of them. Arin was shaking as hard as the walls, but she was too frightened to cry anymore.

Something pounded at the door, and Arin whimpered and burrowed deeper into their mother's lap, pushing Daleina out. She thought she heard her father's voice.

"Daddy?" Daleina whispered.

"Stay here," Mama commanded.

Daleina began to pull away. He was calling. Wasn't he? It was difficult to hear a single voice within the screams and the cries and the crashes and the thuds. Listening, she focused, trying to separate the strands of sounds—there, Daddy! She heard more pounding at the door. He was here, out there, trying to get in! Wrenching herself away from her mother, Daleina ran toward the door.

"Daleina, no!" Mama cried, her voice a rough whisper.

"It's Daddy!" She yanked at the bolt, pulling it back.

Behind her, she heard Mama push to her feet, but she was slowed by Arin, who stuck to her like a pricker bush. A weight on the door shoved it inward, and a shape fell inside, hard on his knees—*Daddy!*

A squirrel-size tree spirit clung to his shoulder, its teeth dug deep into his flesh. Daddy's face was slicked with streaks of red, and blood speckled his hair. He surged to his feet, and the spirit gripped him harder.

"Get off him!" Daleina screamed. She grabbed at the spirit's waist while Daddy pushed at its face. Its claws tore his shirt and chest. One claw sliced the back of Daleina's arm, and a thin bead of blood popped onto her skin. "Leave him alone!"

It hissed and spat.

And then Mama was there, a rolling pin in her hand. She bashed at the spirit's head and back. "Get out! Out of my house! Away from my home!"

It twisted its head and fixed its eyes beyond them.

Arin.

Releasing Daddy, it ran toward Arin, faster than any of them could grab it.

Scrambling underneath the kitchen table, Arin screamed, high and shrill.

No! Don't hurt my sister! Daleina felt as if her whole mind and body were screaming the words, as if they were ripped away from her and thrust outward. "Stop!"

And, amazingly, it did.

The spirit halted, mid-run. It pivoted its head to look directly at Daleina. Its eyes were red with veins that spread outward from its red pupil. It shifted from foot to thorny foot, hissing.

"Go away!" Daleina said. "Leave us alone."

"Again, Daleina," Mama said, her voice low, strangely calm. "It's listening to you."

"Leave us alone," she repeated.

"Again."

Leave us alone, leave us alone, leave us alone. "Leave!"

The spirit tore its gaze away to look again at Arin. Its spindly fingers reached toward her, but its feet didn't move, as if it were rooted to the wood of the floor.

"Leave us alone!" Daleina shouted, and she shoved every bit of fear and anger inside her into those three words, driving it all out through her body. She felt as if something were shattering inside her from the force of her shout.

As if the words were physically shoving it, the spirit ran, skittering and shaking out the door—and Daleina caught a glimpse of outside. The bridges were broken, swinging from the upper branches, and the nearest house had collapsed. A man in green raced from branch to branch, a sword in his hand. Before Daleina could ask what was happening and who he was, Daddy slammed the door shut, and Mama slid the bolt.

The house began to shake harder, and Daleina heard scraping at the roof, as if something were tearing the shingles and shredding the wood. Mama and Daddy dragged the cupboard in front of the door, and they upended the table and pushed it against a window.

"Command them," Mama ordered Daleina.

Squeezing her eyes shut, Daleina repeated, "Leave us alone, leave us alone, leave us alone." Thrusting the words out of her, Daleina sank to her knees. The cries outside drew back. Arin whimpered, and Mama and Daddy shushed her, and still Daleina kept chanting. The scraping on the roof stopped.

Outside, through the walls, she still heard terrible sounds, but they were more distant now.

At last—at very long last—it was quiet.

Daleina pried open her eyes. Her eyelids felt gummy, as if they'd been glued together. In the corner of the room, she saw her family. Her father was slumped against the wall, breathing heavily. Her mother was pressing a cloth hard on his arm. The cloth was soaked red. Arin was curled in a ball underneath one of the chairs. Tears had stained her cheeks so they looked slick. "Daddy?" Daleina asked.

"Did they hurt you, Ingara?" Daddy asked, pausing between each word to suck in air. "Daleina? Arin?" He winced as he tried to sit, and he clutched his side.

"They're all right, and you aren't dead, and I want to keep us all that way. Tell me how badly you're hurt," Mama commanded.

"I'll be fine." He puffed.

"Liar."

Daleina rose shakily to her feet. She looked at the door. A crack ran, jagged, through it. Her legs felt as trembly as a newborn deer's as she walked toward the door. She pressed her face to the crack, trying to see through, and saw a sliver: sunlight and green but that was all.

She pressed her ear to the door, listening.

She didn't hear screaming anymore. Or anything. Just silence. Horrible silence that was somehow worse than all the noise. Stepping back, Daleina stared at the door.

Daddy's breathing was the loudest sound.

"You need a healer," Mama said to Daddy.

"Don't," he said.

"It's quiet," Mama said, standing. Daleina thought she'd never seen her mother look like that, so fierce and frightened at the same time, and in that instant, she decided she wanted to be exactly like Mama when she grew up. "Whatever the spirits were doing, they're done."

Grabbing her wrist, he stopped her. "Or they're waiting for us to feel safe."

Mama removed his hand. "I'll never feel safe again." She took a rolling pin in one hand and a kitchen knife in the other, the long knife that she always kept sharp enough for meat. "Open it, Daleina, slowly."

Taking a breath, Daleina slid the bolt and cracked the door open. She braced herself, ready to shove it shut with all the strength in her ten-year-old body, but nothing pushed against the door. She inched it open more and peeked outside.

What she saw didn't make sense.

Widening the door, she stared out and tried to understand. All she saw was trees, just the unclaimed forest, thick with trunks. No bridges. No houses. Leaning out, she looked up—all the higher branches had been shorn off the tree. Only their house was still attached. She looked down, down, straight down to the forest floor. A mass of broken boards lay tangled on the forest floor. She saw a chair and a table, upturned. Clothes were strewn between the branches, like ribbons leftover from a birthday party.

"Are they out there?" Arin asked, still under the table.

"No," Daleina said. Her mouth felt dry, as if she hadn't swallowed water in a very long time. "No one's out there."

"What do you mean, 'no one's out there'?" Mama asked, nudging Daleina aside so she could fit in the doorway. Side by side, they looked out at the pristine forest, above the wreckage. Sunset was coming, and the shadows stretched long between the trees. The wind was still, and nothing moved. No spirits. No animals. No people.

Nothing.

"Fetch the healing kit."

Daleina didn't move.

"Now."

Hurrying, Daleina ran to the cabinet over the sink. She pulled out a basket filled with bandages, tonics, and dried roots and herbs. Sunlight slid through the cracks in the closed window over the sink, as if it were a beautiful, ordinary day outside. Daleina didn't want to open the window.

"Mama?" Arin asked. "What are we going to do?"

"First, we fix up your father." Returning to Daddy, Mama opened his vest and peeled his shirt away from blood-sticky skin. "And then we go out and see."

"See what?"

"If there's anyone left," Mama said.

Arin began to cry again.

Wordless, Daleina helped Mama, fetching water from the kitchen sink, as well as bandages and herbs as instructed. Mama washed out the wounds—there were many—on Daddy's neck, legs, arm. His thick clothes had blocked some of the bites, making them bruises instead of punctures, but there were still so many that his once-white shirt was speckled red all over. While Mama worked, Daleina listened for the sounds of their neighbors—surely someone had seen Daddy rush in, injured—but no one came to check on them or help them. She thought of the man in green she'd seen, or imagined.

"Spirits aren't supposed to hurt people," Arin said, her eyes glued to the bandages and Daddy's shirt. "The queen won't let them."

"I know, baby," Mama said.

"Why did she let them?" Arin asked.

"Maybe she couldn't stop them this time," Daleina said. "Maybe she was sick or distracted. Maybe she didn't know what they were doing. Maybe the spirits decided we're too far from the capital for her to know." *And maybe they're right,* she thought.

"But she's the queen," Arin said. "She's supposed to keep us all safe."

"We aren't safe here," Daddy said. "We need to find the forest guards, before the spirits come back. Alert them to the danger. Tell them there may be villagers who need healers." The fact that Daddy was able to say so much without gasping for air made Daleina feel better. She had her parents, whole and safe, and they'd take care of her and Arin. Everything would be all right, and this would become one of those stories that Rosasi told at night.

After Mama bandaged Daddy up as well as she could, she rigged the basket on the pulley—the one they used to lift heavy supplies from the forest floor—and climbed in. "Everyone, in. We stay together. Daleina . . ." Mama hesitated. "The spirits listened to you. Can you make them listen again, if you have to?"

All three of them looked at Daleina, and she shrank back. No, their parents were supposed to take care of them, not the other way around! She'd just begun to feel safe. "I . . .

I don't know." She didn't know how she'd done it, or why it had worked. She'd never been able to command spirits before, and no one in her family had ever shown any affinity for them. Maybe it was a fluke. Or a coincidence. Maybe it wasn't her at all.

"You can do it," Mama said. "You did it once; you can do it again."

Daddy smiled at her—a weak ghost of a smile, but Daleina saw it as she climbed into the basket, alongside Mama and Arin. "We always knew you were special," he said.

Arin stuck out her lower lip. "I'm special too."

"Of course, Arin." He smiled at her, a real one this time, as he climbed in with them, and then as Mama lowered the basket, his smile faded.

From the basket, it was clear that of the twenty homes that used to fill the village's tree, theirs was the only one left. All the others had been torn from their branches and then ripped apart and scattered on the forest floor. Kitchen tables, pantries, food, bowls, cups . . . beds, chests, toys, sheets, clothes . . . all the innards of two dozen homes were spilled below the trees and mixed together. Daleina saw the strand of laundry, clothes tangled in it, that belonged to old Mistress Hamby. And then she saw Mistress Hamby, her body twisted by what was once a door. Her eyes were open. She was missing her arm, and her chest . . . Daleina looked away. The basket jerked lower, and she saw more.

Legs. Arms. Faces. The faces were the worst.

"Don't look," Daddy said, but it was much too late.

Rosasi. Sweet, funny, work-averse Rosasi, who told such wonderful stories. Her throat looked like a red flower. Her hands still clutched her knitting.

She saw her friends: Juju, Sarbin . . . She didn't see Mina. Didn't want to. But she couldn't stop looking, her eyes roaming over the tangle of their torn village, until she stopped on the figure of a man in dark green, alive, walking toward them.

He was flanked by two men and a woman, one in white and two in black—a healer and two guards. The man in green held a sword. His eyes swept the branches above them while the others poked through the debris.

"Over here!" Daddy called and waved.

When the strangers reached them, the man in the white healer cloak darted directly for Daddy and began checking his wounds. The two guards flanked them in protective stances while the man in green considered them and their intact house. "Which of you has the affinity?" he asked.

Mama and Daddy both gestured at Daleina. "Our daughter, sir," Daddy said. "But we didn't know it until today."

The man in green looked at Daleina, and Daleina felt as if he were looking through her skin to study her bones. His eyes were pale water-blue, and his face was scarred beneath his black beard. He still held his sword, and Daleina saw it was thick with tree sap and specked with rustlike red. "She must be trained." Without waiting for a response, he said to the guards, "Take them with the other survivors."

"Oh, thank the queen, there are others!" Mama said.

The healer laid a hand on her arm. "Only a few, I'm afraid."

"Then we shouldn't say thank you," Arin said, clutching Daleina's hand. Her pudgy fingers were slick with sweat, but Daleina held on to them. "The queen didn't help us. We shouldn't thank her."

"Hush, Arin," Daddy said.

"Daleina should be queen," Arin said. "*She* kept us safe."

Mother clapped a hand over Arin's mouth. "Arin! Quiet! This is a *champion*!"

Daleina stared at the man in green—she'd never seen a champion before. There were only a few, charged with training the heirs and protecting the queen. She never imagined one would be in her village, or what was left of her village.

For a brief instant, she imagined him sweeping her away, taking her to the capital, and proclaiming her his chosen candidate. It happened that way in the tales: a champion would appear in a tiny village, test the children, and pluck one to be trained to become an heir, and the heirs became legends themselves, creating villages, securing the borders, and keeping the spirits in check, in conjunction with the queen. She imagined herself in the palace, a circle of golden leaves on her head, with her family beside her, safe because of her power. Never again huddling afraid in a hut in a tree.

Her story should have begun right then, in that moment. Fate had declared that her power would emerge in her village's tragedy, and chance had put the champion in the nearby trees at the moment the spirits attacked, too late to save the village but in time to meet Daleina. It should have been the beginning of a legend, the moment he recognized her potential and she embraced her future with both arms.

But it wasn't.

The champion looked away, across the ruined village and the broken bodies. "Only the best can become queen. And she is not the best." Daleina felt his words hit like slaps, and then he added the worst blow of all: "If she were, these people would still be alive."

Champion Ven knelt in the ruins of the village. Sifting through the rubble, he lifted out a broken doll, its pink dress streaked with dirt and its pottery face cracked.

There was always a broken doll.

Why did there always have to be a damn doll?

Other stuff didn't bother him—the broken dishes, the bedsheets, the clothes, all the evidence of lives lived and then cut off—but the dolls got him every time. He used to collect them, in the wake of whatever tragedy had struck this time, take them to a toymaker to be cleaned, and then give them to kids in nearby villages. After a while, though, he decided that was too morbid.

He tossed the doll aside. There weren't many survivors. Two children. A handful of adults. They'd be taken to another village, given new homes and lives. The older girl would be trained and maybe become some village's hedge-witch someday. If she was lucky, she wouldn't see anything like this again. But she'd always have nightmares.

Ven knew the nightmares well. He hated sleep. A day like this, he wasn't fond of being awake either. Straightening, he admitted that he wasn't going to find any other survivors, and the spirits weren't going to come back to let him beat on them more.

He wished he could track the ones responsible, make them pay, or at least make them understand. . . . But they'd never understand that what they'd done was wrong, and destroying the spirits would only hurt the forest and leave more people homeless.

"Champion Ven?" It was one of the guards. He'd forgotten her name. She favored an ax and left her right side open for a half second too long when she fought. She was decent with throwing knives and slept lightly, waking often to check their camp. He'd traveled with her for five days. Still didn't remember her name. "The survivors want to bury the dead."

He shook his head. "The queen will take care of it." She'd have the earth spirits subsume the village and cleanse the entire area with water spirits.

The guard flipped a piece of wood with her toe. Underneath it was a hand, gray and bloodless, already stiffening. "Like she took care of them when they were alive?"

Ven raised both his eyebrows. He knew that look could quell most people. This guard, however, was made of sterner stuff, or else she too was unnerved by how thoroughly the spirits had decimated this village to care about his best fiery expression. This village—what had it been called? Greytree?—might have been on the outskirts, but it was within Aratay's borders. It should have been safe.

The guard met Ven's eyes steadily. "Is she dead?"

He flinched at the word, picturing the queen's body broken, like one of these villagers, but it was a fair question—after a queen's death, the spirits always went wild, until the heirs called for a coronation, suspending the spirits' power. "I heard no bells." Three tolls for the death of a queen, repeated across the forest. "Even if she were, she has many capable heirs." If Queen Fara died, they would undergo the coronation ceremony, and one of them would reaffirm the queen's commands. That was the entire point of heirs, and the purpose of champions. Champions found and trained potential heirs, to ensure that Aratay would always have a queen and that the spirits would always be controlled.

Except they hadn't been controlled here, Ven thought, echoing the guard's snark.

He swore under his breath, colorfully and thoroughly.

If he wanted to be sure this didn't happen again, he had to find out *why* it had happened here, why the spirits had defied the queen, and he wasn't going to find an explanation in the outer forest. He had to go back to the capital, talk to Fara, determine why her protections had failed. He was a champion. It was his responsibility. It was the only way to find the answers he needed, the answers that these people deserved. "I'll speak to the queen."

"She must be told," the guard agreed.

"She won't be pleased to see me. I'm not welcome at the palace." He winced, aware that sounded perilously close to a whine, which was not behavior becoming a champion, especially in the wake of a tragedy he'd been unable to prevent. Assuming a sterner voice, he said, "See to it that the survivors are settled safely and then resume patrols. I'll return as soon as I can."

"Just try not to break any heirlooms."

"It was an accident," he ground out.

"You broke her *crown*."

"I thought she was being attacked!"

"She's the queen," the guard said. "She could have defended herself against a vicious twig." The queen's crown was made of twisted living branches that grew flowers every spring and leaves every summer, despite being severed from the earth. He'd thought it was turning on its wearer. He wished that story hadn't spread. It made him look like an idiot. Just because he'd *acted* like an idiot, that didn't mean all of Renthia had to know.

"Send word if there are any more attacks," he said.

The guard sobered. "Run quickly, Champion Ven."

He nodded once and then he sprinted for the nearest trunk. Using the village's anchors, he climbed up, looking back only once to see the guard kneel in the wreckage and pick up the broken doll.

IN THE CITY OF MITTRIEL, THE CAPITAL OF ARATAY, IN the heart of Renthia, the white limbs of the palace tree shone in the moonlight. The shadows seemed softer, and Ven felt as if he was coming home, even though he hated the place.

He'd traveled through midforest, watching for other signs of unrest among the spirits, but hadn't seen anything out of the ordinary. In every village and town, men and women went about their lives without fear—or at least with no more fear than usual. When you lived surrounded by mindless, powerful creatures whose primary instinct is to murder you, a little healthy fear is normal. Even champions weren't fearless. *We just carry larger knives,* Ven thought.

Crouching on a branch just outside the perimeter of the palace, Ven eyed the spirits who served the queen. Tonight there seemed to be more than usual, or maybe he was just sensitive to them. He'd never liked the way they flocked around the queen, as if they were loyal, as if they wouldn't gleefully rip her throat out if her control ever slipped. Above the north spire, two air spirits chased a banner around a pole, winding it, then unwinding it, playing with the wind. On the spiral stairs, a fire spirit lit the candles, dancing within each flame. Below, earth spirits tended to the queen's rose garden, coaxing black roses to bloom for the night.

Maybe what happened in the village was an aberration. Maybe he'd report to Queen Fara, and she would reassert her will over the perpetrators, and that would be it. He hoped it wasn't a symptom of rot hidden beneath the veneer of beauty.

Rot beneath the veneer.

It sounded so poetic when he thought of it that way.

Clearly, he'd spent too much time listening to the canopy singers and not enough time bashing things. After he had his audience with Queen Fara, he'd take a few hours in a practice ring and knock the melodrama out of his head.

"The queen wishes to know if you are lurking in her trees because you have turned assassin, or if you plan to come inside and present yourself." The voice crackled, sounding like wind between dried leaves, and Ven felt the hairs on the back of his neck stand up. He twisted to see an air spirit dangling upside down from a leaf. Its translucent wings beat fast, like a hummingbird's, and its many-faceted eyes darted up, down, left, right. He hated when she sent the spirits to speak for her.

"Tell her I'm considering my options."

Its wings fluttered faster, and Ven smelled the sweetness of wisteria and also wine. "The queen does not have a sense of humor where you are concerned."

He sighed. "I'm aware of that. I'd like an audience with Queen Fara in the Blue Room. Please ask Her Majesty to keep her archers from skewering me."

"She will consider her options."

The air spirit shot upward, rustling the leaves in its wake. Ven climbed higher, to reach one of the spiderweb-thin unbreakable wires that stretched from the outer trees to the palace core. He attached a hook and hoped the spirit had obeyed. The queen's archers were vigilant and trigger-happy, a fact that he'd appreciated when he'd been in charge of defense. He wrapped a rope around the hook and around his wrists. Kicking off, he rode the line through the air. Wind raced past his ears. No arrows fired.

He landed with a thump, unclipped, and rolled free of the rope. He straightened to the sound of slow applause. Flanked by guards, the queen walked forward, clapping, until she was framed by moonlight. She looked flawless as always, all six feet of her, with curls that tumbled artfully onto her bare shoulders and a blue-white gown that looked woven from a moonbeam. A new tiara rested on her head, a delicate metal vine with a single pearl that hung in the center of her forehead. "You always did know how to make an entrance." He'd met her shortly after she'd been crowned. He'd been a new champion, but she had already had the regal bearing of a queen.

"As do you." He dropped to one knee and bowed his head. "Your Majesty."

"Oh, rise, silly. We're old friends. Or have you forgotten that?" She held out her arms, as if she expected him to hug her like a beloved cousin. Slit above her elbows, her sleeves fell back from her arms. Looking at her bare arms, he remembered how he used to hold her—there hadn't been anything cousinly about it. Her cheeks tinted pink, and he knew she was remembering also. Dangerous thoughts.

Instead of embracing her, Ven stayed kneeling. "My queen, I bring grave news."

"And here I hoped you were visiting for old times' sake." Her voice sounded wistful, but Ven didn't trust it. She was a master at shielding her emotions. For all he knew, this pleasant greeting hid murderous rage. Or at least severe irritation. Last time he saw her, she'd been "irritated" enough to send a fire spirit after him. He'd ended up with scars on his arms from the burns, and she'd only recalled the spirit after he'd almost killed it.

"I've been on the outskirts, scouting the midforest villages—"

"Whatever for?" Queen Fara asked. "You already found me an heir. Lovely girl. Sana, is it? Sata? She trains incessantly. It's a bit insulting, frankly, as if she expects me to drop dead any moment. You should teach your candidates to have more faith in their queen."

"I train them to be ever-ready, and hope they never need it."

"Aw, now there's the charming Ven that I missed. Tell me, what did you find in those backwater villages? Lack of bathing routine? Unfamiliarity with how to cook edible food? I swear, if I had to eat one more boiled vegetable—"

"Death, Your Majesty. Your spirits betrayed you, and a village was slaughtered." He tried to keep his voice measured, reporting the news and not reliving it. He'd seen the aftermath of natural disasters before—forest fires, earthquakes, winter storms, leaving behind broken bodies and broken homes with broken dolls—but this . . . this was the largest instance of *deliberate* disaster he'd ever seen.

Queen Fara went still. "You wait until this late in the conversation to tell me?"

"There's no immediate danger. The survivors have been taken to safety, and the spirits have fled into the depths of the forest. The forest guards are watching the other villages, but so far, there haven't been any signs that the tragedy will be repeated. My concern is: why did it happen at all?"

"Indeed." She waved at her guards. "I will speak with Champion Ven in the Blue Room. You will see that we are not disturbed." Without waiting for a response—there was no need to wait; she was the queen—she swept through the hall toward the interior of the tree. Ven followed. A tiny fire spirit darted up and down the hallway, lighting the candles before her and then dousing them in her wake. It looked as if her shadow were extinguishing the flames. *Nice effect,* he thought.

Rushing ahead of her, the guards threw open the double doors to the Blue Room. Standing at attention, the guards flanked the doorway—knees bent, limbs loose, sword hilts an easy distance from their ready hands—as she and Ven entered. He felt the guards' eyes on him, cataloguing his weapons and calculating the distance between the queen, his sword, and theirs. As a champion, he was allowed to be armed in the presence of the queen. The guards didn't have to like it, though, and as someone committed to the queen's welfare, Ven approved of their mistrust.

The Blue Room was known, in whispers and in tales, as the "death-knell room"—you only requested it when you wished a private audience to speak of serious matters. Legend said that a long-ago queen learned of the death of her son in this room and ruled that from then on, the walls could only hear talk of deaths to come or deaths that have been. One version of the tale said *he* killed her. Another said the queen's son died here, in her arms, and her tears stained the walls blue. Clearly the last was untrue, as Ven knew the sap had been dyed blue as it bled from the walls and had hardened into a sheen that glistened and flickered in the candlelight. But who wanted practicality when a salacious rumor existed instead? He followed Queen Fara in.

A small octagon, the death-knell room had been carved into the center pulp of the tree. Sweeping the train of her dress so that it puddled at her feet, Queen Fara sat in the polished blue throne at one end of the chamber. "Leave us," she told the guards. Bowing, they shut the door behind them.

Ven was aware there were no windows in the room. If she sent a spirit after him, he'd have to fight, again. But it wasn't going to come to that. This wasn't a personal visit, and he had no desire to restart their old argument. He was merely a messenger.

He hoped.

"Tell me everything," she commanded.

He told her about how he'd been ten miles away from the village of Greytree when he noticed that the usual spirits were absent. More than that, the forest animals were hiding, and the birds were silent. He'd tracked the silence, but by the time he found the source, the slaughter was nearly over. The spirits had killed everyone they could find, right down to the babies, and torn the houses from their branches. He'd fought the spirits who remained and called for the forest guards for help. Two were nearby—he'd been traveling with them off and on for the prior week—as well as a healer. "Much of the credit belongs to them."

"You undervalue yourself," Queen Fara murmured. "You're a hero, drawn to defend the defenseless. It's admirable." But she didn't sound as if she were complimenting him, or even listening to him. She stared at the walls and pressed her lips together.

Ven waited while she thought. He used to believe he could tell what she was thinking; he didn't delude himself about that anymore.

"Have you told me everything?" she asked.

"One family of survivors saved themselves. The older daughter, who apparently never showed any affinity for spirits before, was able to keep their home intact. I advised she be trained."

"How old?"

"About nine." He thought back to the girl. She'd been as tall as her mother's shoulder, with still-round childlike cheeks. Fierce but afraid—and rightfully so. "Possibly ten."

"And just showing power for the first time? Then she wouldn't have spoken with them."

He assumed she meant the spirits. It took power and training to summon spirits who were sophisticated enough to speak, and more skill to coerce them to communicate if they didn't want to. "She wasn't able to protect anyone but her family. Her influence ended at her house. Someday, some village will be lucky to have her as a hedgewitch, though I doubt she'll ever say the way she found her power was 'lucky.'"

"Good. And now have you told me all?"

He reviewed the details in his head. "Yes, Your Majesty."

"Then I will send earth spirits to bury the village and will wipe its name from the maps." She sighed, and the word Ven thought of was "wistful," which was an odd way to feel after a massacre. Ven expected shock, outrage, or even disbelief. "I only wish I could wipe the memory from your mind as well. Believe me when I say I wish it had not been you."

"Your Majesty, it could be indicative of a larger problem—"

"There's no 'larger problem.'"

He wanted to let the matter drop at that—he'd informed his queen; his duty was done—but he thought of that broken doll, and the way the little sister spoke about the queen. "We need to know why the spirits disobeyed you—"

"The spirits did not disobey me, Ven." Queen Fara rose. On the dais with the throne, she towered over him, and her shadow stretched blue across the room. "They never disobey me, and you must never suggest that they do. It would weaken our people's faith and endanger us all."

He appreciated her confidence, but he'd seen the evidence with his own eyes. "But—"

"There were traitors in that village, several who plotted against Aratay, against us. It was a breeding ground for betrayal. I have eliminated the threat." She closed the gap between her and Ven, her gown swishing on the floor. Laying her hand on Ven's cheek, she said, "I am sorry you were a witness to it. But I am not sorry for doing what had to be done. A queen must make sacrifices for the greater good."

Ven shifted back so that her hand fell from his cheek. His skin felt burned where she had touched him, and he didn't believe her. She couldn't have caused that tragedy. She'd never have gone that far. "There were children. Elderly. Innocents. You can't tell me the entire village was guilty of treason."

"Enough were. It had to be done."

"There had to have been another way!"

"Don't get agitated, Ven—"

"I am very agitated!" Ven paced through the Blue Room. He didn't want to look into her eyes anymore, her beautiful, guiltless eyes. She hadn't been there. She didn't understand the horror the spirits could inflict . . . *Except that she does understand,* he thought, *because she's queen.* He knew how extensive her training had been. "You are supposed to protect your people, all your people, from the spirits. You aren't supposed to use the spirits against them! Ever. No matter the crime. No matter the danger."

"Oh, you are so tiresome, Ven. I did what I had to do. Do you think I don't feel guilt? Sorrow? Anger? I do! I hate that I must make these choices, but I don't run from them. Like you did, fleeing to the outer villages—don't try to pretend it was anything else. I stay and do what's best for *all* my people, not a few, not myself, not the ones that I like best. That's what it means to be queen."

"There must have been another way!" he repeated.

"It was the best way for all our people."

"How do you even know there were traitors—"

She cut him off again. "I have ways, Ven. Ears in places you can't imagine. Voices that whisper to me on the wind. There are no secrets that are safe from me."

He quit pacing and stared at her again. "You're using the spirits to spy on your people?" This was getting worse and worse. If people knew . . . "Why are you telling me this? You know I won't approve. Can't approve. What you did . . . it was outside of your promises to the Crown. You know I can't allow you to do this ever again. The council must be told, and they will rule—"

"You will not tell them," Queen Fara said.

"Fara, I'm sorry, but I must."

"You don't have the right to call me that anymore."

More softly, he said, "Your Majesty. Can't you see what you are doing is wrong? Using the spirits to spy on your own people? Using them as weapons against your own people?" *Rot beneath the veneer,* he thought.

She laughed, a brittle sound that was devoid of even a

shred of humor. "You ask why I told you: I hoped you'd understand. Oh, Ven, I hoped you'd stand beside me, that we'd be as we once were. I hoped you'd see the need for silence."

No. Ven didn't believe her. It didn't make sense, and he believed strongly in things making sense. If that was her goal, she'd never have confessed to something she knew he'd find abhorrent. She'd never have told him she was responsible for all those deaths. . . . He thought of that family again, of the look in the littlest girl's eyes, and he couldn't imagine what Fara's game was or why she was trying to manipulate him. What he did know was that when he came bearing tales of death and horror, he expected a different response, especially since he did not believe either that the villagers were traitors or that she'd intentionally caused their deaths. "If you value what we were at all, don't lie to me."

Her false smile faded. "The truth then? I cannot allow you to speak to the council. What happened in Greytree was a tragedy—a random, isolated accident—and it must stay exactly that. It cannot be linked to me, and you must *never* suggest to anyone, much less the council, that my power is failing. It is *not*, and to bring a formal accusation . . . Raising such doubts about me would have catastrophic repercussions."

"I have a duty to Aratay, to the council, to the throne—"

"To me!"

"To our people!"

"Then you give me no choice. I must discredit you. Champion Ven, you are hereby stripped of your seat on the Council of Champions. You are exiled from the palace, in full disgrace, with all rights to a private audience with the queen suspended."

He'd thought he'd seen enough of the world that he couldn't be shocked—he, Ven, one of the Queen's Champions, was supposed to be hard and experienced, or at least bitter and jaded—but he felt like a just-born chick caught in the talons of a hawk, too stunned to even squawk. He hadn't committed any crime. He'd never betrayed his queen, even when he disagreed with her, even now. She couldn't—

"I will tell the council that you became distraught and attacked me," she continued, "after I rejected your attempts to rekindle our romance. Any attempt you make to speak against me will be dismissed as the bitter rantings of an ex-lover. You will have no credibility with the other champions or anyone. Between what's known of our past history and the testimony of the guards who witnessed your violent attack on my royal person, everyone will believe me, and peace will be preserved."

"Violent attack . . . ? I would never—"

She raised her voice. "Guards!"

From the lit candles, the fire spirits flew at him. Three of them, each tiny, their bodies made of flame, their eyes like coal, their claws like diamonds. He drew his sword, slowly, his muscles not believing that she was doing this. One of the spirits latched on to his arm, its claws digging into his muscle. He burst into motion kicking and slicing at the spirits, as the door to the Blue Room burst open and the guards spilled in.

All the while, Queen Fara watched from the throne. He thought he saw sorrow in her eyes.

The entrance exam to Northeast Academy was always conducted in front of an audience. Guards were arrayed around the bleachers to minimize the danger to onlookers, and the bleachers themselves kept the audience off the forest floor, but no one pretended it was safe, which was why Daleina did not like that her parents had brought her little sister, Arin, now nine years old, to watch. The three of them were squeezed into the back row—the wealthy parents had secured the better seats, in the center, with a thick layer of other viewers between them and the trees. In the back, Arin was popping bits of crumbled cookie into her mouth, and their mother had bundled her in three sweaters and two scarves.

As an applicant, Daleina wore a white tunic, only a thin layer between her skin and the cold. Goose bumps crowded her arms and legs, and she tried not to noticeably shiver. The other applicants didn't seem bothered by the almost-winter chill—white blossoms of frost had coated the glass windows in the morning and had made the fallen leaves crisp and shrivel. The others were chatting and laughing, clustered by the judges' table. There were about twenty girls, all approximately fifteen years old, like Daleina. Many of them seemed to know one another already. She tried to smile at a few of them, and a few smiled back before they returned to chatting with the others. Others returned much colder looks.

She was the outsider, she supposed—the only girl from the outer villages. For the last five years, she'd been the assistant to Mistress Baria, the local hedgewitch in the village her family had settled in, tasked with gathering herbs and mixing charms and keeping the shop clean, because the hedgewitch's joints bothered her. She was only allowed to practice commands once a week, while Mistress Baria monitored her attempts, in order to make sure she summoned only small, stupid spirits with weak wills, who could be easily dismissed with a few words and charms. Outside the academy, waiting with the other girls, Daleina was acutely aware that her training was, at best, minimal.

But that's why I'm here—to change that, to learn, to test myself. To be more.

Looking up in the stands, Daleina met Arin's eyes. Bouncing in her seat, Arin waved with both arms. It was Arin who had convinced her she was ready. The hedgewitch said she wasn't, but Arin argued she just didn't want to lose her assistant. Daleina had been paid in lessons, a bargain for the hedgewitch. *She'll just have to dust her own cobwebs,* Arin had said, *or make friends with the spiders. You're supposed to be a student, not a servant. You have to do this!*

And so Daleina had announced to her parents that she was ready, and here they all were.

Daleina couldn't help wondering if Mistress Baria was right. She didn't feel ready anymore. She studied the row of judges: five older women, all in black, with hair slicked away from their faces. One had a scar on her cheek. Another had tattoos across her neck, obscuring bunched tissue from old burns. The oldest woman only had one arm. The other empty sleeve was pinned to her blouse. Other teachers were lined up on the side—they'd be the ones to administer the exam. All of them sported scars too and wore uniforms that emphasized them: the ones with arm scars were sleeveless, one with a scar across her stomach wore an open tunic that exposed it, and another had painted her false leg a brilliant red, broadcasting how dangerous this life was. *Not very subtle,* Daleina thought, and looked instead at the other girls again. One with gleaming black hair and a brittle smile stood out. She was at the center of the pack, and every time she spoke, the others rotated to listen to her, as if she were the sun and they were in orbit. Briefly, as if she felt Daleina looking at her, the black-haired girl met her eyes. Daleina tried a smile, but the girl focused instead on another applicant and laughed at words that Daleina couldn't hear.

High up in the trees, a bell rang. Several birds startled from the branches and fled upward, breaking the canopy above the academy. Daleina wondered what the academy looked like inside—it was supposed to be breathtakingly beautiful, as lovely as the palace itself. If she passed, she'd see it for herself before the end of the day. If not, she'd never know.

A woman walked out from a gap in the wall of trees. She wore a black gown edged with dark-green lace. Her white-gray hair was knotted on top of her head. She had no visible scars, but her dress fell to her ankles and the sleeves covered her hands. She carried a slim, unsheathed knife with a jeweled handle. "Applicants, I am Headmistress Hanna. Welcome to the entrance examination for Northeast Academy."

Daleina straightened. This was the headmistress! The woman who had trained Queen Fara before she was chosen. The woman who had predicted and survived the Massacre of the Oaks. The woman who had presided over three coronation ceremonies and witnessed the deaths of two queens. She'd had songs written about her. Daleina wondered if it was wonderful or tedious to listen to songs about yourself.

I suppose it depends on how well they're sung.

Pacing in front of the girls, the headmistress studied each

of them in turn. Daleina told herself not to flinch as Headmistress Hanna's eyes landed on her, then passed on. "You are here to begin on the path to a glorious destiny, but not all of you will walk that path. Be full of courage, full of strength, full of cleverness, and full of compassion, and you will thrive."

Daleina let the words roll over her and fill her. She would be fearless! She would be strong! She wouldn't fail! And yet even as she thought that, she couldn't help but hope her mother didn't embroider the headmistress's words on a pillow. Mama liked to embroider, especially after she finished a difficult whittling job. Their house was filled with platitudes, embellished with tiny roses and stars. Words comforted her, she said, when wood failed to.

Headmistress Hanna was still talking. *Pay attention,* Daleina scolded herself. She shot another look at her parents and sister. Part of her wished she were still home in bed, surrounded by Mama's embroidered pillows. ". . . begin your path, you must *find* your path," Headmistress Hanna was saying. "Your exam is simple: find your way through the maze." As the onlookers gasped, the headmistress plunged her blade into the nearest tree. It sank in, and sap oozed. Above, an unseen spirit shrieked, and a crack spread below and above the knife blade.

With an echoing snap, the tree split apart, and the crack yawned open. The knife clattered to the ground at the base of the gap. Whispering to one another, the girls clustered together and inched forward.

The gap was only wide enough to fit one at a time, and through it was darkness. Daleina looked up. She couldn't see beyond the thick weave of branches to tell what was on the other side of the gap: open sunlight or suffocating shadows, towering trees or a snarl of brambles.

"Who will enter first?" Headmistress Hanna asked.

Daleina squared her shoulders, took three deep breaths, tried not to look back at her family, and prepared to take a step forward—but the black-haired girl was already striding through the clump of applicants, elbowing the others out of her way. She stopped in front of the headmistress. "My name is Merecot," the girl said, "and I will conquer your maze."

"That's excellent," the headmistress said, "but I don't care who you are until you come out the other side. Leave any weapons behind. You go in with only your mind, heart, and soul."

The black-haired girl, Merecot, pulled a knife out of her waistband, then bent down and removed a dagger that had been secured to her ankle. Raising her tunic, she unstrapped another from her thigh. Her eyes fixed on the headmistress, she also extracted a needle-thin blade from within her hair and then removed a coil of metal from around her upper arm. She dropped it all in a pile her feet. Daleina had only one knife. She again felt unprepared.

"One other thing: you will be timed," the headmistress said. "Go now."

Merecot pivoted and ran into the maze.

Another followed her, leaving a sword behind, and then another.

And then all the remaining girls pressed forward, pushing to be next into the maze, and Daleina was elbowed back. She entered third to last.

As soon as she crossed the threshold, she was in darkness. Shadows enveloped her, and she faced a wall. *Right or left?* She listened for sounds of the others—there was a scream to the right, thin and sharp. She went left instead.

Hand on the wall, she half walked, half jogged down the left path. Leaves crunched under her feet. The ground was uneven, full of roots and rocks. She slowed as the last tendril of light from the entrance faded behind her. Feeling her way forward, she found a turn in the maze and took it. If she kept her hand on the wall, she could at least feel the shape of this place.

Ahead, she saw a sliver of amber light. *Aha, daylight!*

She hurried toward it and then plowed directly into another girl. The other girl scrambled past her, a tangle of arms, knocking Daleina down, and then the girl continued running in the opposite direction without a word.

Getting to her feet, Daleina didn't move. She held still and listened.

Ahead she heard a *whoosh, whoosh,* like a breath of wind, but rhythmic. The amber sliver of light bobbed up and down.

Not daylight, she thought. *Fire spirit.*

Rather than staying to determine how large a fire spirit it was, Daleina backtracked to the last intersection. Switching to another wall, she headed into a different dark tunnel. *Of course there are spirits here.* This was supposed to be an aptitude test. All the judges must have seeded the maze with them and were watching to see how the applicants would react. It occurred to her that she hadn't displayed any power or bravery or brilliance by running, but at least she'd showed common sense. *That's a valuable trait.*

Right?

Through the maze walls, she heard the footsteps of the other applicants. Occasional screams. A thud. And ahead, a trickle. Water spirit? There was more light here, streaming from a slit above, and she tried to keep her footsteps silent so that she could hear the direction of the drips.

The maze walls were smooth wood that stretched up to the canopy. No footholds, no hooks, no anchors, no ladders. The floor was a mass of roots. As she turned another corner, the roots felt squishier—moss. So maybe the trickle wasn't a spirit. Maybe it was water, and that's why there was moss. Listening, she didn't hear any of the other applicants near her. She seemed to be alone in this stretch of the maze. She wondered how large the maze was and if any of the others had found their way through yet, and she pictured her parents and Arin, out in the bleachers, worried. She'd better find her way through, fast.

She hurried forward, rounded a corner, and then halted. Suspended across the path was a cat-size translucent spider with a child's face. Its legs were braced against the walls of the maze, and tears poured from its eyes.

Definitely a water spirit.

Daleina froze, unsure what to do. She'd run from the fire spirit, but what if that wasn't the right choice? What if she was supposed to go through it? What if the only way through the maze was through the spirits? The more she thought about it, the more logical it seemed.

Carefully, the way the hedgewitch had taught her, she shaped a thought. One word was easiest, if you didn't know a specific chant for what you wanted. You had to hold the word in your mind, wrap it in your feelings, and then send it out. One word was an arrow she could aim.

Down, she thought.

She sent the thought spinning out of her.

The spiderlike spirit scuttled its legs as if half of them wanted to crawl down and half wanted to reach toward her.

Down.

It sank its head lower and opened its mouth. Water gushed out of its mouth and pooled on the moss below. Daleina walked forward.

Down.

It hulked down, its legs still braced but twitching, and then slowly it began to inch down toward the ground. Holding its gaze, Daleina kept walking, though she wanted to turn and run the other way—as soon as she had that thought, her hold on the command word faltered, and the spirit straightened and scurried upward.

Down!

It dropped down onto the moss. Curling its legs into its torso, it huddled in a ball. Daleina kept to the wall and skirted around it. "Thank you," she told it as she passed. Only when she reached the next corner did she dare turn her back on it, as she stepped around the corner and into mud.

Hands grasped her ankle.

Mud hands that rose disembodied out of the wet earth.

She bit back a scream. *Earth spirit!* Ahead, in the mud, she saw the shape of two girls, pinned by the mud to the earth. The closest one was trying to claw her way forward, her body stuck from the waist down. The farther one was trapped up to her neck. She'd tilted her head up and was muttering, "Free me, free me, free me," but it was clear that she was panicking instead of concentrating. *Concentrate,* Daleina told herself, as the mud stretched up her calf to her thigh. It encased her leg as she pulled against it. She wished she had some charms. If the spirit would retract even a bit, she could think! *Stop,* she tried. *Down! Release!*

"For spirits' sake, are you all idiots?" It was Merecot, the black-haired girl. As she ran past Daleina, she grabbed her arm and pulled. Daleina felt the mud hands tighten around her thighs, holding her in place. Spinning, Merecot commanded, "Water!"

Behind her, Daleina heard a trickle and then a rush. And then a torrent of knee-high water raced around the corner, ridden by the spiderlike water spirit. It swept through the mud, washing it away. Free, Daleina ran to the other girls and helped pull them out of the diluted mud. They gasped for air and leaned against the walls as the earth spirit slunk back into the ground, the last of the mud burping behind it. Looking up to thank Merecot, Daleina watched the black-haired girl disappear at a run around the next corner.

"I'm surprised she helped us," one of the girls said. "Perhaps I misjudged her."

"Are you all right?" Daleina asked.

"She's just trying to make herself look good," the second girl said. "We'd better go. I'm Revi, by the way." She was short, with bark-brown skin and clipped brown hair.

"I'm Linna," the first girl said. She tried to wipe some of the muck off her shirt. Beneath all the mud, Linna was a beautiful green-skinned girl with curled hair and yellow eyes. She had jewels woven into her hair, like a courtier or a palace artist favored by the queen, and her voice had a hint of an accent.

"Daleina. Do either of you have any idea which way to go?"

Revi shook her head. "I can tell you five ways *not* to go. Don't follow me. I have terrible luck. I keep finding dead ends, like this one."

"I'm not sure it is a dead end," Daleina said—after all, the girl Merecot had kept running and hadn't returned. "I think maybe we're supposed to go through the spirits. Part of the test."

"So they can see which one eats us?" Revi asked. "Whoever dies in the least embarrassing way passes? Great, sounds like a fun plan."

"Well, we can't stay *here*," Linna said, and Daleina was able to place her accent. Definitely court-bred, most likely raised with speech trainers and etiquette masters. Courtiers were supposed to sound musical when they spoke, their laughter like a harp chord and their sneezes like notes on a flute, or so she'd heard. "They're timing us."

Together, the three of them trotted forward. *We need some kind of plan.* Her current approach—choosing random directions and bumbling into spirits—wasn't working. "If we could only see the maze from above . . ." Daleina began.

"Easy, if you're part squirrel," Revi said. "I haven't seen a single thing to climb. Unless you're that water spirit. Ever seen one that looked like a spider before?" She shuddered.

"Horrifying. I'll be having nightmares about that one for weeks, thank you very much."

"Why do this if spirits give you nightmares?" Linna asked.

"*Because* spirits give me nightmares," Revi said promptly.

Daleina thought about her own nightmares and had to agree. Not doing this would be letting the nightmares win, and she'd promised Arin years ago that that wouldn't happen. Arin told her often enough that she slept well because she knew Daleina could protect her, but after five years with the hedgewitch, Daleina knew she didn't know enough yet to protect anyone. The academy was the answer.

She heard a crackle up ahead. "Stop."

The others obeyed. Linna whispered, "What is it?"

"Something unpleasant," Revi answered. "I can feel it. Can't you? Like a shiver in the air." She crept forward and peered around the corner, then retreated. "Yes, I was right. This one's an air spirit. They're trying them all out on us. I'm not good with air yet. Are either of you?"

Daleina wasn't sure if she was or not. She'd never succeeded in summoning an air spirit, but then Mistress Baria had never let her try. She'd only proven an affinity for earth and wood.

Linna raised her hand. "I am."

"Can you make it leave?" Daleina asked.

Inching forward, Linna peeked at it then returned. "It's small. Hummingbird small. I think I can do it. But I can't see what's beyond it. It could be a dead end or another trap. I won't be able to react to that if I'm controlling the air spirit."

Revi nodded. "We'll prepare for the next whatever, if you take this one."

Daleina caught Linna's arm as she started to move. "Wait. How good is your control? If it's an air spirit, it can fly. It can see the way through the maze. You could make it lead us."

Revi swore like a forest-floor woodsman. "Why didn't *I* think of that?"

"Can you do it?" Daleina asked.

Linna smiled—a sweet bow-shaped smile. *Courtier's daughter,* Daleina thought, and wondered how her family had felt when Linna displayed an affinity for spirits. Most courtier families never left the palace, a fortune paid to train their children in courtly graces. "I can try."

"Let's go together," Daleina said. "You take the air spirit. Revi and I will watch for other spirits who try to stop us."

Side by side, the three girls rounded the corner. Thrusting her hands forward, Linna concentrated on the air spirit. It was a six-inch-tall man-shaped spirit with luminous dragonfly wings, and it did not look pleased to see them. In fact, it held a tiny blade that looked like a bee stinger, except that it grew from the spirit's fist. Linna walked toward it, resolutely, step by step. The air spirit squirmed, writhed, and zigzagged back and forth. Linna raised her hands in the air, and the spirit soared upward. They watched him as he reached the top of the maze.

Sweat glistened on Linna's forehead. Her delicate hands began to shake. Daleina saw her jaw was clenched so tightly that the veins in her temple throbbed. And the air spirit dove down, hovered in front of them, and then zipped forward.

The three girls ran after him.

Right, left, straight . . . Left, straight . . . And then they burst through a narrow opening and were again in the practice arena in front of the academy. Seeing them, the audience clapped and cheered. Daleina saw her family in the stands, Arin jumping up and down, and her parents hugging each other. Several girls were already out, in a clump by the judges' table. Most of them were stained with mud, drenched in water and shivering, or sporting scrapes and fresh bruises . . . except for Merecot, who was spotless, as she drank a cup of water.

Meeting Daleina's gaze, Merecot winked, and Daleina couldn't tell if it was a mocking wink or a friendly one. She *did* help them pass the earth spirit, though, even if she didn't stay with them. Daleina opted to smile back and nod, hoping the other girl interpreted it as thanks. Daleina's smile faded as she saw another girl, lying on a stretcher, with red staining her white tunic. Healers hovered around her and then obscured the girl from sight.

Beside Daleina, Linna clapped her hands and squealed. "We did it!"

"Not bad," Revi said. "Right? We aren't the last ones? Okay, not the first, but not last. Do you think we made it in time?"

The judges were barely looking at them. Daleina scanned the crowd for the headmistress and didn't see her. "I hope so," Daleina said. The headmistress had final approval over all applicants—legend said she'd even predicted that a young applicant named Fara would become queen. Legend also said that a halo of butterflies had landed on the young queen-to-be's head, and some in the audience swore they heard trumpets. Daleina guessed that was an exaggeration. At any rate, there weren't any instruments playing today, and it was too cold for butterflies.

"Let's go with yes, until someone tells us otherwise," Revi suggested.

Linna nodded and linked her arms in Daleina's and Revi's. Together, they approached the judges' table. Looking up, Daleina saw Arin and her parents waving at her, as if she'd already won the queen's crown.

CHAPTER 4

The headmistress's office was filled with sunlight. It poured in through the windows in the ceiling and the wide window behind her desk. All the glass had cost a small fortune to have shipped from the islands of Belene, but Headmistress Hanna thought it was worth it. Her office was situated at the top of the academy, close to the forest canopy, where no branches blocked the midday light. Hands clasped behind her back, shoulders straight in perfect headmistress posture, Hanna faced the largest window and let the sunlight soak into her.

She hated this day, entrance examination day. All the applicants came so full of hope, and it was her job to crush that hope out of them before the academy crushed them. It felt like being cruel to sweet, fluffy kittens.

Behind her, the door squeaked as it opened, and she heard the shuffle of feet on the thick carpet. She knew without looking that the applicant was trying to step gingerly, trying to keep the muck and water from the maze from soaking into the rug. Listening, Hanna waited while the applicant found a spot of wood floor to stand on, where the mess wouldn't cause too much damage, but Hanna knew without looking that it required standing in the center of the brightest sunlight. It was all strategic, of course, designed to make the applicants feel uncomfortable and out of place, but it was hell on the carpet.

"So, you believe you can become an heir," Headmistress Hanna said without turning.

"My little sister does, and I won't let her down, ma'am."

Hanna closed her eyes. *Spare me the heroes,* she thought. The ambitious ones were easier to take. Disappointment just made them angry. The altruistic ones were always so sad. "It doesn't matter what she thinks. She isn't here. And she won't be here, if you stay. You won't see your family daily anymore or even monthly. You will live at the academy, sleep here, eat here, breathe here. You will work until your muscles feel like sponges and your mind feels like dust. You will have neither the time nor the energy to worry about what your little sister thinks of you. You will need to find the strength from an internal source, not an external one, and if you cannot do that, you will not last."

"I can do it," the girl said instantly.

Of course she thought she could. All the girls thought they could. All of them were optimistic, idealistic idiots, with no idea of the cost of failure. Few, if any, had ever witnessed the danger of a rogue spirit. They had no concept of the level of destruction even one could cause, much less the thousands that a queen had to control. "Do you have any idea of what an uncontrolled spirit can do?"

"Yes, ma'am. My village was destroyed by them."

Hanna was grateful that she still faced the window so that the girl couldn't see the expression on her face. It was rare, very rare, that villages were destroyed, but when they were, the spirits were usually thorough. She'd never met a survivor. To have one come here . . . Schooling her expression, the headmistress turned to study the girl.

Standing in the sunlight, the girl was a mess. She had mud in her hair, and her clothes were soaked. She'd left a mucky puddle at her feet. She was average height, average size, average everything. Without the mud, her hair might be striking—it was streaked red and gold and orange, like leaves in fall—but right now it was caked with brown muck. Her cheeks still had baby pudge to them, and her arms were tan, showing she spent a lot of time outside. Her fingernails were worn down to the tips of her fingers. She looked very young to have faced such tragedy. But then, all the students looked young. "I am sorry for your loss," Hanna said at last.

"Thank you, ma'am. It's the reason I'm here. I don't want it to happen again."

Studying the girl's determined eyes, Hanna revised her usual speech. "I am going to be blunt, because you need to make your decision with facts instead of emotions. You did not do well in the entrance exam. Yes, you passed, because you made it out of the maze in the time allotted"—she saw the girl's shoulders visibly sag in relief—"but you did not excel. You only used your power once and you expended a great amount of effort in order to control a single, weak spirit with a simple command. To excel at this academy, you must show great proficiency and innate talent, and frankly, I do not believe you possess it."

The girl did not move, speak, or react. Hanna admired her for that. She'd seen other girls break down in tears at even gentler assessments of their abilities.

"That said, you could still be of immense service to Aratay. You do not have to enter this academy for your life to have purpose and your power to do good. You could work with the forest guards or become a hedgewitch or—"

"It's not enough," the girl said.

Headmistress Hanna raised her eyebrows. She wasn't often interrupted.

"I'm sorry, ma'am, but my village had a hedgewitch. She died. It's not enough. I want to learn more than how to make charms and chant a few simple commands. I want to learn . . ." As if intimidated by the headmistress's expression, the girl petered out and ducked her head.

"You may not be able to," Hanna said, more gently. "We all have limits."

"Then please, I want to find them."

Hanna nodded. She'd intended to talk this girl out of staying. She'd watched the test, seen her performance, and while she had shown some intelligence and leadership ability, she hadn't shown much raw power, not like the first girl through the maze, Merecot. *That* was a girl with power. But it might be nice to have a student with some actual maturity and real-world experience, for a change. The headmistress hoped she wasn't becoming soft. She couldn't afford to let sentiment weaken her decisions. It wasn't fair to the girl, or to Aratay. "It is your choice, then. You have passed, and you may stay. But if you do, be prepared to work harder than you've ever worked before. And tell your little sister to be prepared to bury you if you fail."

The girl bowed. "Thank you, ma'am."

"Don't thank me," Headmistress Hanna said. "This is not kindness."

DALEINA WANTED TO DANCE OUT OF THE HEADMIS-tress's office. She'd passed! She couldn't wait to see Arin and hear her say, "Told you so!" Running down the stairs two at a time, she blew past the other applicants, who were still waiting for their audience with Headmistress Hanna.

"New students, this way," a woman commanded, and Daleina veered in the direction she pointed. She charged through an archway and then halted.

This wasn't outside. It was *in*.

Below her, above her, and all around her was the academy. It was a circle of trees whose trunks had been fused together into a ring and whose bark had been smoothed and polished to gleam like marble, a hollow tower with rooms within the walls. Spiral stairs ran up the inner ring, edged with ornate vine-coated banisters that looked like lace. On each level, the stairs produced a platform that cut into the air and also recessed into an archway that led into the interior of the tree. Along the stairs were windows as well, all edged with intricate designs. She guessed they were student rooms, or classrooms. High above, the trees stretched to frame a perfect circle of blue sky.

Far below, on the forest floor, was the practice ring. She'd heard about this: the famous academy ring. So many heirs had trained here: Heir Malliyn, who was said to have fought three rogue water spirits at once and created the Elder River; Heir Rubina, who became the third queen of Aratay and built the first palace; Heir Saphiral, who founded the first border guards and (according to legend) kept back an avalanche for long enough to save everyone except herself; and of course Her Majesty, Queen Fara. It looked like a manicured garden, with a waterfall that trickled down from a spout in one of the trees, and mossy paths between bloom-covered rocks. A thick grove of seemingly mature trees was in the center. Their leaves were lush summer green, in defiance of the season. If the stories were to be believed, these trees could have been grown in a single afternoon and could be felled by dawn. The practice ring was ever-changing, under the constant manipulation of the students. All her tests would be there, as well as some of her classes. She pictured herself there, wielding her power with ease, like an heir in the tales. . . .

A woman in blue thrust a stack of clothes at her. "Clean yourself. Baths are two levels down. Deposit your old clothes in the bins. You'll bathe every day, after survival class and before the evening meal. You'll keep your room neat and bring your clothes to me for a new set when you outgrow them. You also will come to me when you are ill or injured, and I will give you a pass to the healers. Unless you are unconscious, in which case a pass will be sent with you."

"Um, thank you." She wondered how often students were knocked unconscious, if that was part of the standard welcome speech. "I'm Daleina. It's a pleasure to meet you."

The woman gave her a withering look, all her wrinkles deepening until her face looked like a squeezed cloth. "Room 27B. Your schedule will be on your door. Do not be late. *Ever.*"

"Where can I find my family? To say goodbye. They'll want to see me, and I want to tell them I passed." She held the clothes gingerly, away from the mud that clung to her tunic. Her family would prefer to see her clean and unbruised, even if it took an extra minute. It would help erase her parents' worry and bolster her sister's impression that this would be a piece of cake.

"You're in the academy now," the woman said. "You don't have time for family. Everyone has been dispersed, and your parents will be told of your status by messenger."

"But I didn't get to talk to them—"

"Bathe and settle in. We are your family now." She turned from Daleina to shove clothes at the next student, a girl with wide eyes and pinched lips who looked as if she'd rather bolt up the tree like a squirrel than stay a second longer. Daleina wondered what the headmistress had said to her. She lingered for a second more, trying to think of what she could say that would convince the woman to let her see her parents and Arin. She only needed a moment, a chance to tell them that everything would be fine. Finishing, the scared girl scooted over to her.

"Hurry," the girl whispered. "You don't want to be on her bad side. That's Caretaker Undu."

The name meant nothing to Daleina, but she followed the other girl down the stairs. The steps were smooth and curved, as if they had been worn by hundreds of feet over hundreds of years. "What's a caretaker?"

"Teachers run the classes, and caretakers run everything else. Caretaker Undu is the head caretaker. She has zero sense of humor and zero tolerance for nonsense. You aren't from the capital, are you?"

"Outer villages, midforest. I'm Daleina."

"Marilinara. You can call me Mari." Away from Caretaker Undu, Mari didn't seem so scared anymore. She strode into the bathing room as if she'd been there before. *Maybe she has,* Daleina thought. *Maybe everyone else knows where to go and what to do, and I'm the only green one.*

"Where are you from?" Daleina asked.

"Here." Selecting a slim door, the third in a long row of doors, Mari opened it. Daleina caught a glimpse inside: a tub with steaming water and a pile of towels. "Caretaker Undu is my mother." She then closed the door, leaving Daleina by herself.

Half of the bathing stalls were full. Walking past them, Daleina picked an open one and shut the door behind her. She stared for a moment at the hot bath. Usually baths at home involved a pitcher and a bowl at their feet to catch the water. Mama sometimes heated the water over the fire. Sometimes she overheated it. Sometimes she didn't heat it at all. It was usually a surprise, and Arin always insisted Daleina go first. She'd then howl in laughter at however Daleina reacted. Arin would have been fascinated to learn that the baths here were hot without any sign of anyone heating or filling the tubs. And to hear about the maze, the headmistress's office, and the inside of the academy . . . Daleina swallowed hard. She didn't want to start her first day at the academy with any trace of sadness. She'd see her family soon enough, and she'd tell them everything. Steeling herself, she striped off her filthy, wet clothes, then plunged into the hot water and tried to scrub away all the doubt, fear, anxiety, and the rest.

It didn't work, of course. But at least she ended up cleaner.

She dressed in her new academy uniform: a pale-green tunic with black leggings, a black sash, and a black ribbon to hold back her damp hair. Clearly, the no-goodbye was meant to make them feel off-balance and vulnerable, just as calculated as making them face the headmistress while still covered in mud from the maze. *They want us to feel small and powerless,* she thought. *But it's not going to happen.* She'd come to the academy to learn how to be powerful, and she wasn't going to let them break her. She wondered if she was still being tested. Probably. Definitely. Always.

Leaving the bathing rooms, Daleina climbed the stairs again, searching for room 27B. Circling up the spiral, she found it off a small platform, a small round room with a chest for her new clothes, a desk with a chair, and a cot. All the furniture had been grown from the tree itself. Even the chair was rooted to the floor. She stood in the center of the room for a moment, but she had nothing to unpack. Going to her door, she read her schedule: a full lineup of classes, including history and politics, etiquette and diplomacy, magical theory, survival skills, and summoning.

Her heart beat faster at the word "summoning." She was going to learn so very much, well beyond what Mistress Baria could teach her. She was going to study nonstop, be the top in her classes, and—

"Oh, delightful. You'd think they'd house me near someone my equal." Merecot opened the door to the second room on the level, 27A. "Please do yourself a favor and quit now."

"Excuse me?"

"You don't have what it takes. Anyone can see that. I'm not being cruel; I'm being honest." Merecot paused, wrinkling her perfect forehead as if in thought. "Well, yes, I *am* being cruel, but the fact remains, you won't last." She shut her door behind her.

Daleina stared at the closed door.

A second later, it reopened. "What?"

"You want me to doubt myself so I will fail," Daleina said. "You want to undermine my confidence, because you're afraid you're not the best."

Merecot's lips quirked into a smile that she tried to suppress. "I know I am the best. I just want you to quit sooner so I can have your room. You have the better view." She shut her door again.

Behind Daleina, from the stairs, Revi said, "Nice. Guess she isn't here to make friends."

"She could use an extra class on diplomacy." Daleina thought of how Merecot had washed away the earth spirit in the maze. She hadn't had to help Daleina, Revi, and Linna. "Still, I like her."

"No accounting for taste." Revi opened the door to 27C and checked her own schedule. Tucked behind the schedule was a map of the academy, with class locations circled. "Hey, looks like we're in the same classes."

Daleina compared the two schedules—she was right. She then calculated the time, based on the timepiece she'd seen in the headmistress's office. "And we're late to our first one. Come on!" Knocking on Merecot's door, she called, "Hurry! Class has started!" and then she grabbed the map of the academy and sprinted out to the stairs. The classes were held below the living quarters, above the dining hall.

Revi trailed after her. "How can we be late? We just got here!"

"They're going to make everything as unpleasant as possible, in hopes that anyone who is going to quit will quit and not waste their time. I'll bet anything that means we start today." She ran faster down the stairs, and the two of them burst into a classroom that matched the number on their schedules. Other students shifted in their chairs, turning to watch them enter, proving that Daleina was right—and also late.

Slowing, they walked to two empty desks and sat. Trying to quit panting, Daleina scanned the rest of the room—most were older students, their hair neatly tied back and their uniforms crisp and clean. A few with still-wet hair were new arrivals like Daleina and Revi. They faced the front of the room, with their backs straight and hands clasped on their desks. Several empty desks were scattered around the classroom, and Daleina wondered how many of the other new students were missing their first class. Not everyone had even met with the headmistress yet. She didn't see Linna, though the caretaker's daughter, Mari, was already there, with her wet hair impeccably braided.

Only a few moments later, Merecot strolled into the room. Her hair, Daleina noticed, was dry. She had no idea how Merecot had managed that. Sitting beside Daleina, she opened her notebook and dipped a quill into an inkpot. She waited, quill poised.

Oh no, I didn't bring anything.

Looking around, Daleina saw everyone else had notebooks and textbooks, except her and Revi. She hadn't thought to grab one; she wasn't even sure she owned one. She hadn't checked the desk for supplies. Without even glancing at her, Merecot handed Daleina an extra notebook.

"Thank you," Daleina whispered.

Merecot ignored her.

"Hey, do you have another extra?" Revi whispered.

"No."

"Just 'no'?"

"Shh." Merecot put her finger to her lips and then pointed at the teacher.

"You can share with me," Daleina whispered to Revi.

The teacher was, to Daleina's surprise, a man. She'd expected them all to be female, since only girls were born with an affinity for spirits. He was older, with tufts of white hair, and he shuffled as he paced in front of his desk. Mid-lecture, he didn't acknowledge the new, late arrivals, and Daleina was grateful for that. It was bad enough to have the other students staring at them. ". . . in the third generation, the queen of Semo worked in concert with the queen of Chell to shrink the eastern mountains, in order to create what would become the northern fields of Chell. Doing so eased the burden here"—he tapped a map on the wall, one that showed all of Renthia—"but forced upheaval in the west. Literal upheaval. This mountain range increased in size by thirty percent. The results would have been catastrophic if the region hadn't been evacuated . . ."

Daleina focused on the map. She'd never seen such a detailed one of all of Renthia. It showed the five lands: their own Aratay with its vast forests, the mountains of Semo, the farmlands of Chell, icy Elhim, and the island chain of Belene. Beyond the known lands were the untamed wilds, where no humans lived. At the heart of Aratay was their capital, Mittriel, drawn in minute detail, with its interlocking trees and spiraling pathways. The Northeast Academy was, as the name suggested, in the northeast corner of the capital. Other academies were located in other cities, each drawn with as much care.

"Consequences," the teacher said, thumping his desk. "Every command has consequences, whether it be large like the thrust of the plates of the earth, or small like the life of a butterfly. You must think through all the ramifications before you act, or you will forever be reacting. And reacting poorly. Turn to chapter two, and we will discuss those whose reactions did *not* bring about the desired effect . . ."

History and politics class ended with the assignment of reading, plus a paper on the relations between Aratay and the neighboring land of Semo for the past fifty years. It was due in three days. Daleina and Revi hurried next to magical theory.

The teacher for magical theory acknowledged the new students by making them stand at the front of the class and answer a barrage of questions: how intelligent are spirits (it varies), can any female develop an affinity for spirits (yes, it can manifest in any family), can anyone with an affinity learn to sense spirits (yes, with proper training), can spirits sense humans (no, but they're drawn to the use of power), and so on. "Correct, correct, correct," the teacher, Master Bliara, said. "Now, tell me what happens when a queen dies."

"Death," Merecot said.

"Correct. After a queen dies, the spirits are released from her commands and obey only their base instincts, causing upheaval in the land and slaughtering any humans they find. Many years ago, it was discovered that women with affinity, working together, can override these instincts if and only if they issue one specific command. And what is this command that renders the spirits powerless?"

All of them chorused, *"Choose!"*

"Correct! This command triggers an almost hibernation-like state in the spirits, suspending their powers and their will. They remain in this state for seven days—a boon for us because it allows us time to gather our best heirs in the Queen's Grove. After seven days, the spirits choose the best heir to be queen and infuse her with enough power to command them all."

One of the students raised her hand. "But why? I mean, they hate us. Why give one of us more power?"

"Ahh, excellent question, Zie. It's the wonder of nature, protecting herself, ensuring the continuation of the species. Why does a river fish swim for miles and miles to reach a particular bank to lay her eggs?" The master paused. "That was not rhetorical, students. Marilinara?"

"Because it's safer there? Or the water is better for baby fish?" Mari glanced around her as if checking to see if anyone else had a better answer. Daleina was glad she hadn't been chosen to speak. She didn't want to be singled out on the first day—especially not about fish. "There must be something about that spot that makes it more likely that her offspring will live."

"Ah, but does the mama fish think to herself, 'Oh, that riverbed is a delightful place to raise children? It has nice weather. Great schools . . .' Please, you may laugh at my pun."

No one laughed. Daleina managed a smile, which seemed to be enough for Master Bliara. She continued on. "No! The mama fish doesn't *think*. She doesn't decide in a rational way, weighing the pros and cons. It's instinct! The same for the spirits. They act on instinct. Even the intelligent ones are ruled by their instincts. Do not expect them to think like we do. They can be smart, but do not mistake that for human logic. Now . . . what are the two primary instincts that drive the spirits?" The master looked directly at Daleina.

Daleina shrank back, and then squared her shoulders. "To kill humans."

"And?"

"To . . ." Daleina glanced at Revi and then at Merecot, who was watching her with a faintly amused expression. "Well, fire spirits start and spread fires. Wood spirits grow trees . . ."

"Precisely. To destroy and to create! And what is the problem inherent in those two instincts?" The master continued to look at Daleina expectantly.

Daleina swallowed. *Why me?* There were plenty of other students in the class, including older students who probably knew exactly what answer Master Bliara was looking for. Daleina hadn't even seen, much less read, any textbooks yet. "They're contradictory?"

"Exactly. *That* is why they crave a queen. As much as they hate us, the spirits need a queen to manage that contradiction and keep them—and our land—balanced. But never be fooled into thinking that *needing* a queen is the same as *wanting* a queen. A queen must never forget that the spirits both require and revile her."

A traitorous thought sneaked into Daleina's mind: *Why would anyone want that kind of life?* She squelched it down. Like the spirits themselves, she wasn't here because of what she wanted. She was here because of what was needed.

"You will each write a ten-page research paper on the positive and negative effects of this unique command, quoting historical sources, as well as speculation on *why* it's effective, due by the end of the week."

Last class of the day was something called survival skills.

Daleina and Revi, as well as Linna, who had missed the earlier classes, found their way down to the practice ring. This was the first class of the day with only the new students. Clustered by the waterfall, they all held their books and notebooks and wondered if they were supposed to sit or stand. Only thirteen out of the original twenty had made it through the entrance exam. Daleina had heard a rumor that one applicant had gone home with a broken leg, another with a concussion, and a third with burns on her hands so bad that her fingers looked shriveled. Daleina realized she'd been lucky to pick the path she did and find the other girls.

"I can light a fire with sticks and string," Linna said. "If that's on the syllabus, I'll help you. Do either of you know any other survival skills?"

"I can recognize a few edible plants," Daleina offered. She knew more than a few. Living in the outer forest, she had to scavenge for a lot. It was one of her primary tasks for Mistress Baria, finding the correct herbs for the hedge-witch's charms and meals.

"I don't know anything useful," Revi said. "Oh, wait, yes, I have the secret ability to mock anything and anyone who threatens me."

"A terrifying power," Daleina said solemnly. "Use it wisely."

Leaves rustled behind them, and the students turned in time to see a wolf trot out from between the manicured trees.

A wolf.

Here.

Its pelt was thick, and its muscles were bunched. Stopping at the edge of the trees, it bared its teeth and growled, a low rumble that Daleina felt in the base of her stomach. Her muscles froze. She didn't run, twitch, or even breathe.

From above, a voice said, "You encounter a wolf in the forest. What do you do?"

Merecot answered first. "Summon an earth spirit to pull it into the ground."

"Or merely to hold it still," Mari said, shooting a look at Merecot. "You don't need to kill the poor thing."

"The 'poor thing' wants to eat us," Merecot argued. "I say it should be discouraged from thinking humans are lunch. We have enough enemies."

Another girl raised her hand. "A water spirit could wash away the ground under its feet. Make it difficult for the wolf to chase us."

"Air spirit," another said. "Throw it into the air."

"Or make the spirit push it back." Another.

Ideas flew around them: making a tree spirit wrap the wolf in vines, creating a hole beneath him, blowing a tree down on him, and setting his fur on fire. As the others talked, the wolf paced back and forth.

Daleina opened her mouth to say that maybe the best thing to do was *not* to stand in front of it, discussing options, but the others were talking too loudly for her to squeeze in her opinion. She tugged on the sleeve of her closest class-mate. "Linna? Revi? Merecot? We should climb, while we can." But they were all too involved in the discussion.

With her eyes on the wolf, Daleina inched toward a tree. The wolf was watching the students who were talking most animatedly. There was something not right in the way it was behaving. *It should have fled,* she thought, *or attacked.* Looking at it, Daleina became more and more convinced that it wasn't there to prompt a theoretical discussion. "They're testing us, always, remember? Including right now." Daleina stepped onto a branch and climbed up onto it. She continued to move slowly, smoothly, as she climbed several branches up, until she was beyond the wolf's reach, even if it were to rise onto its hind legs. As one of the girls stepped forward to be heard, the wolf snapped. It darted into the group, aiming for the closest girl.

The girls screamed and ran.

Low and fast, the wolf chased them, snapping at their heels.

"Grab my hand!" Daleina called. Leaning over, she reached out. Revi got to her first, and Daleina helped pull her up to the branches. Linna was second.

From one of the circular platforms above, the teacher dropped into the practice ring. She put two fingers in her mouth and whistled. The wolf halted and then trotted to her side. She scratched between its ears and dug a treat from her pocket.

The girls began to return. "That's your *pet*?" Merecot asked.

"Tell me what you learned just now," the teacher said.

Merecot folded her arms. "Don't trust teachers with pet wolves."

Mari raised her arm. "Don't assume wolves are safe just because they haven't attacked. We should have already been reacting, instead of having a discussion. Not everyone knew he was your pet."

"You knew," the teacher said to Mari, "but you didn't share that information."

Many sets of eyes glared at Mari. She stuck her chin out. "It was a lesson," Mari said. "I didn't think I was supposed to." Daleina shook her head, wanting to say they weren't in competition—they were all here to learn. But she knew that wasn't exactly true.

"You withheld knowledge," the teacher said. "And the rest of you posited impractical solutions. You must work with the power you have."

"It wasn't impractical," Merecot argued. "I could have done it."

"You *didn't*," the teacher said.

"You wouldn't have liked it if I'd killed your pet."

To Daleina's surprise, the teacher didn't point out the obvious fact: Merecot hadn't known the wolf was the teacher's friend, yet she still hadn't used any power. To be fair, it hadn't even crossed Daleina's mind to call on any spirits either. It had all happened fast.

"Today in survival class, you will use the resources you have to evade my wolf. Anything else in the ring is yours to use. But you may not summon any spirits—that class will begin tomorrow." Letting her words sink in, the teacher met the eyes of each girl. "I would prefer it if you didn't kill him, just as we would all prefer it if you didn't wantonly kill anyone or anything. Save yourselves, and do no harm. Let that be your mantra during your years here and beyond. *Do no harm*." Last, the teacher met Daleina's eyes. "You, girl in the tree. You will assist my wolf."

Daleina gulped. *Me again?* She didn't know if it was good or bad that teachers kept calling on her. From the looks of pity the others were shooting her, she guessed bad.

"I'm sorry, Master"—she paused, not knowing the teacher's name—"but I don't understand."

"You already showed you can survive. Come down here, and show me you can thrive." Hands on her hips, the teacher surveyed them all. "You will call me Master Bei. The wolf is Bayn. Come on, girls, look lively. Bayn wants another treat. Rule is: his teeth touch you, and you're out."

As the other girls scattered around the practice ring, Daleina climbed down the tree and cautiously approached Master Bei and Bayn. The wolf watched her with yellow eyes. Daleina had seen enough wolves on the forest floor to know this wasn't a wolf-dog hybrid. This was pure wolf. Keeping her distance but trying not to look as if she were keeping her distance, Daleina approached their teacher. She stopped several yards away.

Master Bei's lips quirked, as if this amused her. "Bayn is well trained. Keep him safe and help him hunt."

"You want me to *hunt* the other students?" Daleina wondered if Master Bei was really a teacher, or if this was another test of some kind, to see whether she was gullible enough to turn on her new classmates. "I can't do that." The other students weren't her enemies, right? Or was she utterly naïve?

"You will, if you want to pass this class. And if you don't pass, you don't stay."

aleina held her hand out, palm up, as if the sleek, muscled, rather-hungry-looking wolf were just a skittish puppy. The wolf ignored her. Daleina put her hand down. "Okay, Bayn, um, we need to find the other students. A lot of them will have climbed trees. So, um, you use your nose, and I'll use my eyes, and we'll search, all right?" Daleina glanced at Master Bei. "How much does he understand me?"

"Completely, or so I've found. He's a highly intelligent animal. More so than most of the students I've seen pass through here, that's for sure."

Daleina nodded. She felt as if she were on the verge of embarrassing herself spectacularly. Worse, if she failed or refused to try, she could be kicked out of the academy without finishing a day. She'd have to go back to her parents and Arin and tell them she'd washed out after a single afternoon. Her mother would act pleased, going on and on about how dangerous it was anyway. Her father wouldn't say anything but would shoot her looks that were both sympathetic and disappointed. And Arin would be crushed. She'd look at Daleina as if Daleina had ripped apart her favorite dress and drowned her doll. "Follow me," she told the wolf.

At a jog, she plunged into the grove of trees in the center of the practice ring. Here was where the trees were tallest, the best choice for climbing to safety. As soon as she entered, she slowed. The wolf's paws were silent on the path, and Daleina switched to walking silently as well, stepping over twigs and dried leaves and tiptoeing across moss and roots. All kids from the outer villages learned to walk through the woods quietly.

Kids from cities . . . did not.

She and the wolf heard two tromping through the underbrush, loudly, ahead of them. "Go get them, Bayn." The wolf darted forward, and she followed, arriving in time to see him nip at the heels of first one, then the other girl. Both of them shrieked, even though he didn't break skin.

In a nearby tree, Daleina spotted a flash of red—there, another student. The girl was puffing as she climbed higher, slowly and painfully. The scrawny tree bent and swayed as the girl climbed. She must have chosen it because of all the easy branches that jutted ladderlike from the trunk, but the trunk was too pliable. If she climbed much higher, the tree would bow beneath her weight. She seemed to realize that, though, and stopped climbing. An idea began to form in Daleina's head.

Circling the tree, the wolf looked up at the girl.

"Be ready," Daleina told the wolf. She scurried up a nearby tree, scrambling from branch to branch, keeping to the side of the trunk away from the other student, out of sight. Soon, she'd climbed higher than the student. When she was even with the top of the scrawny tree, Daleina stopped and gauged the distance. She was reasonably sure the tree was healthy enough not to snap. If it bent slowly . . . *This could work,* she thought. Or it could be a painful disaster. Question was: How badly did she want to stay in the academy?

Do it, Daleina told herself.

Jumping off her tree, she landed on the scrawny tree. It bent under her weight, bowing. Clinging to the tip, Daleina rode the tree downward. The other girl screamed and hugged the trunk as it dipped toward the ground—and the wolf.

The wolf nipped lightly at the girl's leg, not leaving a mark, and then howled.

Gotcha.

She began climbing down the trunk. The lower she got, the more the trunk lifted back into the air, until Daleina reached the other student. "Sorry," Daleina told her. "Did the wolf hurt you?"

The other student shook her head without saying anything.

"You can probably climb down now."

The other student nodded but didn't move.

Daleina tried to remember if she'd heard any teachers say her name. "Lyda? Is that your name? Are you hurt?"

The girl's eyes were wide as a deer after it felt an arrow in its haunch, but she shook her head. "Just going to . . . rest here . . . for a minute. That was . . . I think, maybe, I hate it here."

"It's just the first day."

"That's what scares me."

Daleina hesitated for a moment, and then maneuvered past her and climbed down to the ground. She couldn't help with Lyda's epiphany. "Next?" she asked the wolf.

His tongue hung out of the side of his mouth like a happy dog.

In the end, they only caught three more: one who had hidden behind the waterfall, another who had tried to camouflage herself in the dirt, and a third who tried to trick Bayn into a trap, which Daleina spotted because it was the kind of trap her father used all the time.

When Master Bei called them all back, Daleina trotted beside the wolf. She didn't know if she'd done well or not, and Master Bei didn't say, but she resolved to find a treat for Bayn as soon as she could.

IT WAS NEARLY IMPOSSIBLE TO STAY AWAKE DURING dinner. All the new students sat together, crammed side by side, on a few benches. Caretakers served a stew, ladling spoonfuls into bowls, while the students passed around a chewy nut-flour bread stuffed with dried berries. Daleina dipped the bread into her soup and forced herself to eat—she knew she'd need the energy for whatever waited for them tomorrow. Plus there was still reading to do and papers to start. And as Lyda said, this was only day one.

"Do you think it gets easier?" Revi groaned. "I mean, they're just hazing us, right? Throwing us into full-fledged classes after we just finished the maze. It'll be better next week."

"Obviously it gets harder," Merecot said, helping herself to another chunk of bread. Of all of them, she was the only one who didn't look exhausted, though Daleina noticed she still had a streak of dirt in her hair. She must have hidden from Bayn on the ground, an unusual choice. She was surprised he hadn't sniffed her out. Thinking of the wolf, she sneaked a strip of meat into a napkin to feed him later. "If you can't take it—"

"Why are you obsessed with what others do?" Linna asked. "Any number can be heir. The more heirs there are, the safer Aratay is. The queen would be delighted if all of us were chosen to be candidates."

"Only one can be *queen*," Merecot said. "And it will be me."

All of them rolled their eyes at her.

Merecot shrugged and ate another spoonful.

"We're a long way from becoming queen, any of us," Revi said, and groaned again. "I think I left half my skin on the bark of that tree. Why oh why did you have to get us all climbing trees, Daleina?"

"It's the most logical way to escape a wolf. Won't work

with cats. Or snakes. Certain bears." Daleina thought of the bears that roamed the forest floor beneath her old village. All the berry patches had to be guarded every autumn, but keeping the stores above worked fine. "Haven't you climbed before?"

"I live in the capital," Revi said. "We use bridges like civilized people. And ladders. A few of the shopping areas even have rafts on pulleys that you can ride on to travel from tree to tree. Yes, woodsgirl, we don't all get around like squirrels."

"Where did you learn to climb like that?" another girl asked. "Hi, I'm Evvlyn. You almost caught me today. I was two trees over from you when Master Bei called time." Daleina recognized her—she was one of the girls who had come out of the maze before her. She had multicolored hair, cut short enough so you could see her scalp. Tattoos of birds trailed up her neck and behind her left ear.

"I'm from an outer village, midforest," Daleina said. "This is my first time anywhere near the capital. My family and I came just for the entrance exam." She felt a lump in her throat that she was sure wasn't a wad of bread. By now, Arin and her parents had to be heading home. It cost too much to stay in the capital, and there was still so much to be done to prepare for the winter storms. She wondered if they'd stopped somewhere to eat too, if they'd camped or found a way station, and hoped they'd set up enough charms and were being careful. She knew they knew how to take care of themselves. It wasn't as if they needed her. But still . . . "How about you? Where are you from?"

"North, near the border with Semo," Evvlyn said. "My parents are border guards."

The others introduced themselves as well, a dozen at their table, all the new students. Daleina realized that the one she'd caught in the tree, Lyda, was missing and wondered if she'd quit. She hoped not. She didn't like thinking that quitting was an option. She'd rather think of this as something she had to do, like hauling firewood or helping the hedgewitch with her toenails. Except with more magic.

The older students were clumped together and didn't look nearly as exhausted, except for the oldest students, who ate without speaking. Daleina studied them. There were only four of them, and they shared a table with the headmistress, but they didn't look up from their stew. They ate as if it were their sole task in the world. One of them twitched every time someone passed near her.

"What's wrong with them?" Evvlyn asked.

"There's a champion here who wants to choose a candidate," Mari said with the air of someone who knows everything that's going on—which she most likely did, as the head caretaker's daughter. "The teachers always push the oldest ones the hardest, hoping she'll pick one of them. Don't worry. That won't be us for a long time."

Watching them, Daleina barely tasted her stew. If that was what students looked like *after* they'd been trained . . . But just because it wasn't easy, that didn't mean it wasn't worth it. *I can do this.* She had the feeling she was going to be telling herself that a lot. The key was to never doubt it, which was hard when she felt her doubts and fears pitching tents in the back of her mind, sparking a fire, and settling in for the long haul. She knew she wasn't powerful enough, smart enough, clever enough, knowledgeable enough, talented enough . . .

Stop it, she told herself, but her doubts just ignored her and roasted a sausage over their campfire. *Stupid mind.* She wondered if Headmistress Hanna had felt any self-doubt when she faced the spirits at the Massacre of the Oaks. Or Queen Hunerew when she rode a hurricane out to sea to protect the islands of Belene. Or Queen Phia when she commanded the spirits to grow the first city in Aratay, the Southern Citadel, on the shores of the Iorian Sea. Or . . .

"Is everyone ready for tomorrow?" Linna asked.

"Why? What's tomorrow?" Daleina asked.

"Tomorrow is when we learn who really deserves to be here," Merecot said, as if relishing the idea of people quitting. "Our first summoning class. Better not get too friendly with anyone. Not all students survive their first summoning."

Putting down her spoon, Daleina didn't feel like eating anymore. In fact, she felt sick. "Truly? Students have *died*?"

Merecot began to nod solemnly and then broke into laughter. "I don't know. It's my first day too. But you should have seen the look on your face."

"It's official," Revi announced to the table. "I don't like her." The other students glared at Merecot too, at least those who had enough energy left to glare.

"I don't need you to like me," Merecot said, still smiling. "I only need to win."

HEADMISTRESS HANNA HAD PERFECTED THE ART OF eating while watching her students without appearing as if she were watching her students while she ate. It was the only way the students would eat enough. She'd found over the years that if they thought she was observing them, they'd universally lose their appetite. She had enough students passing out from exhaustion as it was. She didn't need to add to that number with malnutrition. Digging into her stew with gusto, she peeked at them as she swallowed.

"New crop of students seems promising," Master Klii said.

The headmistress didn't answer. All new crops seemed promising, so full of hope, until it was drained out of them. She tore a hunk of bread off a loaf and dipped it in her stew. By the time they reached their final year, most were shells. She looked at the older students, their eyes downcast, their shoulders slumped. She didn't know if any had the inner strength left to become viable heirs. "Tell me, Klii, what do we do here? Do we build heroes, or break them?"

Master Klii stared at her as if she'd sprouted spirits out of her ears. "Headmistress?"

Hanna forced a small laugh. "Ignore me. I'm having a pensive day." The arrival of a new set of students always made her feel this way, as if she were taking young innocents and robbing them of their childhood, never mind that the students volunteered and were always welcome to leave. Children couldn't possibly understand what they were being asked to give up, and by the time they realized it, they were too immersed in this life to imagine any other way.

One of the caretakers scurried over to her and whispered in her ear. "Urgent message for you in your office."

Hanna put her goblet down and rose.

All eyes turned toward her, and conversation ceased. "Continue your meal." But the sounds of forks and knives on plates didn't resume until after she had left the dining hall and was climbing the stairs toward her tower.

Her knees ached by the third level up. This was the flaw with choosing an office at the top of the academy. One day, her joints wouldn't be able to take it. Of course, that would probably be the day that the spirits took her, so it didn't matter.

Yes, definitely a cheerful mood today.

She felt lighter as she climbed, as if the air were fresher higher up. Perhaps it was because she was farther from the sounds of the dining hall, or the lingering stench of sweat from the practice ring, or perhaps it was only an illusion. With the sun low in the sky, it didn't penetrate the heart of the academy, but it still bathed the top of the stairs.

It would be lovely, she thought, *if the "urgent message" brought happy news.* A new grandbaby. A full harvest. Another peace treaty with one of the other queens. Hanna climbed into the amber light and then entered her office.

The message was on her desk, a piece of parchment that had been tied to the leg of a falcon. One of the caretakers had cut it off and taken the falcon to be fed. Sitting at her desk, Headmistress Hanna looked at the parchment without touching it.

At last, she picked it up, broke the wax seal, and opened it.

It held the name of a village, Birchen. Below the name were two words in the queen's distinctive curled handwriting: "Tell him."

Setting the note down, Hanna put her face in her hands.

She breathed in and out and counted slowly in her head, forcing down the fear that rose like a threatening tide inside her. She still had time, didn't she? The message had just arrived.

Rolling the message back into a scroll, she sealed it with shaking hands, then tied it with a ribbon that bore her own mark. Her bones creaking even more than when she'd been climbing, Hanna pushed herself off the chair and crossed to a window. She opened it, closed her eyes, and called to an air spirit.

One came easily, as always—her best affinity had always been air. Opening her eyes, Hanna held out her hand, and the spirit alighted on her finger. It was shaped like a miniature child with translucent butterfly wings and a tail of feathers.

Hanna gave the message to the spirit, who tucked it beneath its spindly arm. "Find the disgraced champion." Lifting her hand, Hanna raised the spirit higher. Wings outstretched, it dove from her palm and pierced the air between the branches below. Hanna watched it until it disappeared and prayed she'd done enough.

CHAPTER 6

S ummoning classes, according to Mari (their expert on all things academy), were always in the practice ring. At dawn, after the bells exploded in a flurry of chimes, Daleina and the other students piled out of their bedrooms, into the bathing rooms for a frenzy of tooth and hair brushing, and then down the spiral staircase. The first thing they noticed was that all the trees were gone. Manicured bushes, gone. Rocks and flowers, gone. Waterfall spilling into a pool, gone. The practice ring was a wide circle of dirt.

"What's going on?" Daleina whispered to Mari.

"You'll see."

"She doesn't know," Merecot said.

"Do too."

"Ugh, can we not argue this early?" Revi said. She still had sleep crusted in the corner of one eye and looked like a bear woken from hibernation. "Some of us actually worked on our papers last night."

Daleina hadn't even tried. She'd collapsed onto her cot within seconds of the night bell. Her dreams had been thick with wolves and her family and the dark corners of the maze. She woke with her sheets sticking to her sweat.

Six teachers waited for them in the practice ring, one for

each kind of spirit, each wearing a ribbon around her waist to denote her specialty: air, earth, water, fire, ice, or wood. A few of them had been judges at the entrance exam; the others Daleina didn't recognize. All the students lined up in front of the masters. Daleina felt as if she were back in front of the maze, about to be tested again. And of course that's exactly what's going to happen . . . again and again and again. *I'll pass every one,* she promised herself. *Whatever they throw at me, I will catch. Or dodge. Or whatever I'm supposed to do this time.*

The master with the green ribbon spoke. "The primary purpose of this academy is to identify and train those girls who possess the necessary abilities to be queen. At the end of your time here, several of you will be chosen by champions as heir candidates. Those candidates will receive specialized training and undergo the trials, and the best will be selected to be heirs and prepared for the coronation ceremony, in the event of the current queen's death, may she live long and never falter."

All the students were silent; even their breathing felt hushed. None of the master's words were new to them—all Renthians knew this—but somehow hearing it here felt weightier, as if this were a ritual rather than a lesson.

"At the coronation ceremony, the spirits will select the queen from the pool of heirs, choosing the strongest and best. It is our job here to see that you are prepared for what Aratay—and indeed all of Renthia—will demand of you."

"We ask much of our queens," the next teacher said, "and your classes here will provide you with a valuable knowledge base to draw on, if and when you are called upon to serve our people."

Another took up the speech. Daleina wondered how many students they'd said this to over the years, and how many had lasted to become heirs. "Make no mistake, it is service. It is not glory. The queen exists to protect us. She must be selfless, determined, brave, intelligent, compassionate, and wise, as well as strong in will and power."

"It is the last that this class is designed to address," the fourth said. "In this class, you will learn to summon and control spirits, singly and in groups, in close proximity and at a distance. You will learn to sense the presence of spirits and determine their level of hostility and ability to cause harm. By your final year here, this class will dominate your days."

The fifth: "All of you have shown an affinity for one or more spirits. By your final year, you will show mastery of all six, or you will be asked to leave."

Daleina glanced at the other students to see if this made them nervous too. All eyes were glued on the masters. A slight frown on her face, Revi was chewing her lower lip. She didn't look tired anymore. Linna's expression was close to worshipful. Mari looked terrified. Merecot somehow looked bored.

The sixth and last teacher: "Today we will assess your abilities as they currently stand. You will be divided into groups and will rotate between us." She consulted a sheet. "When I call your name, please step forward. Iondra, Zie, Linna . . ."

Daleina didn't have much experience with summoning spirits. In the outer forest, the spirits were mostly something you avoided, and the hedgewitches worked to keep them away from villages, not invite them in. They safeguarded the woodcutters from tree spirits who resented the felling of trees, they monitored the drinking water for signs of a vengeful water spirit, they kept the fire spirits from stoking cooking fires into brushfires, they guarded the bridges and ladders against destructive air spirits, and so on. Moreover, a lot of their work was done through charms and ritualistic words rather than pure power.

"Merecot, Daleina, Cleeri, Tridonna . . ."

She scooted forward to join Merecot and two other students with the teacher in the red ribbon, a stern-faced woman with a burn scar beneath her left ear and clawlike scars on her arm. "I am Master Klii. You will follow me."

Master Klii marched them to the center of the practice ring. "For fire spirits, it's best to summon them as far from structures as possible. Your clothes are flammable, which is unfortunate but unavoidable." Reaching into her robe, she pulled out a jar of white goo and held it up. "This is burn ointment. Be generous with it while you are here, and sparing when you are away from a steady supply. The healers keep us well-stocked." Dropping down to sit cross-legged in the dirt, she said, "Sit, and begin."

There was zero other instruction. Daleina had expected another lecture, or a demonstration, or at least a hint of how exactly they were expected to summon a fire spirit.

The master pointed at one of the other students. "You first."

Sitting cross-legged across from Master Klii, the girl closed her eyes and inhaled deeply. Her lips formed a word: "Come."

Watching her, Daleina tried to glean any hints. "Come" was a vague word. She had to be targeting a specific spirit, but how?

"Look," another student breathed. She pointed to one of the lanterns that lit the spiral stairs. In morning, the candles within were unlit, but a bright shape danced behind the glass.

"Come," the student whispered, beckoning with her fingers.

The dancing flame slipped between the panes of glass. It tumbled down the stairs in cartwheels and then rolled over the dirt. The student held out her hand, and the teacher quickly pulled a leather glove over the student's fingers as the flame leaped to land on her palm. It was a tiny spirit, its height rising and falling as it danced, spinning in circles. Its laugh sounded like the hiss and pop of a fire.

"You"—the master pointed at Merecot—"make it light the blue cloth but not the red. Take control of it." She tossed two strips of cloth onto the dirt, one blue and one red.

Pressing her lips together, Merecot focused on the fire spirit. "You," she said to the spirit, "will obey *me*." It tensed and then twitched once and stiffened. Moving her finger, she guided the flame toward the blue. "Burn the blue, only the blue."

The flame spirit pounced on the blue fabric. It smoldered, and then flames licked over the cloth, darkening and curling it. The spirit danced as the cloth blackened, and it crumbled beneath the spirit's feet.

Smugly, Merecot smiled at the teacher. Her smile faltered when Master Klii merely moved on to the next student. *She must be used to more praise,* Daleina guessed.

"Now the red," the teacher said to the third student.

The third student began to speak in a singsong voice that at least was similar to what Daleina had witnessed hedge-witches doing. "Burn the red until it's dead, burn it deep before you sleep, burn the red . . ." And the spirit engulfed the red cloth, spinning in the dirt with it until it disintegrated into ashes.

Master Klii sniffed. "We're training heirs here, not hedgewitches. Spoken word is unnecessary for our students. You"—the teacher turned to Daleina—"banish it, without the peasant chant."

Daleina felt nearly dizzy with relief. *This I can do.* Sitting cross-legged, she focused on the fire spirit. "Leave," she told it.

It danced, stomping on both the red and blue cloth.

She was aware of eyes on her, the other students and

the teacher. Sweat prickled her armpits and the back of her neck. "Leave," she repeated.

It ignored her.

She pretended the others weren't there, that she was home, that the only thing that mattered was convincing the fire spirit to *leave now*. Clenching her fists, she tried again, pouring all of her energy into the word. *"Leave!"*

Startled, it met her eyes. Its pupils were tiny orange flames, and its lids were charred. For an instant, it was frozen mid-dance, and then it darted across the practice ring and back up to the lantern. It writhed on the wick, and Daleina imagined it was glaring at her.

"Good, all of you," the teacher said. "Switch to the next spirit."

Shakily, Daleina stood. She swayed as the practice ring tilted. She felt a pressure on her elbow, a hand, and looked to see Merecot beside her. "Deep breaths," Merecot murmured. "You pass out, and that's all anyone will talk about. Seriously, was that hard for you? You had the easiest one."

Concentrating on breathing evenly, Daleina went with the other students to the teacher with the blue ribbon, on one side of the practice ring. The teacher laid her hand on the smooth white trunk of the tree. "Your task here is to summon a waterfall from within the tree. Right now, three water spirits are blocking the water that would naturally spill out of the cracks. Convince them to release the water and recreate the fall that should be here."

Three spirits at once? And where were the spirits? Behind the wood? She felt as if everyone else had been given lessons that she'd missed. Maybe this was Mistress Baria's fault. Daleina hadn't had proper training. *Or maybe I'm not like the others.* Maybe her power wasn't as useful as she'd thought. Maybe the headmistress was right, and she was destined to be a hedgewitch or a guard.

"Each of you target one of the spirits."

Daleina licked her lips, cleared her throat, and asked, "How?"

The teacher looked at her as if she'd violated a sacred law, then she sighed and tapped Daleina's forehead. "With this. Your mind. Picture it like a hand and reach out."

She took a deep breath and tried. Carefully, she imagined her thoughts in the shape of a hand, reaching out toward the wall. She reached *through* it—and she felt a shiver shudder along her "arm." A spirit! She'd heard that queens and heirs could sense spirits, but Mistress Baria had never been able to explain how it was done. Yet it was so simple!

"Visualize water pouring," the teacher said. "Use the word 'release.'"

Those were at least concrete instructions, but Daleina had never successfully commanded a water spirit before. Trying to push her self-doubt away, she focused on the word and on the spirit at the other end of her mental hand, through the wall. She felt as if she were fracturing—she couldn't hold both the word and the hand. "Release," she said out loud. She heard the other girls as well: "Release, release, release." She imagined the water spilling through the cracks in the wood. But she didn't feel the words burn inside her.

Water spilled from the cracks. It tumbled down the surface of the wood.

"Well done," the teacher said.

Daleina felt Merecot looking at her. She met the other girl's eyes. *She knows I didn't do it.* She waited for the other girl to call her out, to tell the teacher that she'd failed—that one of the others had commanded her spirit, that Daleina might not have enough power after all—but Merecot didn't say anything.

They moved together to the next teacher, earth, to summon small mole-like spirits from within the dirt. Merecot succeeded in summoning a dozen. The other students summoned one each. Daleina failed to summon any, but the earth-spirit teacher was kind. "Don't worry," she told Daleina. "Some affinities manifest later than others."

For air, Merecot forced a tiny air spirit to blow a dried leaf in figure-eight patterns in front of the teacher. Others were able to cyclone a few leaves. Daleina was only able to convince the spirit to blow the dried leaf into the air a few inches, which was, thankfully, enough to satisfy the teacher.

To Daleina's relief, everyone in their small group failed with the ice spirit. "In the mountains of Semo or on the glaciers of Elhim, this is an easier task," the teacher comforted them. "Ice spirits are rare in Aratay. Rare or not, though, the principle is the same: the key to summoning any spirit of any kind is will. Your need for them to obey must be greater than their need to resist, and they are born with the need to resist. They are born hating us. You must replace that hatred with obedience. The images you choose, the words you use, are merely conduits to focus your will—that is why you will hear so many hedgewitches using chants or traditional words. But in truth, the words themselves aren't necessary—the *focus* is. We will teach you to choose the best conduits for your power."

Last for Daleina's group was wood. She *should* be able to handle this. Wood spirits were the most prevalent spirit in Aratay, as evidenced by the mighty forests. The spirits and the land were linked. If she'd started the class with wood, she might have done well. But by the time her group migrated over to the teacher with the green ribbon, Daleina felt as if her insides had been scraped out with a spoon, mashed together, and then poured back in.

They knelt in a circle around a circle of seeds with one simple task: ask a wood spirit to grow the seeds into plants. Daleina had done this, helping the hedgewitch aid the forest farmers, casting charms to encourage the spirits to tend to the plants, and hurrying the growth of certain necessary herbs. Usually, they'd entreat the spirits and then leave the area, letting the spirits do their work in peace, but that wasn't an option here. *This isn't so different,* Daleina told herself. *You've done this. You can do it.*

Again, one by one, the others succeeded. One grew a three-inch flower. Another sprouted a row of beans. Merecot, of course, exceeded them, causing a carrot to thicken until it was edible and then plucking it out of the earth while the spirit howled.

On Daleina's turn, she focused on one spirit and one seed. *Please,* she thought at it. *Make it grow.* Out loud, she said the words she'd been taught by the hedgewitch, "*I am the sun, I am the rain, I am the soft earth. You are the life, the need, the heart. Grow in light, grow in rain, grow in soft, soft earth.*" But the spirit continued to rail in its tiny, unintelligible voice, shaking its twiglike fist at all of them. Winking at it, Merecot bit into her carrot.

"Without the words," the teacher said.

Daleina felt sweat pop onto her forehead. Without the words, it was difficult to concentrate. Around the practice ring, the other groups were working through their tests. To their left, she heard applause as water gushed out of the tree by the water-spirit teacher, and to their right, she saw the dance of flames in front of the students working with fire. Near another group, tiny earth spirits were tumbling across the dirt in every direction.

Focus, she ordered herself. She had the will. She simply had to harness it. *Grow, please.* Abandoning the chant, she tried to push the words out of her, from the inside, from her heart, and she felt as if her blood were burning. She gasped as the practice ring spun again.

Around her, everything blackened and blurred. She blinked, feeling her eyes fill with water. Her hands were shaking. She was shaking. She felt hands on her shoulders, and a voice saying, "Steady." The voice sounded as if it were underwater. She tried to breathe deep, to steady herself, but the world tilted sideways.

"Stop!" a voice commanded. And cold water splashed in her face. Spitting and gasping, she fell backward and landed on her rear.

Then Merecot was helping her stand. "Hey, look, she did it!"

Daleina looked at the dirt, and one of the seeds had sprouted. Lying on its side rather than in the dirt, it had produced a tendril of green and a misshapen pink blossom.

The teacher grunted, "Good."

As the students began to move to congregate in the middle of the practice ring, Daleina stayed behind, staring at the sprout. "I don't think I did that," she said softly.

"You didn't," Merecot admitted, also quietly.

"Why?" Daleina asked. "Why help me?"

She shrugged and didn't meet Daleina's eyes. "The entire class, you were the only one who dared ask a question, the only one who cared more about learning than being their performing monkey and passing their stupid tests. Frankly, I need someone to talk to, and you're the only one who seems to have half a brain."

Daleina studied her face. *She's lonely,* she thought. "Thank you."

"Granted, given your lack of skill, your life will certainly be short, but I'll enjoy your company until you're torn to bits."

Less gratefully, Daleina repeated, "Thank you," as they joined the other students to hear who had passed and who had failed.

V en hooked his knees over a branch and began sit-ups. He was at the top of the forest, and every time he swung his torso up, he had a view across the canopy. Sunrise streaked the sky in lemon and pale blue, and the autumn-gold leaves glowed where the light touched them. The canopy singers were heralding daybreak with a complex harmony. He couldn't see any of the singers, but he listened to them blend their music to the birdsong.

So close to the sky, it was peaceful. Not many lived this high. Dedicated singers. A few artists, hermits, and other loners. The weaker limbs were more dangerous, and it was a long way from the more abundant resources of the forest floor. Also, it was a very, very long way to fall. But Ven liked it. If he had to choose a place to live, he thought he'd pick the canopy. Fewer people was a definite bonus.

"Champion Ven?" a voice called—Healer Popol. "Much as I don't want to question your choice of camps, my apprentice and I would be much more comfortable if we could return to our customary paths."

Ven crunched his torso faster, completing twelve more sit-ups before answering. "You hired me to keep you safe. You should trust my judgment."

"We do! Of course we do! But . . ." The healer paused

as if choosing his words carefully, and Ven smirked. The healer hadn't been this deferential earlier. He supposed the change was due to the way Ven had caught dinner last night. He'd hit the squirrel mid-leap with his knife, a clean kill through the neck, and had it skinned and on the fire for dinner before Popol and his apprentice had finished laying out the bedrolls. Had to keep his skills fresh somehow. Plus the look on the pompous healer's face was priceless. ". . . your skill is unparalleled, so it seems to me that you could keep us just as safe on less . . . precarious terrain?"

Stopping the sit-ups, Ven caught the branch with his hands, flipped his legs over, and then landed on another branch a few feet below. Healer Popol and his apprentice, a young boy with green-gold eyes and black skin called Hamon, were huddled in the thin crook of the tree trunk. Ropes held their camp in place—they'd used their bedrolls like hammocks. Ven doubted either of them had slept much, though the boy hadn't complained. He rarely spoke at all, which Ven liked. Popol spoke enough for all three of them.

"We're expected in Ogdare by midmorning," Popol said. "Given how long it took us to reach this height, we will need to send word that we'll be late. I dislike being late. People expect their healers to be punctual." He switched his words to lecture his apprentice. "You must appear to be in control of the uncontrollable when you're a healer, or else people will worry and make your job that much harder. Appearance matters, my boy. You must be clean, neat, well dressed, calm, and in control of your temper at all times, even when your patients are being idiots. It can be challenging. People in pain are often idiots."

Ven would have broadened that to say people in general were often idiots. He'd seen so many forget the most commonsense basic security measures, such as refreshing their charms or reinforcing the walls and doors of their homes.

Or ignoring the advice of a trained champion.

Ex-*champion*, he thought with just a touch of bitterness.

Or more than a touch.

As Popol talked, the boy Hamon was packing up the camp, efficiently rolling the bedrolls into their packs. He left the spiderweb of ropes in place, to hold his master's weight, but he wasn't relying on them himself, Ven noticed. Very sensible.

Popol switched back to addressing Ven. "When we reach Ogdare, I expect you to take full responsibility for our tardiness. Explain it was your excessive concern for our welfare. It may turn out for the best, if they think our skills are so valued that we are in danger of being targets."

"Your skills *are* valued, Master," the apprentice said.

Accepting one of the packs, the lightest one, Popol waved his hand to dismiss the boy's words. "Of course they are. Perception, my lad. It's a tool just like the surgical knife. Belief in the healer can help a patient heal as much as the right herb."

"But isn't it better to actually heal them?" the boy Hamon asked.

"Both is best. Then the healthy heed your advice and don't need future healing."

Taking a rope from Hamon, Ven looped it around a branch. "We won't be late to Ogdare."

"I don't see how that's possible," Popol said. "It was a three-hour climb up."

Ven smiled and knew it was *not* a nice smile. "Down is much faster." Taking the remaining pack, he hooked a harness around Popol. The boy Hamon, quicker on the uptake than his master, secured himself to a rope as well. And then Ven released the knot that was holding their camp in place. They plummeted.

Ignoring Popol's screams, Ven watched the branches flash by, the autumn leaves blurring into golden streaks. At midforest, he caught the rope. It yanked and would have burned his skin if he hadn't worn thick leather gloves, which he always did—he'd learned that lesson the hard way, after an accident with a pricker bush when he was eight. His mother had left the prickers in him so he'd learn from his mistake. He still had a few scars from that. He tightened his muscles, and their plunge jerked to a stop, knocking off a spray of crinkled red leaves.

Popol gasped in air. "You are trying to cause a heart attack."

"Good thing we have a healer here to stop it." Ven lowered them slowly onto a bridge and then flicked the rope so that it came tumbling down after them. It collapsed into a pile at his feet, and he wound it back into a coil.

"I am never hiring you again," Popol said.

Inwardly, Ven sighed. He should really try not to antagonize his clients. It was just so very difficult to resist. It was the only amusement he got these days.

"He has kept us safe," Hamon pointed out. "And we've covered more territory—"

"I know, I know." Popol waved his hands like bird wings again. "But every—"

Ven heard a breath of wind in the trees. "Shh." Holding up one hand, he listened. The wind was above them, southeast, a tiny disturbance in the leaves, too localized to be true wind.

Both healer and apprentice fell silent and scanned the trees with him.

Hamon spotted the spirit first. He pointed wordlessly toward a translucent shape that watched them from a few branches up, perched on a patch of mottled bark. It was a child-size spirit with translucent butterfly wings. It held a bulge under one of its arms.

Ven put his hand on the hilt of his knife.

Up in the canopy, the tree spirits had largely ignored them, but now that they were back on the path, more would be watching them. The spirits didn't like it when humans traveled through the woods. Sometimes they showed their dislike in malicious ways. While they didn't dare defy the queen enough to directly harm a human, they could make travel difficult: weakening a bridge, cutting a rope, causing an animal to attack . . . little acts that couldn't be proven to be their fault.

For all that, though, it was unusual for one to show itself like this. "Stay in the center of the bridge," Ven said in a low voice. He'd take the rear, since the spirit was behind them. Drawing his knife, he herded the healer and apprentice forward.

The spirit flitted between the trees, pacing them.

"What's it want?" Popol asked, in what for him was a hushed voice. It still grated on Ven's ears. The man had no idea how to preserve himself in the forest. City-bred idiot.

He didn't dignify the question with an answer, and neither did the apprentice. All spirits wanted the same thing: the eradication of humans. Short-term, though? There was no way to know. Spirits didn't think like people or like animals. Their intelligence level varied dramatically within their own kind as well. Some were capable of a measure of reason; most weren't. It could be this spirit was curious. Or it could be judging them, seeing if they made easy targets. Ven scanned the other trees, to determine if it was alone, a scout, or, worse, acting as a distraction for others. He'd known that to happen: one spirit would draw attention while others would attack. It was one of their more clever maneuvers. It required a spirit that could plan, rather than one that acted on pure instinct, but there were such spirits, contrary to what people safe and snug in the cities liked to think.

He bet the apprentice Hamon was from one of the outer villages. He moved like he knew the danger. Popol moved like a blundering bear, woken too early from hibernation.

Next time Ven picked someone to guard, he'd choose some-one who was slightly less accustomed to safety.

The spirit flew between the trees, weaving to keep them in sight, veering closer and closer. They'd definitely caught the spirit's attention, for whatever reason. "If it attacks, drop and curl into a ball," Ven told Popol. "Present the smallest possible target."

"I'm not small," Popol objected.

No kidding. "I'll guard you."

"You'd better."

Ven resisted saying that's what his fee was for. If Ven had been able to act as a proper champion, he wouldn't have needed to sell his services this way. The crown would have continued his steady income, and Ven wouldn't have had to seek work like a common mercenary, but these days, Ven had to be practical. "Drop now."

Obeying, Popol thudded down and curled his head against his chest. He wrapped his arms around his head.

"You too," Ven told Hamon.

"I can help." Hamon drew one of the surgical knives. It wasn't suited for fighting, but it was sharp. Ven didn't bother arguing with him, especially once he noted that Hamon was clever enough to position himself behind Ven—he'd be a second line of defense for Popol, but he was smart enough not to try to be front line.

The spirit swooped onto the bridge. It landed lightly, like a leaf settling onto the ground. Without a word, it pulled a roll of parchment out from under its arm. It held it out toward Ven.

For an instant, Ven stared at the parchment and then at the spirit. *Someone had* sent *this?* Who? Queen Fara? Dare he hope . . . a pardon? An end to his exile? Perhaps after five years, she had realized the needs of Aratay were more important than the needs of the moment, or she'd realized the error of what she'd done and was ready to admit the truth and restore his reputation . . . Except that Fara never admitted errors.

Kneeling on one knee, he took the message from the spirit.

Without a word, the spirit darted back into the air and then disappeared between the trees.

Behind him, he heard Popol shift. "Is it gone? Did it go to fetch others? Is it coming back? Are we still in danger?"

Hands shaking, Ven untied the ribbon and unrolled the parchment. He saw his queen's handwriting. He touched the lettering as he read it. *Birchen. Tell him.* He checked the ribbon and recognized the mark on it: Hanna, headmistress of Northeast Academy, the school where Fara had trained many years ago.

It wasn't forgiveness.

It was . . . a warning? A plea?

A chance.

He rose. "We'll send word to Ogdare. You will be late."

FAST, AND HE'D LOSE THE HEALER THAT THE VILLAGers of Birchen might need.

Slow, and there might not be anyone left to heal.

He didn't know when the queen had sent the message to the headmistress, or how many days it had taken the air spirit to find him. The attack could have already taken place. Or he could be misreading the message, and there might not be an attack at all—it could be a surprise birthday party or a special sale on armor or . . . no, definitely carnage. *Tell him,* his queen had said, and the headmistress had decided that he, the Disgraced Champion, was that "him," which meant that whatever waited in Birchen would not be pleasant. He had to be prepared for anything from a rabid raccoon to a disaster like Greytree. Beside him, Healer Popol puffed and wheezed. His pack bounced on his back, and Ven reached over, grabbed it, and lifted it off, adding it to his own. Meanwhile, the boy didn't complain. Head down, lips pressed together, he was running along the bridge without a word. Popol didn't have breath left for words. Otherwise, Ven was certain he'd be hearing many.

He pictured Greytree, the destroyed village from five years earlier, the rubble on the ground, the family all alone amidst the debris, the bodies strewn around them. He never knew what had happened to that family. He should have checked on them, he supposed, listened to them thank him for coming when he did, or not thank him, since he'd come too late. Besides, hadn't they saved themselves? It was blurred with the memory of other fights, other disasters, other tragedies, perhaps none as broad and thorough as that—a whole village. Spirits picked off occasional travelers, hermit houses, herders, or other solitary woodsmen and woodswomen, but that kind of attack was, thankfully, rare.

Here, though, another village. A name. A warning. He hoped. His thoughts spurred him faster until Popol and the boy fell behind him.

There had to be a faster way!

Higher. He could go up.

Yes. "Do you trust me?" he asked, rounding on Popol and the boy.

"Of course. Hired you, didn't I?" wheezed Popol. "You might not be good enough for the capital anymore, but you're good enough for an old man. 'Course I trust you."

It wasn't a rousing endorsement, but it was acceptable. "Get out the harnesses," he ordered the boy.

"Wait, what do you have in mind?" Popol asked.

Ven didn't answer him. He scanned the trees for a reasonable path up. Hamon took the harnesses out of the packs and began strapping them around his master and himself. He then turned to Ven with the clips outstretched. Despite the circumstances, Ven smiled. *Bright boy,* he thought. "There's a wire path above us. Canopy singers use it."

"Oh no," Popol said, backing up. "No, no, no, thank you very much, but that is out of the question. I do *not*—"

"Do you want to explain to the people of Birchen why there was no healer to help them? Word will reach the other villages too, how you were too cowardly to travel quickly. It won't do good things to your reputation, the frightened healer who valued his own comfort over the lives of his patients. That kind of blow to the reputation can take years to recover from." As the healer's pasty face paled even more, Ven added, "Believe me, I know about tarnished reputations."

It was the last that decided him, Ven could see. Everyone knew about the legendary Champion Ven's fall from grace. Queen Fara had done her best to spread word far and wide, about how he'd attacked her in a spurned lover's rage.

Popol squeezed his eyes shut, took a deep breath as if to fortify himself, and then nodded.

Even with cooperation, it took the better part of an hour to travel the bridges to a spot where they could access the wire paths, and then they had to climb a ladder up the trunk before they reached the platform. "All you need to do is hang on," Ven told them. "And even then, the ropes will hold you. You'll be cargo. I'll do all the work."

Popol looked too terrified to speak, which Ven thought was an improvement. He and Hamon positioned the packs on Ven's back and then attached the harnesses so that Popol and Hamon were strapped to him as well. Then Ven clipped himself to the wire paths.

"Ready?" he asked.

"Are you serious?" Popol demanded. "I am *not* ready. And if you—"

Ven kicked off the platform. They sailed down the wire,

between the trees. Wind whipped against them. Leaves and branches smacked Ven's legs, and he felt the others huddle against the packs. A grin pulled at his face, a fierce grin.

This time, he would not be late.

Faster, they flew through the air. He readied the next clip. As they approached the intersection of wires, he counted down . . . three, two, one . . . He clipped on to the next wire and a half breath later, unclipped the old so that they sailed onto the new path without interruption.

This fast, he couldn't hear the birds, only the wind. Leaves blurred into a smear of green, gold, brown, and burnt red. He watched the wires ahead, every muscle alert for the next switch. Miss it by a second, and—

"Watch out!" Popol screamed.

But Ven was ready. He switched wire paths effortlessly. Again and again.

Below, down in midforest, signs pointed to their destination. It wasn't easy to read them or spot the landmarks at this height and speed, and Ven felt as if all his senses were heightened, every fiber of his body awake and vibrating.

"Brace yourselves!" he called.

"For what?" Popol yelled back, terror driving his voice an octave higher.

Aiming, Ven raised his feet into the air. He tensed his arm muscles—and then slammed into the side of a tree, feetfirst, absorbing the impact with his knees. He braced, keeping Popol and Hamon from crashing into the trunk, and they all hung for a second from the wire.

"Grab that rope ladder, would you, Hamon?" Ven asked.

Leaning over, Hamon pulled the rope ladder closer. Ven climbed onto it, unclipped from the wire, and climbed, carrying his two passengers and all the packs, down to the midforest bridge. Once there, he undid the harnesses. Hamon landed lightly, and Popol collapsed into a heap.

"Let me catch my breath!" Popol pleaded.

"Almost there," Ven said, hauling him up. He missed his years training candidates, when he didn't have to feign sympathy in his voice. He had no sympathy for people who let their own comforts endanger others. Healer Popol should have prepared himself before leaving his cushy city home. On the other hand, at least he *had* left it. Not many did. He added, "The people of Birchen will be grateful for your heroism."

"Yes." Popol straightened. "We do what we must."

Ven and the boy Hamon exchanged a look, and then they were moving again, quickly along the bridges, toward the village.

They heard the screams long before they saw anything through the thick trees. "Stay behind me," Ven ordered, and drew his sword and knife. One in each hand, he charged forward. His feet were silent on the bridge.

He burst out of the leaves into the town square, a platform suspended between a trio of trees. It was market day, bright-colored tents set up in a row, and people were running between them as air spirits flew around them, talons outstretched, tearing flesh as they flew past. Bodies already lay on the ground.

"Inside!" he bellowed to the people. "Take cover!" And then he ran forward to give them the distraction they'd need. Leaping and slicing, he threw himself into the center of the market.

Shifting their target, the air spirits flew at him—three in all, each medium size, with jewel-colored wings, angelic faces, and more deadly claws than any natural creature should have. They whipped in a circle around him, and he spun to keep his eyes ready for movement. His knife was tucked by his side, blocking his torso, and his sword was ready to strike.

With ear-piercing shrieks, the spirits howled at him, and then they attacked. He didn't think. He spun. He struck. He sliced. He jabbed. As one scraped its knifelike claws down his calf, he leaped, stepped on a crate, and launched himself up on top of the tents. The canvas bowed beneath his weight, and he ran across the tent poles, forcing the spirits to fight higher, above the level of the fleeing villagers.

Keep their attention, he thought. *Draw them away.*

The three spirits darted around him, wary now of his sword. He ran across the tent poles and then slid on his feet down an awning. Two spirits—where was the third?

As he hit the end of the awning, the third flew up from below him, aiming for his throat, its ethereal face twisted. He sliced, his sword catching the spirit in the torso and flinging it backward. It smacked into one of the houses, and the house shook.

The other two spirits screamed with so much rage that it poured into Ven, and he had to fight to keep his mind clear. Their scream dove deep inside him, fusing with his bones, until he could taste it in the air he breathed.

He had to lead them higher.

Leaping off the awning, he ran at the fallen spirit. Sword raised with both hands, he prepared to strike: a clean swing, slice its head from its neck. Not even a spirit could recover from a strike like that. But before he could land the blow, wind blasted in his face, driving him backward. Spinning through the market, the other two spirits used their power, spiraling the wind faster and faster, ripping fruits and stacks of clothes and blankets and tools and nails from their stalls and flinging them through the air. Ven dove for the ground, behind one of the stalls, until they ripped the stall itself back.

Howling, the two uninjured spirits flew at him, and he dropped his sword, reached into his shirt, and pulled out two charms. As their mouths opened, he hurled the charms at them, first one and then the other. The charms hit the backs of their throats.

"Go!" he shouted, standing, his sword again in his hand. "Leave this place, and don't come back."

Whimpering, the two spirits fled. The third crept behind them, its wings weakened, scuttling over the side of the platform and then disappearing.

Only then did Ven realize he'd been hurt.

He sagged as pain radiated from his ribs.

Blackness crept into his vision, and his last sight was the healer boy Hamon leaning over him. "Your turn," he said to the healers. As he lost consciousness, it occurred to him to wonder why his queen had sent this warning—why him, why here, why now? But he had no answers.

Only darkness.

CHAPTER 8

Queen Fara surveyed the Council of Champions and thought, *They're all idiots. All they do is talk, talk, and talk.* A few of the older ones should have retired years ago, but try explaining that to them. Her own champion, the one who had chosen and trained her, had stayed until he was delirious and ill, dying in the middle of a council meeting. The others had seen that as admirable. She'd been horrified. Of the current crop, many had flab instead of muscles, while others seemed to be there purely to show off their muscles. *Spare me the posturing of hypocrites and innocents.* None of them understood what had to be done to keep Aratay thriving. No concept of the sacrifices or of the choices she had to make. And they were supposed to be her staunchest supporters. Surrounded by her best allies, Queen Fara felt the most alone.

She leaned back in her throne and let their words wash over her like the rain. Concern over the border, over trade, over what coronation gift to send to the new queen of Chell, over how to appease the berry farmers and still please the timber barons—as if any of their babble mattered. No amount of discussion could fix the problems or fulfill the needs of Aratay. Only action.

Her action.

Champion Ambir had the floor, and he was using it, pacing back and forth over the inlaid wood, until Queen Fara wondered if she should worry about the shine. "The population of the capital bursts at the seams. We need more infrastructure: bridges, paths, ladders, to handle all the people coming in and out of the shops and schools every day. As it is, the crowds are too much of a temptation for the spirits."

There, at least, someone was saying something remotely useful. The spirits *were* drawn to crowds, resenting them even more than solitary travelers. Crowds caused harm to the forest, wear to the trees, hardening of the soil, overharvesting of the fruits and berries, overhunting of the animals, all of which riled up the spirits. But paradoxically, crowds were also safer. Spirits would rarely attack a large number of people, especially so close to the palace, where there were an overabundance of hedgewitches, guards, and overeager heirs itching for more practice so they'd be ready when their beloved queen died. As such, Ambir—like the rest of them—was wasting her time. "You don't need to concern yourself," Queen Fara said. "The capital is strong, and the spirits may salivate, but they won't act against us."

"If we had more bridges—"

"It will be done. Next?"

Next, apparently, was that more schools had to be built and rebuilt. And a few of the towns to the east were clamoring for a new hospital. There were petitions for additional secure orchards, a new area to harvest walnuts, permission to plant more blueberry bushes within an area not granted that kind of protection, even libraries and playgrounds that needed her approval. One of the cities, the Southern Citadel, wanted new housing for its poor, as they lacked the funds for fixing it themselves, due to the inconvenience of poverty.

She didn't know when being queen had become about minutiae. But no one wanted to live or work anywhere that the queen hadn't sworn to protect. As the champions prattled on, Queen Fara held up her hand. "Compile me a list. Rank it in order of importance, and I will attend to it. What is your report on your candidates?"

This was what the council of champions was supposed to worry about: the security of the crown. Her security, and the assurance that if she were to fall, the forests of Aratay wouldn't fall with her. One by one, the champions reported: all of them had candidates, and a few were overseeing heirs—about thirty-five heirs at present. Her people would be well cared for if she were to fall. Not that she had any intention of falling. Truthfully, she never liked listening to the champions report on her replacements. It made her feel expendable, and she was not that.

Never that.

"Enough." She waved them silent. "I have matters to attend to, as do you." Rising, she stood in front of her throne as each champion bowed to her and filed out of the council chamber, then down the stairs that spiraled down the outside of the palace tree. One of the last champions handed her the list she'd requested, all of the demands distilled from the various factions who petitioned the champions for the ear of the queen. Probably bribed them too. Fara took it without looking at it and instead watched her champions leave.

Soon, the Chamber of the Queen's Champions was empty, except for the queen. She breathed in. The chamber always smelled like flowers. White blossoms wound over the archways in clusters that looked like snow. She'd never seen anyone tend the flowers, and she'd never cared for them either. They merely grew there, every season, even in the worst of winter when the branches were laced in ice and the chamber was slick with frost. The chamber had been grown by one of her predecessors, shaped from the top of the palace tree, with arches that surrounded it and a throne that grew out of the center. It was open to the sky.

Standing by her throne, Queen Fara watched the blue

expanse above. Her visitor always knew when she was alone here, no matter how carefully the champions checked for assassins and spies. Clouds stretched and separated, forming shapes that looked as if they were fleeing from one another. It was late morning. By now, the deed was done, and Champion Ven had either received her message in time or he hadn't. Sending the message to Headmistress Hanna had been her one burst of inspiration, her one gesture of defiance.

As usual, she didn't see the spirit arrive. One second she was alone, and another . . . it perched on her throne.

It was a wood spirit, with the face of an owl and the body of a woman, with owl wings that lay down her back. Her feathers were patterned with a hundred shades of brown, as if she wore a mosaic of all the bark of all the trees of the forest. Her bare feet had talons in place of toes, and they were digging into the soft wood of the throne.

"Are you satisfied?" Queen Fara asked, and she couldn't help the hostile tone creeping into her voice. She tried to swallow it back. It wouldn't help to let the spirit see her emotions. The spirit wouldn't understand, as it had none itself. Except rage. And now the satisfied smugness of a hunter who has claimed her prey.

"Yes, indeed," the owl woman said, her voice nearly a purr.

Queen Fara thrust the list of demands at her. "This is what my people need. Your spirits will assist me."

"Of course," the spirit said. "We honor our promises."

And unfortunately, so do I. Queen Fara kept her face blank. "Do not grow accustomed to this arrangement. This will not happen again."

But she knew she'd said those words before.

aleina pinched the flesh under her arm, hard, to keep herself awake. Exams, reports, lectures . . . She stayed on top of those, but this—summoning—still didn't come easily, even after two years at the academy. She sat cross-legged on the floor of her bedroom. The wolf Bayn curled around her back, a comforting cushion. He didn't mind that Daleina wasn't asleep yet.

The trick was to clear her mind of all other thoughts. She had to focus purely on what she wanted the spirit to do. Years ago, when Greytree was attacked, fear had instinctively focused her, but everyday life didn't include that kind of mortal danger. Even after two full years of academy training, she still had difficulty controlling her mind. All the thoughts from the day tumbled through: the facts from the day's lessons, how tired she was, how she still had to study for her diplomacy test, the way her arm ached from a miscalculation in survival class. She breathed in and out, as she'd been taught, and picked a single image: a candle flame.

She'd set a candle on the floor in front of her, in an iron candlestick that she'd borrowed from the dining hall with Revi's help. Revi never minded pilfering items from the common areas. They're here for our use anyway, she rationalized. And besides, what better cause was there than practicing their lessons? Daleina couldn't argue with that, but she did intend to return it, once she'd mastered this. "You are going to dance for me," she whispered. "Come and dance."

Gently, the wolf began to snore.

Daleina pushed Bayn's rumble out of her head. She pushed away the clatter of footsteps on the spiral stairs outside her window. She ignored the bells that called for the younger students to be in bed. She ignored the chatter from Revi's room—Revi, Mari, and Linna were having their usual study season for tomorrow's history exam. Daleina hoped she'd studied enough. She thought she had. She'd been cramming facts into her head all week, names and dates of queens, their miracles and their deaths, battles and treaties, ready to rattle them off—*No, focus,* she reminded herself. *That's why you're in here, not over there.*

Another deep breath. "Come and dance," she whispered.

She wasn't supposed to say the words out loud. It was a crutch, the teachers said. All summoning should be all internal by now. She shouldn't need to even think about it; it should be instinct. Yet it wasn't, not yet. But it *would be*, even if she had to forgo sleep for the next week.

"Come and dance."

She knew the spirits were out there—she could sense them, little shivers in the air, wrinkles that she could "feel" when she reached her mind out. She'd become adept at sensing spirits, one of the best in her class, in fact. It had been such a relief that at least one skill had come easily. But it wasn't enough. The spirits teased the edges of her awareness, twisting and slipping and sliding out of her grip. Sometimes it felt as if they were pieces of her that she could feel—extra limbs that felt smooth, soft, hot, cold—but couldn't move.

She'd left the window open intentionally, and the curtain shifted as wind blew. She glanced up. A spirit? Just a breeze. It carried the scent of tonight's dessert: a chocolate melt cake, a reward for all the students who passed last week's diplomacy exam. She'd never tasted chocolate before. It looked like mud but tasted like what she imagined sunset would taste like, if it had a flavor. And there she went again, mind drifting. Maybe she should try this first thing in the morning, before she was cluttered up with thoughts from the day. Except morning came with the remnants of dreams, and then crowded with the rush to begin the day's lessons. She'd do this now. No more excuses.

Flexing her hands, rolling her shoulders, and taking a few more cleansing breaths, Daleina tried again. This time she focused, reaching toward a small shiver in the air outside on the stairs. A tiny fire spirit, one of the ones that liked to inhabit the lanterns around the school, skittered over the sill of her window.

"Come," she coaxed. She beckoned it toward the candle.

It darted closer and then stopped, a little closer and then stopped again, as if it were shy. It was a beautiful thing, a living dollop of flame, with fiery hair, coal eyes, and a dress of glowing embers. It climbed onto the iron candlestick and then shimmied up the wax candle to the wick.

And then it danced.

It danced!

Twirling and spinning, it swayed and leaped in the melting pool of wax. *Dance! Yes, dance!* She wanted to clap her hands and shout, even though she knew first-year students did this all the time. She'd done it, herself, with no help. *Dance!*

And then there were more, pouring in through the window, dozens of tiny fire spirits. Some climbed the curtains. Others cavorted over her bed.

Oh no, not this many.

Daleina pushed to her feet. "All right, that's enough. Stop now. Go."

Growling, Bayn backed to the door. He then turned tail and fled for the stairs, pure wolf instinct. Sensible instinct. Daleina thought maybe she should run too.

Flames licked up her curtains. They raced over her desk, curling the edges of her notes. The corner of one book crumbled into ash. *Stop,* she told them. *Stop now!*

But the fire spirits didn't listen. There were too many, swirling together, laughing in their crackling voices. Fire, true fire, whooshed up from her bed, and smoke gathered.

"Stop!" she commanded. Her voice rang, and the fire spirits halted where they were and looked at her, all the coal eyes looking at her. And then they fled, pouring out the window, but leaving the fire behind.

Daleina ran to the door and flung it open. "Fire!"

Merecot threw her door open. "What did you do?"

"They danced," Daleina said.

Opening her door, Revi shrieked. Linna tossed a pitcher of water toward the flames. Mari bolted down the stairs, calling that she'd fetch help.

"Seriously, all of you?" Merecot rolled her eyes. "Try thinking instead of panicking." She raised her hand, and water spirits dove through the window, bringing a cascade of rain into the room. They drenched everything, including Daleina, and then they funneled out of the room. Returning up the stairs came Mari with a bucket of water. Behind her was Caretaker Undu.

Daleina wished she could vanish out the window like the spirits.

Standing in the doorway, hands on her hips, Caretaker Undu surveyed the mess that was Daleina's room: soaked and charred at the same time. "Who is responsible for this?"

Slowly, Daleina raised her hand. "I am."

"The rain was mine," Merecot chimed in.

Revi peeked in around them. "Adds a nice touch to the décor. Sort of post-shipwreck chic."

Daleina rushed inside. "Oh no, my books! My notes!" All her textbooks, her notes . . . two years of notes! Ruined!

"I can call a fire spirit to dry them," Merecot offered.

"No more spirits in bedrooms," Caretaker Undu said firmly. "You will clean up this mess, and then you will report to me for appropriate punishment." She swept out of the room and down the spiral stairs.

In her wake, they stared at the mess that was Daleina's room.

"You know, in a few years, you'll look back on this and think it's hilarious," Revi said.

Linna patted Daleina's shoulder. "You'll tell your future kids the anecdote so many times that they will be able to tell it back to you."

"If she has kids," Merecot said, "which she won't, because she's going to die young."

Revi, Linna, and Mari glared at her, but Daleina looked at the wet curtains, with char that dripped black on the sill, and she started to laugh.

Concerned, Linna approached her. "Daleina?"

"I set my room"—she laughed harder—"on fire. And she"—she pointed at Merecot, and her finger shook as she laughed more, bending over to put her hands on her knees. She couldn't explain why it was so funny.

"Yeah, we know," Revi said, looking at her as if she'd hit her skull a bit too hard, "we were here."

"Sorry about my mother," Mari said. "I didn't mean to bring her."

Daleina couldn't stop laughing. "It's just"—she gasped as she laughed—"she thinks she's so good, and I think I'm so . . . *not* good, and together we destroyed—" Tears popped into her eyes.

Merecot began to laugh. Slowly, it spread to Revi, Mari, and Linna, until all of them were laughing, clutching their sides, with tears running down their cheeks.

———

Oᴜᴛsɪᴅᴇ ᴏɴ ᴛʜᴇ sᴘɪʀᴀʟ sᴛᴀɪʀᴄᴀsᴇ, Hᴇᴀᴅᴍɪsᴛʀᴇss Hanna paused, listening to the sound of laughter from the students' rooms. Laughter, such a rare, beautiful sound within the walls of the academy. Hanna stood listening for as long as it lasted.

Iᴛ ᴛᴏᴏᴋ ᴀʟʟ ꜰɪᴠᴇ ᴏꜰ ᴛʜᴇᴍ sᴇᴠᴇʀᴀʟ ʜᴏᴜʀs ᴛᴏ ᴜɴᴅᴏ the mess that the spirits had caused. Even then, Daleina's books and notes would never been the same. She'd left them to dry by the fires of the academy kitchen, but she knew the pages would be forever crinkled and curled. Linna had taken all of Daleina's smoke-filled, water-logged clothes down to the laundry, and Daleina now had fresh linens on the bed and no more curtains on the window. After scrubbing everything, it all smelled like lemons. Surveying the room, she thought it looked and smelled as if she'd never lived there. After two years, she thought there would be more evidence that she'd been here than this. Her life ought to have made a mark on the room, other than a few scorch marks that she couldn't scrub away. Instead, it looked as though she'd moved out—*or worse, as if I'd never been here.* She had the urge to clutter it up again, to prove it was hers.

"On the plus side, you'll pass room checks," Revi said with a yawn.

"Go to bed," Daleina told them. "You can get at least an hour before the bells ring."

Nodding, Linna padded toward her room. Revi gave Daleina a quick hug. "Everything will be fine. Well, after Mari's mother finishes skinning you alive."

"Sorry." Mari cringed.

"It's okay," Daleina said. "My fault." She turned toward Merecot. "I'll tell her that, too. You don't need to come with me. I was the idiot who called too many spirits. You were the hero who stopped the fire before anyone was hurt. It could have spread and endangered the entire academy."

"Obviously I'm coming with you," Merecot said. "You can't face the dragon by yourself. Your magic isn't good enough for the kind of punishment she could dole out."

"Ouch," Daleina said, though she couldn't argue, with the lemon-fresh evidence in front of her.

"Ouch for me too," Mari said. "My mother's not a dragon. She's just . . . serious."

"True," Merecot said. "I'm sorry. She's serious." As Mari headed for her own bedroom, Merecot added, "—ly dragonish."

Daleina shut the door on the room that didn't look like her room anymore, and she and Merecot headed for the spiral stairs. It was possible that Caretaker Undu would be asleep and didn't mean for them to come the instant the bedroom was clean, but Daleina thought that was unlikely. The head caretaker never seemed to sleep. She was everywhere, all the time, and was the reason that the academy ran so smoothly. She took the concept of organization to a higher level, conducting the other caretakers in the art of preparing dinner, washing the laundry, and cleaning the academy as if they were instruments in her orchestra. "She'll be fair," Daleina said, as much to soothe herself as Merecot.

"She hates me," Merecot stated. "All of them hate me, which is fine because it's mutual."

"You don't really hate them."

"They're jealous of me."

"No one is jealous of you." Daleina resisted the urge to roll her eyes. Sometimes Merecot got in these moods. Daleina was never sure if she meant it or not. Merecot never *sounded* upset, but she excelled at hiding her feelings.

"Except you."

"Except me, of course," Daleina said, "but it's not because

of your incredible powers, or the fact that you're at the top of every single class."

"Oh, really?"

"It's because of your hair," Daleina said with a straight face. "You have the best hair."

Merecot smirked at her as Daleina knocked on Caretaker Undu's door. She waited, listening for footsteps. Once again she prayed that maybe they'd get lucky, and the caretaker would be asleep. Then she could collapse in bed for a few minutes before it was time to be shoved through the cheese grater that was an ordinary day. She was never going to make it through all her classes completely awake. Maybe if she kept poking herself with a quill, that would keep her alert. Or she could bring in a stash of crackers to nibble on— sometimes that worked. Summoning class was doomed to be a disaster, and she hated to think what Master Klii was going to say. She'd be back to herding mole-sized earth spirits around the ring. Again.

She heard footsteps, and then the door opened. Caretaker Undu was in full robes, as if she'd been awake for hours. Most likely she had. "Good. You finished before dawn. Come with me." Without waiting for a response, the head caretaker swept past them and up the stairs.

Exchanging glances, Daleina and Merecot followed. Punishment was almost certainly going to involve some sort of cleaning and suck away any extra time they had, the time they used to practice, study, and write papers. But it could involve more studying and practice—in fact, that would be logical. Perhaps Caretaker Undu was going to hand them over to Master Klii or one of the other masters, and they'd have to review the basics for hours on end.

Except that Caretaker Undu kept walking higher.

Above, the circle of sky visible from the academy was gray, lightening with the touch of predawn. The few stars were pale, and the shadows within the academy were flat.

Daleina wondered what the sunrise looked like from the top of the academy, above the forest canopy. She was always busy at sunrise: beginning her day to the toll of the morning bells. A few birds were singing, but other than the birds, all was quiet.

"Caretaker Undu? For the record, it wasn't Merecot's fault," Daleina said. "It was mine and mine only. I was alone in my room, and I made the decision to summon spirits alone."

"You'll discuss it with the headmistress," Caretaker Undu said. "She wishes to speak to you."

Daleina swallowed and exchanged another look with Merecot. Neither of them had said more than a few words to the headmistress, not since the day they were admitted two years ago. She was a distant presence, always there, always watching, but never involved. Certainly never in any disciplinary action involving students, at least to the best of Daleina's knowledge. Was what she had done so very bad? Surely other students had had accidents with spirits. Lots of accidents. The teachers were always telling cautionary tales about former students who had summoned spirits too large for them to control. Sometimes those tales even included tours around the academy, pointing out locations where students or teachers had died or been dramatically injured. Not that Daleina had ever seen it happen. The masters were careful to have their students summon only controllable spirits—that was the point of the training. Don't mess with the big ones. You needed the extra power that came with coronation to tangle with those. Every teacher sported scars from times when past students had tangled with the wrong spirits—they were all living object lessons, at least those who still lived.

At the top of the spiral, Caretaker Undu knocked on the headmistress's door. In response, it swung silently open, with no one touching it. Daleina peered around, looking for spirits who could have opened it, but saw none. "Thank you," came the headmistress's voice from inside. "You may leave us, Undu."

Bowing, Caretaker Undu retreated past them down the stairs. She didn't look back.

"If she lowers my scores because of this, I'm not forgiving you," Merecot murmured to Daleina.

"She won't," Daleina said. "It wouldn't be fair." She stepped forward. "I'll go first."

Merecot blocked her. "I will. She won't be as angry at me, since I did keep the academy from burning down."

"But you shouldn't be punished at all—"

"I know. And I'll speak up for you."

"I'm not going to let her—"

The headmistress's voice cut across them. "Predawn wanes. Come in before old age claims me and all that remains is bones."

Both of them walked in together—with a little maneuvering and brushing of shoulders against the jamb—side by side.

At her desk, the headmistress was crowned in candlelight. An array of candles flickered behind her, the reflection of flames shimmering on the windowpanes. She had parchment on her desk, notes and maps, and a pile of half-eaten fruits and breads lay beside her, as if she'd been there and working for some time. *Does anyone in this place ever sleep?*

The spirits know I haven't.

Daleina bowed, and Merecot, a second later, followed suit. "Headmistress Hanna, I take full responsibility for my actions—"

"And I for mine," Merecot jumped in.

"I was attempting to practice, and I lost control," Daleina said. "Merecot was merely trying to contain the damage I'd done. She stopped an accident from becoming a tragedy. I don't think she deserves to be punished—"

"And you?" the headmistress asked, looking at Merecot. "Do you believe you deserve punishment?"

"I don't," Merecot answered. "And neither does Daleina. It was an accident. Daleina has difficulty controlling spirits. She's easily overwhelmed if they come in either strength or numbers. It wouldn't surprise me if the nearby spirits noticed this and came in droves on purpose."

That was a bit more honest than helpful. Daleina shot her a less-than-friendly look. The headmistress didn't need to know all of Daleina's failings. It would have been far better if the headmistress hadn't noticed her at all, at least not for two more years, until after she'd passed her exams and been chosen by a champion.

Headmistress Hanna folded her hands on her desk. "Accidents happen. They are part of how we learn. And you are here to learn."

Daleina bobbed her head hard. "If my punishment could be more practice, I'd appreciate it. I'd rather not lose time in the classroom. We're so close to midterm exams."

"Yes, exams." The headmistress tapped her fingers on a stack of parchment.

Merecot frowned and craned her neck as if trying to read the papers. "Are those mine?"

The headmistress pushed back from her desk, walked toward her window, and clasped her hands behind her. "Can you tell me why this academy exists?"

"To train those with the affinity for spirits to use their powers," Merecot said, promptly and loudly, as if answering a drill.

"Indeed. Why?"

"So that the champions can choose the best candidates to become heirs," Merecot said. "The queen must be the best of the best."

"And why do we need a queen?" the headmistress asked.

Daleina glanced at Merecot. That felt like a trick question. Only a queen could touch all the spirits at once. After the coronation ceremony, her powers were magnified, her strength and range increased until she could impose her will on all the spirits within her borders. She and she alone could maintain the do-no-harm command for every spirit and keep the spirits from destroying everyone. "To protect the people," Daleina said. "A queen must use her powers to ensure the well-being of everyone in her land."

"It is an enormous responsibility, to be queen. It requires sacrifice, compassion, and wisdom. A queen must be morally unassailable. She must be strong of character, as well as affinity. It is seldom discussed, but the fact is that a bad queen can be as dangerous as no queen."

Daleina wasn't sure that was true. No queen meant certain death. Her village, writ large. It was the reason that *every* woman, regardless of level of power, was taught the coronation command—after a queen died, the spirits had to be, in essence, frozen so that they didn't slaughter everyone before the next queen was chosen. *Choose.* That simple command suspended their bloodlust, their power, the forest itself. Drastic but necessary. To be without a queen . . .

"This academy exists not only to shape the kind of power required to be queen but to shape the kind of *person* required to be queen," the headmistress said. "Your courses in history, politics, and ethics are of equal importance to summoning and survival."

"With all due respect, Headmistress, we know this," Merecot said. "Please just tell us our punishment so we can return to our studies."

Daleina winced. She might know diplomacy was important, but Merecot still needed to work on it.

Headmistress Hanna turned from the window to face them again. "I took the liberty of requesting your records, after the incident last night, and I'm afraid I found a disturbing trend. Your papers and your exams over the last two years in history, politics, theory, and ethics . . ." The headmistress gestured at the stacks of parchments. "I believe you two have engaged in unethical behavior, repeatedly. Your work is too similar for any other explanation, unless you would care to offer one?"

Daleina stared at the headmistress as the words linked and unlinked in her head, her brain trying to make sense of them. The headmistress couldn't mean . . . She couldn't think . . . "We didn't cheat. Not on an exam. Or a paper. Or anything. Ever."

"I worked hard," Merecot said. "I deserve my scores."

"Merecot has helped me in summoning classes," Daleina said, "but only during classes and practices, not during anything official." Not much, anyway. Not enough to constitute cheating. Everyone helped one another.

Headmistress Hanna shook her head. "Summoning classes don't concern me. I am concerned with your coursework in your other classes, with your written assignments and exams."

This didn't make sense. It was unfair. Untrue! "We study together, a lot." Or at least Daleina studied with Revi and Linna. Merecot didn't come to their study sessions. Still . . . "It makes sense that our answers would be the same. We learned at the same time, from the same books and same lectures. We discuss the lessons. We're supposed to do that!"

Headmistress Hanna plucked two papers from two different stacks and laid them side by side. "First-year exams, history." She pointed to answers, one after another. Leaning forward, Daleina read—she remembered this exam. She'd studied hard. Some of the answers had been obscure, and she'd been proud of herself. She'd even written to her parents and Arin, telling them how she'd done. They'd been proud of her, even sending her a necklace of whittled wood

as a congratulations present. "And this, second year, ethics."
The headmistress drew out two papers and displayed them
before Daleina and Merecot.

Daleina looked up from the papers. "You're mistaken.
We did our own work."

"Test results don't matter anyway," Merecot argued. "It's
the power that matters. The spirits chose the strongest and
the best. They won't choose anyone to be queen who hasn't
mastered all six kinds of spirits. The greater the control, the
greater the queen."

"Power without ethics is a recipe for disaster beyond
imagining," Headmistress Hanna said. "And this sort of
rampant disregard for the integrity of your own work concerns me greatly."

No, this can't be happening! She'd studied. She'd ago-
nized over papers, pounded facts into her head, and pored
over textbooks. All the notes that were drying in the kitchen
were proof that she'd done her own work! Except that
she'd be lucky if any of them were legible—her proof was
charred and shriveled. Her stomach felt like a charred stone
inside her.

"Give me a reason why I shouldn't ask you both to leave
this academy." There was sadness in her eyes, Daleina
saw; the headmistress didn't want to do this, but she believed
they'd both cheated. Daleina felt sick, the charred stone
churning over.

"Because I am the best student you've ever had," Merecot answered without hesitation. "Because I *will* be queen."

"And you, Daleina?" the headmistress asked.

A thousand answers tumbled through her. Before she
could answer, though, Merecot spoke again, "Because she
didn't cheat. I did." Sauntering up to the desk, Merecot rifled
through the pages and then flung them on the floor. They
fluttered together like fallen leaves. "All of this . . . it's a
waste of time. The only thing that truly matters is the spirits.

How strong you are. That's how I chose to spend my time. Every waking moment, I've honed my power. See?" Holding out her hand, Merecot faced the window, and an air spirit slammed into the glass.

Daleina jumped back as the window shattered.

The spirit flew directly to Merecot's hand and alighted on it. Merecot stroked its head as if it were a pet. "Aw, you broke a window," Merecot said to the spirit. "We must fix it."

Nodding once, the spirit flew to the shards of glass. It gathered them in its arms, oblivious to how the shards cut into its thin skin. Blood dotted the bits.

"Merecot . . ." Headmistress Hanna began.

Merecot held up her hand again. "I'm not done yet."

More air spirits swarmed through the window, gathering the bits of glass. They held the pieces into place. And then fire spirits ran over the cracks, and the glass heated, brightening to a glowing orange. The cracks melted together, fusing back. With a flick of her wrist, Merecot dismissed the spirits, and then turned to the headmistress.

Daleina walked to the window. She'd never seen Merecot do anything like that. She'd never seen *anyone* do anything like that. She hadn't even known it was possible. Reaching out toward the fused cracks—

"Don't touch," Merecot warned. "Still hot."

She withdrew her fingers. There were streaks of reddish pink within the glass, where the air spirits had bled on the shards, and the healed cracks were still visible. It was far from perfect, but the level of power and control—"I used my time to practice, instead of wasting it with irrelevant nonsense," Merecot said. "Is that so very wrong?"

"This"—the headmistress tapped her desk and the few papers that hadn't been scattered—"is indeed so very wrong. And the fact that you admit it with pride and do not seem to comprehend the seriousness—"

"I have a gift, and I want to use it!" Merecot said.

"Why?" Headmistress Hanna asked. "Why do you want to be queen so badly?"

"Because it's what I was born to do," Merecot said. "It's why I exist. It's why everything that's happened to me has happened. It's my purpose, my life."

The headmistress turned to Daleina. "Why do you want to be queen?"

Daleina swallowed and thought of her sister Arin. Her answer was the same as it had been on the day she took the entrance exam. That hadn't changed. "To protect people." But that sounded so weak next to Merecot's claim of destiny and her display of power.

Merecot snorted. "Seriously? You're parroting back *that* answer? Can't you be honest with yourself at least about why you're here? You aren't as good and pure as all that."

Daleina shook her head. It wasn't about goodness, and she wasn't trying to get the right answer. Whenever she thought about why she was here, whenever she closed her eyes at night, whenever she sat in the practice ring or listened to a teacher wax on about the importance of their studies, whenever she was so tired that she wanted to quit, she saw her village, except now the torn bodies were her family and her friends: Revi, Mari, Linna, Merecot, her teachers, the caretakers, her parents, her sister . . . It was their bodies she pictured in the wreckage. "I think not wanting people dead is a reasonable answer. Be honest: it's your answer too, Merecot. You want to protect people too. You have this incredible power, and you want to use it to be everyone's hero."

Merecot exhaled so heavily that it sounded as if she were deflating. "Yes. Exactly. You can't fault me for that. I'm not 'unethical.' I'm driven."

Headmistress Hanna studied them both. Under her gaze, Daleina felt as if her skin were peeled back and her innards examined. The silence stretched for longer than a comfortable moment. "Merecot, you admit that Daleina was not involved?"

"She had no idea," Merecot said.

Daleina opened her mouth and then shut it. She didn't know how to defend Merecot when all of that was true. She'd had no idea, not even a suspicion, that Merecot had been stealing her work and copying her exams. Scooping up the pages, she saw more similarities—papers that looked nearly identical, research that matched point for point, analysis that followed the same logic. She'd spent hours and hours on all of this, and Merecot had just taken it, without ever asking or telling her—

"Then, Merecot, I have no choice but to insist that you repeat these courses, or leave this academy," Headmistress Hanna said. "I cannot permit you to be chosen until this is rectified. You will also report for specialized ethics training, since those lessons in particular seem not to have made an impact."

"Repeat *all* the courses? From two years?" Daleina clutched the papers. "You can't delay her like that. Look how incredible she already is. She'll make an amazing queen! With her as queen, we'll all be safe." She was aware that she should be promoting herself, that she was supposed to see Merecot as her competition, but it wasn't fair!

"With her as queen, we'd all suffer." Headmistress Hanna's eyes were fixed on Merecot. "Do you understand, child?"

"I understand," Merecot said stiffly.

"I don't think you do. But your obedience will suffice for now. You are both dismissed."

"Wait, surely there can be some kind of compromise." Daleina made herself put the exams down, neaten them, then straighten them again. "She could do a special study with one of the teachers. She could retake the exams, on her own, and then you could judge. She could—"

Merecot laid a hand on Daleina's shoulder. "It's all right. Let's go."

"But, Merecot—"

"She dismissed us." Merecot pulled her toward the door. "And the morning bells have already rung. You're going to be late for class."

Daleina hadn't heard the bells. But dawn was streaming through the once-broken window and spilling onto the floor, shadowy lines in the light marking where Merecot had healed the breaks. She let herself be led out of the headmistress's office, though she swore to return later, after class, and argue again. It wasn't fair to ask Merecot to retake all of the classes. She was the best in the academy, albeit maybe not in coursework . . . "Why didn't you ask me for help? I could have, I don't know, tutored you. We could have studied more. . . ."

"It doesn't matter," Merecot said. "I don't regret what I did. I only regret that the headmistress blamed you too."

"You've helped me plenty. I wouldn't be here if it weren't for you. I could have helped you!" If Merecot had asked for help in their other courses, Daleina would have given up sleep to help her. She could have had a separate study hour for her.

"You *did* help me. You just didn't know it." Merecot quirked her lips into an almost-smile. She hooked her arm through Daleina's as they climbed down the stairs. "I want you to promise me something: you won't believe what the masters say about you, what I say about you, what you say about yourself. We're all liars. You have power within you. Enough power."

"Not like you," Daleina said.

"The way they teach here . . . It's not right for me. I realized that a long time ago, but I thought I could stick it out, fool them, and focus on what I needed. I was wrong about that, I guess. But, Daleina, it's not right for you either. You need to find what works for you. Practice as much as you can, even if it means burning down your room a dozen times. Don't do what's expected. Don't just follow the rules. The spirits don't follow their rules. Why should we?"

The other students were spilling out of the bedrooms and heading toward their classes.

Merecot stopped at their bedrooms and took Daleina's hands in hers. "You might even do amazing, once you're not in my very impressive shadow anymore."

Automatically, Daleina began, "Your shadow's not that—" She stopped. "You're leaving? Merecot, you can't! After all the work—"

"I've gotten as much as I can get out of this place. It's time to move on. Learn someplace else. Someplace that will appreciate me more. Someplace that needs me."

You can't leave! Daleina wanted to yell at her, shake some sense into her, but Merecot was wearing her most mulish expression—which was saying something. There was no arguing with her.

She hugged Daleina, and Daleina hugged her back. And then with a smile that on anyone else would look forced, Merecot headed for her room.

Following her, Daleina watched her pull clothes from drawers and her cache of personal weapons, the ones she'd arrived with, from under her bed and stuff them all into a pack. "Wait, you're going *now*? Right now? Don't you want to say goodbye to everyone?"

"I'm not good at goodbyes. Tell them for me. Consider that paying me back for stopping your fire from completely destroying the academy, which you'd think the headmistress would have brought up as more serious than my academic issues." Merecot shook her head. "She doesn't have her priorities straight. But that's no longer my problem. Try not to make it yours. And, Daleina, try not to die."

Daleina felt tears in her eyes. "You too."

By the end of her third year at the academy, Daleina could summon all six kinds of spirits, as well as sense them at distances up to a quarter mile. By the end of her fourth year, she could control them. Sometimes. If she worked at it. And if she chose small, weak, not-so-smart spirits. Merecot had been right: without her acting as a safety net, Daleina was pressed to work harder. And she had. She passed her exams, year after year, and so did Revi, Linna, and Mari, as well as the others who had joined their study group: Zie, Evvlyn, and Iondra. Every night, all seven young women crammed into one bedroom after dinner to discuss magical theory, argue about the history of Renthia, and agonize over the next hurdle the teachers wanted them to leap. In the spring, that hurdle was their largest yet: champions looking for potential heirs were spotted at the academy. Two, to be specific, Champion Piriandra and Champion Cabe. Daleina had caught a glimpse of them as they were greeted by Headmistress Hanna.

"Details, please," Zie begged as the usual study group crowded into Daleina's room.

"Both of them look strong." That had been Daleina's first, albeit brief, impression: contained strength, like a coil held in tension. "Champion Cabe's muscles have muscles. And Champion Piriandra is just skin on top of muscles."

"And bones," Linna corrected primly. "The expression is 'just skin and bones.' "

"I don't think she has room for bones with all the muscles." The champion had also been alert, her eyes snapping to every corner of the room. She'd spotted Daleina instantly. She was the kind of champion that Daleina wanted—smart, aware, serious. Someone who could take Daleina's training to the next level. After four years, all of them were chafing to be out in the world. Others their age were marrying, having children, running shops, becoming journeymen and masters—in other words, living their lives, not still preparing for them. *It's our turn now.*

"There will be tests tomorrow," Mari said. "My mother had caretakers washing our uniforms, even though they weren't dirty. She had strict orders about the stains."

"Your mom thinks stains are a personal insult," Revi said.

"So what do we do to prepare?" Linna asked.

"Everything that we've done for the past four years has been to prepare," Iondra intoned. She was always intoning, proclaiming, or decreeing things. She was from the forest canopy, the daughter of a drummer and a singer, and she treated speech as if she were performing.

"Best thing we can do is get a full night's sleep," Daleina said.

All of them looked at her. Revi raised one eyebrow. Daleina felt her lips twitch. And then they all burst out laughing. She waved them silent. "Obviously we'll practice. Air spirit? Who wants to start?"

Concentrating, Mari summoned a tiny air spirit into Daleina's bedroom. It danced on her sheets. As they took turns commanding the creature, they compelled it to create a gust of wind that blew papers around the room like birds. The spirit flew with the papers, spiraling up the ceiling, then darting out the window. Next: an earth spirit, which crawled, oozing with mud, up the stairs and into the room. At Zie's command, it shaped itself into a snake and then a salamander, sprouting legs of mud. They ended with a fire spirit, causing it to light and then douse all the candles on their level of the spiral staircase.

When all the candles were out and the fire spirit dismissed, the others shuffled off to bed, leaving Daleina alone in her room. Lying on her bed, she told herself to go to sleep. She had to be well rested for tomorrow. Two champions to impress. Two chances to be chosen. Two chances to make all of this worthwhile, to prove she could do this, to have the opportunity to do something real with her power, not just practice and study.

She wished Merecot were here. Not for the first time, she wondered what had happened to her friend, if she'd found a new academy, if she'd been chosen by a champion, or if she'd gone home to her family—wherever and whoever they were. She hadn't realized until after Merecot was gone how little she'd truly known about her. Because of that, Daleina had made even more of an effort to get to know her remaining friends beyond what kind of students they were. Zie was a middle child and had never left the capital. Revi had scores of cousins, all city-dwellers too, plus two mothers, who visited constantly. Mari was the youngest of ten, the only child who had shown enough power to enter the academy. She was convinced her family would never forgive her if she failed. She wanted her mother's approval so badly that it hurt, but Caretaker Undu never wanted to show favoritism. Evvlyn was the daughter of border guards and had been born while her mother was on guard duty, alone, in the middle of winter. She often said that nothing she could ever do could match the fierceness of her birth, but she wasn't going to stop trying. As well as having famous musical parents, Iondra had an older brother who was renowned as a canopy singer, a baritone, who had never been to the forest floor, considering it a place of wolves, bears, and ruffians. Linna was a courtier's daughter, the first in her family to braid her own hair and not wear silk. She'd been raised primarily by a governess, who quit when she discovered her charge playing with spirits. Since she'd enrolled in the academy, Linna hadn't seen her parents once.

Daleina wished she saw her own family more. It had been a month . . . no, two months. Three? Had it really been that long since she'd seen them? Arin grew taller all the time. Last visit, she'd been past Daleina's shoulder, and her cheeks had lost the baby pudge. She was braiding her hair now, festooning it with flowers, and talking about the baker's boy who made her laugh. Daleina wondered if they knew the champions were searching for candidates and imagined telling them the news she'd been chosen . . . and then she imagined telling them she hadn't.

The door creaked open, and a wolf trotted inside.

"Close the door behind you," Daleina told Bayn.

He nudged it shut and then jumped onto Daleina's bed. Daleina scooted over to make room as he settled his furry bulk next to her. Bayn didn't always come. Often he was with Master Bei. But he must have known somehow that Daleina wasn't going to sleep well tonight.

With the wolf beside her, she did.

SHE WOKE TO THE CALL OF THE MORNING BELLS. Springing out of bed as if she'd never slept, she bolted to the bathing room, washed, dressed, and then headed for the practice ring. She skipped past the dining hall, too keyed up to eat. Inside, Iondra was stoically eating a plate of poached quail eggs, while Mari picked at a piece of toast. Seeing Daleina at the doorway, Mari waved. Daleina waved back but didn't stop. She'd go to the ring early, settle herself, maybe practice more.

She wasn't the first to the ring. Two students were already there: Cleeri and Airria. Nodding to Daleina, the two didn't stop their summonings. Cleeri was skilled with water spirits and currently had three of them splitting the waterfall to irrigate the flowers that were growing at the base of the spiral staircase. She was thin, with white-to-the-point-of-nearly-translucent hair, and was missing one arm below her elbow. She'd lost it in a training exercise in her second year, when she'd summoned an earth spirit too large to control. It had taken an earth master plus the combined efforts of six senior students to subdue it. As far as Daleina knew, she had no family—at least none that had come to visit her while she was in recovery.

Airria was known for her precision in summonings, and in everything else she did. Her hair was always neatly pinned into a bun, and her gold-tinged skin never seemed to bruise or even get dirty. She was halfway up a tree with an air spirit perched on her palm. She was from midforest, like Daleina, but from a larger town, closer to one of the cities in the south. Daleina liked both of them, though they weren't part of her usual study circle.

She scanned the practice ring, looking for a spot to settle in, trying to decide if she should work with the earth spirits this morning or the wood spirits. She was best with wood spirits, but she could use—"Youch!" Airria leapt down from the tree. "It bit me!" She put her finger in her mouth and sucked it.

"Need a bandage?" Daleina offered. She kept extras in her room.

Airria glared at the spirit, which was cavorting on a branch as if it had done nothing. "Just a flyswatter." To the spirit, she held out her hand. "Come. Now."

Its wings drooped, and it flew to land on her hand. A

second later, Airria threw her hand upward, and the spirit launched itself into the air. It flew up, high up, until it reached the window to one of the storerooms and disappeared inside. Daleina watched, glancing at Airria, whose eyes were focused on the window, staring as if the spirit's disobedience were not an option.

A second later, it burst out, with a round object in its thin arms. It plummeted down, its wings flapping fast to slow its descent. Straining to control its flight with the object in its arms, it veered erratically, like it was fighting with the air. It swooped through the tops of the trees, and then, shakily, aimed at Airria. She held out her hand imperiously.

It landed on her hand and released the object—a woundberry.

Airria picked the purple berry up and squeezed it. White goo oozed out, and she smeared it in her cut. "You may go," she told the spirit, and it fled, its wings buzzing so fast that they were invisible.

It was all so effortless.

With Daleina, it was never effortless. Yet Airria had executed a string of commands and had them obeyed, without her breaking a sweat. Like it was easy.

Movement caught her eye, and she glanced to see one of the champions, Champion Cabe, standing at the base of the spiral staircase. He nodded approvingly at Airria, and she beamed back. Daleina felt her heart sink. She tried to muster her shreds of self-confidence, as the second champion, the other senior students, and several teachers filed down into the practice ring. The two champions led them through the day's exercises.

BY THE END OF THE DAY, CHAMPION CABE HAD CHOSEN his candidate: unsurprisingly, the prodigy Airria, after she flawlessly executed commanding a wood spirit to speed the life cycle of a flower. She presented the flower to the champion by having an air spirit carry it to him as he emerged to congratulate her.

Champion Piriandra ended the day without choosing anyone, which gave Daleina hope that maybe she had broader requirements for a candidate than just power. Over dinner, the students speculated about whom she would pick, whether she'd even stay, or whether she'd switch to another academy and choose one of their students. There was no rule that a champion had to choose any of them—or anyone, for that matter. The champions could wait for years for the right candidate to train.

I'll make sure she doesn't want to wait, Daleina told herself. She'd be chosen tomorrow. She was sure of it. Again, she woke early, bypassed breakfast, and prepared herself for the day.

Daleina pushed herself harder than she ever had, focusing on every task, calling spirit after spirit until her muscles shook and her hair stuck to her forehead and cheeks. But it didn't matter. At the end of the second day, Champion Piriandra chose Linna.

Helping her friend pack, Daleina told herself she'd have other chances. Linna would make an excellent candidate and an even better heir. Champion Piriandra must have seen that and known they'd make a good fit. "I'll be back," Linna promised. "Champion Piriandra is taking me for deep-woods training first. But next semester, I'll split my time between training with her and classes here. She says the academy is a valuable resource, and I've still a lot to learn that is better done in a controlled environment. Oh, Daleina, she's taking me outside the capital! She believes in practical experience."

"That's wonderful," Daleina said, trying to put as much enthusiasm in her voice as she could. She was happy for her friend, truly. "You'll do great."

"Don't worry, Daleina," Linna said, hugging her. "You'll be chosen. We'll face each other in the trials. And someday, we'll be side by side at the coronation ceremony."

"Of course we will," Daleina said.

Stepping back, Linna surveyed her room. "It looks like I was never here. Do you think they'll put another student here, or keep it for me when I come back?"

"I don't know," Daleina said. "Ask Mari."

Linna nodded. "I can do this, right? I'm ready?"

"Absolutely."

A knock sounded on the open door. Champion Piriandra filled the doorway. She was dressed all in dark green that hugged her body, showing the many knives and weapons that she had attached to her hips, thighs, and upper arms. She carried a slim pack as well. "Your belongings will be put into storage. I will provide the supplies you need, and we will sustain ourselves with food the forest provides."

"Oh!" For an instant, Linna looked disconcerted. Even after all their survival classes, Daleina was sure that Linna hadn't truly thought about what it meant to leave the safe cocoon of the academy. A week with Champion Piriandra would fix that. That was part of what the training with the champion was for: to take them out into the world, to change what had been theory into reality, before the fate of everyone depended on them. Daleina wished with every scrap inside her that she'd been the one going out to learn all that the champion could teach her. Linna plastered on her smile again. "Let me say goodbye to everyone, and then I'm ready!"

As soon as the champion inclined her head granting permission, Linna scampered out the door, leaving Daleina alone with the champion. Silently, the champion studied her, as if cataloguing her faults and failures. Daleina searched for something to say. "You chose well. Linna deserves this."

"It's not a reward; it's a responsibility."

Daleina winced. She hadn't meant it to sound that way. "I know. I meant . . . she's talented and she'll work hard. And she's a good person. She may seem delicate, but—"

"I will cure her of any delicacy."

"I didn't mean . . ." Daleina trailed off. She hadn't meant to imply that Linna had any flaws. She'd meant to praise her friend.

"I watched you as well," the champion said. "I saw how hard you worked."

"Uh, thank you." She wanted to say, *Then why didn't you pick me?*

"Your technique is solid. It is obvious that you are dedicated and work hard. But if you want a little friendly advice . . . that is your problem. You work hard at things that should come naturally to a candidate."

Daleina felt her stomach sink. *But I'm doing the best I can.*

"There are many ways to serve Renthia. With academy training, you could work in the palace, or be invaluable at the border. You could join the guards and protect one of the towns. Your skills and dedication would also make you a boon to places relying on a hedgewitch with merely one affinity. To have someone with six would be miraculous to them. You would be valued and provide value. It's a worthy path. Not everyone can be queen."

She knew the champion was trying to be helpful. She couldn't know how every word felt like a spoon shoved into Daleina's heart, scooping it out. "But this is what I'm meant to do."

Champion Piriandra studied her for a moment more. "Then I am sorry."

Sorry that she didn't choose Daleina? Or sorry that Daleina's best wasn't good enough? Sorry that she'd never be chosen? Sorry that she'd picked an impossible dream? Sorry that she'd wasted years of her life? Sorry that she was never going to do what she'd promised her little sister all those years ago that she'd do? Sorry that she was going to fail?

I won't, Daleina thought. *I can do this. I'm* meant *to do this. And if Champion Piriandra thinks I'm wasting my time, then that's the only reason she should be sorry. . . .*

Because she's wrong.

She watched as the champion claimed Linna, and the two headed down the spiral staircase. Linna had a skip in her step and a bounce in her curls, and every few stairs, she paused to wave back at her friends. All of them waved back, including Daleina.

CHAPTER 11

The heir Sata crouched on a tree limb above the thieves and sighed inwardly. Three of them, and they hadn't once bothered to look up. Not that she wanted to be seen, but honestly, have a little self-respect. You live in a three-dimensional world; you can't just check right and left when you want to be sneaky.

Kids, she guessed. Probably dared one another to break into the palace. Or maybe it was more than a lark, and they were down on their luck. Whatever their reason, they should have started smaller, trained, and then tried to hit the palace. Not that she wanted lots of trained thieves running around. But still, she resented the unprofessionalism. It was keeping her from her well-earned sleep.

She'd been dreaming all night of snuggling into her downy bed, closing her eyes, and not opening them again until the smell of honeyed toast drifted into the bedroom. Her husband had hinted strongly that the morning would be theirs. He'd been granted half the day off from guard duty, and since she had the night shift . . . As soon as she took care of these so-called thieves, she'd be done.

Careful not to rustle any leaves, she followed above them as they crept closer to the palace boundaries. A clear stone wall marked the line between palace and city. Flecked with mica, it reflected in the torchlight. That is, except for here, a stretch of shadows close to the treasure pavilion, where the Crown displayed a few of its possessions for the public to enjoy. *Silly children,* Sata thought. *Don't they know the shadows are always watched?* She lived in the shadows. Ever since she became heir, that had been her place. The night was her specialty. Also, anyplace with the word "treasure" in its name was obviously going to be guarded.

Idiots.

The thieves climbed the wall, crossing the perimeter, and inched together toward the display room. Encased in darkness, the pavilion was lovely in its inky blackness. Sata slipped down one of the pillars. She held out her hand, palm up, waiting, and she listened.

Scuffling. Shuffling. They were here.

Silently, she reached out with her mind. *Light.*

A fire spirit darted into the pavilion and alighted on her gloved palm. Its dancing body shed light on the pavilion, the treasures, the thieves, and her as she lounged against a pillar beside the three necklaces of Aratay, the pearls of Belene, and the chalice of Chell. "Looking for these?"

The boys—they were three boys, all young, all suddenly terrified—froze. A more sensible reaction would have been to run, but if they were sensible, they wouldn't be here. Sata called out again silently. *Hold them.*

Mud hands reached up through the gaps in the stone floor and clasped their ankles. The boys started to struggle and scream and babble incoherently. "Don't hurt me!" "We just wanted to look!" "Let us go!" "We didn't do anything!"

"You can't tell me you accidentally crept across the perimeter."

"It was dark!" one of them tried.

She rolled her eyes at him. "Tell it to the palace guards." Sata sauntered past them and plucked a knife out of one of their pockets, relieved another of a short sword and the third of a dagger tucked into his boot. She passed a trio of guards who were rushing toward the pavilion, and handed over the thieves' weapons. "Three young idiots. Nothing to get too excited about. Just threaten to tell all their girlfriends and every potential girlfriend they may ever have that they were caught within two seconds of trying to commit their crime."

One of the guards grinned at her. "Thanks, Heir Sata."

"And now, I'm off to sleep and enjoy time with my husband, not necessarily in that order." With a wave, she headed out of the pavilion. Catching a hand on a branch, she swung up into a tree. She was thinking about young thieves and bad life choices when the attack came.

There was no warning. None at all. And she'd had the best of training, relentlessly drilled by Champion Ven, one of the finest champions that Renthia had ever seen. He used to hide in the bushes at daybreak and send spirits after her while she slept, to try to catch her off guard. She had a few scars she owed to that little exercise, but by the time she was proclaimed heir, even he couldn't catch her by surprise.

But these spirits did.

Six wood spirits melted out of the trees. They formed a ring around her, closed hands, and then melted their bodies into one another, until they grew into a solid ring of wood.

Let me pass. She pushed the words at them as she pushed forward.

The ring tightened.

"Let me pass," she said out loud. She hurled more power into the words, wrapping the command in all her exhaustion, frustration, desire, ambition, and every other thing she'd felt in the last few hours. It should have sliced right through them and sent them scuttling away from her, but it didn't. Instead, the spirits continued to meld together, their bodies fusing into a single bark-encrusted circle. Their faces stretched and spread until they were only hideous lengthened grins. "Why are you doing this?"

None of them spoke.

She pulled out her knives, one in each hand. Ven had taught her this too, in case of a time when her power wasn't enough, and she'd kept up her training, even after he pronounced her perfect. She became a whirl of blades, slicing at the wood.

But for every slice she landed, the spirits coated the gash in bark, thickening it into a wood scar. There were no faces to hurt, no limbs to slice. She realized that their bodies had melted into the branches below her, solidifying into a solid bowl. Looking up, she leaped, reaching for the limbs above her.

But the limbs retreated, slipping away from her fingers, and she fell backward. She was back on her feet instantly, but not fast enough. The wood sealed above her, closing off the sight of the forest and the night sky. The wind was suddenly silenced, and she was in complete darkness, not her familiar shadows. She felt the wood bump her shoulder—it was closing in on her. She felt it touch her head—the ceiling was shrinking.

She was forced to her knees.

Gathering a breath, she focused. She was a trained heir, able to control numerous spirits. They hadn't disobeyed her in years. She took that confidence, wove it with her desire to be free, her need to see her husband again, her duty to her country and the Crown, and threw it into a command, *Release me!*

But the wood, now a sphere, closed in. She was forced into a ball. Hitting it with all her strength, she pounded her knives into the wood, trying to carve her way out. Soon, the wood was too tight around her to move her arms.

Only then did it occur to her to call for help. She'd never needed help before. She was an heir, a protector. Others called her for help. But now, with the wood closing in around her, she called, "Help! Spirits attacking! Someone, help me! Stop them!"

She felt dizzy. The air—there wasn't enough. She tried to conserve, tried to stay calm, tried to reach out beyond the wood shell to any spirits who could help her. Fire, to burn the wood away. Earth, to decompose it. Air, to break it apart. She felt the spirits respond . . . and then they stopped, as if commanded to ignore her orders.

No! she cried. *Help me!*

And during all this, the sphere closed tighter in, squeezing her body until her arms pressed against her ribs and her knees jabbed into her chin. Her head swam as if she'd been shoved underwater. She couldn't string her thoughts together.

She lost consciousness as the wood crushed the life from her body.

Only one death this time. Ven didn't say that out loud. The berry picker wouldn't see it as a blessing—his wife, the village's schoolteacher, had been killed. As Ven bandaged the man's arm, he didn't say a word. There were no words that could make this easier and no point in calling for the healers. Ven could patch up an arm, but no one could heal the empty look in the man's eyes.

"You'll send word to the queen?" the berry picker asked.

"She'll be told," Ven promised. He still always reported the deaths, even though after four years of acting on her cryptic warnings, he had no proof that Queen Fara ever acted on his information. "I'm sorry for your loss."

"Only woman who could have ever loved a lout like me. Used to make me charms. Keep me safe from the spirits. Made extra charms too: keep me safe from falling trees, keep me safe from spoiled lunches, keep me safe from the bookseller's wife—she always admired me. Just pretend charms. Except the spirit ones. Those were real and strong. They should have kept her safe. The queen should have kept her safe."

"Accidents happen," Ven said, and then winced at himself. What an asinine thing to say. It was never an accident when a spirit killed. Spirits *wanted* to kill. Ven knew that better than anybody.

The man met Ven's eyes. He wasn't crying, thankfully. Ven wasn't good with tears. But there was a sheen in the man's gaze as if he were perilously close. "Why? Just tell me why. The queen . . . she built us a library, you know? In the center of our town. Gorgeous thing, inside a tree, with books that came out of the pulp she'd had the spirits carve. Spirits flew for days, back and forth, taking the books to the wordsmiths, bringing them back printed up nice, with tales inside. Have you seen our library?" As Ven shook his head, the man continued, "My wife, she loved it. Loved the carvings in the bookshelves. Said they looked like every flower in the forest. And she loved the books. She learned to read when she was a kid but hadn't had much chance to after that. But since the queen built the library, she's been hauling home stacks of books and reading them to me at night. Puts me right to sleep every time. She'd tease me about that. But I think it made her happy, whether I slept or not. She called that library our own miracle. So tell me, why, if the queen could make such a miracle, couldn't she protect my wife? How can there be miracles like that and still 'accidents'?"

"It shouldn't have happened." That was true. Maybe not comforting, but true.

"If she can't protect her people, doesn't matter how many miracles she can build. My wife . . ." Tears finally streamed out of his eyes and down his cheeks. The berry picker looked away, his fists clenched in his lap. "Makes a man wonder if the spirits chose the right woman to be queen." He squeezed his eyes shut. "Forgive me."

Fara had been the perfect heir. She'd been the shining star at her academy, and she'd excelled throughout the trials. No spirit had ever harmed her or even come close. She'd escaped unscathed while the other heirs struggled. She'd been a natural choice, both for the champions and the spirits.

She was also instantly beloved by the people: regal, beautiful, smart, wise. They showered every adjective on her. And Ven had worshipped her right alongside them.

And yet he couldn't help wonder if the berry picker was right . . . and that worried him.

Ven finished the bandage on the man's shoulder. He knew he should leave right away, send a pointless message to the capital that would be ignored, and resume patrols that never seemed to put him where he was needed, but instead he sank onto the branch beside the berry picker and looked out at the dark-green leaves, heavy pinecones, and thick mat of vines. The forest was calm now, the wind still, and the birdcalls a low warble. "What's your name?"

"Havtru. And I love our queen, Champion Ven."

"Relax. I don't blame you for what you said. And I'm just Ven now."

He snorted. "Uh-huh, that's why you're roaming the woods, saving people like me, because you're ordinary folk now. Yeah, I've heard of you. We've all heard of you. My wife used to talk about you, you know. Said that we were blessed to have a legend looking out for the common people."

Ven felt the guilt twist like a knife inside his rib cage.

"I don't blame you for not saving her," Havtru said. "It happened too quickly. In fact, you gave her that gift. If you hadn't come, the spirit would have made it slow. And I'd have lost her all the same."

Intellectually, he knew that Havtru was right. He couldn't have saved her—he'd been busy saving the children caught by spirits inside the school at the same moment she was trying to save those outside the school. He couldn't be everywhere he was needed when he was needed. Only the queen could be everywhere at once. And she wasn't.

Why? It was an excellent question, and there were only two answers:

One, the queen had sent the spirits to kill on purpose,

because she suspected traitors. That was what she'd told him nine years ago to explain Greytree, but he didn't believe it then and he didn't believe it now. He'd found no hint of any rebellion in the outer villages. Besides, if she did intend for people to die, then the cryptic warning notes she sent through the headmistress made no sense—she couldn't be certain he'd save the correct people.

Two, the spirits were killing on their own, and she wasn't able to stop them, even when she knew their plans. She was losing control and soon she'd lose control entirely, and they'd kill her, instead of random villagers.

He hated both answers. He hated everything about this.

"Please, can you ask her to stop the deaths?"

Ven flinched. "Told you I'll send word. That's the best I can do." Pushing himself off the branch, he landed on the bridge below. "Keep yourself safe. Stay in the village until the guards are sure there will be no more incidents. And see a healer about your arm. I recommend Popol's assistant, a young man named Hamon. He has real skill, and he won't drive you crazy with babble."

"I've met Popol. He's a talker."

"Hasn't changed."

Havtru raised his bandaged arm. "Thank you."

Ven thought of their beautiful queen, whom he used to believe was more perfect than the sun, and of the berry picker's wife, dead because of the queen's weakness. "Don't thank me."

Running across the bridge, he stretched his muscles. If his queen was really failing, then it was more imperative than ever that he keep moving, keep patrolling, keep protecting the people he could. And when she fell—he forced himself to think the thought—when she died, an heir would take her place, and maybe he wouldn't be needed out here anymore. He could be a champion again and do what he was supposed to do.

He reached the healers, Popol and Hamon, who were working on the villagers' injured children. He'd sent them a message as soon as he could, and as always, they'd responded quickly—he hated that after four years, this had become depressingly routine. He should consider asking one of them to travel with him permanently so there would be no delay between the headmistress's warning and the healing. As he stopped beside them, Hamon looked up.

"She didn't make it; he did," Ven reported. "Here?"

"Just injuries," Hamon said. "But . . ." He hesitated, and his eyes slid to his master.

"There's news from the capital," Popol said, his voice booming. All the villagers were watching them. A few of the kids were crying, but quietly.

Ven tensed. *Fara,* he thought. It had happened already. But then why hadn't the heirs frozen the spirits? When a queen died, the heirs had to issue the coronation command—

"One of the heirs has died," Popol said. "Dreadful business. They should be taking precautions. You never know—"

"Who?" Ven asked.

"The heir Sata," Hamon said quietly. "I'm sorry."

VEN HAD KEPT AWAY FROM THE SO-CALLED GLORIOUS city of Mittriel, the capital of Aratay, for nine years. But by keeping to the wire paths, he was able to return in a mere three days, in time for Sata's funeral. She was to be buried in Heroes Grove, with the other fallen queens, heirs, and champions.

By the time Ven arrived, it was full of mourners, including a chunk of the palace guard. The other heirs had coaxed flowers to cover the ground and now the blossoms were crushed underfoot, and he could smell the thick perfume of their scents. It permeated the air so strongly that his head began to throb. He slipped in with the crowd, steering clear of anyone he knew. He wasn't here to talk to anyone. He was only here for Sata.

She was one of the best heirs he'd ever trained. Always had a sense of humor, even when they were drenched with rain, covered in mud, and beset by overly irritated spirits that they'd intentionally annoyed. When she was a child, she'd had dreams of being one of the forest acrobats, the Juma, who traveled from town to town, performing for people who never traveled more than a few miles from their homes. But when she'd shown an affinity for the spirits, her family had encouraged her to enroll in one of the academies. She'd excelled there, and that's where Ven had found her. She'd liked him because he valued her physical ability as much as her power, and he'd liked her because she'd laughed at his admittedly bad jokes and never complained, even when he pushed her hard. She'd been an excellent heir and didn't deserve this.

No one deserved this.

He'd yet to get a solid answer out of anyone as to what had happened to her, but he knew she'd been working with the palace guards. He could talk to one of them later, when he wouldn't be seen by the queen or any of his former colleagues. He didn't want to hear their smug sympathy, or their relief that it wasn't their trainee who had died. Standing in the crowd, he kept his hood up.

The ritual began with bells, first chiming softly from high above and then cascading down until it became a waterfall of bells ending in a low tolling bell in the center of the grove. A man in all end-of-summer green—his face painted green, his hands covered in green gloves—hit the final bell one more time, its low ring vibrating through the forest, radiating out from the grove, and then all the bells fell silent.

Her body was carried in by her closest kin and friends—all palace guards, he saw. He knew she'd been working with them in recent years. She lay on a litter and was draped in a white lace cloth that covered her entirely. Usually, the cloth was translucent, so the mourners could see the hint of the face and shape of their loved ones, but Sata was covered first in a thick summer-green sheet with black trim.

How did she die? he wanted to ask. He'd heard crazy stories as he'd traveled: she'd been crushed by a tree, she'd been trapped inside a trunk, she'd been smothered by spirits. It wasn't the kind of thing that happened to an heir, especially one as skilled as Sata.

The guards carried her body into the grove, and the mourners parted. As one, they laid her at the base of a tree, cradled in its roots. One by one, each of them spoke, sharing a moment, a memory from Sata's life. Her husband spoke last, in a voice that was thick with unshed tears but strong, the way Sata had been strong.

Ven wanted to step forward. He'd been her champion. He'd chosen her, trained her, known her better than anyone, at least for those few years until he'd taught her everything he knew. She was the best thing he'd ever done. She could have been queen. A great queen. She was meant to be. She deserved . . . so much more. But he didn't know what words to say that would encompass all that. There was no one moment that personified Sata to him. It was a compilation of all the moments: the way she'd woken up cheerful, even when they'd barely slept at all, thanks to the wild wolves that howled all night; the way she refused to eat snake for the first few weeks of training and then the day he found her chowing down on leftover water snake. Good with pepper, she'd said. She'd been clever. Quick to learn how to be silent in the woods. Fast with a blade. And economical with the way she used the spirits. She preferred not to, if she had a choice, and he'd liked that about her. She didn't see them as toys, the way some candidates did, the ones who hadn't seen or couldn't imagine the damage they could do. She saw them as tools, and she used them for serious purposes. She took her role as candidate and then heir seriously, and he'd been proud of her. He should say all of that. But his throat felt thick and clogged with the perfume of all the flowers, and before he could decide to step forward, Queen Fara swept into the grove.

She looked unaged from the last moment he'd seen her, nine years ago. Her golden curls were piled on top of her head and wreathed in vines that tendrilled down from her crown. She wore black and green, the traditional mourning colors, and she looked every inch the strong, regal queen that she was supposed to be. Looking at her, it was hard to picture the berry picker's wife and the other deaths in the outer villages and think that she was in any way responsible. A queen this perfect could not have let that happen.

But it had happened. And Sata had happened.

He wanted to stride across the grove, shake her shoulders, and yell, *Why?*

This wasn't the place or the time, though. This was for Sata, and he would not disgrace her memory by causing a scene. He'd keep his memories to himself and his presence a secret.

He watched the queen glide across the grove toward Sata's body. "We thank you on behalf of Aratay, on behalf of all of Renthia, for your service and your sacrifice." She said other ritual words, ones he'd heard too many times and didn't think he would hear applied to Sata. He'd had such faith in her. She was supposed to live. Even outlive him. She was supposed to be queen, when Fara died.

He stared across the grove at Queen Fara, as if his gaze could pierce the royal shell that she wore and reveal the real woman beneath the ritual. Fara may be his past, but Sata had been the future. She was supposed to make everything right, control the spirits, protect their people—all the people, even the ones in the outer villages. He knew there were other heirs, ready to take the crown as soon as they were needed, but he didn't *know* those heirs. He hadn't chosen them, tested them, trained them, prepared them, shaped them like he had Sata. Other champions had done that. Some he respected, and some he didn't, but none he trusted to have trained an heir as capable as Sata.

Queen Fara never returned his gaze, but then again, he didn't want her to notice him. Finishing the words, she raised her hands. Silently, the earth opened beneath Sata's body, and the roots parted. Spirits killed her, and now they helped bury her.

Sata's body sank into the earth, and the dirt closed over her. Roots sealed on top of her, and tiny white flowers, hundreds of them, blossomed all over where she lay, at peace.

But the queen wasn't done.

She kept her hands up, and the air above them exploded with spirits. Dancing in the air, dozens of winged spirits swirled, each carrying a white rose. They spiraled in a circle as if Queen Fara were stirring them, and then they released the flowers. As the roses spattered onto the grove, white doves burst from the branches of the tree. They funneled up toward the open sky. And then Queen Fara closed her hands, and the spirits all fled. Ven thought he saw a hint of a satisfied smile on the queen's lips before she bowed her head.

He left the grove without a word to anyone, happy to be away from the cloying scent of her flowers.

He hadn't seen or spoken to Sata since his exile. He'd avoided everyone from that life, as if he truly had done something wrong. Maybe that had been a mistake. Maybe if he'd stayed closer, she'd still be alive. Maybe if he'd taken her with him, she could have helped him in the outer forest. But he hadn't wanted his disgrace to spill over to her. Her reputation was pristine, and if she was to be queen, she would need the approval and support of the people. He hadn't wanted to tarnish her, or her future, or the future of Aratay.

He didn't slow until he'd crossed half the capital and realized he'd gone *into* the city, rather than *out* of it. Part of him, the unthinking part, had already decided to stay, at least until he had some answers to how a queen with as much control as Fara had just displayed could have allowed an heir to die. He owed Sata—and the future she should have had—at least that much.

If he was going to stay, he needed a place to go. So he spent the afternoon on mundane details that distracted him temporarily from the reality of Sata's death: He found a place to live, hunted for his dinner, and rounded up a few other necessary day-to-day items. He paid the landlord a week in advance, out of the money he'd earned from guarding the healers. He hadn't told the man his name, and the man hadn't asked. It was that kind of area.

The place wasn't much more than a few boards lashed together to be the floor and a tarp overhead to protect against the rain, plus a brick-lined area for a cooking fire that funneled smoke up between the branches, but it was close to the wire paths and far from neighbors. He'd stuffed his green armor into his pack and wore a tan tunic common among the laborers of the capital. He wasn't hiding per se, but just like at the funeral, he wasn't going to announce his presence either.

As he crisped a skinned squirrel over the fire for his dinner, it occurred to him that he could have come back to Mittriel anytime, as long as he didn't try to enter the palace uninvited or speak with the queen alone. He'd stayed away from the capital by choice, and truthfully he hadn't missed it. He'd missed the council, the work, the feeling that what he was doing mattered. And yet, at the same time, he didn't miss the way the sounds of the city blotted out the sounds of the forest, and the way he couldn't smell the trees over the scents of other people's meals and, worse, their garbage.

He lifted the squirrel off the flame and blew on it until it cooled. And then he drew his knife and in one quick motion threw it toward the roof of his tarp.

It embedded in the fabric, and he heard a shrill yip. A shadow fluttered. He plucked the knife out of the tarp and used it to cut the cooked meat off the bones, as the air spirit limped through the doorway.

"I don't like spies," he told the spirit.

Glaring at him, it handed him a scroll of parchment, and then it limped out.

Heart beating, he unrolled it, expecting to see the queen's handwriting and the name of a town he was now too far away to help. But it wasn't. Instead, it was the headmistress's own lettering: "You are still welcome here." She'd signed it with her name and title, headmistress of Northeast Academy, as if defying anyone who intercepted the message.

Ven held the parchment over the flame until it caught fire and crumpled into ashes. He then packed up the squirrel meat, washed his hands with water from a pitcher, and took his weapons with him. He wondered who had seen him at the funeral and reported to her. Or had she merely guessed he'd come? It didn't matter. He wasn't going to say no, not to the woman who had helped give his life a purpose over the last few years.

He remembered the way to the academy easily. Joining the people on the bridges, he made his way through the crowds. Most were heading home from work, their thoughts most likely on dinner or their families or the minutiae of their days. Head down, he didn't meet anyone's eyes. He doubted there was anyone who would recognize him, or care, but he didn't want to have a conversation explaining why he was here, where he'd been, or what he was doing next. Or really, any conversation at all. The people around him were chatting with one another as they strode or strolled down the bridges. He heard fragments of their conversations: about what was for sale at the market, about what the queen had worn at her last address, about the condition of the bridges, about the newest library that Queen Fara had built, about the weather and if it would rain. It grated on his skin like a hundred fingernails, lightly clawing him. None of these people knew what it was like beyond the comfort of the capital. *And they shouldn't,* he reminded himself. The queen was supposed to take that worry away from them. But what would happen when she couldn't? Who was the next best heir, now that Sata was gone?

Ahead, the academy soared, the jewel of the northeast corner of the capital. The low sun bathed it in its amber light, filtered through the leaves. The trees around it all held homes, crammed onto the branches, but the outer walls of the academy were smooth. Every window, he knew, faced inward into the center court. It was designed to keep its students isolated and focused. Cut off from the rest of the world. Their interface with the outside world was supposed to be the champions.

Ven jumped off the bridge without bothering with the ladder. A few of the citizens glanced at him before he remembered he'd decided to play it low-key. Oh, well. He didn't intend to stay in the capital for long enough for the queen to care. He strode in through the main gate of the academy. "Ven to see Headmistress Hanna," he told the caretaker at the gate.

The woman studied him head to foot.

He added, "Per her invitation." He'd always been admitted to the academy before without any question, but this time, he'd deliberately left off his title, "Champion." He wasn't sure if he was one, and not just because of his status with the queen. Since he had neither a candidate nor an heir, he didn't know if he had a right to claim the title anymore. His hands clenched as he thought of Sata, and he forced his fingers to relax.

"Please wait here. I'll inform her."

He waited, pacing back and forth. Everything felt familiar and distant at the same time. He'd been in this foyer many times over the years, yet it felt like it was from another lifetime—the smooth curved walls, the pillars of spiraled wood, the chairs that had been grown from the roots that crisscrossed the floor. He'd known that of course everything continued, of course the academy continued to train students while he was gone, but a part of him expected it to have disappeared. To see it still here, still the same, while he felt as if he'd lived a dozen lives . . .

"She'll see you in her office. Do you need a guide, sir?"

"She still likes her osprey nest?"

The caretaker smiled. "She enjoys the view."

"How is she? It's been . . . a while."

He had the sense that the caretaker knew exactly who he was and exactly how long it had been, but she was too polite to point that out. "She's well. She ages but won't acknowledge it, so we don't acknowledge it either, except to include more juice with her meals."

"Good." He was glad they were taking care of her. Even better that they were doing it without her noticing. Knowing Headmistress Hanna, she'd probably forbid them to and order them to focus only on the students. She'd never admit that she was the heart and soul of this place, not the students who revolved in and out barely leaving a mark.

He wondered if that was what he was like, drifting through places, barely leaving a mark for all his efforts to be everyone's protector. His mark had been Sata, and now she was swallowed by the earth and crowned only in flowers. He headed for the spiral stairs.

As he walked up and looked down at the ever-changing practice ring, he realized how much he would have liked to call a place like this home. In another life, maybe he would have been a teacher at an academy like this one.

Faces were pressed against windows, watching him as he

climbed the spiral stairs. Classes were over for the day, he guessed. If the schedule was the same as it used to be, the students were supposed to be squeezing in extra studying before dinner. Had they always looked so young? He remembered them as older, but now he could barely tell the youngest from the oldest. Surely, Sata hadn't looked this young when he'd started training her, though she must have been. He wondered what her life would have been like if he hadn't chosen her, if she'd never become heir. She could have become an acrobat, traveling and performing, like she'd wanted—though she still would have had the affinity. The spirits still would have been drawn to her. At least with his training she could defend . . . She should have been able to defend herself.

Dammit, Sata, what happened? His girl could handle anything. She was beyond capable. He hadn't worried about her because she was *fine,* always fine. She was supposed to outlast him.

Higher, he was free from the stares and whispers of the students. If only there were a height to free himself of his own internal whispers.

Stopping at the door to the headmistress's office, he knocked. Immediately, the door swung open. He peered inside but didn't see any air spirits.

"It's on a string." The headmistress smiled. "I don't tell many that. Maintains the mystique, but there's a thin wire that leads to my desk, plus the door is angled so its weight tends inward. Pull the string, it unlatches, and gravity pulls the door open. Magic. Don't tell the students."

"I wouldn't dream of it." He shut the door behind him.

Headmistress Hanna looked exactly the same. A few deeper wrinkles on her cheeks. Thinner. He hoped the caretakers were feeding her more than just juice. But she had the same warm smile that he remembered. Her office too was as warm and glowing in the sunlight as always. The wide window behind her had thin cracks in it that looked as if they'd been inexpertly seamed together. Given the number of women with power in the building, he was surprised she hadn't had it done correctly.

"It's good to see you," he said. "You look great."

"You didn't add 'for your age.' I appreciate that."

"Objectively great. Being headmistress hasn't killed you yet."

"Being the Disgraced Champion hasn't killed you yet either." She stood, crossed to him, and embraced him. "They've written songs about you, you know. Horrible songs with meandering verses that go on and on about your fall from grace and your rise as the savior of the outer forest. You've gained quite a reputation."

He thought of the berry picker's wife. He didn't deserve a shiny new reputation. Especially when it meant he hadn't been here to save Sata.

"Tell me: has your exile ended? Has she forgiven you?"

Crossing to her window, he studied the fused glass. Outside, it was sunset, and the sky was stained amber. Looking out across the top leaves of the forest, he could see the spires of the palace tree, rising up above the capital. On one spire was the council chamber, perched like a crown. Another spire was the Queen's Tower, where she could see across the forest or look at the stars. In the failing light, the pale bark glowed rose. He'd been up there once, with Fara, shortly after she became queen. She'd been so very beautiful that night, beyond the beauty of any of the stars. "You can see the mountains of Semo from that tower."

"You are changing the subject. Badly, I might add."

"Does she go up there anymore, to look over the forest? It was built to remind the queens that they rule more than a single tree. To remind them that there's more to the world than what they see in their throne room every day."

"Fara hasn't come to visit me in longer than you have."

Ven considered that. Once, Fara had considered Hanna like a mother. It wasn't good that that had changed. "Have you visited her?"

Hanna's tone was guarded. "I have."

"And? How is she?"

"If you're looking for me to say she misses you, I won't," Hanna said. "I went to plead with her, twice, on your behalf. Once, shortly after she exiled you. Again a few years later. You should have kept things simple between you."

Ven sighed and ran his fingers through his hair. "With Fara, nothing is simple."

"True enough. But she should have forgiven you by now. I thought . . ." She trailed off and fidgeted in her chair, as if she were a child about to confess. "There's a thought I had, and it is . . . You will not like it."

"Tell me."

"I believe she's losing control, slowly but inevitably. Worse, she is in denial and is deliberately hiding the fact from everyone. And you"—she paused, and the pity in her eyes made Ven flinch—"are enabling her. With you out there being a hero, she doesn't need to feel guilt about her failures. She has no need to address them or even admit to any loss of control, if you are there to ameliorate her disasters. I believe she hasn't rescinded her exile because she's using you."

The words felt like a punch. "She wouldn't . . . That's not . . . I saved people! Not all. But some. It wasn't . . ." He paced back and forth, tigerlike. The problem was, it *did* make sense. He stopped, took a breath, and focused on another thing she'd said. "You believe she's losing control?" It was of course the most likely explanation, but after seeing her today he was less certain. Her display at Sata's funeral— that wasn't the act of a queen losing control.

Hanna nodded. "Sata shouldn't have died."

"But I saw at the funeral . . ."

"I know. I was there. Why do you think she did that? To

silence those who doubt her. To prove she isn't losing control. Overcompensating."

He ran his fingers through his hair again. "How did Sata die?"

"She was found encased in a sphere of wood near the palace. Crushed and smothered. I'm sorry, Ven. I wish it was otherwise, but it was clearly a deliberate act by multiple spirits. Queen Fara has been in damage-control mode ever since, trying to prove that her people are safe. She's spread a lie that Sata's death occurred outside the city, far from the palace. She's even . . . Word from the palace is that Sata was to blame. The people prefer to think that, rather than believe their queen is weak."

"Sata wouldn't call more spirits than she could handle." Ven noticed he'd clenched his fists. He deliberately opened them before his next instinct was to bash his fist into a wall.

"And yet that's what they say she did."

"She wouldn't. I trained her."

"I know." Hanna was watching him.

Ven felt as if she were looking inside his skull, watching his thought process. Either Sata provoked the spirits, or Fara's control was truly failing. As much as he wanted to deny it, he couldn't hide from the truth. He'd seen it in the outer villages. No, there was no other explanation. Fara's control was failing, and she was trying desperately to hide that fact, starting with the day she'd exiled him. "Why won't she admit—"

"Why do you think? She doesn't want to die. If people think she's not a strong queen, they'll want a better one. And what's the only way to get another queen?"

He sighed heavily. "The old queen has to die first." Fara didn't want to die. He almost laughed at the thought—no one *wants* to die—but the queen was almost religious about it. She clung to life more fiercely than anyone he'd ever known. That was one of the things that had drawn him to her in the first place. Sinking down in an empty chair, he put his face in his hands.

"Exactly," Hanna said. "We both know Fara's always been a fighter, willing to do what was necessary to assure her place. In the beginning, that kind of drive and ambition was exactly what was necessary, and we applauded her ascendance to queen. But Sata died—an heir killed so close to the palace—and that means Fara's control is slipping even more, no matter how much she tries to hide and deny it. But neither you nor I can say that. You can't, because she's already discredited you. And I can't, because I'm needed here. I can't afford to lose the Crown's blessing, or I will lose the academy. But while we can't directly address the problem, we *can* be part of the solution."

He lifted his face. "You have a plan?"

"Not a plan. A request." She was smiling.

"That's an ominous look. What?"

"Don't you see? While you are out there in the outer forest, cleaning up after her, she doesn't have to face what she's done. But without you there . . ."

"Without me there, people will die." She couldn't be suggesting he just stop trying to save people. He couldn't ignore the warnings.

"People are dying anyway. Like Sata."

He shook his head. "I can't just stay here and not do anything. You must keep sending me her messages, and I must keep—"

"Did you bring your uniform?"

"I have it, but I didn't think it was appropriate—"

"It is, if you are to take a new candidate." She smiled again, sadly this time, as he gaped at her. "Take on a new candidate. Train someone to be heir. Be ready for when Fara falls." Moving to a cabinet, she pulled out sheaths and rolls of parchment. "Evvlyn is one of our best students. Her specialty is fire, though of course she's proficient with all the spirits. Marilinara—she goes by Mari—is exceptional as well. Organized thinker, with a logical approach to her summoning. Very consistent. Tridonna is exceptionally strong with air."

"I can't take on a candidate." He'd failed with Sata.

"You must. It's your duty. The heir you trained is gone. You must replace her."

"I've been exiled, remember?" He wasn't a champion anymore. At best, he was the Disgraced Champion, a figure from a song—and not very good songs, from the sound of it.

"From the queen's presence. Not from the capital. Or from here. Or from the forest. You do not need Queen Fara's permission to perform your duty to Renthia. Ven, we need an heir of Sata's caliber for when Queen Fara falls." She stared at him. "And she *will* fall."

The way she said it, the way she looked—Hanna truly believed what she said. Ven was starting to believe himself, but still . . . "The queen won't be happy with me. Especially if you're right that she's using me. Whatever girl I choose won't walk an easy road."

"You of all people should know I don't train my girls for easy roads." She thrust the papers at him. He didn't move, and she continued to hold them. "I train them for necessary ones."

"And what of the deaths that I don't prevent because I am busy training a candidate? What if the queen sends more notes, predicting more attacks? Do you expect me to just ignore them? Let the people die?"

"If that's the road that makes the most sense."

"Hanna, you know I can't—"

"Like my girls, a champion must make hard choices," she said. "The few for the many."

"There are other heirs and other champions."

"Not like you, and not like Sata. She was the best, and she was not just because of her talent but because of her training. I will send any new messages to the forest guards. Protecting the outer villages is their responsibility. Yours is here. You must train another heir, and you must do it well. You are meant to be a queen maker."

He took the papers.

"Choose carefully, Ven. Sata's death indicates that the queen's control is slipping faster and faster. I believe the ones who are being trained now . . . I believe one of them will be called to serve. You *must* choose carefully, Ven, because there won't be time for a second choice."

CHAPTER 13

Because she couldn't sleep, and because Bayn was with Master Bei, Daleina invited one of the caretaker boys to her bed. His name was Andare, and he was only one year older than she was, with soft amber hair, smooth skin, and an easy smile.

He knocked on her door after the night bell, a soft rap that she would have missed if she hadn't been listening for it. She opened the door, and he slipped inside. Candlelight danced across his face as she reached up to cup his face in her hands. "You shaved. For me?"

He'd had soft fuzz on his cheeks and chin when she'd spoken to him after dinner. "It seemed appropriate." He had a nice voice, low and buzzing. He probably sang well. She wondered if he'd sing for her, if she asked.

"You understand what I'm asking?"

"For comfort. For peace. For this." He leaned down and placed his lips on hers. He'd kissed before, she could tell, as his lips whispered against hers.

She breathed again when he stepped back. "I'll need to wake early. And I'm told that I sometimes snore."

His lips quirked into a smile. He had a nice smile too. He had been a good choice. She'd been watching him for a while—he worked in the practice ring, raking the dirt between classes or tending the plants when they were there. She'd also seen him in the dining hall, carrying the overburdened platters to the long tables. "I snore too," he confessed. "Like a bullfrog."

She laughed. She hadn't expected to laugh tonight. An extra bonus. Taking his hand, she led him to the bed. "May I?" she asked, and lifted his shirt over his head. Her fingers traveled down his chest and stopped at a scar close to his heart.

His hand closed over hers. "It was a long time ago. And I'm safe now. Here."

She wanted to ask what happened, who or what had allowed it to happen, how he'd come to the academy, where he was before, but he forestalled her questions by kissing her. She let him distract her, and she pulled him onto the bed with her. The mattress sank beneath them, cocooning them in sheets and blankets and pillows.

Eventually, she slept, more than she'd expected, to the rhythm of his snore, with the weight of his arm across her stomach. Before the morning bell, as the first hint of dawn poked through her window, she woke and slipped out from under him. She tucked a sheet around him and lightly kissed his forehead, soft as a butterfly. He didn't stir as she dressed.

She did feel rested. Ready. Today would be different, she could sense it. Slipping down the spiral staircase, she headed for the practice ring. As she walked across the grass, she tied her hair back and stretched out her arms. By the grove of trees, she stopped and began her stretches. For the first time since the champions had begun coming, she didn't feel the knots in her muscles. Maybe it was because there were no champions on the schedule today, or maybe it was because of Andare. She should invite him to stay another night, except she'd have to be careful to be clear he couldn't form any expectations. As soon as she was chosen, she'd be gone.

If she was chosen.

When I am chosen, she corrected. *When.*

If, her mind whispered.

Shut up, she told her mind, and resumed her stretches.

Midstretch, she saw him: a man in green with a pepper beard and clipped hair. He was on his stomach, crawling on his elbows between the roots of the grove. He had moss and leaves draped over his back. When he quit moving, he blended in so effectively that Daleina had to look twice.

She guessed he wanted to observe how they acted if they thought they were unwatched. *Guess he doesn't know we're always watched.* There were always teachers, caretakers, other students, not to mention the headmistress, who always seemed to be nearby observing every time Daleina had a disastrous class.

Very aware the champion was there, Daleina continued her warm-up ritual, clearing her mind of as many thoughts as possible, calming her breathing, steadying her heart rate. She stretched her arms and legs, rolled her neck until the muscles were loose again, and clenched and released each muscle in her arms, legs, and hands, until she'd regained the relaxed feeling she'd had when she'd woken up in bed not alone. By the time the other students came from the dining hall, she felt centered and calm and all the things she was supposed to be.

Spotting her friends, she crossed to them.

"Daleina!" Zie grabbed her arm and pulled her into their circle. "Have you heard about the headmistress's visitor? He went into her office last night and didn't come out."

"I don't think you should be gossiping about the head-mistress," Mari said.

"She could be sleeping with him. Or murdering him. Or both."

"Zie!" Mari stomped away from them.

Zie grinned. "Aw, what did I say? Daleina, what do you think? Does our headmistress have a sensual side?"

"First, ew. Second, I have more important information." Daleina shot a look at the grove. The lump that was the champion hadn't moved.

"Like you and Caretaker Andare?" Revi asked.

Daleina shot her a look.

She feigned innocence. "It's only that you've been working so very hard, and we've all been concerned. It's about time for you to treat yourself."

"He's very nice, and if you tease me about him, or him about me, I will dump a bucket of water on your bed."

Revi grinned. "You can't use water spirits for pranks. Definitely against the rules."

"No spirits. I will borrow a bucket, fill it with water, and dump it on your bed. Very simple. Very wet. Now, do you want to listen for a second? There's a champion hiding in the grove. No, don't look. We're not supposed to know he's there."

Hands on her hips, Revi scanned the grove. "I don't see him."

"You're as subtle as a hammer," Daleina said. "I said he's *hiding*. Zie, can you spread the word to everyone? We're being judged today. Again." She tried to feel gratitude at having another chance, but she mostly felt tired.

Zie nodded, serious for once, and scampered to tell the other students. Rejoining them, Mari asked, "Who is he?" She was shooting looks at the grove, trying and failing to be subtle. Daleina thought it was a good thing that becoming an heir didn't require spy work. With the exception of Zie, her friends would fail dismally.

"I'm sure he'll introduce himself when he's finished communing with the moss," Daleina said. "Leave him alone. It's nearly time." She pointed to the stairs—their teacher, Master Sondriane, was descending from the dining hall. Master Sondriane was a tall, gaunt woman with skin mottled like a tortoise shell and a scar on one cheek. Stories about that scar abounded, each more wild than the last, but most involving three lovers, a waterfall, and between one and twenty spirits.

As Master Sondriane reached the bottom, a water spirit burst out of the pool beside the waterfall. Water sprayed in a fountain upward, and the spirit twirled. It was a long, thin spirit, with sharklike skin, seaweed green hair, and "fingers" of kelp that dangled from the ends of its wrists. "All right, students," Master Sondriane said, "your lesson today is simple. Control *that*."

The water spirit opened its mouth and screamed, high-pitched and so loud that Daleina felt her bones rattle. She fell to her knees. On either side of her, she saw the other students clutching their ears, also doubled over. Still shrieking, the spirit sped through the practice ring, pulling the waterfall behind it like a comet tail. It splashed over the students.

Sputtering, Daleina struggled to her feet. She had to focus, but she couldn't think over the screeching. The spirit swooped back and pulled more water from the crack in the tree. Soon, it was gushing through. It carried the water with it as it swirled around them, faster and faster.

Revi shouted, "It's. Spout. Need. Stop!" The shrieking of the spirit and the roar of the water drowned out her words, but Daleina could see what the spirit was doing too: forming a waterspout around them.

Water sprayed out of it, battering Daleina's face. She put her arm up and forded over toward Revi. "It's the shrieking!" Revi cried. "I can't—" The last word was swallowed by a crash.

The spout stretched taller, toward the first floor, and veered closer to the grove. It uprooted a tree, tossing it in the water. *Oh no, the champion!* Surely he was smart enough to get out of there—unless he expected them to protect him, unless saving him was the test.

"Hold hands!" Daleina shouted to Revi. "Find everyone!"

Hand in hand, they pushed through the water, linking

hands with the other students. She was shivering, hard, as the water soaked into her skin. It was hard to see as the water hit her face. Closing her eyes, she yelled, "Fall! Tell the spirit to make the water *fall!*"

Fall!

And the water fell from the sky. It crashed down around them, sweeping and tugging at their feet. Daleina hung on tight to the women on either side of her. "Don't let go! Send it out! Out!"

The water flowed out, led by the spirit. It gushed past them, narrowing into a raging stream before being funneled out the gate of the academy to disperse through the forest floor. Daleina realized she was gripping Revi and Evvlyn's hands so hard that their fingers were mashed together. She released them. Everyone released hands and sagged together. They shared a few tentative smiles.

Daleina sneaked a look toward the grove.

The champion was gone.

He was either unimpressed or drowned. For a brief instant, she wasn't sure which would make her happier.

SIDE BY SIDE, SOGGY AND SHIVERING, DALEINA AND the other students stood in the swampy mud that was the practice ring. Her wet clothes chilled her skin, until she felt like frozen meat. Master Sondriane surveyed them all. "I am highly disappointed. You should have done that much more quickly and with much less mess. If this were a field, the crop would have been ruined. If it were a village center, the market would have been destroyed. Livelihoods and lives will depend on you. Act like it." She swept away, leaving them to shiver together.

Daleina felt her heart sink. No wonder the champion had left, if that was the master's assessment of them. She tried to think what she could have done better, or at least differently.

Stayed in bed, she thought, and then pushed the mutinous thought down.

"All right. Who's up for liberating some towels from the bathroom?" Revi started for the spiral stairs, but before she could climb more than three steps, Master Klii strode into the practice ring.

"And where do you think you're going?" Master Klii said.

"Um, to dry off?" Revi said. Her foot hovered over the next step. She didn't put it down.

"Class is not over. Not until you are dry." She snapped her finger and pointed to the ground. "Each of you, summon a fire spirit, make a fire, and dry yourself out. Once you've done that, you can leave class." She fixed her eyes on Daleina. "No lanterns, no firemoss, no shortcuts, and you must work alone."

Daleina flinched. She wanted to say it had worked, regardless of how, but she knew better than to argue with Master Klii. Instead, she headed for the grove.

Behind her, others were already calling fire spirits to them, more than Daleina could comfortably call, especially when she was this cold and tired. Zie already had a circle of them around her, dancing over her arms, but Daleina knew she'd have better luck if she could find some brush she could use as kindling and invite one of the fire spirits from the lanterns to play in it until the fire caught, rather than relying on the warmth of the spirits themselves.

Combing the grove, she looked for dry branches. Everything was soaked and soggy, or too green and alive. She plucked some moss from the side of a tree and rubbed it between her damp hands to dry it. She saw blazes lighting up all around the practice ring. Returning to the edge of the grove, she tried to quit shivering long enough to summon a fire spirit.

One flew from a candle and danced around her. She held

out the moist kindling. *Dry this,* she told it. Her hands shook as she held it steady. Kneeling, she laid it on a rock. *Burn.* She cupped her hands around the kindling.

Several of the others were heading up the spiral stairs already, dry and done. She felt tears prick the corners of her eyes. Again, she was failing. "Come on," she whispered. She felt so very cold, as if the water had seeped through her skin and muscles straight into her bones.

The bundle of kindling smoked. She blew on it, as her father used to when he lit a fire in their hearth. She pictured her parents and Arin. She hadn't seen them in months. She wondered how they were, if the house was ready for winter, if Arin had kissed that baker boy, if her mother had taken care of the mouse problem they'd been having, or if all her news was so old that it wasn't even relevant anymore. She wondered what they'd think if they saw her now, shivering, with a pathetic smoldering ball of debris.

A flame licked at it. She coaxed the spirit to stay and added more twigs. Glancing up, she saw that nearly every other student had a hearty fire going, or at least it seemed that way. Bonfires dotted the practice ring. Evvlyn had even set part of the grove on fire. Huddling next to her pathetic fire, Daleina thought she'd never be warm again.

A soft weight landed around her shoulders, and she jerked backward, before she realized it was a blanket, only a blanket. Oh yes, a blanket! She curved herself inside it and hugged it close.

"Catching hypothermia is not a good way to train," a man's voice said.

She looked up and saw a man with a black-and-gray beard and pale water-blue eyes—and instantly, she felt transported to being ten years old, her village in rubble at her feet. She couldn't speak. Her throat felt clogged, as if the memory itself were stuffed down her throat.

He squatted opposite her, and then swatted the fire spirit away. It scampered off, and she didn't try to call it back. It had done its job well enough. She had the start of a fire—it could dry out the larger branches.

"Thank you for the blanket." Reluctantly, she lowered it from her shoulders. The air hit the cold cloth of her shirt, chilling her skin even more. "But I don't think Master Klii would approve."

He reached over and pulled the blanket back onto her shoulders. "Master Klii is not in charge of you anymore. I am."

She stared at him, certain that the wet and cold had addled her hearing. "I'm sorry?"

"Why did you tell the others where I was hiding? You could have had an advantage, as the only one who knew I was there. The others would have treated this like an ordinary class and not done their best."

"They're my friends. I'm not in competition with them."

"Yes, you are. There are more of you than there are champions. Not to mention that we can draw our candidates from anywhere, not just an academy—any village with a hedgewitch who shows affinity for all six spirits is fair game. Simple mathematical odds say if the others lose, you win."

"Champions choose the best, not the sneakiest."

"How do you know what the champions look for?"

"I don't, but . . ." She searched for a way to articulate what she felt more as an instinct. "The other students are not my enemy. And the ones I don't know—from other academies or from the villages or wherever—they're not my enemy either. The spirits are. I won't forget that." She saw her village again, crisp in her memory. Rosasi, who used to tell stories. Her little friends who used to play on the branches with her. She hadn't forgotten them. She wouldn't ever.

He studied her. She couldn't read anything in his expression, not with his beard masking his lips and the shadows in his eyes disguising his thoughts. "It was your idea to link hands and combine powers."

"The teachers don't like it when we do that."

"You use the resources you have. Life isn't like the practice ring. The only rule is do no harm, and save who you can when you can."

She resisted pointing out that was two rules.

"Okay, that's two rules." A smile flickered across his lips and then was gone. "Tell me: why do you want to be queen?"

"You know," she said. "You were there."

He looked startled. At last, an expression she could read.

"I'm from Greytree. You might not remember it. It was a tiny village in the outer forest, and it doesn't exist anymore. But you were there, scaring the spirits away." She smiled then, not at the memory but at the thought of Arin, her stubborn always-right sister. "My little sister will say this is fate, your choosing me."

He was silent for a moment, and her smile faded. She wondered if she'd said the wrong thing, if she'd scared him off, if she'd misunderstood him.

"You *are* choosing me, aren't you?" She hated the way her voice wavered, as if she were still a child, but she couldn't help it. To be so close and fail . . . it would be worse than never being chosen at all.

He was silent again, and Daleina felt as if the world around her was brittle. One wrong word and it could all shatter. But then he spoke a single word, the right word: "Yes."

The headmistress drummed her fingers on her desk. "Daleina?"

"Yes?" Daleina said.

But Hanna wasn't talking to her. She fixed her eyes on Ven, as if she could peel back his expression and see his thoughts, or maybe just shake some sense into the man. Exactly what was he thinking? Yes, Daleina was a well-intentioned girl—now a young woman—who worked hard, but year after year, she eked by, excelling in her written exams but barely passing the practicals. She was hardly the star that Sata or Fara had been. The other champions hadn't even considered her. One, Champion Piriandra, had even recommended she be expelled, to save her heartache later. But Hanna didn't want to say that out loud in front of the poor girl, so she merely repeated her name. "Daleina?"

"Yes," Ven said. Firmer this time.

Crossing to her cabinets, Hanna rifled through and drew out of a sheaf of papers. She carried them back to her desk and leafed through them: Daleina's records, from her entrance exam to now, including teacher and caretaker comments. Oh, everyone liked her fine. She was bright, a team player, conscientious. The caretakers appreciated that she never left her towels on the floor and also replenished the soap on her own. Her teachers noted that she was never late to class. She studied hard and excelled at all her academic classes, as well as in survival. Everyone agreed she tried hard at commands. And she'd undoubtedly shown improvement. She could summon all six spirits. But she wasn't a natural, and you couldn't learn that. "Let me be blunt," Hanna began.

"That's never a good opening," Ven noted.

"I can tell you what she's going to say." Daleina stopped in front of the wide window, touching the seams of the once-broken glass, and Hanna waited, allowing her to speak. "You shouldn't choose me. There are more powerful girls here. Girls with higher test scores. Girls with glowing reports." She delivered it as fact, with no self-pity in her voice. Hanna felt her rib cage loosen. Maybe this wouldn't be so difficult, since the girl understood the situation.

"Your reports aren't bad," Hanna said. "All your academic scores are top-notch. We're all proud of what you've accomplished."

"Especially since you didn't think I'd make it so far?"

Again, no self-pity. Hanna glanced at Ven. She expected to see concern etched on his face, or a hint of chagrin. Instead he looked a bit smug, as if he'd pulled off a trick. "She's naïve," Hanna told Ven.

"That will change."

"She's inexperienced."

"I will provide the experience."

"It's one thing to make it through here, where the teachers are always on hand to correct for errors. You take her out of our walls, expose her to the world—"

"I want this," Daleina interrupted.

Both Hanna and Ven looked at her. She shrank back at first, then squared her shoulders and lifted her chin, as if remembering she wasn't a child anymore. "Daleina, dear," Hanna said, "I know you want to, but sometimes our abilities and natural talents don't match our dreams, and reality—"

"I can both sense and control all six kinds of spirits." She turned to Ven. "I have power within me. Enough power."

Hanna sighed and felt a headache pinch between her eyebrows. She rubbed her temples. "All right. We'll alter your schedule. You can continue half your classes here, and half independent study with Champion Ven."

"I'm taking her out," Ven said.

Champions often did that—took their candidates out for a crash course in reality, taught them woodland survival the hard way, exposed them to the true dangers of the spirits—and then later returned them for extra classes, like Champion Piriandra intended with Linna, but just as many chose to stay in the capital, especially if their candidate still needed to develop her core skills. In Daleina's case, the choice seemed clear. "You'll be given a room here, Ven, unless you're particularly attached to your loft."

"I can't stay."

Hanna glanced at Daleina and wondered if she had any idea who her new champion was, what his history was. She had no doubt that her fellow classmates would fill her in. She debated what to tell her. "I doubt Queen Fara—"

"It's not about her," Ven said. "I'm needed in the outer villages."

Instantly, Hanna knew what he meant. He wanted to keep playing the hero and cleaning up the queen's disasters. "You can't expect to continue on as you have been." They'd already discussed this, and she'd made her views clear. She'd thought he agreed.

"I can, and I will," Ven said. "Keep sending the messages."

Hanna tapped her fingers on her desk, which she thought was more polite than wrapping them around his neck. Why did champions have to be so stubbornly dense? They always wanted to save the world, everywhere, all at once, and it simply wasn't practical. "You have to choose, Ven: train her or patrol the villages. You can't take her out so far, as green as she is. The spirits will be drawn to her. She has enough power to be a danger to herself and to you."

"She will have accelerated training," Ven said. "I know what I'm doing."

Hanna wasn't convinced he did. He'd been sulking in the outer forest for so long, avoiding the capital as if everyone here had shunned him. She considered whether it would be bad form to call him an idiot in front of his chosen candidate. "Remember what I said? My thought on *why* we've been sent the messages?"

"I can't ignore them. Even if you are right."

"And this is your decision? I can't dissuade you?" She drummed her fingers again, faster. *This could be a disaster.* She wondered if she should have been more explicit in describing how Sata had died, how close she'd been to the palace, how much pain she must have felt. If that could happen to an heir, then how were they supposed to protect the candidates? Especially away from the academy? She turned to Daleina. "Champion Ven has been on the front lines, protecting villages who lack protection. He comes to their aid whenever there is an attack. He's often first into dangerous situations, well beyond anything candidates usually face. With him, you will be exposed to more danger and hardship than a typical candidate. And you may not have the queen's blessing for this unconventional training."

"Queen Fara hates me," Ven told Daleina.

My, that was blunt. "I wouldn't have put it that way," Hanna said, "but yes, you may inherit political baggage that shouldn't be your responsibility."

"First Headmistress Hanna tried to convince me that I don't want you, and now she wants to convince you that you don't want me," Ven said. Damn man sounded amused. "The fact is that you do get to decide, Daleina. It's not only me choosing you; you must choose me as well."

"Is this what happened with all the candidates?" Daleina asked. "When they came to see you. Did you try to talk them out of it?"

Her bright eyes were fixed on Hanna, and the headmistress shifted in her chair. She should lie, for the sake of the girl's feelings, but under her gaze, it didn't feel right. "This is an unusual case."

"Because I'm a mediocre student, and he's a disgraced champion?" Daleina turned back to Ven, and Hanna couldn't help admiring the thread of stubbornness that ran through her voice. That determination, she remembered, was why she'd allowed a barely qualified girl to enter the academy four years ago. "Do you think I can help protect the outer villages?"

"Yes," he said without hesitation.

"Then I choose him," Daleina said.

Hanna looked from one to the other, at their identical mulish expressions. She sighed heavily. "Just tell me one thing, Ven: why her?"

"Because she knows why she's here," he answered. "She knows who the enemy is."

And that was the moment that the headmistress began to feel a trickle of hope.

DALEINA WALKED DOWN THE SPIRAL STAIRS BESIDE her new champion. Her stomach rolled and flopped, and she realized her hands were shaking. That hadn't gone the way she'd hoped. She'd expected . . . She hadn't known what she'd expected, but not that humiliation.

"That wasn't a ringing endorsement for either of us," her champion said. He didn't sound upset, but he had to be second-guessing his choice after all the headmistress said.

"Maybe you *should* choose someone else." It hurt to say that, but what if she was taking the place of someone who would be better? She was being selfish, and that was wrong. "Aratay deserves the best."

He stopped on the steps, forcing Daleina to stop beside him. "Then you will need to become the best. It won't be easy. I'll push you hard. You won't like me very much most of the time."

She looked at him, at the pockets of shadows under his eyes, at the grayness in his hair, at his sinewy muscles. "Can you teach me how to keep a village from being destroyed?"

"I aim to try."

"That's all I want." Side by side, they headed down the stairs. He left her at her room, to pack and to say goodbye. "I can be ready in five minutes," she told him.

"You have two."

"Are you saying that because there's somewhere we have to be in two minutes, or because you want to demonstrate your power over me?" The instant the words were out of her mouth, she wanted to pull them back. She didn't mean that to sound as disrespectful as it did. She knew better. But again, he surprised her, this time with a smile that flashed across his bearded face then vanished.

"Both. Move quickly."

She spent a few precious seconds watching him leave, then she sprinted into her room. She packed fast—a few changes of clothes, a knife, as well as various ointments and herbs, including burn cream, herbs to stop her monthly bleeding and prevent making a baby, and salves to prevent infections and ease bruises. She'd watched the other chosen candidates pack and had imagined this moment for herself so many times that she knew exactly what she wanted to grab.

She heard a clatter, then murmurs, and turned as her friends crowded into the room, a mixture of worry and hopeful happiness on their faces. "Is it true?" Zie asked. "Were you chosen?"

"By Champion Ven," Daleina confirmed.

They all tumbled in, and then everyone was talking and hugging and laughing and shouting all at once. She hugged each of them. Revi. Mari. Zie. Evvlyn. She nodded through all the good wishes and good-lucks and outpourings of advice.

"I don't know when I'll be back." *Or if I'll be back.* "We're going to the outer forest. He doesn't want to stay in the capital."

There were gasps at that. The other candidates were all expected back soon. Daleina was going to miss seeing Linna and Airria and Iondra when they returned. She hugged them all again, and then she darted out of the room and down the stairs. Looking back, she saw her friends pressed together at her bedroom window, waving at her, as she'd done for others before her. She waved back, smiling so hard that her cheeks hurt.

She found her champion in the entrance hall, talking to one of the caretakers. Shifting from foot to foot, she waited for him to finish. She heard footsteps behind her.

"Daleina?" Master Bei, the survival class teacher. Beside her was the wolf Bayn.

Daleina knelt and rubbed the fur on his neck as if he were a dog. She scratched his ears. "I'm going to miss you," she told him.

"He wants to go with you."

Daleina looked up sharply at Master Bei. "But he's yours."

"He's his own. And he wants to see the outer forest again."

Behind her, Champion Ven said, "Wolves can't climb, and we will be ranging everywhere."

"It's what he wants," Master Bei said. "He'll follow from the forest floor. You don't need to worry about him or adjust your plans in any way. Just drop a smooth stone when you switch camps—he'll find you."

"Are you sure?" Daleina asked, her hands still deep in the wolf's fur. She then addressed the question to the wolf. "Are you sure?" She'd never been certain how much he truly understood.

Like the pet dog that he wasn't, the wolf licked her cheek.

"Ew, and thank you. Truly, thank you."

The champion grunted, and Daleina didn't know if that meant he approved or "this is a terrible idea," but he didn't protest again. She stood and bowed to Master Bei. "Thank you for all your instruction."

Master Bei nodded and then swept away, though not before Daleina saw a hint of moisture in her teacher's eyes. Daleina stroked Bayn's neck again and then stood.

"Are you ready now, or is there another pet you'd like to bring along? Perhaps a raccoon? Or an elephant?"

"His name is Bayn, and he can understand you."

Bayn bared his teeth at Champion Ven.

"You keep up or you don't," he told the wolf. "And you're responsible for your own food. We won't hunt for you or wait for you."

Daleina hoped the same rule didn't apply to her.

"Have you ever taken the wire paths?" Champion Ven asked her.

"No, sir," she said, though she knew what they were. Knew, for example, that they were very, *very* high up.

"You'll like it," he said. "Nice view."

Obviously he was joking.

Wasn't he?

He headed for the nearest tree, and he didn't look back as he climbed. She followed and did look back every few feet to look at the academy as they went higher and higher, past platforms and past houses. When he reached the upper midforest, he waited for her to catch up. Once she did, he headed down a bridge without a word. Daleina kept looking back until she could no longer see the gleaming white wood of the academy. Green closed around them. Far below, on the forest floor, Bayn kept pace with them. Occasionally, Daleina caught glimpses of him: a streak of gray fur winding through the cultivated bushes and herb borders—few lived on the forest floor, but many harvested from it.

Out in the capital, Daleina felt like a first-time visitor. She'd meant it when she said she hadn't left. It wasn't expressly forbidden, but students had so little free time that it was impractical. She knew some of the others liked to see friends in the city. Visit the tea houses. Shop in the boutiques. Drink in the taverns. Dance in the halls. Stroll through the markets. She wondered if she'd missed out by not doing those things. But she'd been happy at the academy, and there had never seemed to be enough time.

Ven kept striding through the crowds without meeting anyone's eyes, and Daleina stuck close, half a step away, so close that if he stopped she'd walk into him, but she didn't want to lose him in the crowd. She wasn't certain he'd come back for her. He might decide it would be a good lesson for her to navigate on her own.

The light felt different out here. Inside the academy, the sun filtered through the wide circular opening at the top. Midday, it flooded everything, but mornings and evenings were shadowed. Here, it was dappled with patches of light. Streams of sun penetrated the canopy above and then pooled here and there on the houses, the bridges, and the platforms.

She wondered what the people did all day every day, and realized she hadn't ever thought much about it. She knew what her family did, and others in the outer villages, where the challenge was to feed your family, keep everyone healthy, and keep a solid roof over your head. But in the capital, only a few feet from where she'd spent four entire years? She passed a woman who had braided gemstones into her hair and wrapped her body in shimmery lace and then a man with what looked like bits of glass embedded in the fabric of his shirt. They stared as openly at Daleina as she did at them.

Farther out, the men and women looked more familiar, mostly dressed in tan tunics, often carrying tools—
this was obviously the laborers' section of the city. They
passed through it, and the living quarters became smaller
and seedier. Instead of houses, the homes were platforms
lashed together with tarps, boards—sometimes even a door
hammered on as a roof. Laundry was strung between them,
and there were a few kids draped over a branch, passing a
jar back and forth between them. "Don't make eye contact,"
Champion Ven told her.

She swung her head to stare just at Ven's shoulder blades.
He strode quickly through the area and then he climbed
another ladder. She followed him up to an empty platform
with a tarp. "Where are we?" she asked.

"My place, for the week. I rented it."

"We're staying here?" She tried, and failed, to keep the
judgment out of her voice. She'd pictured them heading
much farther out, into the forest.

"I paid for it, but since I won't be using it as a home . . ."
He drew out a knife and sliced the tarp from the roof. He
rolled it up, tied it with a rope, and slung it on his back. "Our
portable camp. Consider it your first and last luxury, at least
until we reach a village." He then began to climb up, beyond
the end of the ladder. "Let me show you the other reason I
chose this place: location."

She opened her mouth to ask where they were going next
and then shut it. She'd find out soon enough. It didn't matter, as long as he trained her. Higher, they reached the canopy, and she found him looking at her. She wondered if she'd
done something wrong.

"You aren't afraid of heights, are you?"

"I don't think so." She'd climbed the spiral stairs daily,
and she'd never blinked at it. He pulled a rope with a clip
out of his pack.

"You wrap this around your wrists, attach the clip to

the wire, and then you kick off. Whatever you do, don't let go." He handed the clip to her, and then he got out his own, wrapped it fast around his wrist, reached up, clipped it to a wire, and then without another word, he kicked off. Dangling from the clip, he sailed through the branches, breaking through the leaves, with the whoosh of wind in his wake.

"Wait! I . . ." She stared down at the clip in her hands and then swallowed. No wonder traveling the wire paths was considered insane. "Don't let go. All right." She'd wanted this, she reminded herself. She'd taken plenty of survival classes, though they'd always been either on the ground or very close to it. None of them had involved hurtling through the tops of trees. She took a deep breath and then another, and she wished she were traveling the forest floor with Bayn.

She hooked the clip onto the wire, and she wrapped the rope three times around her wrist. Testing its strength, she lifted her feet. It held. She couldn't see where the wire led. It disappeared into the leaves only a few feet from her. She didn't see any motion and had no idea how far the champion had gone. She couldn't let him get too far ahead of her.

Kicking off the tree, she held on tight. She gritted her teeth so she wouldn't scream as she soared down the wire. Wind whistled in her ears, and branches slapped at her arms. One sliced her cheek. She turned her face away and closed her eyes, then forced them open again.

Ahead was a tree and a platform. The champion was waiting for her. It was almost over! But how to stop? She clung to the rope and felt as if she were increasing speed. She lifted her knees up to her chest, trying to protect her body, and she tensed for impact. She squeezed her eyes shut again—she couldn't help it—and then she slammed into something soft.

The champion grunted as he caught her, and she felt him take a step, only one, backward, then he steadied himself and her. Slowly, she lowered her legs down. She didn't stop clutching the rope.

"Unclip yourself."

Shakily, she unclenched her hand and unclipped from the wire. "Are we going down?"

"Hardly. Next lesson." He pulled a second clip with a rope out of his pack. "To travel from wire to wire, you need to clip on to the next wire at the same time—or more accurately, an instant before—you unclip from the prior wire. Try not to lose momentum."

"What?"

She saw where a second wire came into the tree. He reached over and clipped on to it. "You hang on with one hand, and you ready the second clip with the other. Think of a monkey swinging from vine to vine. It's like that."

But I'm not a monkey, she wanted to say, but didn't. More important, she'd never even *seen* a monkey. All she knew of them was that they were native to the islands of Belene and liked to throw rotten fruit and feces at intruders. Charming creatures.

She was starting to have the same feeling about Champion Ven.

Regardless, he was her teacher, her only one now, and she knew better than to argue. "Will you . . ." She licked her lips. Her mouth felt dry. ". . . go first?"

He grinned. "Stay close. And remember: this is the fun part." Clipping on, he kicked off and hung from the rope by one arm. He held the other ready.

"Right. Fun part." She clipped on and followed. In her other hand, she held the other clip. Up ahead, she saw him make the switch, clipping on to the next wire and sailing smoothly onto it. "You can do this, Daleina," she told herself. "Ready . . . one, two . . ."

On two, she hit the end of the wire. Her feet swung up and bashed into a limb, and the force jerked her arm. She felt as if it were going to pull out of her shoulder. Wincing, she dangled, and then she clipped on to the next wire. Slowly, she slid down it, gathering speed.

She shook her arm out as she flew down the wire, and she readied the clip. She kept her eyes focused ahead of her. Ready, ready, ready . . . There! *Now!* She clipped on to the next wire and soared on.

Again and again, she switched wires, following behind Ven, catching glimpses of him through the branches. Wind whooshed past her, and she felt as if the world had narrowed to just this area of forest. All her focus was on the next branch, the next switch, the next tree trunk. By the third switch, she was smiling. By the fifth, she was laughing.

At last, she saw the champion ahead, waiting for her on a platform. She raised her legs up, feetfirst, as she'd seen him do. She tensed her arms, ready. He hadn't mentioned how to stop. The trunk came at her fast, and she saw the champion was leaning against it idly, no intention of catching her. And an instant later, she was there, feetfirst, hitting the trunk. She bent her knees, absorbing the impact as best she could, though it shuddered through her.

She lowered her feet to the platform. For a minute, she could not make her hands open to release the rope, but then her muscles obeyed. She unclipped. Her arms ached in a way they never had before. Wincing, she swung them around in a circle.

"How good are you with a knife?" he asked.

"I did well in survival class. But not with shaking arms."

"You'll learn. Get out your knife. Next lesson." He pointed to the next tree, at a crook between two branches. "Hit that."

She pulled her knife out of her pack, wrapped a charm around the hilt so the spirits wouldn't object, and then held it up, aiming at the tree. Her arms were shaking. She tried to calm the muscles. "Can I wait until—"

"Throw."

Deep breath. Steady. She threw.

The hilt hit the trunk, and the knife plummeted. It bounced off a branch, then another, then lower, before it landed on a wider branch.

"Get it, climb back, and try again."

She obeyed, even though her arms ached. Climbing down from branch to branch, she lowered herself down to where the knife had landed, and then she crawled to it. Reclaiming it, she climbed back up to the champion. Her arms were shaking worse now, and her cheek stung from where a branch had nicked it. She wondered if there was blood. Later, she'd deal with it. In the meantime, though . . . She took another breath, focused on the crook in the branch, and threw.

This time, it embedded itself in the tree, three feet down from the crook. She looked at him. "Get it, climb back, and try again," he repeated.

She climbed again.

And again.

And again.

"Enough," Ven declared. "We'll camp here."

"Here? As in, right here?" She felt him watching her, judging her. "Here is fine." He handed her the canvas, and together they set up camp, creating a nest of ropes.

Suspended between trees, Daleina tried to sleep. After so long closeted inside the academy, she'd forgotten what the open forest sounded like at night. The owls called to one another in long, low notes, while the wolves howled far below, echoing the howls of other packs. Insects clicked, buzzed, and hummed, and the wind whispered through the leaves. It was extremely irritating. Plus she couldn't get comfortable. The makeshift rope hammock wasn't woven evenly, and every time she shifted, she accidentally stuck an arm or a leg through a too-wide hole.

"You need to rest," Champion Ven said, his voice much too awake for this late at night. She supposed he was keeping watch, another thing she hadn't had to worry about inside the academy. She missed her walls, and she wondered if Bayn had found a comfortable place to sleep on the forest floor. She wished they could have camped down with the wolf.

"I know."

"Relax," he said. "Think soothing thoughts. I know the academy teachers taught you control and focus. Use that to coax your body to sleep."

Daleina didn't answer. She didn't want to sound disrespectful, but she couldn't force herself to sleep. The more she ordered her body to relax, the more it tensed.

"Or you could summon a few spirits to sing you a lullaby."

"Is that a joke or an order?" She wasn't sure champions were allowed to have a sense of humor. She'd never pictured them ever laughing. Lifting her head, she tried to see him in the darkness. They were tucked in the shadows, and he was only a shape, sitting on a nearby branch. She thought she saw a sword balanced on his knees.

"There are several nearby. Can you sense them?" He was looking out, and his profile made her think of a hawk, alert, ready to hunt, or maybe he was more like an owl, watching the trees for any hint of movement.

She stretched out her awareness. It felt like straining one's ears to hear a muffled whisper, except it was more closely linked to the sense of touch. She concentrated first on the feel of the rope hammock, biting into her skin, and the feel of the air that moved beneath the tarp they'd stretched as a roof. She then "felt" beyond her, to the sturdy trunks of the trees, the empty air between them, the thin life of the branches . . . Her mind brushed over an owl and then a few crickets before she encountered the first spirit.

It felt like a small one, huddled in a nearby tree. She reached farther and touched two more. "What are they doing?" she whispered.

"Watching us," he answered.

"Do you think they'll attack?"

"Only if we do something stupid."

"Like what?"

"Like this," he said, and swung his sword and lopped off a branch. "Did your teachers ever tell you about the most important ability that champions possess?" he continued conversationally.

Struggling to sit up, Daleina scrambled out of the ropes. "What are you doing?" He hadn't taken any precautions—no charms on him or the blade.

He hacked at another branch, and then another. "The ability to"—hack—"thoroughly"—hack—"piss off"—hack—"spirits."

"Champion Ven!"

He stopped and said in a calm voice, "Your turn. Keep them from killing us." Sitting on an unchopped branch, the champion propped his legs up and leaned back, his hands behind his head.

Daleina heard the spirits shrieking. Leaves rustled as they ran along the branches and flew through the trees. Three wood spirits. One looked like a raccoon skeleton, draped with leaves, with a face made of bark. Its eyes were like black rocks embedded in mud. Another looked like a beautiful green girl with hair of leaves. The third looked like an insect, with a hard, glistening shell for a body and many legs. She could feel their rage shivering in the air. *Stop*, she tried. But the spirits weren't listening, and Champion Ven pursed his lips together and began to whistle, breaking her concentration.

Focus, Daleina, she told herself. *Four years of training.*

You can do this. A first-year could do this. All she had to do was make them leave.

Casually, the champion reached over his head and plucked a leaf from the tree.

These spirits were larger, stronger, and wilder than the ones in the city. *Go,* she told them.

They fought her command. She felt them fighting—their strength was like the core of a tree, solid and deep, and like the steady rain. She felt the press of their minds against hers.

And she had an idea.

She changed the command: *Grow.*

She invited them closer. Picturing in her mind an image of the broken branches, healed and growing, sprouting, spreading, thickening . . . she pushed the image toward them, layering it with leaves and blossoms.

Crying in triumph, the spirits soared closer. Out of the corner of her eye, Daleina saw the champion tense. His hand closed around the hilt of his sword, but otherwise, he didn't move.

The wood spirits circled around the broken branches, and the tree began to grow. New branches shot out from the broken wood. They split and spread, sprouting leaves, and the branches thickened. The spirits rode them upward, circling around, and Daleina felt her soul flying with them, reveling in the tree as it strengthened and grew.

When the spirits finished, Daleina realized her cheeks were wet. She wiped them with the back of her hand as the three spirits dispersed into the leaves.

"Since you're wide-awake now," Champion Ven said, "how about you take first watch?" He then curled up against the newly grown branch and, as near as Daleina could tell, fell instantly asleep.

CHAPTER 15

D awn came with new sounds: birds that trilled, chittered, and warbled. Daleina felt stiffness in all of her
muscles. Rubbing her neck, she sat up. Ven was already
awake, having taken the second shift. He handed her a hunk
of cheese and cold, leftover squirrel meat. "Champion Ven?
Those spirits last night . . ." she said, unsure if she should be
saying this or not. She decided she'd already started, though,
so finished, "I didn't expect them to be so strong."

"The academy shelters its students. You were never asked
to control a spirit stronger than what your teacher could control, and the teachers actively monitor which spirits are in
the vicinity. Out here, there aren't any restrictions like that.
Any spirit can swing by for a visit. Also, you can drop the
'Champion.' Just call me Ven. I'm out of practice with the
title."

She considered his words. "Then they weren't really preparing us."

"Their job is to teach you the basic techniques; it's my
job to give you a chance to apply them in the real world."
He efficiently rolled up their tarp roof and unraveled their
rope hammock. She helped him squeeze the supplies into
their packs. "In other words, I'm going to push you until
you break."

"I won't break." She added his name: "Ven." Daleina didn't know if she was lying or not. She suspected she was, but she was never going to admit that. Especially not to him.

All he said was, "We'll see."

And from there it began: they traveled eastward, away from the capital. Every few hours, whether they'd stopped or not, he deliberately irritated the nearby spirits, and she was forced to find ways to deflect them. She let a rain spirit drench them and encouraged an air spirit to blow them onto the next bridge. She guided an earth spirit into shifting some rocks, and she left another flock of tree spirits in a grove, coaxing new saplings to sprout. A few times, she slipped: one wood spirit sliced her arm before she was able to shift its anger away from her, and another weakened the branch they were on, causing them to fall to the next branch. Over the course of a few days, she encountered a wider variety of spirits than she'd ever seen.

Out in the forest, the spirits ranged in size, strength, and intelligence. She saw tiny air spirits, the size of dandelion fluff, drawn to their camp and then distracted by rustling leaves. Others tracked them for days, working together to coordinate clever, vicious attacks. Once, a beaver-size earth spirit created a sinkhole to try to trap them while a fire spirit deliberately danced flames on their supplies. Another time, three air spirits held a broken bridge in the air, releasing it only when Daleina and Ven were halfway across. Even with all her history and theory classes, she hadn't fully grasped the breadth, variety, and viciousness of the forest spirits.

In between irritating the spirits, her champion also worked with her on her knife skills. He had her practice hitting targets, in between fending off spirits. Eventually, he combined the two, removing the charm from her knife hilt so that a spirit would come investigate every time she impaled a tree.

She lost her knife in that training exercise.

By the fifth day, Daleina and Ven had a trail of spirits, six or seven that kept just out of sight, watching them from the trees. Ven told her to stay aware of them as he hunted for dinner.

Waiting for him on the forest floor, Daleina kept her senses open as she extracted a burr from Bayn's paw. The wolf had had a run-in with a pricker bush. He'd been chewing the burrs out, but when Daleina started helping, Bayn had sat and lifted up the offended paw. "You seem to be doing well, other than the prickers," Daleina said to him. The wolf's pelt was still soft, and he'd clearly been finding food.

In response, the wolf let his tongue hang out like a happy dog.

"You're having fun?"

He thumped his tail.

"Want to know a secret?" Daleina leaned toward the wolf's ear. "Me too."

Ven didn't ever criticize her technique. He cared about results and didn't demand that she channel her power in specific ways or use particular commands. He acted like he didn't regret his decision to pick her, and she had no intention of ever making him regret it. She scratched behind Bayn's ears. "It's nice to feel like I'm doing well."

And that was the moment that the earth spirit tried to kill her.

She felt the wolf stiffen as she plucked the last burr out, and she twisted around, expecting to see Ven stride into the clearing. But he didn't. None of the leaves rustled. She cast her senses out, checking for the spirits—and beneath her, the earth dissolved.

"Bayn, run!"

The solid dirt shifted into a mucky sand, and she sank to her waist. Ignoring her command, Bayn lunged for her and snapped Daleina's shirt in his jaws. Daleina wrapped her arms around the wolf's neck. Bayn scrambled his paws backward, trying to yank Daleina out of the shifting sand, but the sand was oozing outward, dissolving more of the solid ground—it was going to trap the wolf too.

"Get Ven!" Daleina ordered the wolf, and then she released his neck. Her shirtsleeve tore as he refused to open his jaws. "Now!" The wolf obeyed, releasing her and bounding into the forest, as the sand pulled Daleina faster, down to her armpits.

She cast her mind down—the earth spirit was beneath her. This wasn't a tiny spirit. This one's mind felt old, smart, and aware. It extended far under the earth, embedded in the bedrock, with tentacles that reached through the stone, deep.

She knew instantly it was more powerful than she was, so she cast upward toward the other, smaller spirits. *Help me,* she commanded. To the wood spirits, she called, *Grow the roots.* She pushed a picture toward them, thickening the roots, growing them toward her, and the wood spirits emerged from the trees. Gleefully, they pounced on the roots.

To the water spirits, she called, *Wash the sand away! Flood it!*

The roots thickened and spread through the loose sand. Rain trickled between the leaves, and then fell harder. Daleina reached for the roots. As she tried to kick her legs, the sand seemed to melt around them. She sank up to her neck.

Grow faster!

More wood spirits piled onto the roots, and they continued to thicken, plumping like loaves of bread in an oven. She grabbed one. And then she felt a meaty hand clasp around her ankle and yank her downward.

She lost her grip on the root. Her mind screamed for the wood spirits as rain poured into the sand, but not quickly enough. The sand closed over her head, stinging her eyes, filling her nose, and seeping into her mouth. The hand pulled her deeper, and she flailed her arms as she screamed with her mind. Her lungs burned.

Help me! she called to the spirits.

She felt them above her, growing the roots and flooding the sand with water, but neither the roots nor the water reached her. She sank too quickly, deeper and deeper, with the hand clutched tight around her leg, its fingers reaching from her ankle to her thigh. Her leg ached from the pressure. Her whole body felt compressed by the sand, as if it wanted to shrink her.

Ven will come, she thought. Bayn will find him. He won't let me die.

Unless this was a test. And she was failing.

She tried to cling to those thoughts as her mind fragmented. Her mouth opened—to breathe? To scream? Sand poured down her throat. It tasted, she thought, like burnt toast.

And then she thought and felt and tasted nothing.

VEN LINED UP HIS SHOT: A PLUMP SQUIRREL, ABSORBED in trying to crack a nut by bashing it on a branch. One flick of his wrist, and it would have a knife through its throat. A quick death. He pulled a charm out with one hand and draped it onto the hilt of the knife. The wood spirits would ignore his blade buried in the tree, at least for long enough for him to retrieve their dinner.

"Champion Ven!" a voice boomed. Popol, the healer.

The squirrel froze, and then, clutching the nut, scampered out of range. Sighing, Ven lowered the knife. "You couldn't have waited?"

"You asked us to meet you," Popol said, genuinely perplexed.

Apologetically, his assistant Hamon held up a bag, which

Ven assumed held food. He hoped it was fresh. Ven accepted it. "I've taken on a candidate," he said with no preamble.

Popol blinked. "You what? But I thought you were in disgrace. Oh, that's splendid news! The queen has lifted her exile? I knew her benevolence—"

"She hasn't," Ven interrupted. "But I have my duty."

"Oh." For once, Popol was out of words.

"I am about to initiate the next stage of her training, and I need a healer on call. I don't plan to go easy on her, and I don't want her dying unnecessarily."

Popol frowned. "I am depended upon by upwards of twenty villages for—"

"I'd like Hamon," Ven cut in.

Popol's eyes widened. "Hamon? But he's just a boy."

"Actually, I grew up," Hamon said. "Time has that effect." He said this without any hint of disrespect in his voice, which Ven found impressive.

"It's time to grant him journeyman status," Ven told Popol. "Past time."

Popol looked at Hamon as if seeing him for the first time. The boy had grown into a young man with clean-shaven cheeks and well-earned muscles. "But he's the best assistant I've ever had."

"Exactly why you should set him free."

"Exactly why I need him," Popol said. "The outer villages need him. I'm—we're—stretched thin enough as it is. The demands—"

"He will also have the chance to gather and study rare plants and herbs, found only in the less-populated areas—I remember he was interested in that. A unique opportunity." The trick with Popol was never to let him work himself into a rant. He was a good man, but he liked the sound of his own voice and he was overly impressed with his own sense of logic. "Truthfully, it isn't your decision. It's Hamon's."

Popol huffed. "It's the master's right to declare when the student is ready."

"And you already said he's the best you've ever had," Ven said, trying to stay patient. Popol should have released Hamon a year ago. "Hamon? What say you?"

Hamon bowed to Popol. "It has been an honor to serve and be trained by you, sir. You are a credit to healers, and songs should be written about you. Now it's time for me to humbly take my training out in the world, so that more can see the results of your mastery."

Popol preened. "Well. Yes. But I'll miss you, boy."

The goodbyes were suitably awkward, and Ven spent a while watching the trees while they each praised each other and wished each other well, repetitively. At last, Popol trundled off down the bridge, toward the nearest village.

"Laid it on a bit thick, didn't you, boy?"

"Master Popol feeds on praise the way other men feed on bread. Besides, it costs me nothing to make him happy." Hamon attached his pack to his back. He flashed Ven a rare smile. "I trust you don't require constant compliments?"

"Just a few now and then."

Straight-faced, Hamon said, "I'm honored to be working alongside someone with such expert woodland knowledge, superior battle skills, and an impressive beard."

Ven stroked his beard. "Indeed you are."

They left the path, heading back toward where Ven had left Daleina. Hopefully, whatever Hamon carried in his pack would make up for the dinner that Ven had failed to shoot. He knew Daleina would be hungry after the intense training from earlier in the day. He was working on her physical reflexes, climbing up and down the trees and practicing her knife throws—she was surprisingly adept at both, most likely thanks to her outer-forest upbringing, but he also had to credit the survival classes. Unlike some candidates, she hadn't neglected those. With a fully trained body, she'd be free to devote her mind to her powers. Her muscles would know how to react on their own, freeing her mind to focus on the spirits.

"Tell me about your candidate," Hamon said.

"She's too concerned with doing things perfectly, a habit from the academy. Though they'd deny it, they teach that it's more important to be strong than smart," Ven said. "I'm trying to break down the structure they've imposed. Their training is excellent for a certain type of student, but for Daleina, she needs to allow herself more flexibility in her thinking—"

He heard branches break. Automatically, he stepped in front of Hamon and drew his knife. Crouching, he prepared to strike, as a wolf burst through the underbrush.

"Hold!" he told Hamon.

It was Bayn.

He knew instantly something was wrong—he'd never heard the wolf be anything but stealthy. Without waiting to explain to Hamon, he ran after the wolf. He heard the boy—young man—scramble after him, as Ven swung from branch to branch, leaping while the wolf ran just ahead of him below, leading the way.

The wolf burst into a clearing and then halted abruptly and howled.

Ven ran after him toward the clearing. Jumping in front of him, Bayn snapped at Ven's legs. He stopped just on the edge of a morass of loose sandy earth. The wolf howled again, and the message couldn't have been clearer if he spoke:

Daleina is down there.

Quickly, Ven dropped his pack and yanked out a rope. He secured it around a tree and then tied it around his waist. He then sucked in as much air into his lungs as he could, and he dove into the shifting sand.

He kept his eyes squeezed shut, but felt the sand fill his

ears and nostrils. It moved around him, shifting, as if he were diving through oatmeal. He kicked his legs, propelling himself downward, and his hands encountered soft flesh. Daleina!

He closed his hands around the limb—an arm—and he grabbed back at the rope, pulling on it. But Daleina didn't budge. He pulled harder—it didn't matter. Something was holding her. He pivoted and dove down farther.

His lungs began to burn. He had to work fast, release whatever was holding her. He expected to find a knot of vines. Instead, it felt like stone, clamped around her. *Dammit, release her!*

Moving his arm through the sludge of sand, he drew his sword and plunged it into the stone. *Let her go!* The stone loosened, and Ven tugged Daleina upward, yanking himself up on the rope.

The rope itself began to pull upward. He burst out of the morass and gasped in air. Sand filled his mouth, and he spit it out as he hauled Daleina out of the quicksand.

Hamon and Bayn were both pulling the rope, helping him out. Hamon rushed forward and dragged Daleina out and lay her on her back. Ven crawled out on his elbows beside her. "Is she alive?" Ven spat out sand.

"No," Hamon said as he tore open his healer's pack.

aleina woke in darkness. Her eyes felt as if they'd been scalded, and when she blinked, it felt as if knives were being plunged into the back of her skull. She reached up to wipe the grit from her face, and her wrist was caught by a hand. "Don't fight," an unfamiliar voice said.

Every instinct screamed at her to claw the sand from her eyes and to run, far away from the shifting sand, from the monster, from the pain. But then she felt cool water poured over her eyelids. A cloth was rubbed gently across her face, and then more water. Her head was tilted to the right, and she coughed, splitting up bile mixed with sand. It scraped her throat like a thousand fingernails, and tears popped into her eyes. The tears were rinsed away, along with more sand.

Reaching with her mind, she felt deep into the bedrock, for the spirit . . . Nothing. No monster beneath the rocks. The water continued to pour, washing her eyes. Moving hurt. Breathing hurt. *Who are you?* she wanted to ask.

"Is she going to live?" Ven's voice.

She clung to his voice as if it were a rope tossed to her as she drowned. She wanted to say yes, she was alive, she wasn't beaten.

That he hadn't broken her yet.

"Her heart stopped," the unfamiliar voice said, calm, as if commenting on the weather.

"I know, but is she going to live?"

My heart? It was impossible to imagine. Her hand twitched, and she raised it to lay over her heart. She tried to feel the heartbeat through her sand-encrusted shirt.

"Yes. But there may be damage."

"Fix it," Ven said.

"Stop talking, please." The other voice was mild, calm, and male. She couldn't tell the age, but she thought he must be a nice singer. His voice was a smooth baritone. "Relax, Daleina—you're safe now."

She lay still and let the healer continue to pour water over her eyes. At some point, she must have lost consciousness again, because the next moment she became aware, she tried to open her eyes and couldn't—her head was swaddled in soft cloths. Reaching up, she touched the bandages. "Hello?" she tried to whisper. Her throat felt raw, as if it had been scraped with a fork all the way down to her lungs. *Ow.*

"Lie still," the baritone said. "You need to rest."

"Who are you?" There, that sounded louder, more human.

"My name is Hamon. I'm a healer." His voice flowed over her, like the water. It made her feel as if everything was all right, as if she was being taken care of, as if she were home. She'd never heard a voice with that kind of power in it.

"Where's"—she stopped, tried to swallow, tried again—"Champion Ven?" Her voice creaked, like a rocking chair made of brittle wood. *A thousand times ow.*

"He's hunting. Said he wants to make you soup." Hamon sounded amused. "I didn't know he knew how to make soup. His usual cooking technique is to stick meat into a fire until it's burnt."

She knew she should smile, but her face felt stiff. "My eyes?"

"Need to heal." She felt his hand laid over hers. His hand was warm, like a blanket.

"How long?"

He didn't answer. "How are you feeling?"

She considered being stoic and strong. She was a candidate, after all—she wasn't supposed to be slowed by pain—but he was a healer, and it felt stupid to lie. "Everything hurts."

"You have no breaks, miraculously, but your body was under tremendous strain. You were the rope in a tug of war. Do you remember any of it?"

She shook her head and then wished she hadn't as pain blossomed fresh through her skull.

"Champion Ven dove into the quicksand after you and stabbed the spirit with his sword. I don't think anyone has ever fought a spirit within the earth before. As he told it, the spirit was surprised enough to release you, and Ven pulled both you and himself out."

"Why?" she asked.

"What do you mean, 'why'?" He sounded startled, unusual in such a soothing voice. His voice reminded her of chocolate, she decided. "He wanted to save you."

"I failed." She wanted to elaborate, but every word still scraped her throat. She'd failed her test. She was unworthy. By all rights, he should have left her in the soupy earth. As soon as she was well enough to move, he'd be taking her back to the academy, dumping her on the doorstep. Some hero she'd turned out to be. She couldn't even protect herself. No one wanted a queen who needed saving.

"You encountered an old, strong spirit," Hamon said. "There's no shame in that."

"Lots of shame. I can't move." The truth of that last sentence echoed in her head. "Why can't I move?" She tried to shift her leg.

She felt calming hands on the sides of her face. "I had to give you a large dose of medicine—a mix of firebrand and moon-moss, which if you combine three to one and . . ." Hamon began then stopped. "Your muscles will remember how to move. In the meantime, you need to be patient and rest. The forest won't fall down around us if you sleep a little more."

"And my eyes?"

He was silent for a moment. "You need to be patient—"

"Am I blind?"

"Your eyes were scratched by the sand. They need to rest."

"But will I—"

She felt fingers pressed to her lips, stopping her. "Rest," Hamon told her.

Daleina tried, truly tried, but her mind churned, replaying every second that she could remember, trying to pinpoint what she did wrong and what she could have done differently. If she'd summoned the spirits faster . . . If she hadn't clung to Bayn . . . If she'd been more aware to begin with . . . She spread her awareness out as she "rested," and felt the location of every spirit around her, from the tiny ones in the upper leaves to the ancient slumbering ones within the trees. She'd never felt one as large as the one within the bedrock before, and she couldn't find it now. It must have fled the area, or burrowed deeper.

She heard Ven's voice. "How is she?"

"Stubborn. Like you. She pretends to cooperate, but she's lying there, awake, most likely berating herself for not being instantly well. Speaking of which, you should let me examine you."

"I'm fine. Will she recover?"

"It's too soon to tell. Give her another few days to sleep, and then we'll see."

She wanted to speak up then, tell them she couldn't sleep

for a few days, she couldn't afford to lose the training time, she didn't want to fail . . . But then she felt sweet, syrupy liquid on her lips.

"Drink," Hamon commanded. "It will help."

She drank. And then she slept again.

At some point, she woke and ate soup, which tasted like burnt meat. Some time later, she woke again and was able to sit up. Later, Hamon helped her stand. He steadied her as she relieved herself, and she realized he must have been cleaning her before now. She was grateful for the syrupy liquid after that realization. Maybe it would erase the memory of how terrible it was to feel so helpless.

She didn't know how much time had passed before she was strong enough to feel her way over roots without help. Bandages were still wrapped around her eyes. Underbrush scraped her legs. Bayn nudged her knees, guiding her behind a tree so she could relieve herself on her own. It was her first triumph since her failure with the quicksand.

That night, she sat still as Hamon unwrapped the bandages. Ven told her he'd douse the fire so the brightness wouldn't hurt her eyes. She blinked them open. The lids felt crusty.

"Tilt your head to the side," Hamon said.

She obeyed, and he poured water gently across her eyes. After he finished bathing them, he tilted her chin up, as if he were examining her. "How can you examine my eyes in the darkness?" she asked.

"It's not dark," Hamon said quietly.

"What do you mean?" But she felt her heart constrict.

Gently, he rewrapped the bandages. "Your eyes need to heal for a while more."

Reaching her hands forward, Daleina felt around her, and her palms felt heat—Ven hadn't extinguished the fire. "But . . . they should be better!" The rest of her had healed. Why not her eyes?

"The corneas should heal themselves," Hamon said. "Most likely, your sight will return on its own, but you must continue to rest them. All you need is time."

"Is she well enough to travel?" Ven asked.

"Yes, except for her eyes, she's fully recovered," Hamon said. "She was remarkably lucky, in many ways."

"Then we'll start for the academy at dawn—"

"I'm not going back," Daleina interrupted. He'd said she was recovered. That wasn't grounds for sending her back to the academy in shame. She felt along the edges of the bandages. Their softness was comforting now, after the water. "I'll heal out here."

"You can't continue your training like this," Hamon said gently. "In a few months—"

"In a few months, the queen could call for the trials." The queen could call them whenever she wanted, regardless of whether Daleina—or anyone—was ready. And Champion Ven could find another candidate, one who wasn't injured, one who was more powerful. It would be worse than not having been chosen; she'd be the rejected one.

"It's not possible," Ven said. "You can't climb without your sight, and you can't train on the forest floor—it's too dangerous, especially since we can't predict when another earth spirit will decide to grab you—"

"Of course you can predict it! It was your test, wasn't it?"

"Daleina, that wasn't a test."

She was silent for a moment, absorbing that—he hadn't been testing her, which meant she hadn't failed, not really, not in her champion's eyes. At least, not yet. Not if she showed him that this wouldn't stop her. That was one thing she could do as well as or better than any other candidate: be stubborn.

"It's the healer's purview . . ." Hamon began.

"But my decision, right?" Daleina interrupted.

Hamon began to protest again, but this time Ven stopped

him. Daleina listened to their breathing. She heard the crackle of the fire and Bayn's soft panting beside her, as well as the wind in the leaves above and the rustle of night animals in the underbrush. Stretching her awareness out, she touched the spirits that lived in the trees nearby. "What are you suggesting?" Ven asked her.

"If I become queen, I won't have the luxury of hiding if things get difficult," Daleina said. "If I'm not strong enough for just myself, how can I be strong enough for Renthia? I have to do this. I can't stop."

"You're injured," Hamon said. "No one expects you to continue to train while—"

"I'm supposed to stay with Champion Ven. Learn from him. I can't learn if I'm cocooned away somewhere." There was no guarantee Champion Ven would want her as a candidate anymore if he had to wait for her to heal. He could choose someone else, and what if no one else ever chose her? Especially with an injury, her chances were far worse. If he didn't keep training her, if she didn't continue, she may never get another chance. *It was a miracle I was chosen at all.* Headmistress Hanna had made that clear.

"Only until you're well enough," Hamon said. "Then you can train all you want."

"It's just my eyes, isn't it? If I could see, you'd let me train, no objection."

"You need your eyes—"

"The people need a queen, not a squirrel. I don't need to be able to climb easily; I just have to control the spirits." Daleina buried her hands in Bayn's fur. "Bayn will help me on the forest floor. And when I have to climb higher . . . I've climbed at night before. This won't be so very different. Please, Ven, don't dismiss me. I can still do this."

"I don't advise it," Hamon said.

"You're not supposed to advise it," Daleina said. "You're a healer. You're supposed to coddle people. Ven, I know I can do this, but I can't do it without you. Please. You chose me. Choose to believe in me again."

He was silent for a long moment. She listened to the night sounds. A distant wolf howled, but Bayn didn't echo him. Insects buzzed, and night animals rustled in the bushes around them, scrounging for food. No spirits were nearby.

"Very well," he said at last.

SHE TRAINED ON THE FOREST FLOOR.

Her champion drilled her on sensing spirits. How many could she feel? How far could she reach? She'd never done it without sight before, and it was both easier and harder. She couldn't depend on seeing a leaf rustle, but she could hear it, and without the distraction of her eyes trying to guess where the spirits were, she began to trust her mind more. For an entire week, that was all she did: practice reaching with her mind.

They kept to the camp for the most part, with Bayn on guard against wolf packs, irate badgers, ground snakes, and the other wildlife that kept most villages up in the trees. The wolf also acted as her guide, helping her move quickly around the trees and over the roots. Daleina keep her hand on the wolf's back so she could feel when Bayn leaped over a root, and Bayn would nudge against Daleina when it was time to move around a tree. The wolf stuck by her side constantly.

The earth spirit in the bedrock didn't return, but Daleina stayed alert for him. When it was time to sleep, she climbed into a hammock above the dirt, and Bayn lay beside her. She hoped that was enough to keep them safe.

Gradually, she became used to feeling her way around the camp. She had a sense of where the trees were, and each step didn't feel so much like plummeting off a cliff.

"You're going easy on me," she told Ven one morning. "You haven't had a spirit attack me yet."

Hamon spoke up. "You *want* to be attacked?"

"I want to stop an attack," Daleina corrected, turning in the direction of his voice. He was grinding some of the plants that he'd gathered—she could hear the pestle and mortar. When he wasn't tending to her eyes, he used his time to search for rare plants, herbs, and berries. He'd found ripe woundberries, as well as the root of a jump flower (used to prevent seizures), a rare bush of deadly nightend berries (used to ease the passing of a terminal patient), the pow-dered petals of a glory vine (used to slow the symptoms of a disease called the False Death), and many others. Daleina couldn't remember them all, but Hamon liked to rattle off their properties as he worked.

"I don't want to risk waking that earth kraken again," Ven said. "We'll resume the attacks when we can be midforest."

Very well, if that's what it took, that's what she'd do. She hugged Bayn, and he leaned his head against Daleina's cheek. Daleina then stood up and, with her hands in front of her, felt to the nearest tree. She knew from ducking under it that this one had a low branch, and she knew from sensing the spirits run up and down it that there were multiple limbs above her.

"He didn't mean right now," Hamon said.

She climbed slowly but steadily, reaching up for the next branch, climbing by feel. It wasn't so different from climb-ing through her old village at night. She missed the shadows and bits of light that filtered through the trees, but other than that, she knew she could do it. Beneath her, she heard the sound of climbing—Ven was following her.

Clinging to the braches, she stretched her mind out to the nearest spirits. She kept her mind open, waiting for the attack that she knew would come—and it did come. She "saw" the wood spirits converge, heard them chittering to one another, and she focused on them.

Grow berries. She guided them with her mind to the

berry bushes that ringed their campsite, imagining the bushes bursting with fat, ripe berries, and the spirits veered down to attend to the bushes.

"Is that the best you can do?" she asked Ven.

He laughed. She thought it was the first time she'd heard him laugh. It sounded like a rumble, as if a bear were laughing.

From there, the training resumed as intensely as it had been before. He tested her often, calling spirits to their campsite and ordering her up into the trees to face them. She wasn't fast, and she often came down with extra scrapes and bruises and the occasional more serious gash.

Hamon patched her up each night. "I can see why Ven wanted a healer along."

"What were you doing before this?" Daleina asked him.

"Helping my master in the outer villages. All the usual sicknesses and injuries, plus childbirth complications."

She leaned her head to the side so that he could smooth a salve on a scrape that crossed the back of her neck. She'd miscalculated on a branch, and it had snagged her as she jumped to the next one. Jumps were the scariest, since she had to trust Ven was right about the distance—he'd call it out, and she'd do it. As long as she didn't think too much before she jumped, it went fine, usually. At least she hadn't broken anything yet. "Why did you become a healer?"

"The same reason most do, I suppose. I want to help people."

"But why?"

"You don't want to hear the sob story. It's not particularly original. My father was ill when I was young. If I'd known more about medicine, I could have helped him. As it was, he died." He unwound the bandages from around Daleina's eyes. She cracked them open. They felt as if they'd been glued together.

Looking around, she thought she saw glowing orbs,

orangeish. That was progress, wasn't it? "I see a glow, there." She pointed.

"That's the fire. Good." He began to wash out her eyes again.

"I'm sorry about your father."

"It was a long time ago." Gently, he wiped her eyes with a soft cloth. They didn't sting as much. She tried again to see the fire, trying to force it into a crisp shape. The glow undulated. "My mother did not take his death well, and so I left for an apprenticeship as soon as I could. Not an unusual story. Your childhood pain is more unique."

"Ven told you?" She thought she saw a hint of movement, but it could have been her imagination. She closed her eyes again as he rewrapped the bandages. "Our stories aren't so different. I wasn't good enough to save them."

"I understand how that must have shaped you. Survivor's guilt, it's called; it's an illness of the mind. I have been trained—"

Curled at her feet, Bayn tensed. Immediately, Daleina sent her senses out, as well as down and up—there was a spirit with Ven, several yards from their camp. She didn't sense anger, but she leapt to her feet, tense, ready.

"What is it?" Hamon asked.

Daleina heard Ven barrel into the campsite. "Got a message. I have to go. Bayn, take care of Hamon and Daleina." She listened as he threw items into a pack.

"What do you mean, 'a message'?" she asked as Hamon asked, "Where?"

"North Garat."

"I'll come," Hamon said. "You'll need me." She heard him begin to pack as well.

"No, I need you to stay with Daleina," Ven said. "She can't be left alone out here. Not on the forest floor, and not when we've been drawing spirits. Not until—"

He stopped short, and Daleina knew he was going to

mention her eyes. She clenched her hands and forced her voice to sound calm, reasonable, competent. "What's happening?"

"He gets messages with warnings, about rogue spirit attacks," Hamon explained when Ven didn't answer.

"Then I'm coming too."

"You can't keep up on the forest floor." Ven's voice wasn't cruel, just factual.

"We can travel the wire roads," Daleina said. "I don't need to see to fly. All I need is someone to call out when it's time to switch wires." She managed to say it as if she thought it would be easy, even though the idea of hurtling through the air unable to see the end of the line was terrifying. "I can help. You know I can. This is why you picked me, why you brought me out here, isn't it?" She remembered the conversation with Headmistress Hanna, the cryptic remarks about messages that hadn't made sense at the time. "This is why we're here."

She braced herself for an argument, but it didn't come.

"Fine," Ven said. "Let's go."

All three of them began to climb.

s she climbed, Daleina felt the air change. On the forest floor, it tasted damp, thick with the smell of earth and moss. By midforest, the air was sweeter, mixed with the scent of nearby villages, of smoke and cooking meat and drying clothes. Higher, near the canopy, it was like breathing fresh, cold water. She felt the wind on her face and heard the whispering of leaves.

Below, Ven called, "The platform is to your left."

Stopping, she reached around the trunk with her foot, feeling for it. Her toes brushed the edge. Intellectually, she knew how high she'd climbed, but she pretended she was only a few feet from the forest floor as she shifted weight and lunged onto the platform. *Just like climbing back home, right?* Wind whipped around her, and she clung to the tree trunk. Feeling above her, she found the wire.

Soon Ven joined her, and then Hamon, panting. "This is insane," Hamon said. "Daleina, you can't do this." He caught her shoulder, and she shrugged him away.

"Tell me when to switch wires," she told Ven, and then she hooked herself on to one. She held her other clip in her free hand and breathed deeply once, twice, three times. *You can do this. No fear.* She heard Ven clip on behind her and felt the wire tremble.

"We'll have to make three switches and then climb down to the bridges," Ven said. "Be ready. If you can't do it, stop and I will come back for you later." *And then deliver you to the academy,* he didn't say, but Daleina heard.

"I can do it." Hoping she wasn't wrong, she kicked off the platform. Wind hit her face, her arms, her legs, and her back so hard that she felt wrapped in wind. Branches slapped her legs, and one caught her hair, yanking out several strands. Tucking her chin down, she kept her free hand out, the other clip ready. She listened, as if she could somehow hear the end of the wire, but for all she could tell it went on endlessly.

"Three! Two! One! *Now!*"

Daleina reached forward, and her arm hit the next wire, stinging as the wire sliced her skin. She clipped on and released the first clip. She swung wildly, her arm wrenching in its socket as she switched, and then she was going, speeding up again. She felt the wire shake as Ven switched behind her and then again when Hamon switched.

She sailed between the trees, and for a moment, she felt free, for the first time since she'd been pulled beneath the earth. She felt as if she were all that existed, soaring through an empty world.

"Three, two, one, now!"

She switched again, and then again, until at last Ven cried, "Brace!"

She held out her feet, knees bent, letting gravity tell her which way to face, until she felt the impact of the tree reverberate through her body. She collapsed onto the platform and unclipped. Her arms ached, and her legs stung where branches had smacked into her. She felt and heard Ven land beside her. Standing, she pressed against the trunk, hoping she was out of the way enough as Hamon landed beside her.

"Let me look at your wounds," Hamon demanded.

"There's no time," Ven said. "Climb down."

Hamon kept his hand on her, letting her use him to guide

her to the ladder. She then climbed down by feel until she reached the bridge. Reaching out, she grabbed Hamon's hand, and he held it as they ran along the bridge, following the sound of Ven's footsteps, pounding on the wood as the bridge shook beneath them.

She heard screaming up ahead. Multiple voices. And the rip of wood. Instantly, she was plunged back in her memories to when she was ten years old. Her breath, already harsh in her throat, felt even faster, and her heart raced. Every muscle wanted her to turn and run in the opposite direction, but she kept running toward the screams. Her hand was gripping Hamon's so hard that sweat stuck their palms together.

Ven stopped her with his hands on her shoulders. "Hide here, both of you."

Hamon pulled her down behind what felt like a wall. Her fingers touched the seams between wood boards—the side of a house or just a crate. She couldn't tell which it was. She heard Ven pull his blade from its sheath, the ring of drawn steel, and she cast her mind outward, feeling for the spirits.

There were six. Small but vicious wood spirits, tearing through the houses, biting any flesh they saw, ripping any cloth, breaking any wood. She felt them like vibrations in the air, tiny earthquakes in her mind. *Stop!* She sent the thought out, and it was swallowed in their whir. She doubted they even felt her. They were all whirling rage and joy and ecstatic, blood-crazed destruction. She wasn't going to be able to overpower them; she'd have to redirect them, somehow.

Growing a few branches was not going to be a tempting enough substitute for the bloodlust. She needed to offer them something grand. Like a palace. Or a fortress. Or the academy. Drawing a picture in her mind of soaring spires and fused trees, she crafted her command. She'd have to hold it firm and be—

"What do we do?" Hamon whispered in her ear.

"I talk to the spirits; you keep me safe." Standing, she threw everything in her into that picture and sent it spiraling out toward the six spirits. *Build!* she commanded. She held the picture of the spires.

The spirits shrieked. She felt them rip into a woman's leg. Distantly, she heard screams, but they faded as she bore her will down on the spirits. *Build!* She painted the picture for them, beautiful and tall. And she felt the spirits swirl around one another, faster and faster, in a cyclone, and then they burrowed into the trunks of six of the village trees. They wanted this: unfettered growth, wild birth.

The trees began to grow, and she felt as if the growth was being pulled out of her own body. She swayed and felt hands on her shoulders, steadying her. She kept the pressure on the spirits as sweat poured down her forehead and trickled down her back.

Build!

The trees burgeoned wider and burst upward, stretching and soaring and twisting together. The spirits fused them and, laughing, spread the branches into a lacework canopy above. The wood was hollowed and peeled, its bark flayed and split, and she felt as if it were her flesh being peeled, and she felt her throat aching, as if she were screaming, but she couldn't hear herself. She couldn't hear anything. Couldn't feel her own body. She was the trees, growing and widening and stretching.

And then she felt nothing.

She collapsed.

WHEN DALEINA WOKE, HER FACE FELT CHILLED. SHE touched her cheeks and then, gently, her eyelids. The bandages were gone. Carefully, she opened her eyes and saw a yellowish glow above her. It was framed by blurred light green.

"Good," Hamon said. "You're awake. Ven? She's all right."

She saw a shadow shift beside her. A shadow! Eagerly, she tried to force it into a shape, but it stubbornly refused. "What happened? Is the village okay?"

"You have an interesting mind," Ven said. "I'm not sure anyone has ever controlled the spirits quite the way you do. No wonder you didn't test well. You seem to be more effective when the spirits are already agitated."

"Did it work?" She struggled to sit up. Her head pounded, and she blinked. For once, it didn't feel like knives slicing her. The yellowish glow stayed above her. Sunlight? She tried again to shape the shadows and glowing orbs into recognizable bodies and faces.

"You turned the village into . . . well, I don't know what it is. Spires? Towers? A palace?" Hamon said, awe in his voice.

"I had to redirect them, and it had to be something big."

The shadow moved again, and she heard heavy footsteps on the bridge, felt the boards tremble—Ven's footsteps, receding. She heard his voice, lower, muffled, and then another voice replied. He'd gone to talk to someone else.

With his usual gentleness, Hamon helped her stand. All her muscles ached, and she couldn't tell if it was from the trip across the forest or from the magic. She reached out with her mind, trying to feel for where the spirits had gone, and pain shot through her temples. She staggered backward, but Hamon didn't let her fall. "How do you feel?" he asked.

"I've felt worse."

"I'm sure you've felt better too."

"You're not wrong."

"You might not want to do something like that again for a while."

She rubbed her temples. "Probably a good idea. How are the villagers?"

"Three dead, fifteen injured, but the vast majority are safe, only minor injuries, and getting over their terror," Hamon said. "Lean on me. You need a softer place to sit."

"You need to help the injured."

"Once you're taken care of."

"I'm fine. Go, Hamon. This is why you're here."

"I'm here for you. Because of you. No, *for* you." He touched her cheek gently, and then he took his hand away and her cheek felt chilled without it.

Softer, she said, "Go. If anything tries to hurt me, I'll make it build a shed."

He insisted on helping her shuffle a few more feet, and then she sank onto the wood floor of whatever platform she was on—the village? her new building? a bridge?—so that he had to leave her and help the ones who needed it more.

She lay on her side, cheek against the warm wood, and just breathed without trying to focus her mind on any particular thought, except how nice his touch was. The village smelled like an odd mix of burnt wood and freshly planted grasses. She heard lots of voices, talking, some crying, their words mixing together. She didn't try to separate them out.

"Hello? Are you dead?" It was a girl's voice.

"I don't think so," Daleina said, "but thanks for asking."

"Are you a queen?" she asked.

"No, just a candidate."

"I thought only queens could build things."

"These spirits had a lot of energy," Daleina said. "I told them to do something else with it."

"Oh. It's pretty."

Daleina didn't know what to say to that. "Good." She wasn't sure exactly what she'd done or what the spirits had built. Opening her eyes, she tried to focus on the girl. She saw a blob that bobbed in front of her. It seemed vaguely girl-like in shape.

"You're pretty too."

"Uh, good?"

"Except for the blood. I got a cut too. See?"

"I hurt my eyes a while ago, and I can't see very well." *Or at all.* Except that she could at least see glows and shadows and blobs. She tried to squint at the blobs, and her head ached as if her skull were a bell hit by a hammer.

"My granddaddy can't see very well either. He mostly stays inside. But that's because his knees hurt him too. I don't know if he's dead."

"Is your mother or father nearby?" She hoped the spirits hadn't made the girl an orphan.

"My mommy is talking to the green man. He scared the spirits away from my little brother. I'm glad the spirits didn't eat my little brother, even if he fusses a lot. Mommy said we're going to be great friends when we get bigger, but I don't think that's true. I never wanted a brother. I wanted a sister so we could play queens together. Do you want to be a queen?"

It was hard to follow the tumbling words with the way her head was pounding. "Yes, I do."

"Mommy says that people who want to be queen don't live very long, so I don't really want to be queen. I want to be a woodcarver and make beautiful butterflies out of wood. But I need a lot of charms to do that without angering the spirits, and I don't have very much money. Mommy says maybe I can apprentice when I'm older. Are you an apprentice?"

"Sort of. Yes. I am."

"Do you think Mommy will let me live in the spires if I ask her?"

"I don't know." Daleina thought about sitting up and then decided it was nice lying right where she was. At least while the child was talking, she knew nothing bad was happening. She was certain she couldn't handle another attack right now. She wasn't even sure she could command her legs to move, much less command a spirit. "Can you tell me what it looks like?"

"It's like a palace!" In a happy burble, the little girl described six trees, fused together and spiraling up to pierce the canopy. The bark was stretched smooth, like skin pulled taut. "Like this," the girl said, and Daleina guessed she was demonstrating. She then continued to describe the soaring structure that Daleina had pictured in her mind.

It had actually worked. She'd done it.

Maybe she *was* meant to do this.

SPRAWLED ON A DIVAN, THE OWL WOMAN LICKED CHOColate off a spoon. "He brought a woman with him this time, a powerful one."

Queen Fara sipped her pine tea and schooled her face to show only pleasant interest. "Oh? I hope this woman didn't cause problems. Please, have more."

Discarding the spoon, the owl woman dipped her hand into the chocolate and then licked her many-jointed fingers, one at a time. Each finger ended in a talon. "My spirits were not displeased. With the addition of the woman, they were able to create both death and life."

Fara knew perfectly well who "he" was, but she hadn't known he'd chosen a new candidate. She made a mental note to have her gatherers make inquiries, discreetly. "I am glad everything was satisfactory, despite the disruption."

"Indeed." She shifted, her wings fluttering, then lying flat on her human back. "But today is not for talk of business. I came to play." Before dawn, on the night of the first full moon, was the time for bargains—lately, the owl woman preferred the poetry of it.

"But of course." Fara studied the garden. A few gardeners toiled in the flower beds, creating spreads of blossoms to complement her topiaries. Her latest addition was a miyan set, comprised of snarls of branches tethered to the ground by vines. As long as the vines were intact, the living game pieces could be moved. Flicking a finger, she sent an order to a small, docile spirit next to her piece. It cajoled the plant to pull the piece three spaces.

The owl woman twitched the feathers on her shoulders, and one of her game pieces shifted to the left. "Still . . . The young woman must have been very strong, to have placated my spirits. I am curious why you allow yet another to grow in power, knowing she will only hunger for your death."

Fara stood and crossed to the table behind the divan to pour herself more tea. Her cup was already three-quarters full, but the owl woman reeked of churned mud from a marsh in summer. She should have known the conversation would shift this way. It was her own fault for opening the door to the possibility. This spirit was far more intelligent than any other she'd encountered—*and ambitious,* Fara thought. Unnervingly so. "It's tradition."

The owl woman twisted her head more than one hundred eighty degrees to look at Fara. "You're the queen. You set tradition."

Fara tried not to show how disturbing she found the owl woman's statement. Bound by their own instincts, most spirits would never think to question tradition. Spirits weren't supposed to be aware enough to question the way things were. "An heir must always be ready. If I should die—"

"They would rejoice, but I would mourn my dearest friend." Without any obvious signal from the owl woman, one of the game pieces shifted two spaces diagonally, blocking Fara's move. "Truly, if you must have heirs, why must it be one trained by the very man you hate and who hates you?"

Fara bit back a bitter laugh. "Be honest, dearest friend: you're trying to manipulate me." She considered the game board again. In three moves, she could capture the spirit's token. Two, if she risked exposing her own token. She wondered if the owl woman would predict the maneuver. Hidden from the sight of the gardeners, she didn't have as clear a view of the garden. Fara made her move.

"They are simply so very eager, always meddling where they shouldn't. You and I have an understanding, dear heart. The heirs are like bumbling babies. It would be simpler and safer for you and for us if they weren't in the game." The owl woman took Fara's token, sliding another game piece in from the side. "You left yourself exposed."

"As did you," Fara said, taking her token as well, tying the game. She told the spirits on the board to unroll the vines, and they did, snaking them around the pieces in the pattern that her moves had laid out. The longest unbroken vine would win.

Other vines chased across the board, tangling and twisting around Fara's. For a moment, they were both silent, concentrating, and then the owl woman said, "She will plot against you. They all will."

"If they do, I will act."

"Ahh, but then it may be too late. You must know they are only waiting for you to die. Until then, they must taste the drink of unfulfilled destiny, and it is bitter, my love." The owl woman flicked her finger, and a game piece that had been tucked to the side swept forward to corner Queen Fara's token. The queen's token fell.

Fara smiled, though it felt like her cheeks would crack to smile at this monster. "Well played. But I believe you distracted me with talk of business, despite your love of the full moon."

The owl woman laughed, a sound like talons scraping against rock. "Perhaps I did. But I spoke only truth. You will see. Call for the trials, and he will bring her, the woman he has trained to replace you. Call them now, and then judge for yourself who is a danger. If you wish it, I will swear to protect you from her and all those who covet your crown, as would every spirit who answers to me." Opening her hand, the owl woman sliced her own palm with her talon-like nail and let three drops of blood fall onto the floor, a sign of her sincerity. The blood sank into the floor as if the wood were drinking it. A rose blossomed from between the wood tiles. With a sweep of her wing, the owl woman plucked it and handed it to Fara. It was an unsubtle reminder of the way to make a blood oath: drink three drops of blood to seal a bargain.

Fara inhaled the rose's scent. "Lovely. Another game?"

Ⓣraining intensified.

"You do best if you don't try to control them," Champion Ven said outside the village the night they left, after the funerals and the celebrations and the wretched attempts to immortalize the events in song—Daleina sincerely hoped everyone forgot the lyrics by morning—"which explains your test results at the academy—they teach students to command, control, and coerce, but your strength is in redirection, as you so clearly demonstrated in North Garat. So tell me, what do the spirits most want?"

"To grow, and to kill."

"Douse the fire," Ven said. "Your way."

Daleina shifted to kick dirt on their campfire but stopped when she felt his hand on her wrist. "Oh, we're done with the magical theory discussion? Of course we are." Settling herself, she considered the task—he didn't want her to reach for fire spirits the way she'd been taught: fire to handle fire. Instead, she reached into the earth and located a small earth spirit burrowing under a nearby root. She invited him to come, showed him what she wanted him to do, and then watched as he crawled from beneath the fire and covered it with dirt, creating a mound in its place.

"Exactly," Ven said.

He set her to tasks: seeking out the nearby spirits and guiding them to tasks that they *wanted* to do. It didn't feel like commands, not precisely. More like suggestions. In truth, it wasn't so different from what she'd always instinctively done, but now she studied and honed her skill instead of treating it like a backup plan or a kind of shameful trick. Soon, she began to have a feel for which spirits would be guided and which resisted. The younger, smaller ones were eager for direction. Older, stronger spirits ignored her, and at Ven's direction, she let them, for now, focusing instead on the ones that she could influence.

"Power won't always be a problem," Ven said. "When you're crowned queen, the spirits will confer power on you. You need to master technique."

"It won't matter how much power I'll have afterward if I don't have enough before. To be crowned queen, you need power. The spirits always choose the heir who projects the strongest command. But even before the coronation ceremony, the queen will expect me to command at the trials."

"She'll expect you to survive."

Hamon was puttering nearby. She heard him chopping herbs and mashing them into his various medicines. It was a familiar sound. All the rare plants he collected while they trained—he crafted them into salves and poultices that he traded for bread and other items in the surrounding villages, except for those he kept for his own studies, like the nightend berries and the clippings of glory vine. "You must. I didn't go through the effort of putting you back in one piece just for you to be torn apart again."

"You will survive," Ven said, "but you'll do it your way. Even a handful of gravel is a useful weapon when thrown at the right time. My mother embroidered that on a pillow."

"She did?"

He shook his head. "You are still so naïve."

"It's only that you never talk about your family." She

couldn't picture Ven as a child. He seemed as if he'd been born in green armor, a knife in his hand. "Plus my mother embroiders sayings all the time. Every pillow bears a platitude."

"Our mothers are nothing alike. Start a new fire. I'll be back with dinner." She heard his boots hit the ground as he stood, and then she heard branches and leaves rustle and knew he was climbing up, higher from their midforest camp.

"Don't mind him," Hamon said. "He enjoys being an enigma." She felt his hands touch the bandage around her eyes and begin to unwind it. "Let's check on how you're doing. The sun is down, so it shouldn't hurt to try. If you face me, you won't be looking directly into the fire."

She sat still as he unwrapped the bandage. Her eyes didn't hurt anymore, or maybe their pain was overshadowed by the pain of her scrapes and bruises from clambering around the forest.

"Ven's mother used to be a champion," Hamon said.

"Really? Used to be?" She hadn't known anyone ever quit being a champion. Most kept the title until they died.

"Do you know 'The Song of Sorrowfield'?" Softly, in his baritone voice, he sang:

Dearest, do you hear them, calling through the trees?
Calling me to Sorrowfield,
Dearest, can you feel them, coming through the trees?
Taking me to Sorrowfield,
Dearest, can you take me there, lay me down,
Carry me to Sorrowfield, before they come around . . .

It was about an elderly queen and the champion who helped her end her life. Her power was fading, and she wanted to choose the time of her death—it had a soaring melody leading to the moment she drank the juice of a dozen deadly nightend berries while lying on a bed of flowers in a field. The new queen caused a forest to grow where the field had been, to honor the old queen's courage in dying before she was killed. It was one of those songs that was seldom sung but everyone knew.

"That was her, the champion?" Daleina asked.

"She quit being champion after the queen's death. But she raised her children with the expectation that one of them would follow her footsteps and serve Aratay. One became a border guard, one a canopy singer, and then there was Ven, the youngest. When he was disgraced . . . Suffice it to say that he has not seen his family in a long while."

She felt the last piece of bandage fall from her eyes. "How do you know this?"

"My former teacher, Master Popol, researched him thoroughly before hiring him. Master Popol liked to talk." He shrugged, and she was close enough that she could feel the movement. "Open your eyes and tell me what you see."

Daleina carefully opened her eyes. At first, it was all an amber blur, and she felt her heart sink. *Still not better,* she thought. Against her will, she felt tears well in the corners of her eyes.

"Yes, that's it," he urged. "Let them fall."

She blinked, and the tears washed her eyes and then slipped down her cheeks, a rivulet. She raised her hand to wipe them away with the back of her hand, and he caught her wrist.

"Good. Now look at me. Try to focus."

The tears ceased, and she focused ahead of her, at the blur that was his face, caught in the amber light of the campfire. He had black hair and black skin that bled into the shadows. His lips were parted as if he wanted to speak, but he was silent. His eyes were gemstone green, bright against the whites of his eyes, blurred but visible. He was staring at her unblinking with those green, green eyes, and she thought that green was the most gorgeous color she'd ever seen in her entire life. Greener than a fern in springtime. Greener than the canopy at daybreak. Greener than her own eyes, which were staring at him, *seeing* him for the first time.

His lips—she could see his soft, beautiful lips!—curved into a smile. "You're looking at me. I can tell you are. You see me."

Yes was too small a word. There were no words. She couldn't speak, think, or breathe. She could only stare. Her hand trembled as she reached up, gently, to touch his cheek. It was soft under her fingertips; even his stubble was soft, like the underbelly of a hedgehog. *Where did that thought come from?* She felt a laugh bubble up from her stomach and shake her arms.

She saw his expression shift into concern—his lips turned downward and a small crease appeared in his forehead, wiggling as she tried to focus on it. He was looking at her as if she was the most important thing in the world. Not like a healer looks at a patient, but as if she was special and cherished . . . and she realized she treasured that, the way he cared about her, the greatness of his heart and depth of his kindness. She also realized she hadn't answered him yet. Leaning forward, she touched her lips to his, her eyes open. His lips softened, and he kissed her back.

Scooting closer, she wrapped her arms around his back. She felt his back through his shirt, the muscles from climbing, and he folded his arms around her and drew her in against him. She kissed him as if the rest of the world didn't exist, and within his arms, she felt safe.

THREE MONTHS LATER, AT DAWN, THEY CLIMBED UP beyond the wire roads so that Daleina could watch the air spirits tumble in the clouds—her sight was at last no longer blurred, and this was her reward. Hamon came too, though there was no specific reason for him to come. No reason other than to be close to her . . . a reason she thoroughly approved of.

He braced himself on the thin branches beside her, tossing a rope to secure himself. Ven didn't use a rope, and neither did Daleina—Ven because he was Ven, and Daleina because he told her not to, despite Hamon's objections. "She's in training" was Ven's answer, which convinced Daleina that he was going to push her off the tree. But for now she was free to watch the spirits.

At first, she didn't see any, though she sensed them, high above the clouds. But then one burst through. Its white-furred, sinewy body undulated between the clouds. It spread black wings that spanned several feet on both sides and ended in handlike paws. Clapping those together, it plummeted, and then spread its wings and soared up. It looked, she thought, like a six-foot-long ermine—with bat wings.

She then heard chittering of laughter from a trio of tiny air spirits—they looked vaguely human in shape but with wings, like something a child would draw: sticklike arms and legs, broad smiles for mouths, and dots for eyes. They lacked noses but had hair that flowed into a feathery pelt down their backs. The trio danced on the tops of the leaves, hands clasped. Their laugh was as beautiful as a bell.

Out of the corner of her eye, she saw Ven shift to turn to her, but she didn't need to see to know what was coming— she'd felt the branches quiver. "Can you wait until they fly again before you push me?"

He scowled. "How do you know I'm going to push you?"

"You want to see if I can call the spirits fast enough to catch me."

"Can you?"

"I don't know. Why don't you push me and we'll find out?"

Hamon wrapped his arm around her waist. "That's a terrible idea. Are you two crazy?"

Ven turned his scowl on Hamon. "I told you: she's training."

"She's been training nonstop. Give her a few minutes."

"She doesn't get enough free minutes when she's kissing you?"

Daleina loved seeing Hamon's dark skin blush, even though she knew her own cheeks were afire. He was sputtering as he failed to come up with a response.

From across the canopy, Daleina heard drumbeats. The trio of air spirits looked at each other and scattered, diving down into the leaves, rustling them in their wake. A low voice sang out a clear tone that echoed across the sky. It was joined by a second tone, higher, but matching it, and then a third. The chord shifted higher and then lower, echoing as it was picked up by other singers, spreading across the forest.

I know this song . . .

"Now?" Ven's frown deepened.

"It's too soon," Hamon objected. "She's supposed to have more time."

"The time isn't codified. It can be called any season. It's simply that Fara"—he corrected himself—"Queen Fara usually calls the candidates every third year. We should have had more time."

Daleina listened to the music, trying to remember when she'd last heard it.

"She's calling the candidates to the capital," Hamon whispered. Releasing Daleina's waist, he fiddled with the knot in the rope, preparing to climb down.

The trials. She felt as if her head were spinning. She wasn't ready! She couldn't—

Ven shoved her shoulder, hard. Losing her balance, Daleina fell to the side. Hamon's fingers brushed her arm as he reached for her, shouting her name. Her arms pinwheeled, and for a second, she was too surprised to react. Branches slapped into her back, and she reached for them.

She grabbed a branch, and her arm jerked in its socket as she snapped back—and then the branch broke from the tree.

She called to the spirits in the air, *Dance with me!*

Laughing, the little spirits dove toward her and beneath her, cushioning her fall, and then yanking her upward, higher, higher, higher, far stronger than they should have been. One held each arm, and the winged ermine spirit rode beneath her stomach, lifting her higher, above Ven and Hamon, into the white puff of the clouds.

She felt the mist brush her cheeks, and the world blurred into whiteness, and for one instant, she panicked—she knew she hadn't lost her sight again, it was only the cloud, but it felt far too much like it—and in that second, the air spirits spun her in a circle, laughing. The three little ones pulled both arms and one leg in opposite directions.

She focused on the winged ermine spirit. *Fly.*

It shot forward, and its force knocked the others away from her, sending them somersaulting across the sky. Daleina clung to its shoulders and felt its powerful wings move beneath her.

She felt its joy in its power. Carefully, she framed images of Ven and Hamon. *Return me,* she thought. She pictured the ermine spirit setting her down on the trees behind them, and it laughed, a deep sound that vibrated through her. It didn't want to return her.

She could force it, overpower it and guide it in. But that wasn't what she'd been working on for the last three months. Instead, she told it, *Amaze them.*

It liked that.

Soaring up, it burst out of the clouds, and Daleina saw a field of hills spreading in every direction until they melted into blue. Above, the sky was unblemished and felt as if she were looking at an expanse of pure paint, thick and liquidy. The sun looked as if it had burned away part of the sky, searing away the blue and replacing it with white. Her eyes stung as she drank in the blue. It felt as if she'd never seen sky before. Daleina took a breath of impossibly pure air, and then the ermine spirit dove into the clouds again, faster and faster.

She held tight to its neck. It twisted as it burst out of the clouds above the forest canopy, and then it rotated upside down. She squeezed tight with her thighs as she felt gravity pulling her. It soared upside down inches above Ven and Hamon's heads. Hamon ducked, calling toward her. And she laughed—the look in Ven's eyes. She could see the surprise etched on his face.

You're amazing, she told the spirit.

Twisting right-side-up, it spiraled down to the canopy. She slipped off, and Hamon caught her waist. Ven, she saw, had a knife held casually in one hand, ready. She knew how far he could throw it, though hitting the spirit while he carried her above the clouds would not have been helpful. She was glad he'd resisted.

The ermine spirit turned its bright eyes toward her—and then bit her arm.

Knife in hand, Ven lunged forward, but Daleina stopped him as the ermine spirit flew up and pierced the clouds. Hamon pressed his lips together in disapproval—she loved that she could read his expression instead of guessing his mood from his voice and the length of his silences—and pushed her sleeve up and began cleaning the wound with liquid he carried in his medicine pack.

"What did you do to it?" Ven asked.

"I complimented it, and I meant it."

He snorted. "There have been queens that have tried to parlay with the spirits before. Many times, in fact. You've heard the stories?"

All of them ended badly, very badly.

"Instinct wins over all else," Ven said. "But in the more advanced spirits . . ."

"It just wanted to fly," Daleina said. It was easy to see how much the air spirits loved the air, just as the fire spirits reveled in fire.

He studied her for a moment, then asked, "Do you think your new friend will fly us all to Mittriel?"

"Unlikely." At least, not without wanting to drop one of them. She didn't think she was up to wrestling the ermine for the entire journey. "But I'm glad I got to see above the clouds." That statement seemed inadequate to how it had felt. The teachers never talked about how beautiful working with wild spirits could be. She thought of some of the worst romantic village songs, of young men who fall in love with wood spirits who look like beautiful young girls, and of the widow who hurled herself from the top of a pine tree for love of an air spirit. Always those tales ended in tragedy, but she didn't doubt that they sometimes happened. Some of the spirits looked so close to human, and so many, human or not, were beautiful. They could make even death look beautiful, if you were the kind who swooned over bad poetry. You couldn't ever forget they were the enemy. *Don't trust the fire, for it will burn you. Don't trust the ice, for it will freeze you. Don't trust the water, for it will drown you . . .*

"Wire paths, then?" Ven suggested.

Daleina smiled and drew her clips out of her pockets, thankful that she no longer needed anyone to shout out when to use them. She could do this herself now. They climbed to the wires. Ven first, then Daleina, and last Hamon. Before clipping on, she pulled a smooth round rock out of another pocket and dropped it. It tumbled down the trunk toward the forest floor, a signal for Bayn that they were traveling again. The wolf had an uncanny ability to follow them, even from far below.

Daleina clipped on and pushed off. The trees blurred around her, and for an instant, she felt fear well up in her, like bubbles in her throat—she *knew* it was only because she was flying fast, but she couldn't seem to make her heart believe. It thumped faster and harder. She squeezed her eyes shut. There. That was better. She only opened them again when she heard Ven clip on to the new wire, then she switched wires as well and closed her eyes again.

By nightfall, they'd traveled many miles, and Daleina would have kept going—traveling at night was still easier than traveling sightless. "We have three days to answer the summons," Ven said. "We can stop here. Perhaps even find hospitality?" He turned to Daleina.

"Sorry, but I don't . . ." she began.

"Threefork. Your family's village," Hamon prompted gently.

Daleina felt her cheeks flush. She hadn't recognized it, possibly because she'd never taken the wire paths here before. Looking down, she tried to orient herself. The village her family had settled in had a trio of thick trees at its heart. This—ahh, there they were, the triplet trees, split around a platform.

"At last, beds! Or cots. Or whatever your family has, I'm sure would be fine," Hamon said. "Shall we go down?" He began climbing before Ven and Daleina agreed.

Following, Ven told him, "You lack the heart of a woodsman."

"But I pretend at one so excellently," Hamon said.

"Wait, are you a city boy at heart?" Daleina asked.

"He is," Ven said seriously.

"I think I'm appalled."

"Excuse me?" Hamon said, pausing.

"Revolted," she amended.

"Definitely revolted," Ven agreed. "Rejecting good, clean air and values."

"I'm not sure I can keep talking with him," Daleina said. "Do you think he's been faking woodsmanship the entire time?" He didn't talk about his own family much—

only child, father dead, mother unkind, other relatives uninterested—but she knew he was from one of the northern cities. He was more comfortable in the forest, though, happily gathering his rare plants and berries, as at home as if he were from one of the outer villages.

"I think he slides silk pillowcases over the rocks at night when he thinks we aren't looking," Ven said, climbing too.

"No!" Daleina gasped in mock horror. "And he wears a cravat hidden under his shirt."

"I heard he secretly keeps a pocket watch," Ven said.

"And his boots have heels," Daleina said.

"*My* boots have heels," Ven said. "Better to catch the branches."

"Ahh, but yours aren't lined with fur to keep your toes soft."

Hamon rolled his eyes at them. "I'm going to throw my fur-lined boots at you."

They laughed and were soon on the bridge outside the village. Daleina felt her heart beating faster, and she couldn't explain why. This was her *home*. She should feel as if she were walking into a familiar embrace. Instead, she felt as if she were intruding. She felt both Ven and Hamon watching her, waiting for her, and briefly closed her eyes, resting them. She breathed in, steadying herself, and reminded herself that she faced spirits on a regular basis. Normal humans in a normal village should not make her nervous. Plus these were people who knew her, loved her, and were proud of her.

Except this is the first time I've visited without warning. . . .

Opening her eyes, she told herself to stop dithering, and she marched forward into the center of the village. Everything was the same as she remembered, but also a little different—same enough that the differences were disconcerting. The baker's shop had grown and now sported tables and chairs that extended onto the center platform. Families were sharing dinner together outside, a touch of city life that had spread to the village. The bookshop boasted a new sign, and the door was festooned with ribbons. Daleina didn't recognize any of the books in the display. Nor did she recognize any of the people moving around the town center. Children, laughing, ran through, on their way home from either school or their apprenticeships. She saw the hedgewitch's shop, where she had been an apprentice for five years, and she hesitated again.

Not that it did much good.

"Little Dally, is that you, all grown up? Bless me." The hedgewitch, Mistress Baria, bustled out of her shop. Daleina realized with a shock that she'd aged—her hair was thin and white, her face was creased with wrinkles. She tottered back and forth on plump legs as she crossed the platform to enfold Daleina in a hug.

"*Little Dally?*" she saw Ven mouth. Oh, great, she wasn't going to hear the end of this.

Being enveloped by the hedgewitch made her feel ten years old again. The last few visits her family had come to see her, rather than the other way around. She hadn't seen Mistress Baria in a long time. "You've come for a visit? Oh, this is such a delight! And who are your charming friends?"

"Champion Ven and Healer Hamon," Daleina introduced them, and tried to figure out how to phrase that she wasn't here for a visit, just for a place to sleep.

"A champion, here! And a healer too. I must show you some of my charms. I make the finest concoctions for three villages. Ask Dally. She knows. I taught her everything. She's my shining star." The hedgewitch pinched Daleina's cheek. "I always knew she'd go far. Why, the very first time I met her, she marched into my shop and demanded that I teach her. Yes, she did. I told her no, no, you're too young, your parents should be asking for you, not you."

"That was Arin, actually," Daleina corrected. She felt as if her cheeks were fire-red. It was her sister who had marched into the hedgewitch's shop and informed her that she had to take Daleina for an apprentice. Daleina had been with her parents, shy in the face of a new village. She remembered she'd been looking into the window of the bookshop, wondering if she dared to go in and touch the new books, when Arin had come back, pulling the hedgewitch with her.

"Oh, it was? Truly? No, no, you're remembering wrong. It was you. I know. So precocious so young. I could see the power shining through. You were my prodigy. I was the one who taught her to summon, but she might as well have been teaching me. Such a natural!"

She hadn't been. She'd failed for the entire first year to summon anything. She thought she must have been wrong about her power, until Arin had fallen into a stream and a water spirit had knocked the branches out of her reach, taunting her. Daleina had forced the spirit to release the branches and divert the stream, and the hedgewitch had yelled at her for it, saying she could have killed them both, could have killed them all, if the water spirit had been angry enough. She then assigned Daleina to mashing herbs in the back of the shop for a week, not letting her out until she'd finished and night was falling. Still, Mistress Baria hadn't been a bad teacher. Just cautious. Her first priority was to protect the village as best she could, and Daleina, with her half-formed power, was a danger.

But Mistress Baria was still talking, praising her, saying her power shone through, and everyone had known it. Another lie. Or perhaps just a false memory.

And perhaps one she could leave the old woman with.

Daleina extracted herself. "My family isn't expecting me. It's a surprise visit. So I'd better surprise them before they hear from someone else. You know how villages are."

"Oh my yes. Why, once I had a raccoon break into my pantry, and by breakfast, everyone knew and appeared at my door with pastries—"

Pulling Ven and Hamon with her, Daleina made her escape across the platform. By now, she was certain that word of her arrival had spread to her family. She just wanted to make it there without any more interruptions.

"That explains a lot," Hamon said blandly.

Daleina shot him a look.

Another voice called to them. "Daleina?" This voice was far more welcome: Arin, her sister, who was emerging from the bakery. "Is it truly you?"

She looked so much older than the last time Daleina had visited. She'd sprouted at least three inches, and her hair was pulled back into a bun instead of the braids she used to wear. But most noticeable was the cast that encased her leg from ankle to mid-thigh. She had crutches under her armpits and a bag with bread loaves slung over her back. Swinging her crutches forward, she stopped just outside the bakery door. "If you've come to lecture me about being more careful," Arin said, "I'll hit you in the head with my crutches."

Daleina stared at the crutches. Lacquered black, they'd been carved with their mother's signature designs, curled vines and flowers, and decorated with fresh charms. "I'm not . . ." Words failed her. She hadn't been told of any accident. "Are you all right? Arin, what happened?"

Smacking the wood with her crutches, Arin propelled herself forward. On past visits, Arin had run out of the house and jumped into Daleina's arms. She'd been smaller then. Now Daleina wasn't certain how to greet her, especially with the crutches. Daleina stepped toward Arin to embrace her or kiss her cheek, but Arin's momentum carried her past Daleina toward one of the bridges. "Aren't you coming? Mother and Daddy will be thrilled to see you."

Following Arin, Daleina asked, "How did you . . ."

"Fell out of a tree. It happens. Please don't make a big deal out of it."

If she'd been here, she could have ordered an air spirit to catch her. "Were you pushed? Who did this to you?" As a kid, Arin had been as surefooted as a squirrel . . . Or, no, that was Daleina. Arin had needed help on the thicker branches. But that was when she was little. By now, she should know every inch of the village trees—the ladders, the bridges, the ropes.

"Of course no one pushed me. What a terrible thing to say! I was distracted, and I didn't lift my foot high enough. Caught my toes on the lip of a bridge, and *wheeee*."

"But the railings—"

"Flipped right over. It was remarkably ungraceful, and thank you for making me relive it." Pausing, Arin adjusted the pack higher on her shoulder.

Daleina reached for it. "Let me—"

Arin pulled away. "I can do it. Not an invalid."

"Hamon is a healer. He could look at it later."

Matching his pace to theirs, Hamon began, "I would be happy to—"

"Multiple breaks. It just will take time to heal. So you really didn't come to check on me? I thought Mother would have sent you a message immediately."

"She didn't. Or I didn't receive it. I've been training in the outer forest." But there should have been a way to get messages from her family to her. Headmistress Hanna sent the warning messages to Champion Ven; she could have forwarded a letter, especially if it involved Arin hurting herself. "How far did you fall? Is it just your leg? You could have broken your neck."

"You realize I have heard this lecture daily from Mother and Daddy."

"But not from me yet," Daleina said. "Arin . . ."

"We're home!" Stopping, she waved her arm at the house.

For a fleeting moment, Daleina thought, *It's not my home. Not anymore.*

Last time she had been here, it had been a one-story cottage nestled in the crook of a large branch. The roof had been thatch, and the walls were raw wood, weathered from the wind and rain. Now the roof was pottery tiles, layered in shingles, and the walls had been painted the kind of green that appeared on too-old bread. Charms, both old and new, were around the door and every window, as well as tucked into the shingles on the roof, twice as many charms as on an ordinary house, as if her parents had been adding new ones daily.

"Oh, you haven't seen it with the new paint! Do you like it? I did it myself. And look." She pointed to swirls around the edges that looked like squashed flowers. Arin might have been excellent at baking, but her skill with paint was . . . less impressive.

"Very lovely," Hamon said, and Daleina could have hugged him for that. Her throat felt squashed in on itself. She didn't know why she'd expected the house to stay exactly the same as her last visit. She knew intellectually that time passed. She'd changed. Everyone was older. But there was a piece of her that expected home to remain frozen in time, waiting for her to return and start the clock again.

Flinging open the door, Arin announced, "Daleina's here!"

She heard her parents cry out her name, a clatter of pots and pans as they stopped cooking and then rushed to the door, squeezing through together. Both of them embraced her at once, and then her mother pushed her back at arm's length. "You aren't eating enough. You need more bread. Arin, did you buy extra bread?"

"Of course I did. That's why you sent me." Maneuvering herself inside, Arin carried the bag of bread into the house.

"Should she be running errands, with her leg?" Daleina lowered her voice, but Arin heard her anyway.

"If they had their way, they'd wrap me in cotton and tuck

me back in the crib," Arin said. "Don't you start too. It was a silly accident. It could have happened to anyone."

But it hadn't happened to anyone. It had happened to Arin. And it could have been so much worse. Arin still hadn't said how far she'd fallen or if she'd sustained any other injuries, or if her leg would recover. She could walk with a limp after this. Breaks didn't always heal right. "You should let Healer Hamon—"

"Oh, you're a healer!" Mother said. "Naturally you are. And you must be Champion Ven. I am Ingara. This is my husband, Eaden, and my youngest daughter, Arin. We are so honored by your presence. Come in, please, come in." She ushered all of them inside as Daleina wished she'd been quick enough to introduce them first. Instead she felt as if she were wading through muck, and she couldn't understand why she felt this way. *I'm home. I should be happy.*

"We were hoping we could impose on your hospitality for the night," Hamon said, as graciously as any courtier. She admired how he could slip into city manners so easily, as if they hadn't been sleeping in hammocks strung between branches for the past three months.

"If I'd known you were coming, I would have cleaned." Mother wrung her hands as she looked around the house. Recently washed clothes were drying on various lines throughout the house. Scurrying, Mother collected them into a pile. Dishes were out on the table, stacked and ready to be set. It wasn't a mess, but it occurred to Daleina that home never looked like this when she came for her usual visits. She wondered how much they cleaned up before she came, or why they felt they had to put on a show.

"I can help you," Daleina offered, moving to intercept her mother.

Mother shooed her away. "You, rest! I know how difficult training must be. And you have the trials! Oh, Daleina, we're so very proud of you."

"I know." She looked again at Arin, who had maneuvered her way around the table to begin peeling carrots at the sink. "How have you all been?"

"Well! Of course, well." Mother guided Ven and Hamon to seats, shooing dust off one and moving books off another. She added her pillows, embroidered with platitudes, as cushions, plumping them before placing them on the chairs. Daddy was watching them with wide eyes, as if they might suddenly sprout wings and sparkle. Daleina wished she could have given them a little warning that she was coming. She hadn't realized what a difference it made having her other visits planned so far in advance. They'd had time to adjust their lives to accommodate her. Now she felt as if she were intruding. "Your father works hard. He's been taking on some commissions from the capital. Can you imagine?"

"Some of my chairs will be sat upon by silken—" He stopped himself and changed his sentence. "It's an honor to have my work appreciated."

Ven examined one of the chairs. "You do fine work."

Daddy's cheeks tinged pink. All of them were so very nervous that it made Daleina nervous. *Family should be easy. Not this . . . awkward dance. What's wrong with us? Or is it me?*

Mother beamed at them. "You're in luck—we'd made stew tonight, so there's plenty, and Arin had a hand in the seasoning. She's a natural."

Soon, all of them were seated around the table, chairs squeezed in to fit them all, elbow to elbow. Arin's crutches had been placed in the corner of the room, and her leg had been maneuvered to the side, where no one would knock into it. Mother scurried from the stove to the table, laying out food, while Daddy sliced and buttered the bread.

Carrying the bread to the table, Daddy said, "In the beginning, there was only light and darkness." He distributed the bread, one slice for each plate. Ven reached for a piece, but before Daleina could tell him to wait, he put his hands back in his lap, like everyone else. "And we were alone, hungry, thirsty, and cold. We floated in the light and dark for uncounted time, until at last a child was born, a tiny baby girl, no larger than a fist, who could speak as soon as she took her first sip of her mother's milk. She spoke one word, 'Earth,' and the spirits of the earth were born from her command. They fashioned earth beneath our feet so we could stand. She spoke again: 'Air,' and we breathed freely for the first time. 'Water,' and we drank. 'Fire,' and we were warm. 'Wood,' and we had trees for homes and plants for food. 'Ice,' and we had seasons to grow and seasons to rest. And so we multiplied, until at last there were too many for our patch of the world. We began to fall off the earth back into the air. And she spoke again, one more time, 'Die,' and the spirits who had made our home became our scourge and sought our deaths."

Mother served the stew, ladling it into each bowl, but still no one ate. Daleina felt Hamon's hand brush hers beneath the table. She entwined her fingers in his.

"And we cried out to the baby, 'Save us!'"

Struggling to stand, Arin fetched the drinks. Daleina stood to help her and was shooed back down, without words to interrupt the story.

"So she laid her own body in front of the spirits. Ice froze her skin. Fire burned her. Water drowned her. Air tore her limbs. Earth buried the pieces. And then Wood caused her to grow. From the pieces of her body grew stalks that blossomed, turned to fruit, and ripened. When the seed fell it was in the shape of little girls, and the spirits listened to what they said. The first to fall from the fruit of their mother became our first queen. It is she we thank for this meal, for our home, and for our lives. Her blessing on us."

Mother and Arin repeated, "Her blessing on us," and Daleina joined in belatedly.

Mother smiled. "Eat, eat, please!"

"That's a lovely version of the story," Hamon said as he bit into the bread.

Daleina felt as if her cheeks were red from fire. Her parents hadn't always recited that before meals when she was home. In fact, she remembered once asking them not to, when she was in the academy. *I don't want to be the legacy of some long-ago self-sacrificial baby.*

"We tell it every dinner," Daddy said.

"Except when Daleina is home," Arin said.

"But since she begins the trials soon, it seemed appropriate." Daddy smiled at her.

"Only if the queen approves of me," Daleina said. "It's still not certain. I might have to wait until the next time."

"She'll choose you," Arin said confidently. "You're the best."

Daleina squirmed in her seat, feeling like a child again. She wished Ven and Hamon weren't here, though she couldn't identify why she felt so embarrassed. It wasn't as if her family's faith in her was unappreciated. Their support meant the world to her. Even when her teachers despaired, Daleina knew her family still believed. But it wasn't as comforting as it should have been.

"Tell me how things have been here," Daleina said.

Daddy preened. "Arin has begun her apprenticeship! Every afternoon, after school is over, she works at the bakery. She's even been commissioned to bake the wedding cake for Soria Eversten and Ysi." He paused. "I don't think you know them. Lovely people."

Daleina tried to smile. "That's wonderful! When did you decide you liked baking?"

"I've always liked baking," Arin said.

"And the baker's son," Mother said.

"Mother!" Arin blushed.

Vaguely, Daleina remembered Arin talking about the baker's son. Surely she was too young to be thinking seriously. "Is he . . ." She didn't know what to ask. "Nice?"

Arin blushed harder. "Very. We've promised to wait until we're eighteen, but then we plan to start our own bakery in the next village, Fawnbrook. It doesn't have one, you see, and the villagers travel a fair distance to reach ours here in Threefork. We're going to specialize in fancy cakes, the kind with elaborate decorations, and leave the ordinary bread to Josei and his family, so we won't be taking their business."

"Indeed, that wouldn't be kind, after all they've done for you," Mother said.

"He wants all the same things I want."

"Including children," Mother said. "I want many grandchildren. But only once you're old enough. Start your business first. Settle in your home, not too far away and with no rickety bridges that you can fall over."

"It was one fall!"

"Just one fall can be enough," Hamon said seriously. "I have seen cases of improperly set limbs that healed badly."

"I set it myself," Mother said. "I assure you she's healing fine."

"I meant no disrespect." Hamon bowed his head.

"Let the boy look at her," Daddy said. "He's experienced, I assume. You've been working with Champion Ven? Isn't it unusual for a healer to accompany a champion?"

"Daleina needed my assistance when she went blind," Hamon said calmly.

Daleina closed her eyes and wished she could disappear as her family erupted in shouting, each louder than the other, until her ears rang.

"I'm fine," Daleina said when they'd quieted, somewhat.

Arin snorted. "At least you've all stopped fussing about my leg."

THEY SLEPT, CRAMMED INTO DALEINA'S FAMILY HOME.
Her parents insisted that Daleina take their bed, Hamon
slept on one of the chairs, and Ven chose a spot by the fire,
claiming he preferred that after all the cold nights outside—
the fire was good for his old joints, which Daleina knew was
nonsense, since he didn't have old joints, but worked well
enough to satisfy her parents' need to host them all comfortably. The alternative was kicking Arin out of her bed, and
Hamon pulled his rank as healer to prevent that.

Before sleep, he examined Arin's leg and pronounced it
healing. The fall had happened two months earlier—two
months, and Daleina hadn't known!—and it would be a
while before the bones stitched themselves strong again, but
they would mend.

Daleina slept poorly, dreaming of her sister falling from
the top of the wire paths or being dropped by the ermine air
spirit from above the clouds. She saw Arin's body fall, and
as much as her mind shouted to the spirits to catch her, none
did. Arin plummeted toward thorns on the forest floor.

Daleina woke, sitting upright, with the house still filled
with shadows. The fire crackled in the hearth, burning low,
the embers glowing across the room, and she suddenly felt
as if the walls were too close. She slipped out of bed and
walked silently through the house. She remembered which
boards creaked and which didn't. She lifted the latch on the
door and let herself outside.

Outside, she breathed in. But it didn't help. It still smelled
thick with the scent of cooked dinners and washed laundry.
Daleina climbed to the roof of the house and sat on the cool
pottery tiles, between the bits of charms. She looked up at
the leaves. High above, she saw a strip of night sky, pricked
with stars. She stretched her awareness out, checking for
spirits, and felt a few, around the edges of the village, but
none close.

She sat for a while, trying not to think about tomorrow and the trials, or what it would be like to meet the queen, or what she would do if the queen refused, or what Ven would say. Instead she thought about Arin, who belonged here, and her plans to start a bakery with the baker's son.

She heard the latch below and felt the tiles react when Ven climbed up onto the roof with her. He didn't say a word. He sat beside her and looked up at the sliver of night sky.

"Coming home is hard," Ven said.

"It shouldn't be," Daleina said. "They love me. I love them. It should be easy."

"Once you leave, it's never easy again. Or at least it's never the same. *You're* not the same. You can't expect them to be."

She nodded. "Sometimes they feel like strangers. And still, I'd die to protect them."

"If you think I've been spending all this time to teach you how to die, you haven't been paying attention." Quieter, he said, "You will live, little Dally. You must live."

Last-minute advice was never a good idea, but Ven couldn't help it. He felt like a mother hen whose innocent chick had just been breaded and seasoned. "Don't say you think you'll be a great queen. Don't tell her you're ready. Or eager. Or anything that even vaguely implies that you'd be happy if she were dead. She's sensitive about that." He adjusted the ribbons draped around Daleina's neck, one for each spirit to show she'd demonstrated mastery, and he fussed with a string that dangled from one, nicking off the strand with his knife.

Daleina held still while he circled her, checking for anything out of place that could be misconstrued as disrespectful to Queen Fara. Daleina had been dressed by the palace caretakers in a bead-encrusted gown that looked heavier than his armor. Her hair had been expertly woven into braids so complicated they rivaled the knots that solo climbers used to secure climbs up unproven trees. He'd been forced to wear an equally ridiculously elaborate sash that supposedly told the history of Renthia in embroidery. He felt pity for whatever artisan had been commissioned to spend years sewing tiny depictions of queens and champions on one stretch of fabric. But he hadn't argued, not this time. With Sata, he'd been able to insist on just his plain leather armor, but that had been a long time ago, when he'd been a different man.

"Don't mention the messages. You don't know about them. In fact, it might be wise if you don't talk about what happened in North Garat. But don't lie if she asks about it. In fact, don't lie at all. You can compliment her, if you like, but make sure it sounds sincere. She has people fawning over her all the time and can tell the difference between a genuine compliment and flattery."

"Champion Ven?" Daleina twisted so she faced him as he paced.

"Yes?"

"Relax. Please."

He winced. He was a seasoned warrior. Yet here he was, displaying nerves like an illiterate schoolchild called to recite the alphabet in front of his entire village.

"You believed in me when you chose me. You believed in me when I was *blind*. Believe in me again now."

He wanted to tell her it wasn't her. He *did* believe in her, or he would if he could break her of her habit of calling only weak spirits. She was skilled enough to handle the powerful ones, if she was alert and careful and focused and used her redirection techniques rather than straight coercion. Sata had been skilled too, though. . . . He realized he never talked to Daleina about her. It was too painful. But maybe that was a mistake. He opened his mouth to tell her he believed in her just as much as he'd believed in Sata, but the audience chamber door clanked open. Three of the palace guards strode through and halted in a line. Shoulders thrown back, chests puffed out, they stared straight ahead—traditional honor-guard pose, which was an improvement over the reception he had expected. His last brush with the palace guards had not been exactly respectful. He recalled breaking a few ribs, possibly an arm. Certainly a nose. He studied these faces and didn't see any he recognized.

Obviously, they knew him—the gatekeeper had taken their names when they presented themselves—but no one seemed to be holding a grudge, at least not outwardly.

There was a possibility that Fara meant to lift his exile during this audience. After all, he'd never revealed her secret, regardless of whether she was hunting traitors or losing control. By training Daleina, he were merely doing his duty, the same as all the other champions.

He tamped down the hope, having tasted disappointment so many times before.

And yet I still want it so much. I am a fool.

In unison, the guards pivoted, stomped their heels hard, and then marched forward. He shooed Daleina after them. He matched her pace, automatically adopting a guard's posture. Daleina's chin was lifted, her shoulders back, and her mouth was moving, as if she were practicing a speech or giving herself encouragement or both. She looked so very young, and he wondered if he should have insisted on training her longer and waiting for the next cycle of trials. He wasn't sure she was ready to be on her own yet. She still lacked perfect depth perception, and she hadn't been able to repeat her feat with the castle-like spires in that village. She credited the power of the spirits more than her own skill, which was a problem—an heir needed confidence. Maybe he should have been praising her more instead of constantly pushing her. . . . "You do have the skills," Ven told her, softly. He knew the guards could hear, but he didn't think his voice carried beyond them. She shot him a small smile, and he saw the nervousness in her eyes, churning like a river in springtime. Her technique was near flawless, and she was a quick thinker, able to improvise. Often the most powerful failed—they relied too much on brute strength and never had to worry about strategy. And eventually even the most powerful met a force more powerful, and if they couldn't think and adapt—if they didn't understand that power sometimes wasn't enough, that only queens were strong enough and even the strongest heir could lose a battle of pure power . . .

Daleina will do well, he told himself for the hundredth time, and then he scolded himself. *You're doing it again. Stop being such a mother hen.*

They followed the guards through empty, silent halls that spiraled toward the center of the tree. They saw and heard no one else, which made it feel as if they were the only ones in the palace. Even their own footsteps felt muffled.

Lithe fire spirits jumped from candle to candle. Behind them, the hall plunged into darkness. Ahead a doorway was wreathed in the light from the bodies of dozens of fire spirits. Ven's hand itched to sit on the hilt of his sword. Fara hadn't always been so ostentatious in her displays of power. He tried not to flinch as they walked through the doorway, under the beady, hungry gaze of the tiny spirits. Each one writhed like a flame, but none left their post.

In the throne room water spirits bathed the copper-coated walls in waterfalls that trickled into pools. Each pool was crowned with water lilies, forced by spirits to grow inside, away from the sun. Two air spirits flanked the queen's dais, their wings beating fast so that they hovered in midair, holding the train of her veil or gown or whatever. He didn't know what the name was for that part of a dress, but he did know that Queen Fara had sharpened into a woman even more beautiful than the one in his memory. She rivaled a statue, chiseled and smoothed by a master artist, and wore a serene expression that had his instincts screaming, *Trap, trap, trap!*

Except he couldn't figure out who it was a trap for or why. So he kept walking forward, his own face schooled into as blank an expression as he could manage.

Their procession reached the dais, and the guards split to either side of the queen, while Ven and Daleina knelt on one knee and bowed their heads.

"Your names," Queen Fara commanded.

He'd told Daleina to speak for them, in hopes it would keep Fara's mind off her anger with him and on the candidate, where it belonged. "Champion Ven and Candidate Daleina from Greytree."

Silently, Ven cursed. He hadn't told her not to mention her birth village. It was traditional, yes, but not required. He hoped that Fara didn't recognize the name. Keeping his head down, he resisted the urge to peek and check her expression. This could all end very poorly, very quickly.

"Rise, Champion Ven and Candidate Daleina from Greytree."

He rose, head still bent, hands folded respectfully in front of him. Daleina had worked hard to reach this moment. He was determined not to ruin it for her.

"Tell me, Candidate Daleina, do you believe you are ready to be queen?"

There it was, so quickly, the trick question. He'd warned her. Had she listened?

"No, Your Majesty. I'm not."

And that was not the right answer either. Maybe he should have been more specific.

But Daleina wasn't done talking. "But I *am* ready for the trials."

"The trials are to determine your readiness to be queen, should the need arise. If you are not ready to be queen, then you cannot be ready for the trials."

"Were you ready?" Daleina asked.

For an instant, Ven stopped breathing. This was not a moment he could help with swords or words, and he hated that. Raising his eyes, he stole a glimpse of Queen Fara. Her face was smooth, unreadable, and perfect, as if she'd never smiled, never laughed, never cried, never felt warmth or passion or release, when he knew for a fact that she mewed like a kitten when he . . . Deliberately, he pushed those thoughts out of his head and fixed his eyes on her face, not on the line of beads that teased her neckline. She was the *queen*.

And besides, she hated him.

"No one has ever asked me that before," Queen Fara said, in a voice that implied that no one ever should. He heard the steel in it, as clear as if a guard had drawn a sword, but Daleina didn't seem to hear it.

"Did you ever doubt yourself?" Daleina pressed on. "Were you afraid? Did you have people who meant so much to you that you'd die rather than disappoint them? Or did you do it for yourself, because you knew you could? Did you ever wonder what your life would have been like if you didn't take this route? Did you ever miss what you'd lost, what you never even knew you'd miss, what you never knew you were losing?"

He rolled his eyes skyward and counted slowly to ten. He'd never wanted to gag someone so badly in his life. She chose now to explore her emotions? *Now?* She was supposed to be convincing Queen Fara that she was capable, dependable, and most of all strong enough. He'd hoped that visiting her family would provide the last bit of encouragement by reminding her of why she did this, the people she'd sworn to protect. Not turn her into a philosopher.

He may have miscalculated.

"I have never felt fear or doubt," the queen said. And then she laughed—a sound so unexpected that he jerked backward. "Oh my, candidates are so very *young*. Of course I felt fear and doubt. Only idiots don't, and the throne will not tolerate idiots. Go, Candidate Daleina, tell your loved ones that you will be taking the trials. And Champion Ven, stay. I wish to speak with you."

He stayed as if he were rooted to the floor in the same way as the throne was rooted to the dais, while one of the guards escorted Daleina out of the throne room. She'd passed the interview! He should be elated. But as he listened as the footsteps receded, he was far from jubilant.

"Leave us," Queen Fara told the guards.

"My exile prohibits a private audience," he reminded her.

"I'm the queen."

"Given how our last audience went, I'd prefer a witness—for my own safety if not yours." He wondered if he should have tacked on an apology or other flowery language. He met her eyes and tried to look as unmovable as a boulder. It was a look he had some practice with.

"As you wish." She waved the guards to the opposite side of the throne room, and then she glided off the dais, approaching him. She circled him, as if she were a buyer and he were a prize horse. "You look well, Ven."

"You look exquisite. But you know that."

A faint hint of a smile touched her lips. Not enough to curve them, but enough to make a dimple appear on one cheek. "Your candidate is pretty as well. Greytree? Really, Ven? Did you think I wouldn't recognize the name?"

Inwardly, he winced. Of course she recognized it. "Believe it or not, it was a coincidence. Or partially one, since her origin did shape her. Still, I chose her without knowing her past."

Fara shook her head. "You simply are not subtle enough to play at politics. Does she know you're using her?"

Ven bristled. "I'm training her."

"As a weapon, a figurehead, or a martyr?"

"Your Majesty, it's my duty—"

"You know what I like best about you, Ven?" Stopping in front of him, she trailed her fingertip down his cheek and along his jaw. "Aside from your beard, which I assume my caretakers made you trim. The wild look becomes you more."

His gaze slid to the guards, and he began to wish he hadn't objected to dismissing them. He didn't need Daleina's candidacy complicated with gossip about him, but maybe that was foolish, maybe it was too late for that—as the candidate of the disgraced champion, she was bound to attract talk anyway. "I can't imagine," he said honestly. He had no idea where she was going with this conversation, but he kept his hands firmly clasped in front of him.

She was standing close enough that his every inhalation was full of her perfume. She smelled like gardenias. He'd once brought her a bouquet of them that he'd picked from the southern forest. He'd had to elude a very irate tree spirit, as well as keep the branches alive enough for the journey— it's not easy fleeing with a pail of water on one's back. It hadn't been one of his brightest ideas. She'd laughed at him but kissed him, and that had made it completely worth it. He'd been so young, as young as Daleina was now.

"Even after your exile, after all you've seen, you are still so innocent."

He raised both his eyebrows. He didn't know what game she was playing, but he could play too. Slowly, he let his eyes rake down her from her face to her neckline, to her waist, to her legs, hidden within the folds of her gown but still so beautifully long, and then back up.

She laughed, a light sound like bells. "Not that kind of innocent. You believe in the inherent goodness of people, whereas I know better. There are precious few who are suitable to be queen. Do you truly believe you have found one?"

He knew this was the kind of trick question he'd warned Daleina to avoid. But this was Fara—her laugh, her eyes— and he couldn't lie. "Yes, I do."

She tossed her hands in the air and then stalked away with all the melodramatic emphasis of an actress. "See? Innocent. You know that's not the answer I want to hear. And yes, I was spying on you before you entered. *That's* the true interview, though I have to admit your Daleina was charming in person. Typically candidates are so intent on themselves that it never occurs to them to think of me as anything other than a representation of the duty they may someday perform. But you . . . You come here, to the palace, with a candidate, knowing full well I could declare you both traitors and have you killed within seconds, and no one would doubt my right or even dare question me. You placed your life and the life of an innocent child—for that's what she still is, for all her training—in the hands of someone who has betrayed you before. Why do you continue to trust me?"

It was a real question—from Fara, he sensed, not the queen. He blinked for a moment, trying to formulate an answer. He should be angry at her, for what she did to him, for what she allowed to happen to those villages, for what she was trying to do now, showing off her strength when she knew—had to know—that it was ebbing. But he wasn't mad. He wasn't sure what he was, but it wasn't angry. And so he answered the only way he knew how.

"You're my queen."

Fara looked at him from across the throne room. "Leave us," she told the guards again.

This time, Ven didn't stop them. She was his queen, and either he trusted her or he didn't. Given their past, he recognized that "didn't" would have been the more logical choice. He waited until the guards shut the door behind him before he said, "I know there aren't traitors in those towns. I know your control is slipping. The spirits are breaking your command, and you can't stop them, even when you can predict them. That's why I chose to take on a candidate. Not because I don't trust you, but because I don't trust *them*. The spirits will kill you someday, and I won't let everything you've built and done be destroyed when that happens."

"How long have you been wanting to say that?"

"Since you exiled me."

"Touché." She regarded him, a look somewhere between

amusement and shrewdness. "So you are my faithful, loyal servant, fulfilling your duty for the sake of Renthia."

"Always."

"Then prove it. Show me how loyal you are." She reached up behind her neck, and he heard a clasp unsnap. Her gown slithered off her shoulders, over her breasts, down her waist, hips, and legs, to pool at her ankles. She was naked beneath it, and her perfect body seemed to glow like the sun.

He crossed to her, cupped her breasts in his hands, and kissed her as if she was the most precious treasure in all of Renthia. Because she was . . . even though he spent every day and night preparing for her death.

AFTER SURRENDERING THE LOVELY GOWN AND EXCESsive ribbons, Daleina trudged out of the palace to where Hamon and Bayn waited for her, on the lower bridge. "Well?" Hamon asked.

Bayn growled, ending in what sounded like a question mark, as if he wanted to ask Daleina as well but lacked the jaw shape to form words.

Kneeling, Daleina put her arms around Bayn's neck. She noticed that people on the bridges around them were glancing at the two people and their wolf, but she didn't care. She'd passed! Barely. She should feel more victorious and less like she'd been gripped in the jaws of, well, a wolf and then shaken. "Ven's still in there. She wanted to talk to him."

"But what about you?"

Daleina laughed, shakily. "I made a fool of myself."

"Oh, Daleina, I'm sorry. I know how hard you worked—"

She waved her hand, shooing away his words. "I can do the trials. But it would have been nice if I hadn't turned into a mess of babble in front of the queen. It's only that . . . she's a person, like me. She started as a student, became a candidate, then an heir, and then queen. Same path I'm supposed to be on. But the difference between her and me . . . Have you ever seen her, Hamon?"

"I've not had that honor."

"You feel like you've been granted an audience with the sun. I won't ever be like her. She's as if you took every woman in Renthia, plucked out their best features, and compiled them into a single person."

Hamon laid his hand on her shoulder. "Meeting the queen is *supposed* to be intimidating."

She *knew* that. The palace, the throne . . . It wasn't so different from the show the headmistress put on when she welcomed students into the academy. It was all designed to reinforce the power hierarchy. But knowing it was a show and not reacting to it were two very different things. "I felt fifteen years old again, pretending I belonged in the academy, knowing I'd never measure up." She buried her face in Bayn's ruff, certain that her cheeks were blushing a brilliant shade of red. "Hamon, what if I'm *not* meant to do this? What if I'm just stubbornly clinging to a childhood dream that I should have outgrown years ago?"

"Daleina . . ." He hesitated. "You don't have to go through with this if you don't want to. You have choices."

She lifted her head. "This is not the talk you're supposed to be giving me. You're supposed to say I can do this, not to doubt myself now, I've come so far."

"You *have* come so far, but that doesn't mean you can't take a different path if you wish." He looked so earnest. With the sun streaming between the leaves from behind him, he was lit in a glow that made him look ethereal, as if he were imparting a prophetic message. Unlike the sun of the queen, his seemed to actually give off warmth. She loved that about him, even while he was spouting nonsense. "You have many choices before you, and you are not locked into one merely because you have trained."

"Trained for *years*," she pointed out.

"You could have years of a future as whatever, whoever, you want."

She stood, slowly, her hand still entwined in the wolf's fur, and wondered if she was hearing him wrong. "Are you trying to talk me out of doing the trials?"

"Daleina." He took her hand. "Dear Daleina, I care about you, and I don't want to see you hurt again. Blame the healer in me. Blame my heart. But I want you well and whole." He touched her cheek, gently, and then curled a lock of her hair around his finger.

"This has been my dream since I was a child." She couldn't believe he was saying these words. He had to be testing her, testing her resolve, maybe even on Ven's orders. *He has to know how much this means to me.* "I can't turn away."

"You can. You choose not to. But you can make a different choice. Daleina, dreams change. The future isn't fixed. You can come with me, help in the outer villages. I'll be a master healer as soon as I've taken my tests—"

"And I'll be your personal guard?"

"You'll protect the villages, the way you wanted. You'll still be using your training, and you'll still be doing good for Aratay. But you won't be a target. Heirs seldom have long lives."

She shook her head. After all they'd been through, after all he'd seen her do, all the times he patched her up, all the nursing her through blindness . . .

"Daleina, my Daleina, you work so hard and so nonstop. Have you ever taken a minute before now to think about whether this is still what you want? You've told yourself it is, for years, but is it? Or do you do this because you feel you should? Because you've invested so many years already? Because other people expect it? Because of your sister and your parents and Champion Ven?

"Daleina, tell me, what do *you* want?"

She was saved from having to answer by Bayn's growl—this time, it wasn't a question; it was a warning. Instinctively, Daleina reached out with her mind, and felt the presence of six wood spirits. This close to the palace, it wasn't odd. There were hundreds of spirits of varying sizes. But these six felt different—older, wilder, stronger—and Daleina felt as if they were focused on her. She looked around—there weren't people around anymore. It was supper hour, and only a few people hurried along the bridges that crisscrossed above them. None were close by. From where she was, she couldn't even see the palace guards.

The six spirits flowed out of the trees and linked hands, streaming in a row toward Daleina. Her skin prickled. She didn't like the way their eyes were fixed on her. Standing, she nudged Bayn behind her.

"What do you want?" Daleina asked.

She didn't expect them to answer—she'd never met a spirit that was intelligent enough for conversation. She'd never dared summon one that powerful.

"You," they answered.

All of them spoke, in thin reedy voices, and the effect was like the wind itself.

"There are things you should know. Secrets. Yes, secrets." The words bounded among them until she couldn't tell which was speaking. They didn't have mouths. The words seemed to emerge from them, spread around her, and then disperse.

Bayn growled, low, his hackles raised.

"For your ears, your ears alone. Alone, alone, Daleina, Dally-dally-dally-daleina. Only for you, a secret for you."

Hamon pressed closer to her side.

"You know my name," Daleina said. "How? Who sent you?"

"Who-who, the little owl asks. Oh, little owl, how we have a secret for you, only you, only you. Come." They held out spindly hands, gesturing with their many-jointed fingers as if playing an invisible harp.

"Don't," Hamon whispered.

"But they know my name. Someone sent them." Someone with power. One of her friends, an heir—perhaps even the queen. She should hear what they had to say.

"I don't like it," Hamon said.

"That may have something to do with the fact that they're extremely creepy."

The six spirits continued to hold hands, hovering just a few inches above a branch. All their faces were blank and smooth like sanded and polished wood. Their hands had fused together like a single branch.

"How about we wait for Champion Ven—" Hamon began.

"Alone," the six spirits chanted.

Bayn snarled. Snapping his jaws, he lunged forward toward the spirits. All his fur was spiked. Usually animals didn't react to spirits—they never attacked them—but Bayn had always been different, thanks to Master Bei's training. "I don't trust them either," Daleina told him. "But I can handle this." After all, she'd just claimed she could handle the trials. "Go wait for Ven. Bring him here when he's done."

"Daleina—"

"I have to take risks."

"Why? You don't know what they want."

The six spirits whispered. "Secret. Tell you a secret. Nice secret. Secret for you. You. You alone. Only you."

"The queen handles spirits like this all the time," Daleina said. "I have to start somewhere." And she was curious. Not just curious in the way a child who wants to taste chocolate is curious, but curious in a way that it burned through her body until her veins felt like they hurt. These spirits had come for *her*, before she'd proven herself, before she'd done anything. It had to mean something! Maybe this was the sign she'd been looking for, the answer to her doubts and questions.

"As your healer—"

"As my healer, you know I'm fine."

"As your friend—"

"As my friend, you'll respect my choices."

The spirits continued to wait, hovering in the air, as they discussed this. A few people passed on the bridges. Daleina noticed the spirits had positioned themselves to be out of sight, blocked by branches.

"Stay near the palace," Hamon told her. "Stay where we can find you again."

"Of course. Ask about Champion Ven. I'm concerned that he hasn't come out yet. He should have followed me soon after."

"All right. Come on, Bayn."

Bayn didn't budge.

Daleina knelt in front of the wolf. "Find Ven for me. Bayn, find Ven."

The wolf loped away, and Hamon hurried to follow. Daleina turned to the six spirits. She felt for them—there wasn't anger or rage. She planned a command to redirect them, if she had to. "I'm alone now. What secret?"

The six drifted toward her. They began to melt together as they circled around her. She turned in a circle to see all of them. "Only you," they whispered. "Today. Maybe more, another day? Maybe more, but only one. A secret. A secret, only you."

"What's the secret? Tell me. I'm listening." She spun the words into a command and pushed it gently toward the spirits. They wanted to tell her anyway. It wouldn't be difficult to push them. *Tell me the secret.*

"Death," they said, and they fused into a sphere around her.

The spirits spread, their arms melding into one, legs flattening as if pounded or mashed. Daleina shoved a thought at them, *Grow.* The image in her mind was of them rooting in the ground far below and blossoming . . . but they didn't. Instead, they merged faster, their bark smoothing together into one spread of wood.

Quickly abandoning trying to command the six spirits, Daleina reached beyond them, to the dozens of other spirits, weaker ones, who surrounded the palace. She called them to her. She felt them fly toward her as the wood closed in a sphere around her, cutting out the light. But darkness didn't scare her. She knew darkness.

The six were strong. Scratching against the wood shell, the little spirits weren't hurting them enough—the little spirits didn't want to badly enough. But she knew one thing they did want. *Hurt me,* she told them.

And the little spirits went wild.

They tore at the wood, ripping away the bark, burrowing through it, burning through it. The six spirits shrieked, high, and she heard other voices: cries, shouts, human voices and the shrill pitch of spirits in a frenzy. As soon as a crack was in the wood, the tiny spirits dove through. They attached to her arm. Their tiny teeth plunged into her skin, and she cried out.

But she didn't stop them—she wasn't free yet; the six spirits were still trying to close in on her. *Hurt me more.* More spirits came, dozens more, plastering themselves onto the sphere, tearing at it as the ones already inside tore at her.

Her concentration shattered as pain pierced her from every side, but she saw a sliver of light strike in, and then the sphere shattered away. And the tiny spirits flew inside to her, and feasted.

She felt pain radiate through her, shaking through her, erasing all thought, erasing the entire world. She heard shouting, distantly, and she saw a flash of steel.

And then the piercing stabs ceased as a gray mound of fur leaped onto her body, knocking her away from the teeth and claws that were trying to shred her.

She heard Ven shouting. Her name. *Daleina.* She latched on to her name, let it pull her out of the swimming pain. She felt hands, broad hands, Ven's hands, scooping her up and heard Hamon's voice, "Lay her here. Let me close!"

Other voices too, but those were the ones she focused in on, clung to. She felt cool liquid pour onto the points of pain. "So many," Ven said.

She tried to focus on his face, but her vision swam. *Not blind again,* she thought. She closed her eyes and spread her awareness out, beyond the pain, but her mind fragmented, filled with the buzz of a thousand bees. "Breathe," Hamon said in her ear, his voice calm, deep, still as an untouched pond in the center of the forest.

She breathed.

"Daleina, what happened?" Ven asked, his voice urgent.

She opened her eyes. There. She could see him. She felt herself smiling. She'd survived, and she could see!

"Why are you smiling? Hamon, why is she smiling?"

"Shock," the healer said. "Daleina, I've applied pain-killer. Is the pain fading? Tell me if you need more."

Slowly, she pushed herself to standing. She ached but it

was bearable. Around them was a crowd, a mix of palace guards and overly coiffed city people, whispering to one another. The guards looked ashen. "Six spirits," she told Ven. "Strong, smart ones. They said they had a secret for me, only me, and then they tried to kill me."

Ven dragged one of the palace guards closer. "Inform the queen. The spirits who killed Sata are still free and still hunting." He released the guard's shirt, and the guard bowed before running toward the gate of the palace.

Bayn nudged Daleina's hand, and Daleina automatically buried her fingers in the wolf's fur. She heard a squawk, and looked down to see a spirit dangling from the wolf's jaws, its wings limp. "Let it go, Bayn," she told him. "It was helping me."

"Helping you?" Hamon's usually calm voice shot up an octave.

"I called them." Her head throbbed. She wished they didn't have to discuss it right now. She wanted to curl into a ball and wait for the pain to fade away.

"Good," Ven said.

"Not good," Hamon said. "Are you insane? *Not* good. Very not good. Daleina, you can't compete in the trials. Look at you."

"Hamon, hush," Ven said.

"I will not stay quiet! This is suicide. She can't—"

Ven leveled his sword, slick with the saplike blood of spirits. "I said hush. Not here. Not now. Maybe not ever."

The steel point at his throat, Hamon quieted. His eyes flickered to Daleina. She straightened her shoulders. Ven was right—she couldn't curl into a ball and let them take care of her, as much as she wanted to. She was a candidate, approved by the queen herself, and she had survived this attack. *I'll survive the trials too.* "Let's go," she said.

"Where to?" Ven asked. Interesting that he was giving her the choice, she thought.

"The academy. They have baths. I'd like to look less bloody for at least the start of the trials." She strode down the bridge, past the gawkers. Every step shot pain through her as her clothes rubbed against the wounds. But she wasn't going to show it, not in front of these people, not in front of those she wanted to trust her to be heir.

Hurrying to catch her, Hamon said, "Wait, we need to bandage you. Daleina, let me help you. We can take the baskets—ride to the academy. It's not that close."

She looked up. "Ven, are there wire paths within the capital?"

A smile played on his lips. "Yes." He pointed to a ladder ahead.

She'd show them she could do this. She would not be beaten. She would not be broken. "Excellent." She mimicked Queen Fara's imperious tone as best she could. "Come with me."

HEADMISTRESS HANNA KNEW SHE WAS SUPPOSED TO feel pride. Eight of her most recent students had been chosen for the trials: Airria, Revi, Linna, Marilinara, Zie, Evvlyn, Iondra, and Daleina. It was a record, as Master Klii had pointed out, one she planned to gloat about for months. Concrete proof that their methods worked. It would draw new students and inspire current students. She'd prattled on about it until Hanna had excused herself from dinner. In truth, Hanna wished the queen had delayed the trials, or even refused to admit the newer candidates until they'd had more time to train with their champions. But Queen Fara hadn't bothered to ask for the headmistress's opinion. She was clearly taking advice from elsewhere these days.

Outside, in the practice ring, Hanna walked between a batch of trees that a class had grown. Their trunks were spindly, and their branches mere twigs—they'd been grown too fast. There was no undergrowth beneath them, not even moss, just bare dirt. She stopped by a rock, half formed into the shape of a bear. Sitting beside it, absorbed in her own thoughts, was a girl. Young woman, now.

"Candidate Daleina?"

The girl—woman—raised her head, and Hanna noticed her cheeks were wet, even though her eyes were clear. The tears lingered on the dozens of light scratches that criss-crossed her cheeks. "Are you here to give me words of encouragement?"

Briefly, Hanna considered saying yes and giving the young woman what she needed, but she didn't have the energy to lie tonight. "I was seeking solitude."

Daleina scrambled to her feet. "I can leave."

Hanna waved her back down. "Champion Ven believes you were attacked by the same spirits who murdered Sata. He's blaming himself, of course, since he's the connection between the two of you, and frankly, it's not impossible. He's angered many spirits over the years. You may have noticed he is a bit brusque with them."

"It's in his nature to protect people," Daleina said. "He was probably born with a sword in his hands."

Hanna felt her lips twitch. "That would have been pain-ful. For the mother at least, though having met his mother, it wouldn't surprise me."

"You've met his mother? He doesn't talk about his family."

"She was a driven woman," Hanna agreed. "One of our best." She remembered Ven's mother, a humorless girl who treated her muscles like horses that needed to be bro-ken. She'd had minimal affinity for spirits but incredible instincts. The first time Hanna had met Ven, back when he was an idealistic new champion, she'd seen so much of his mother in him. "He has had to contend with high expecta-tions. You two have that in common."

"My parents aren't pushing me. They just expect me to

succeed, as if it were a matter of course. But it's always been my choice."

"Are you wishing you'd made other choices?" The night before the trials struck all of them this way, forcing them to examine their lives. Hanna suspected it made ordinary citizens feel that way too. The trials were reminders of the fragility of their lives.

"Not exactly. Just wondering what those other choices would have been like."

"Don't," Hanna advised. Such thoughts had never helped her. "Whether you made your choices with your eyes open or closed, they're made. It's not time to regret them; it's time to live with the consequences." Hanna thought that sounded sufficiently encouraging, the kind of statement that a headmistress was supposed to make to a candidate on the eve of the trials, regardless of her personal feelings. As a rule, she wasn't allowed to have *feelings*. They were for children and artists.

"Do you ever regret becoming headmistress?"

"Every day, my dear. Every day."

THE FIRST DAY OF THE TRIALS WAS LOVELY: A QUINTES-sential autumn morning with crisp apple-cider air and leaves so golden they looked painted. Daleina breathed in the air and tried to ignore the way Ven and Hamon were fluttering around her. The night before, Hamon had insisted on examining every single cut, bite, and gash and slathering each of them with the healing salve he'd made himself. She had to admit that it had worked far better than anything she'd ever used before. She felt fine. This morning they'd both showed up in her room with new leather armor, fitted for her, as well as supplies she might need: a knife, a rope harness, clips for the wire paths, a canteen for water, strips of jerky, a bedroll. "The trials might last a while," Ven explained.

"Any rumors on what the challenge will be?" Daleina asked.

"I don't listen to rumors," Ven said.

A familiar female voice rang through the room. "I do."

Zie stood in the doorway, the same cheerful smile on her face but a scar above her eyebrow. She was flanked by Linna and Revi. Daleina broke away from Ven and Hamon and crossed to them, embracing her friends. Others joined them: Mari, Airria, Evvlyn, and Iondra. She waved away their concern over the fading cuts on her face and arms. "Tell me: the trials. Do you know what's coming?"

No two trials were the same. Sometimes the candidates had to prove their worth in challenges like the maze, where the queen set spirits against them. Sometimes they had to demonstrate their ability in real-world situations, such as growing a new grove of trees or cultivating a new orchard. Sometimes the candidates were pitted against one another in a contest of strength. Daleina hoped they'd be able to build: new bridges, a library, a farm.

But none of them had any idea. Even Zie, who ate gossip for breakfast, lunch, and dinner, didn't have any concrete clues as to what Queen Fara had in mind for them. "All I know is that we will have 'unusual' escorts to the palace."

"Caretaker Undu said to gather in the practice ring," Mari said.

"You still aren't calling her Mother?" Revi shook her head in disapproval, and Daleina noticed her friend had honed herself, muscles on her arms that had never been there before, a readiness to her movements as if she were coiled to react to anything. All of them had that same air of readiness, and she wondered if she appeared that way to them. "She should be proud of you."

"She is proud of me. It's you she despairs of."

Zie broke out in a peal of laughter. A little of the tension, and the coiled readiness, drained out of the room, and Daleina caught a glimpse of her old friends under the new hardness.

Iondra shooed them all toward the door. "We cannot be late."

"It would be dramatic if we were," Revi said. "Imagine if we made a queen wait for us."

"We cannot disgrace Headmistress Hanna or the others," Iondra scolded.

"Calm yourself, Iondra, I wasn't serious. I know my duty," Revi said. "You know, time outside the academy tree was supposed to unwind you. Didn't any of you have fun in your training?"

Daleina wasn't sure the word "fun" was applicable. "I rode the wire paths."

"See? Someone had—wait, really? On purpose?" Revi shuddered. "Glad my champion preferred the forest floor. We worked a lot with earth spirits, which was fine by me. Give me a nice muddy earth spirit over an air spirit with a bad sense of humor any day."

Daleina decided not to mention that she'd flown with an air spirit and it hadn't been terrible.

Or that it had, in fact, been extraordinary.

All of them fell silent as they headed down the spiral staircase. They were swept up in a flow of other students, masters, and caretakers. As they descended, Daleina caught glimpses of the places that had once been her whole world: the classrooms, the baths, the dining hall. She remembered her first day here, seeing the oldest students, their seriousness and their silence, and she knew the younger students were now seeing them the same way. Glancing at her friends, she saw the hardness had returned to their faces, overlaid over all the old laughter she knew was there. She also felt the weight of the stares of the students from her year who hadn't been chosen—Cleeri, Keshili, Tridonna . . . and she met the eyes of Andare, the caretaker boy. He raised his hand in a wave of luck.

Below, the practice ring was bare. The thin trees from

the prior night had been swept away, subsumed by the earth. The waterfall that frequently flowed down the wood wall was dry. Together, the candidates clustered in the center of the circle of empty earth, while the other students and teachers—as well as their champions—encircled them.

Bells began to ring—morning bells, evening bells, all at once, a cacophony of chimes that drowned out the ordinary sounds of the academy until it was nothing but the peal of notes falling over one another and mashing together. And then the bells stilled, and there was silence.

Above, a flapping of a great many wings.

Daleina and the other chosen candidates looked up. The sky in the circle at the top of the academy was blotted by winged bodies, and Daleina felt them, spirits, dozens of them, their wings overlapping like the leaves in the canopy. She tensed, and she heard the same whisper ripple through the candidates: *Is this the challenge?* Were the trials beginning now, with this?

"Unusual escorts," Zie said.

"Oh, fabulous. Flying," Revi said. "I shouldn't have eaten breakfast. No one fly downwind of me."

Daleina shot a look at Ven, who was squeezed between two masters, his eyes only on her. She didn't know if she was supposed to fight or accept this—was it an attack or merely "unusual" transportation? She didn't feel any malice in the spirits above, beyond what she usually felt, but then she hadn't felt any in the wood spirits who'd tried to crush her.

He nodded, and the muscles in her neck unknotted.

"If I'm ever queen," Revi said, "I promise everyone will walk to their trials."

"Then you will make an excellent queen," Iondra said.

All of them fell silent again, watching, waiting, ready.

Spiraling down, the spirits soared in a pattern. Their bodies were translucent, each of them reflecting the shards of light that filtered through from above, as if carrying the sunlight down to them. One by one, they scooped up the candidates. Daleina forced herself to relax as two spirits clamped down hard on her arms and lifted her into the air. She could do this.

As if triggered by an unseen signal, the spirits soared together, carrying the candidates up the funnel of the academy. Daleina lifted her face upward as they burst out the top and felt the sun wash over her. *This* was what she loved: this moment, above the world, when she saw Aratay—more than that, Renthia itself—spread beneath her. She saw an unbroken sea of green leaves and, far in the distance, the hint of mountains that could have been clouds, or clouds that could have been mountains. There were farmlands beyond that, she knew, and ice fields. Somewhere, an ocean with islands like jewels. But this, this was *her* Renthia—these forests, these magnificent majestic forests with their tiny villages hidden in trees, waterfalls that tumbled off rocks, sun-dappled groves, shrouded roots that never saw sunlight, thick branches that supported hopes, dreams, lives.

Up here, she felt calm.

She clung to that sense of peace as the spirits flew toward the palace, its spires rising high above the other trees. It seemed to glow in the morning light. They flew toward it and then down. She heard other candidates cry out at the sudden shift, but she didn't. She felt the wind in her face and kept her eyes open even as the air chilled her eyeballs. She saw the ground below them rushing toward them, the branches filled with people, so many people, watching them. When she landed, she looked the air spirits directly where she thought their eyes should be. "Thank you."

They flew upward without acknowledging her. Around her, the other candidates clustered, about twenty-five in total, ranging from recent students like Daleina and her friends to more experienced students who had been training with their champions for several years.

She expected the queen to arrive in a spectacular way as well, carried by air spirits. Looking upward, she didn't see when the queen walked out of the palace. She felt an elbow nudge her—Revi—and looked to see the queen standing before them. Queen Fara was every bit as exquisite as she'd looked in the throne room, everything a queen was supposed to be, as beautiful as the sky. Her hair cascaded onto bare shoulders that had been painted with lacelike vines and leaves. Her pale-blue gown pooled at her feet and spread behind her in a lace train. She wore a necklace of teardrop-shaped stones, and her crown was ivy.

"You have come to serve Aratay." The queen's voice was soft but somehow it carried. It rang throughout the branches, perhaps through all of Aratay. "For that, I thank and honor you. I have been privileged to protect the people of our glorious forests for many years, and it is indeed a privilege, one that asks much of your mind, heart, body, and soul. It is not a responsibility to be assumed lightly, and for that reason, we have the trials."

It felt as if everyone were holding his or her breath. Hundreds of breaths held, all at the same time. It was a silence that felt explosive.

"It's time to prove your mastery over the spirits. Let us begin."

Now?

Now.

The queen raised her arms up, and her sleeves fell back to her shoulders. Her bare arms circled in the air, and Daleina couldn't help thinking that their queen had a flair for theatrics. She tried to push the thought down—she should be feeling respect and awe, not cynicism—but you didn't need to dance your arms to summon spirits. Or maybe you did, if you wanted all eyes on you. The people who had gathered to watch all leaned forward, their breath still collectively held.

Ice spirits sailed through the air toward Queen Fara,

frosting the summer leaves, crafting icicles on the branches, coating the bridges in a thin sheen of what looked like glass until everything glittered. They circled around the candidates, and an ice wall built around them, creating a circle, and then the ice spirits dispersed, melting into the now-frozen earth and skating up the side of the palace. Snow fell in their wake.

"This is your new practice ring," Queen Fara said. "Call your best spirit."

And with that, it began.

One by one, their names were called, and one by one, the candidates stepped into the center of the ring and summoned a spirit. Daleina watched the others as they chose the most impressive spirit they could. A woman with black skin and yellow hair summoned a fire spirit that howled within a column of fire. Another chose an earth spirit that slithered through the earth and curled around her feet, a massive snake with flat black eyes. Its body was thicker than a person. Linna called an air spirit that looked like a beautiful translucent woman with flowing iridescent wings. Mari called a water spirit that flooded the ring in an inch of water that flowed in like a wave and then pooled around Mari's feet. She stood on the spirit's scaled back.

Daleina tossed her senses outward, brushing the powerful minds of the spirits that the others had called. She felt the tiny palace spirits, watching curiously, hidden and wanting to stay hidden. She felt the city spirits, also drawn to watch, and she ran her mind up the trees toward the clouds. She could coerce one of the smaller spirits, but that wouldn't be impressive—it would tremble, terrified, in the presence of the other, stronger spirits. But she didn't think she could control one of the more powerful spirits. Not like these.

She glanced at the audience, which had grown. Ven was there, and Hamon; they'd traveled fast. She met Hamon's

eyes first—worried, of course. And then Ven's. He was, surprisingly, smiling. Why? He had to know she couldn't do
this. She was weak when it came to control. In a contest
of power to power, she was going to lose. Badly, publicly,
humiliatingly, overwhelmingly.

Unless she didn't try to control her spirit. Unless she tried
to *invite* one.

"Candidate Daleina of Greytree," the herald intoned.

Hands sweating, heart pounding, breath fast, Daleina
stepped into the center of the ring. She felt eyes on her, both
human and inhuman, and she tossed her mind up and out as
far and hard as she could. *Come play with me.*

Silence.

And silence.

And then a rush of curiosity as a white streak separated
from a cloud and flew in a spiral down toward her. It was an
ermine-shaped air spirit—the same one? She couldn't tell,
but it dove fast, scooping beneath her, knocking her onto its
back. She clung to it, and it spiraled up, flying her around the
ring while the others watched. Linna waved to her. Revi was
smiling. So was Ven, Hamon, the headmistress . . . She felt
her cheeks stretch and knew she was beaming back at them.

Below, the next candidate was called.

Daleina stayed on the back of the air spirit, circling, as
the remaining candidates each summoned a spirit until the
ring was thick with spirits and their candidates. Everywhere,
she saw feathers and scales and fur, tails and wings, twisted
barklike faces and swanlike beauty. She *felt* their presence
as well, the heat of their anger and hate prickling on her skin
like summer air. Each candidate was focused on a single
spirit.

The queen smiled. "You will be ranked based on the
order in which your spirit leaves the ring—the one who stays
the longest wins.

"Now . . . fight."

*F**ight?*

Surely, she didn't mean . . . But she did. On the back of the winged air spirit, Daleina saw the candidates fan out along the edge of the ice wall that formed the trial ring. Each of them was intent on her own spirit, conducting it. Mari's water spirit drew a funnel of water from one of the streams that fed into the palace and threw it at a fire spirit, dousing the sparks that spread from its fingers. The fire spirit roared back and spun faster, a cyclone of flames that bore down on an earth spirit.

Daleina felt the confused question of her spirit: *Play?*

She didn't know how to answer. She knew it wasn't as strong as the other spirits, and if it was hurt, she wasn't strong enough to force it to stay.

Fly higher, she told her spirit, *but stay within the circle.*

She wanted a better vantage point, to see where she could wade into the fray. She winced as a wood spirit tore the mud-flesh arm from an earth spirit. Spirits didn't normally fight one another. This went against their nature, but the candidates pushed them hard, forcing them to attack over and over . . . until one after another, the spirits balked and fled. Some, because they didn't want to cause pain. Others, because they didn't want to feel it. An earth spirit burrowed far into the earth and out of the ring. An air spirit shot past Daleina and the winged ermine, exiting toward the clouds.

Another air spirit targeted them. Its fingers extended like knives, it dove for them, shrieking. *Don't let it catch you,* Daleina told her ermine. *Don't leave the ring. Game!*

Game! the spirit cried happily.

It evaded the other air spirit, and Daleina clung to its back as it twisted and spiraled. The ermine spirit laughed, a high bell-like sound that sounded too wild for the throat of any real creature. It sounded like raw wind, like a storm fresh from the sea. Daleina's head spun, and her stomach lurched, but she held on.

The other air spirit was close behind them.

Down, Daleina said. *Between!*

Crying with delight, the ermine dove down, flying faster and faster as the earth rushed toward them. Closer, it sped between the other spirits, weaving between them as they attacked one another, drawing the other air spirit into their paths. The ermine then veered up, and Daleina looked behind them—the other air spirit had been caught in the wet tentacle arms of a water spirit.

Yes! She didn't have to fight the others, she realized; she only had to outlast them. Clinging to the ermine, they spiraled up above. She felt the spirit's joy. *Fun,* it seemed to be saying. *Fun,* she told it. *Stay in the circle, but fun.* She then let it do whatever it wanted to do.

It soared.

It dived.

It twisted, twirled, turned, and laughed as it zipped between the other spirits, a bolt of chaos between the serious fighting inside the ring. Daleina saw her friends' faces, fierce in concentration, as they guided their spirits.

It occurred to Daleina that she wasn't playing by the rules. But as the air spirit soared up, wind in her face, she didn't care. It was a solid plan. Last to leave the ring wins. Ven had said that Queen Fara didn't care about how she survived the trials, only that she did. Below, there were only a few spirits left. As she glided above them, she saw a twitch of movement below—one of the remaining spirits had noticed her.

Unfortunately, it too was an air spirit. It launched itself into the air, and the ermine flew higher. *Stay in the ring,* Daleina told her spirit.

The ermine jackknifed and sped past the other air spirit, which looked like a massive winged lizard. The lizard flicked its tail at them, and caught her spirit in the stomach. Her spirit flew backward, and then caught itself, only a few inches from the edge of the ring.

The lizard spirit chased them. Daleina, glancing back, saw its teeth and claws. It would tear into her spirit's soft fur, rend its wings. Her spirit couldn't fight this. Daleina was going to have to let it flee.

As the ermine flew down close to the earth, Daleina let go and tumbled onto the floor of the ring. *Save yourself,* she told the ermine.

The ermine tried to obey, to evade the claws, but it had come too close to the practice ring. Another spirit grabbed its leg and yanked it down.

No! Daleina thought.

She looked across the practice ring. The other spirit was being controlled by Airria. Sweat beaded her forehead. Her hands were clenched into fists—the spirit was clearly fighting her control. And Daleina had an idea. She couldn't order her spirit to attack the other spirit. It would never survive.

But she could order it to attack the one controlling the spirit.

As the ermine spirit cried out, Daleina bundled up all her emotion and threw a command at it: *Hurt her.*

Twisting away from the spirit, the ermine dove for Airria. It raked its claws across her chest. Crying out, Airria lost her grip on her spirit. And her spirit instantly fled.

The ermine dove for Airria again, and Daleina tried to stop it. *Stop!* It didn't want to stop, and Daleina did the only other thing she could think of. *Hurt me.* Twisting, the ermine switched its attack from Airria to Daleina. Knowing it was coming, Daleina twisted at the last second so that the claws would scrape her back. She felt it pierce her tunic. And then the spirit was winging up toward the sky, beyond the ring.

She let it go and stepped out of the ring, fifth to last.

Dropping to her knees, she dug her hands into the ground beyond the ice circle. Her head felt as if it were spinning. She felt Hamon's hands on her back, smearing salve onto the wounds. Lifting her head, she looked across the ring—and saw Queen Fara looking directly at her.

Daleina was certain, bone-deep certain, that the queen knew what she'd done, directing the spirit to attack her friend. Queen Fara smiled.

"Knew you could do it," Ven said, beside her. He helped haul her onto her feet. "Head high, back straight, look like a princess. Everyone's watching."

Daleina nodded. She straightened and watched the two remaining spirits battle in the ring: a candidate she didn't know, plus Mari. She circled the ring for a better view as Mari guided her water spirit to create a geyser in the center of the ring. She must be drawing water from throughout the city. The geyser stretched higher and higher, and her spirit was within it, spinning faster and faster.

The other spirit, a fire spirit, tested the edges of the water, roaring as it turned streams into steam. Steam flooded the practice ring, and then Daleina couldn't see. No one could. She stretched her mind into the ring, feeling for the spirits, and she felt the moment when the other candidate's control broke and the spirit turned on her.

The fire spirit roared down on the girl.

"No!" Daleina cried with her voice and her mind.

She felt the weight of other minds pressing down on the

spirit as well, as other candidates realized what was happening, but they were too late.

The steam cleared.

Mari stood beside her water spirit.

And the other candidate was dead.

ALL OF THEM GATHERED IN DALEINA'S ROOM, LIKE they used to. Except tonight they were silent, and their silence made the room feel small. Mari sat on Daleina's bed, between Linna and Revi. Iondra was perched on the desk. Evvlyn, Zie, and Airria all sat on the rug on the floor. Only Daleina stood.

Linna stroked Mari's hair while Revi held her hands.

"You were following instructions," Iondra said. "This self-flagellation is pointless. Queen Fara does not blame you. The people of Aratay do not blame you."

"*We* don't blame you," Revi said.

"You're all anyone is talking about," Zie said. "You won the trials!"

"First half of the trials," Iondra corrected.

Mari only stared at her hands, entwined with Revi's. "I didn't even know her name."

Zie opened her mouth to say the woman's name, and Daleina nudged her with her foot, hard. When Zie looked up at her, Daleina silently shook her head, and Zie shut her mouth. They fell into silence again. Outside, there were murmurs on the spiral staircase, the current students dispersing after dinner. The night bells were beginning to ring, a cascade that was like a familiar lullaby. Daleina moved toward the window and looked out at the familiar view: the stairs and the interior of the academy. High above, the headmistress would be in her office. Below, the teachers would be preparing the practice ring for the next day. Life went on, even in the midst of the trials. She had to remember this, when she was in the middle of everything. She had to remember who the enemy was. It wasn't anyone in this room. "Airria . . ." Daleina began.

"Don't," Airria said. "You were clever. You've always been clever."

"I shouldn't have—"

"You redirected it, didn't you? Toward yourself. That makes us even."

"But I shouldn't have—"

"Stop, Daleina," Evvlyn said, her voice heavy, old. "All of us do things we regret."

All of them were silent, deep in their own thoughts, until Revi, in an attempt to lighten the mood, said, "For example, I regret that I lied to my champion. 'I shot the squirrel myself.' 'I didn't forget the fire starter.' 'I didn't steal these gloves; they were a gift.' 'Of course I paid for the bread.' 'Of course I can sense the spirits.' All our ethics courses, and I fold in the face of the outdoors and the horror of camping." She mocked herself in a light voice, but the look in her eyes didn't match her tone, and her words fell like rocks into a pond, swallowed whole. She looked haunted. More had happened than she said, Daleina was certain. She wondered how many secrets they each held now and thought of her champion and the notes he received. "A queen shouldn't be a petty thief."

"A queen shouldn't be a murderer," Mari said.

"It's not your fault, Mari," Linna said, covering Mari's hands with her own. "You didn't order the spirit to kill her."

"Of course I didn't!"

"Then it's not your fault."

"She's right," Daleina said.

"But my control slipped," Mari said.

At least you had control, Daleina thought.

"I don't deserve to be here," Mari said.

"You were the best!" Linna said. "What happened doesn't erase that. Mari, you've come so far. Don't talk like that. You're the best of us."

All of them nodded.

"Is this the part where we all hug?" Iondra asked. "Because that is not in my nature."

Mari half hiccupped, half laughed, and then she started to cry. Linna twisted and gathered Mari into her arms so that Mari cried on her shoulder. Revi patted her on the back. The rest sat in silence, listening to her cry, feeling her pain. Daleina wished she knew the name of the candidate who died, wished she knew anything about her, so that the woman could be more than a broken body in the middle of a steam-filled practice ring as the ice melted around her, but she'd been taken away quickly, by her own champion. Daleina didn't know if she should go to the funeral. She thought no. If she were the woman's family, she wouldn't want to see the other candidates, the ones who had survived. Or maybe she had to be there, to show respect. It could have been any of them who fell.

"Did I tell you about the time I tried to gather an egg from a bird's nest? My champion wanted breakfast, and I was determined not to let her down," Revi said, her voice determinedly upbeat.

"Let me guess," Daleina said. "Not a bird's nest."

"Oh, no, it was not. Did you know there are actually flying lizards out in the forest? Well, apparently, there are. And apparently, they don't like egg stealers. And do you know how they express their displeasure? They spit. Goo. All over you. I had it in my hair, up my nose, in my mouth, because of course I opened my mouth to scream, and down my shirt. As a lesson, my champion wouldn't let me bathe until that night." This time, Revi's attempt to lighten the mood worked. Daleina began to smile, almost.

"My champion thought I had to learn to be less 'pretty,'"

Linna offered. "She wanted me to ditch all my hair jewels, go without bathing, and sleep in muck."

"What a strange way to train you," Iondra said.

"I believe she wanted to harden me," Linna said.

"Did it work?" Mari asked in a small voice.

"I'm already hard," Linna said with an elegant shrug. "It just made me dirty. After a week, I made sure to sleep in a pile of skunk cabbage and then stick closer to her for the entire next morning. She let me bathe that same day. Champions do have some odd notions."

"They want the best for us," Iondra said.

"They want the best for Aratay," Evvlyn corrected. She'd returned recently from training and had refused to talk about her experience, but Daleina had seen the way she flexed and unflexed her right hand, as if she couldn't control it anymore. Softly, she said, "I've thought about quitting."

Silence greeted that.

"But I won't, because . . . well, this is who I am now. I wouldn't know who else to be."

Daleina felt herself nodding. She sank onto the bed beside Linna, Mari, and Revi. They stayed up another hour, talking about their training, wondering what the second half of the trials would be like, and sitting together in the silences between the words. *This is my family,* Daleina thought. These women, in this place. This was home, and these were her sisters. When they left for their respective rooms to sleep, she felt their presence linger in the air.

She was still sitting on her bed, thinking about them, her friends, when she heard a soft knock on her door. Standing, she crossed to the door and opened it, expecting to see Mari or Revi or Linna.

But it was Hamon.

He was still dressed in his Healer uniform, as if he hadn't tried to sleep. He probably hadn't. He'd most likely been offering his services to all the candidates. He held a jar of salve. "You're awake. I've come . . ." He trailed off but held up the jar as an explanation. "You need to be pain-free for tomorrow. You don't know what she'll throw at you next."

"Is that truly why you're here?"

"When the wood spirits closed around you . . . I thought I'd lost you. And then today, you were so fierce . . ." He touched her cheek, gently. Definitely *not* a healer's touch.

She drew him inside and shut the door behind him. "I did something unforgivable in the ring today. I turned a spirit on another candidate. A friend. Someone I've known for years, who took classes with me here at the academy, ate meals with me. She may not have been one of my closest friends, but she still counts as one, and I turned a spirit on her to break her concentration. That's the only reason I lasted in the ring as long as I did." The words tasted bitter on her tongue. She watched his face to gauge his reaction, but his face didn't change.

"You turned the spirit on yourself to stop it." It wasn't a question.

"After I let it attack her."

"Let me fix your back. I can't heal what you feel, but I can heal your skin."

She sat on her bed and lifted her shirt over her head. Facing her back toward him, she held her hair up as he rubbed the salve over the mostly healed wounds.

"How are your eyes?" he asked as his fingers rubbed away the remnants of pain.

"Fine." Twisting, she looked at him. She could see him looking at her in the candlelight. His hands moved up to her shoulders.

"And your arms? Any pain from the other day?"

She held out her arms, twisting them for him to see. The cuts from the spirits had faded into pink lines on her skin. He ran his hands down her arms, softly, his fingers feeling like feathers.

"Anything else?" he asked, his eyes locked on hers, as if he planned to never look away. "I want to heal your pain, Daleina. All of it."

She drew him closer, and he kissed her, hesitantly at first as if afraid he would hurt her, and she kissed him back, her hands on his skin, his on hers.

And she felt no pain that night.

*A*fter the funeral, Daleina and the other candidates gathered in front of the palace. The queen waited for them, alone, framed by the arched entrance. The ring where they had fought and the candidate had died was gone, erased as if it never existed, and flowers encircled the queen, cascading from the top of the arch. Side by side with her friends, Daleina felt other eyes on her, people from the city, the champions, and spirits, curious after yesterday. She tried to draw strength from the fact that she wasn't alone.

"Your task is simple. Aratay has many abandoned areas, places where people once lived and now only spirits reside. I have chosen one, a lost village, to be reclaimed for people once again. Your champions have been told where the area is and will share that information with you. Once they have done so, you are on your own. Go. Claim the village. Rebuild it. Make it safe. And then you will have earned your place as heir." She favored them all with a smile. "I wish you the very best."

She then turned and walked into the palace. As she reached the gate, she turned her head and added, "All of Aratay wishes you the very best." And the trees exploded into bloom, flowers bursting to life on every branch, growing from vines that shouldn't have been able to grow in fall, in a riot of colors from spring and summer.

As the queen left, the blossoms burst into flame as fire spirits danced over them and then froze in half-ashen blossoms as ice spirits flew behind them.

"She does know how to make an exit," Revi murmured.

Daleina saw Ven push his way through the crowd toward her. Hamon was close behind him. Ven clasped her hands. "Hate me if you want, but be strong."

Daleina blinked. He looked . . . angry, she thought. It wasn't anything definitive: his face was still blank, but there was a tightness to his jaw that she only saw after a village had been attacked. "What do you mean?"

"It can't be a coincidence, the 'lost' town. She chose it . . . to punish me? To test you? I don't know. I can't pretend to know what she's thinking, but whatever her reason for wishing to put you at a disadvantage—" He cut himself off, as if he realized he was babbling, an unusual activity for a champion and one that was making Daleina feel as if the oxygen was being sapped out of the air. He squeezed her hands again. "Daleina, the lost village is Greytree. It's your village. I am so very sorry. It's cruel."

Daleina felt numb. *Home.* She pictured it as it was, with Rosasi and her friends and their house cradled in the village tree. "She didn't know."

"She *did* know. She's testing you. Why just you, I don't know, except it must be to punish me, because I dared defy her exile and bring you here. She means to hurt me through you. Or test me through you." He closed his eyes, inhaled, and then opened them. "You will need to set aside your emotions, remember your training, and draw on your strengths. Can you do that? If you can't, there is no shame in walking away. We can continue our training and try again at the next trials. No one will think less of you."

"Listen to Ven," Hamon put in. "You don't have to do this."

Daleina's mouth quirked into a smile. "You mean I have a choice?"

"Of course!" Hamon said.

"It isn't fair of her to ask this of you," Ven said. "And I won't ask it of you. I will respect whatever choice you make."

Daleina glanced at the others, also in close conferences with their champions. She doubted the other champions were having this kind of talk with their candidates. She wondered what it meant that hers was trying to talk her out of it, if he thought she wasn't worthy or believed she was going to fail. "It's the kind of thing a queen has to do, isn't it? Heal what's broken? In a way, it's the reason I'm here." Brave words. She wasn't sure she meant them. Then again, she wasn't sure she didn't. *Greytree.* It always came back to that, to the day when she hadn't saved everyone. "I think I'm meant to do this."

Ven snorted. "I don't believe in fate."

"This isn't about you." Daleina covered his hand with hers to soften her words. "Maybe that's how Queen Fara meant it, but that's not what it is. Not anymore. I'm making it about me. Maybe, when I'm done, someone will write a song about it, and your sister will sing it from the top of the canopy. Now, will you both quit worrying about my emotional state and let me go?" On the last word, she realized she was shouting. Gathering up the shreds of her dignity, she marched to the end of the branch and jumped off, grabbing a rope as she did and swinging down to the forest floor.

Whistling, she waited for a moment, and Bayn trotted out of the bushes. Daleina rubbed his ears, and the wolf's tongue lolled out of his mouth. He leaned against her, comfortingly, and she braced herself to keep from toppling over into the bushes. "Guess it's just you and me."

Behind her, she heard a soft thump as someone landed. She turned to tell Ven—

It wasn't Ven. It was Mari. "Is it true you know the way?"

"Yes." She swallowed and straightened, taking strength from the warmth of the wolf by her side. The others from Northeast Academy joined them: Revi, Linna, Zie, Iondra, Evvlyn, and Airria. "I'll take us there."

THE LIGHT WAS FADING TO A MATTE GRAY, FLATTENING the shadows between the trees. Looking up at the moss-coated branches, Daleina called to the others, "We should stop for the night."

Ahead, Linna called, "I found the perfect spot." She beckoned them through the woods into a clearing that was as picturesque as a storybook: a lovely pool of water, reflecting the dimming sky above, beds of soft ferns, blossoms closed for the coming evening, moss hanging from the branches of the bent bows. *All it needs is a deer lapping at the pool, surrounded by singing woodland creatures with ribbons and bows in their fur,* Daleina thought.

As she always did when she traveled with Ven and Hamon, she scanned the area for spirits—she found one, living in the pool of water beneath a tree. "There's a spirit in the . . ."

She trailed off as a half-dozen more spirits swooped in from between the trees. A tiny wood spirit with leaflike wings and berry eyes flew to Mari, alighted on her shoulder, and then dived into a nearby bush—the berries ripened in its wake. Calling to a water spirit, Revi flushed a squirrel out of its nest. Across the clearing, Linna created a fire with only spirits and no kindling or wood, and Zie instructed two earth spirits to kill, skin, and prepare the squirrel to be cooked over that fire. Airria and Evelyn used spirits to plump up the moss and create hammocks out of leaves. Watching them,

Daleina unrolled her plain bedroll. As the air shimmered around her, a part of her kept whispering, *Danger!*

"There are fish!" Linna instructed the water spirit to hand them to her out of the pool. She passed them to Zie's spirits to be cleaned and put on the fire. Soon, they were all sitting around the living flames, eating fish, squirrel meat, and berries, and Daleina had never felt more like she didn't belong.

"Daleina, do you want a hammock? I can make you one," Revi offered. "The trick is to have a tree spirit weave vines."

"I prefer the moss beds," Linna said. "You can contour them to your back."

"I'm fine," Daleina said. "But thanks."

"I've heard Champion Ven prefers the austere approach," Zie said. "I bet he has you hunting for your food with bow and arrow."

"Knives, actually." Daleina felt prickles run up and down her back. The spirits they'd summoned were filling the trees and watching them. There were so many. Aware of them too, Bayn pressed against her legs, and Daleina slid her hands into the wolf's fur, though she wasn't sure who was reassuring whom. The talking continued far into the night, and the fire spirits continued to spin and burn in the campfire. Curled against Bayn, Daleina slept only a few minutes at a time.

She woke at dawn. The fire spirits had fled, but there were dozens of others that watched them from the branches. Keeping an eye on the water spirit, Daleina washed her face in the pool. The water spirit swam in circles, agitated. Seeing the others wake, it froze, and then ducked under the surface of the water.

Airria and Evvlyn bathed in the pool after forcing a fire spirit to heat the water to a bearable temperature. The water spirit huddled by a tree, shivering and glaring. "Sorry for intruding on your grove," Daleina told it.

"There's no point in that," Revi said. Daleina startled—

she hadn't heard Revi behind her. "They will always hate us. You know that."

"I know, but . . ." She couldn't find the words to explain. "It feels as if we're riling them up unnecessarily. All of this, we could have done it without spirits. Instead, we've drawn the attention of all the spirits in the nearby area."

"I know," Linna said, joining them. "It's a strategy. Show them we have power. That way, if we ever face the spirits at the coronation, they'll remember us and choose one of us. They'll know we're strong enough to lead them. Daleina, this isn't foolhardy. We can handle these spirits."

I can't, Daleina thought, and the realization was like a fist in her stomach.

"Different champions have different approaches," Iondra said.

But that's not it, Daleina wanted to say. It wasn't a difference in approach; it was a difference in innate skill and talent. *I'm not good enough.* She looked at each of her friends. She'd known in the academy that commanding spirits came more easily to all of them, but it wasn't until now, out in the world and away from the cocoon of the academy, that she'd let herself see how very stark the difference was between them.

Her friends were still talking, unaware of the realization churning inside Daleina. "In truth, the trial doesn't start at the border of Greytree," Evvlyn said. "It's already started." She looked at the trees above them that housed the hidden, spying spirits. "These spirits will report back to the queen."

"And they'll say we were unafraid," Revi said.

"Maybe it's all right to be a little afraid." Daleina thought of the six spirits and the sphere of wood. Her scratches didn't sting anymore and, thanks to Hamon's salve, were barely visible. In a week, her skin would be smooth again, and there would be no sign at all of any attack, but she wasn't going to forget it anytime soon.

"It's not all right for us," Mari said. "My mother always says that. To be queen is to be fearless. Why do you think I wanted to be queen so badly? If I were that powerful, I'd never feel fear again." She hugged her arms. "I was so afraid before, in the first part of the trials. I think . . ." Her eyes were distant, and Daleina knew she was thinking back to the first trial and the candidate who didn't survive. "I think maybe that's why she died. If I hadn't been afraid . . ."

"Stop it, Mari," Revi said. "It wasn't your fault."

"Remember who the enemy is," Daleina said.

There was silence in the grove, but it wasn't a friendly silence. Daleina was acutely aware of how many eyes were watching and ears were listening. She felt them like an itch on her skin, like new scratches, breaking open the old, and wondered why the others didn't feel it too—another difference between them. Another reason why Daleina didn't deserve to be queen.

In silence, they moved on.

GREYTREE.

Home.

The sign was faded and broken, appropriately, with another sign nailed on top of it: UNPROTECTED. ENTER AT YOUR OWN RISK. It had the seal of the queen. *It's been officially abandoned,* Daleina thought. Somehow that seemed worse than just thinking of it as empty.

She traced the letters with her fingertip, smearing away the mold that had spread in the creases of the words. She couldn't remember who would have repainted the signs. She'd been too young to know which of the adults did what, but she remembered a man with a red beard who used to paint flowers on the walls of the houses. Their house had stencils of ivy painted on the walls, and the kitchen had fat apples painted above the sink. She hadn't thought of that kitchen in years.

"Daleina, are you all right?" Linna asked.

"Of course she's not all right," Revi said. "Daleina, is there anything we can do to help?"

Daleina pulled her hand away and forced it down to her side. She felt as if she'd forgotten what to do with her arms. They hung awkwardly by her side. "It will be good to do this. The village should live again." Ven could be wrong. This might not be punishment at all, or even a test. Maybe the queen felt she was doing Daleina a favor—a chance to fix what was wrong in her past. It could be a chance to change something ugly and painful into something full of beauty and hope. "This way," she said, walking down the bridge.

The bridge was in disrepair, which was putting it kindly. Lichen coated the boards. Several were missing and others were rotted, making the entire bridge look like an old man's smile. Daleina stepped gingerly, testing each board to see if it would hold her weight. She heard the others talking to one another, but it was like a buzz behind her. Her eyes were glued forward, waiting for her first view of Greytree.

Her memory could be wrong. Maybe it hadn't been destroyed as thoroughly as she'd thought. Maybe in a child's mind, it had been skewed into a catastrophe. It wasn't as if the rest of the country had reacted to the loss of Greytree. When they'd moved and she'd told people where she was from, there hadn't been gasps of horror. Just blank expressions, as if she'd named someplace far away. At the academy, most hadn't known of her tragedy, until one of her friends who liked to talk, Zie perhaps, had spread the world. She hadn't minded that they knew. In fact, she'd wanted them to know. It explained why she was there. But bringing them here . . . She was both grateful they were here with her and wished that she were alone.

The bridge ended. Just stopped in midair. Ahead was the village tree. It had been sheared of all branches at midforest level, with no trace of the village that it had once cradled in its powerful arms. No trace except one hut, its roof sunken in, its door hanging on one hinge, but otherwise intact. *This* was home, this broken place, in a way that the charm-covered, garish-green house never was. She'd felt safe here. And happy.

She felt a hand on her shoulder, Mari's hand. She couldn't pull her eyes from her old home. There, she remembered the day that Arin had been born. She'd been like a squalling kitten, and Daleina had been surprised she was so messy. Daleina remembered the breakfasts that her mother used to cook in that kitchen . . . or was she remembering those breakfasts in their new home? The memories were jumbled. She wished she could separate them out clearly.

After a moment, she forced herself to look down toward the forest floor. For an instant, she saw the wreckage again—the just-broken boards, the just-broken bodies—but then her eyes focused, and there was only green, the lush green of bushes spread between the tree roots, as if denying there was ever a tragedy here.

There was no trace of her village below. Only the broken bridge, the missing branches, and her home, alone.

"Are you going to be all right?" Mari asked softly.

"I don't know," Daleina said. "Are you?"

Mari was silent for a moment. "I don't know either."

CHAPTER 23

The other candidates coaxed new branches from the old trunk, thickened them, hollowed them, and shaped them into new houses. Dozens of spirits from the surrounding woods were performing the construction, swooping and soaring among them.

Daleina knew she should be out helping them, but instead, she was inside her old house, sweeping the dust from the half-rotted floor with her mother's decade-old broom. A family of bats had taken up residence in the roof, and she'd shooed a nest of squirrels out of the fireplace. The chimney would need to be patched before it could be used again, and the pulley system that they'd used to haul up water and other supplies had been severed.

When she'd swept out every speck of dirt, she forced herself to walk out of the house and all its old memories. She affixed a rope from inside to a hook and lowered herself to the forest floor. Bayn was prowling between the bushes, sniffing at them.

"They're buried under there," she told the wolf. "Everyone I didn't save." You'd think she would have outgrown the old hurt by now, forgiven herself, and moved on. Kneeling, she pressed her palms against the cool earth. She sent her mind down, as if that would let her touch her old friends, family, and neighbors—

She felt something beneath her. It moved, deep within the earth, like an undulation of a wave. It spread wide beneath them, under the roots of the village tree, its thick tentacles reaching out in every direction.

Oh no.

She'd felt this once before.

The shifting sand.

But it couldn't be the same spirit.

It didn't matter if it was. It was old, impossibly powerful, and beneath them, and it knew they were here. She felt its hatred rolling through the earth. It meant to—

"Run!" she cried.

Bayn obeyed her instantly, sprinting through the underbrush, and she ran after the wolf. Above her, she heard the chatter stop. She felt the eyes of the other girls, friends and strangers, watching her curiously from above. "Don't be idiots!" The tentacles reached far. If they flexed—"It's below us! Reach down. Don't you feel it? It's too strong!" Jumping onto a tree trunk, she began to scale it, shoving her feet into the groves of the bark.

One of the candidates—a girl with silvery hair—laughed, a sound like a bell. Another laughed as well. Daleina ignored them, climbing higher and calling to her friends. "Revi, Linna . . . remember our first survival class? Remember when you were all talking and thought I was foolish to climb a tree, and then the wolf attacked?"

"Yes, but there was no danger," Mari called to her. "It was Bayn!"

"There's danger here! Feel down. Can't you feel it?"

"There's only earth," another said. "Nothing to fear."

Dammit, they weren't going to listen to her. The smaller wood and air spirits could feel it—they were straining to resist commands, to flee the area, and she realized climbing wasn't going to be enough. "The trial isn't about building the village; it's surviving His Highness beneath us." She heard murmurs—about her, about how she was afraid, about how an heir shouldn't fear spirits—and she sensed the earth spirit coil its tentacles, ready. "Fly, everyone. Right now!" She tossed the thought to every air spirit. *Fly! Fly us high!*

Already agitated, they listened to her—she was telling them to do what they already wanted to do: Flee. Three air spirits dove for her, grabbed her arms, and pulled her into the air. Another scooped up Bayn. Around her, she saw other spirits lift candidates up into the air.

And the village tree began to sink.

Air spirits fluttered to the tree, and the candidates were lifted up out of the branches as it sank beneath them, as if swallowed by a vast mouth. The ground around it shifted as if it had turned to liquid, and the other trees undulated. Above, held by spirits, Daleina watched as her home sank toward the earth.

She didn't listen as the other candidates shouted to one another. They were trying to stop it, fight it, control it, but Daleina didn't try. The tree sank, despite their attempts, lower and lower. She wondered how there was so much earth beneath it to claim it, but there was. The trees around it continued to tremble, but none of the others sank. Only the village tree, lower and lower, until at last the tops of the leaves disappeared into the brown lakelike sludge. And then it was gone.

Lower me, Daleina ordered the spirits. They obeyed quickly, plummeting down, and she sensed their curiosity like pinpricks in her mind, the only reason they obeyed so fast—they'd never seen anything like this. But she had. She bent her knees to absorb the impact from landing. Around her, the other candidates flew down on their spirits.

The ground was hard beneath her feet. Kneeling, she felt the soil. Solid.

"How did you know it was going to do that?" one of the candidates asked.

"Because it did it before." Granted, it hadn't done it on such a scale, but she'd felt its power. She reached out with her mind but felt only ordinary dirt and rocks beneath them. "I think it's gone now. We can build the village."

"Is it coming back?" That was Evvlyn.

"I don't know," Daleina said. "But it's not here now."

All of them drew closer, touching her arms and back, and touching each other's hands and shoulders, as if reassuring themselves they were all still here, whole, and alive. They murmured to one another, an overlap of voices that felt like a comforting blanket.

"I'm sorry about your home," Mari said softly, to Daleina. "I know it had memories, good ones as well as the bad ones."

"It's all right," Daleina said, and strangely, it was, because this time . . . this time she had saved them all.

ONE OF THE GIRLS HURRIED OVER TO DALEINA. "WE'RE ready. Where do we start?"

She contemplated the trees for a moment. They'd decided that there wouldn't be a single village tree—without the queen's power, it was too difficult to grow one massive tree, but more important, a single tree was prone to attack from the earth kraken. Instead, the houses would be shaped from the surrounding trees and connected via bridges that would sprout from the branches. "Start with establishing platforms for each of the houses and then construct the bridges between them. Grab everyone who's good with larger wood spirits for that, and we can fill in the details after."

They were listening to her, both because she'd saved them and because she was one of the few that had grown up in an outer village and knew what was needed. She laid out the plan and divvied up the tasks, and then they dispersed, calling to the nearby spirits. Except for her.

It was a hard, bitter-tasting pill to swallow, one that stuck in her throat and scraped all the way down. All of these girls were more qualified, more powerful than she was . . . and these were merely the candidates. There were heirs already out there in the world with both training and experience. If all of them were at the coronation ceremony, the spirits wouldn't hear Daleina calling to choose her any more than they'd hear the cries of an ant. She had no chance.

She watched Linna coax water spirits into creating a well for fresh water, and she watched Revi rouse the fire spirits into hollowing wood into furniture with the heat of their fire. Evvlyn was summoning earth spirits to pile rocks. Others, many whose names she didn't know, were working with the wood spirits to build houses and bridges. All of it was beyond Daleina's skill.

Oh, she could help, and she did. She could command the smaller spirits, assisting the others as much as possible, but they did the bulk. Every shred of confidence she'd developed had dribbled away. She may be able to sense spirits, but she couldn't command them, not in the same way or with the same ease as the others—not unless the spirits were already agitated. If they were worked into a frenzy, she could redirect them, shift them from destruction to creation, but this kind of pure control was beyond her. This was what Headmistress Hanna had been trying to tell her from the very beginning. This was what all her teachers had tried to tell her on every test and in every report. This was what the other champions, the ones who hadn't chosen her, saw.

Her greatest regret was that she would disappoint Ven. He'd believed in her, for some unfathomable reason. Maybe he was out of practice as a champion, or maybe he'd been fooled by a few lucky moments. When the trial was over, she'd tell him, she'd explain she simply wasn't born with the gifts that the others had. She'd never be queen.

But she could *assist* the queen, as heir. She'd play a vital role in Aratay. She was sure of it. She could be the queen's trusted adviser. Her right hand. Surely there was a place for that in the palace. She could coordinate the other heirs, find a way to effectively use them.

As plans went . . . it wasn't bad. In fact, she could feel herself getting a bit excited about it. She'd be like Headmistress Hanna, but for the graduates. She could unite them, even lead them. Yes, this was a future that fit her talents and personality. She wasn't meant to be a star, shining brighter than the rest. She was, as her reports said, a team player. After she became an heir, she'd talk to Queen Fara and propose her idea. She could be a valuable heir, even if she would never become queen. *I could still have a purpose.*

As she worked on the village, she continued to watch the other candidates. Each of them had a preferred kind of spirit, it seemed, though all by necessity could work with any kind. They fell into groups, and each group had their star. She was happy to see that some of her friends shone just as much as the others. Iondra, for example, was adept with water spirits. She funneled them into paths, creating channels for water within the trees—rainwater basins high above that would then run through water-worn paths toward the houses. Another girl, adept with wood spirits, worked with her, creating valves and dams to control the water flow. Each house would have water in its sink. Evvlyn was working with several others to create the bridges, encouraging the wood spirits to thicken branches between the houses. Linna and Revi were a team making houses. Revi concentrated on the structure, while Linna added details like doors and windows. On the forest floor, Zie worked with a group that was cultivating the berry bushes and creating corrals for the villagers' domesticated animals.

But it was Mari who shone the brightest.

She was concentrating on the heart of the village: the marketplace. She stood in the middle of the platform, eyes closed, conducting spirits as if they were instruments in her orchestra. At some point during her training, she'd become the best of them. *She'll make an excellent queen,* Daleina thought, and was proud that she felt only a twinge of jealousy, quickly damped out.

Close behind her in skill was a woman named Berra, who had brown skin and clipped white hair and who controlled air spirits with a dizzying speed, as well as another candidate, Tiyen, a short green-haired woman who worked with a dozen earth and wood spirits at once. And then Linna— after directing wood spirits to create windows and doors, she commanded a line of fire spirits to decorate them, using their fire to etch designs into the wood. It was beautiful, precise work that required exquisite control.

All of them would make strong queens, Daleina thought as she watched them.

On the third night, they slept in the village. Daleina picked a hut that was close to the forest floor—not on the floor, because that would be foolish, but close enough that Bayn could leap up to the platform and come inside.

It wasn't a home yet. It lacked all the details that made it lived in: bedding, curtains, dishes. But the people would bring that when they moved here. This was the shell, the empty nest, that would welcome them. It was, she thought, a fitting tribute to the people of Greytree. New families would be happy here.

All of them had chosen to believe the earth kraken was a onetime event. It hadn't returned, and there was no way to prevent it if it did. It was chalked up to be a natural disaster, not their responsibility, though they agreed to tell the queen about it. Then she would be able to control it, once she knew it was out there.

Daleina offered Bayn a bit of her dinner. He caught plenty for himself out in the woods, but he'd developed a taste for the occasional cooked meat, or at least he never said no when Daleina gave it to him. "The others did a great job, didn't they?" Daleina asked.

Bayn never answered, but it still always felt like he understood more than he should.

"I hope the queen sees that. All of them are worthy." She wondered what the wolf would think of her plan, to assist the queen, to admit she wasn't one of the worthy but still to try to add value. Hamon, she thought, would support her. Her family wouldn't understand.

Daleina heard footsteps outside her hut and then the door burst open. Zie stood in the doorway. "Have you seen Mari? She's missing."

"What do you mean, 'missing'?" Striding toward the door, Daleina signaled for Bayn to come with her. The wolf trotted after her. "Who saw her last and when?"

"No one for several hours. She told Linna that she was going to find some burn herbs. She wanted the new hedgewitch's shop to be set up with some of the basics, in case the new villagers needed any medicine when they first arrived. 'Sickness and injury don't wait for you to settle in,' she said. But she never came back."

"Send out spirits. Get them looking for her."

"Already done. None of them has seen anything."

Kneeling next to Bayn, Daleina said, "Find her, okay? Mari. Find Mari." The wolf raced off the platform and into the forest, plunging into the underbrush.

"She couldn't have disappeared. How have you told the spirits to find her?" She approached a worried group, mostly comprised of Mari's friends. "Do the spirits know who she is?"

"The spirits know who we all are," one said.

Others nodded.

Daleina stretched her awareness out, feeling for spirits, for anything that didn't seem right. She felt the plethora of spirits they'd called, clustered in the trees and flying through the air and spread throughout the forest. It didn't feel any different from how it felt that morning.

"No one can hide from the spirits," Iondra said.

"She's not hiding," Zie said sharply. "Mari wouldn't do that. She'd have come back if she could. Something happened. Maybe that earth spirit . . ."

Daleina plunged her awareness into the earth, to the bedrock. She felt nothing but the ordinary spirits that burrowed through the soil. "It's not near." If it had been near, it had left. "Tell the spirits . . ." She swallowed not wanting to say it out loud. "Tell them to look for bodies." If Mari were . . . gone, the spirits might not consider her Mari anymore. They might overlook her. She heard Linna gasp and Revi hiss.

One of the other candidates, Berra, asked, "Why don't you send spirits out too? Why are you always just giving orders?" She had burn scars across her knuckles, as if she'd once punched a fire.

"Because this is Mari's life we're talking about," Daleina snapped. She wasn't going to trust her own power for this. "And I don't play games with my friends' lives."

"You don't know Mari," Linna chimed in, "so your mind is calmer than ours. You're able to control the spirits better. Please don't argue, not now." Squeezing Daleina's hand, Linna glared at Berra and the others. Daleina wanted to tell them they didn't need to hide her weakness, not anymore. She'd made her peace with it. But now wasn't the time. This wasn't about her and her future; it was about Mari.

They waited. The spirits searched.

Daleina felt them scouring the forest. All the spirits were awakened and buzzing through the air, earth, and trees. Except for a tight knot of motionless spirits. She let her awareness brush over them. They weren't angry. Maybe asleep? She tried to push them away, but it was like pushing on a boulder. She wasn't strong enough. "Revi, to the northeast . . . there are some wood spirits who haven't responded. Can you try to wake them?"

Frowning, Revi concentrated. "Yeah, I feel them. It's like they're curled in a ball."

Oh no. "A ball," Daleina said carefully. "A sphere of spirits. Six spirits?"

"I can't tell. Yes. Maybe . . . yes."

From the forest came a wolf's howl. Bayn.

Daleina took off at a run. The others ran with her. The spirits whipped around them, and Daleina ignored them, all her focus on the sphere of spirits ahead and the lone wolf's howl. She crashed through the brush, making no attempt to be silent. "Break that sphere! Break it apart!"

On the command of the other candidates, all the spirits flew toward the sphere. They tore at it, breaking at the wood. Daleina burst into the clearing, seeing it for the first time, through the translucent bodies of the spirits.

It cracked. She heard the crack, felt it within her body, felt as if her own bones were breaking, and the sphere cracked open like an egg.

Mari's shattered body tumbled out of the sphere.

It should have been a triumphant return, with parades and feasts and joy. Nearly all the candidates had survived the trials, and even better, an abandoned village had been rebuilt. Other years, other trials, the death toll had been higher. But Ven was there in the academy when the news was told to Caretaker Undu. He saw the ashen face of Headmistress Hanna. He watched the reaction of the masters, all of whom had known Candidate Mari. And he knew her champion, an older man who had trained three heirs before her and who, once the news had spread, had confided in Ven that this was it, he was done, he'd never train another.

Ven had understood.

So he was in a less than celebratory mood when the silken air spirit landed on his bed and informed him that the queen requested his company. He was even less pleased when the spirit said it had been sent to carry him. But he squelched down the instinct to toss the spirit out the window and instead sat on its back as if it were a horse. Stronger than it looked, the spirit unfurled mothlike wings that were broader than he was tall, and soared out of the academy window.

Ven eyed the trees as they flew past, his muscles tensed to leap from the back of the air spirit, if necessary, but the spirit flew him straight to the palace and up to the balcony of

Queen Fara's bedchambers. It alighted on the balcony, and
he dismounted.

The spirit hovered for a moment, as if it expected a
reward or praise. Determined not to fight with Fara over
unimportant things when there were important things to say,
he bowed stiffly to the air spirit.

As if satisfied, it flew away, toward the moon, its white
body shadowed as it passed in front of it. Behind him, he
heard the rustle of silk. "They can be beautiful, can't they?"

Ven grunted.

"Come, Ven, even you must admit it."

"The moon is beautiful. The trees. This palace." He
turned to face her. "You." She was. Her silken robe seemed
to float on her shoulders. Her hair was loose and tumbled
around her neck. He wanted to brush that hair off her neck
and kiss her skin everywhere, but he forced himself not to
move. "But they . . . they destroy beauty. Fara, those spirits
have to die."

Killing a spirit was a serious matter. Each death caused
the death of a portion of Aratay, decreasing their forests,
destroying their usable land. Six was a significant number,
especially given how powerful the spirits were reported to
be. Homes could be lost. Orchards. More. But this couldn't
continue. Six powerful spirits were rogue and had to be
brought down. "Once, it was an accident. Twice, unfortunate. Three times . . . it's a pattern. These spirits are defying you."

"And I will tighten my grip on them. Champion Ven, I
am deeply sorry for your losses, but I cannot afford to ter-
minate these spirits." She was using his title. She wasn't
pleased with him. Well, two could play at that game: he
wasn't pleased with her.

"Their deaths would send a message to the other
spirits—"

"The spirits never understand those messages," Queen

Fara said. "You know that. This would be an execution, pure and simple."

"*You* don't need to do it," Ven said softly.

She didn't speak.

"I will do it. It doesn't need to come from the queen. Let me hunt them down." He wanted to be the one to do it—he hadn't been here to protect Sata. And he'd been with Fara, distracting her and distracted by her, when the spirits attacked Daleina. *Destroying them will be my penance.* "I can do it."

Fara was studying his face. "These spirits overwhelmed powerful women, trained to command. What makes you think you have a chance against them?"

"I am certain the heirs would assist me, especially those who were close to Mari. It's possible the entire Northeast Academy would rally for such a hunt, if it was endorsed by Your Majesty, though you may want it done more quietly. One or two heirs would be sufficient assistance."

"It would set a terrible precedent," Fara said. "Punishment is supposed to come from the queen. Otherwise, we'll have vigilantes trying to kill spirits, destroying our land in the process and most likely dying."

"I'm the disgraced champion," Ven pointed out. "I'm not supposed to follow the rules." He held her gaze and thought he saw almost approval in her eyes.

"I have larger problems than a few rogue spirits," Queen Fara said. "There's a new queen in Semo, and she's flexing her muscles. The border spirits are restless. My attention *must* be there, if we don't want to wake one morning and discover our land has shrunk and half our citizens are bowing to someone new who doesn't know our people or respect our forests. As much as our people wish to believe it, I'm not omnipotent." Her gaze locked on Ven, as if they shared a secret, which he supposed they did, though he wasn't sure which secret she was thinking of. "I can't afford the time or energy to hunt for rogue spirits, and I can't afford to worry about protecting other spirits from overeager hunters who think it's open season."

"Perhaps that's what the spirits are counting on?" Ven suggested.

"Perhaps," she said. "It's as fine a theory as any."

For once, she was admitting weakness. For once, she was being honest with him. He felt the muscles in his shoulders unknot. "Then you will allow me to hunt?"

"You must do it secretly, to avoid creating new vigilantes."

And to hide your weakness, he thought but didn't say.

"Begin tonight. It's a full moon, which means the strongest spirit in the capital will be distracted—you should be able to escape her notice. You may take your candidate, of course. I believe she will be motivated to assist you. But I'd ask that you tell no one else."

He touched her cheek, let his hand cup her face. "There's no shame in asking for help."

"There is if you're queen."

"Then don't be queen right now, and ask me as you, as Fara." He touched her lips with his and wondered at the woman who could inspire him to poetry. Perhaps a bit of canopy singer had touched him as well. It did run in his family. "My beautiful Fara."

She kissed him back. "Kill the spirits, Ven. For Mari, for Daleina, for Sata, for me."

"Gladly," he said, and drew her inside the bedchamber.

THE FUNERAL FOR MARI WAS BEAUTIFUL, AND DALEINA hated every second of it. All the students from the academy wore black ribbons and filed in a line to the burial ground. All the masters encircled her body, and the headmistress herself summoned the spirits to bury her deep in the earth. Standing between Revi and Linna, Daleina let her awareness follow the spirits down as they sank with Mari. When it was complete, thousands of white flowers blossomed around the grove, as if snow had fallen. Looking at Caretaker Undu across the grove, Daleina wished she could uproot every single flower and instead give the caretaker back Mari. Joining the line of people, she passed by the masters, clasped their hands, and murmured meaningless phrases, the things you said when this happened, about how she wasn't in pain now, and how she was part of Renthia forevermore, how she'd never be forgotten. She reached Caretaker Undu.

"I'm sorry for your loss," Daleina said, and her throat clogged.

Caretaker Undu held herself as still as a statue. Her hands were clasped in front of her, and her face was like stone. "Thank you, Candidate Daleina."

And that was all she could say, all she could do. She'd never felt so helpless. She wanted to drive her knife into a tree and yell until her throat ached. But she knew that wouldn't bring Mari back or erase one second of pain for Mari's mother.

After the funeral ended, Daleina separated herself from the crowd. Beyond the grove, people lined the bridges, and it felt more like a festival—they wanted to celebrate the end of the trials. Shopkeepers were selling sugared rolls and fruit dipped in chocolate. Children were blowing horns and waving flags. Daleina was even more conscious that Mari should be walking with them, not left behind under the ground in a blossom-covered grove. Veering away, she headed for the academy. She couldn't celebrate.

She found Hamon inside, waiting in her room, as if he'd known she'd come there. He went to her instantly, drew her inside, and shut the door.

"I keep thinking that it could have been you. I'm sorry. I know you're mourning her and I should be too, but I didn't know her. I know *you*, and I keep picturing you in that sphere. It was almost you." He brushed the hair from her neck and wrapped his arms around her, his cheek pressed to her cheek. She let him hold her.

She didn't feel right being in the academy without Mari. It didn't feel like the academy should exist without her. But it was here. They'd come back in only two days, with her body encased in cloth. They hadn't stopped until they reached the tower, and then the candidates had fractured—many to their homes, some to their academies. She had come here, with Mari's body, and been here when Zie had broken the news. She didn't know how her friend had had the strength to form the words. She'd said afterward that was information she never wanted to have to share, and then she'd shut herself in her room and hadn't said a word since.

Their rooms had been preserved—the next crop of students hadn't come yet. Mari's room was still exactly as it had been, with her class schedule on the door, though her belongings weren't there. She'd packed them all away when she left for her training, as they all had. Daleina guessed they were with Caretaker Undu now.

Daleina's room felt like it wasn't hers. All her belongings were still stuffed into a bag. Sitting on her old cot, she felt like a stranger. She held on to Hamon as if he were her link to who she was.

"I know I'm supposed to say a lot of things, like she's at peace, and time will heal all wounds, but that won't help, will it?" Hamon was stroking her hair.

She rested her head against his shoulder. "It won't help."

"What will? Tell me and I'll do it."

She heard the door open. She didn't move, though she felt Hamon's back stiffen as if he wanted to stand at attention, but he stayed with her, arms tight around her.

"I know what will help." Champion Ven.

Daleina lifted her head.

He shut the door behind him. "Queen Fara has given her

permission. We are to find the spirits who did this—and then kill them."

She stared at him. Beside her, Hamon was staring too, his jaw open as if he'd forgotten how to work it. Daleina's hands curled into fists. "You're right," she said. "That will help."

"I HATE THIS PLAN," HAMON MUTTERED LOUDLY.

Ven contemplated telling the boy to leave. He didn't have to be here. In fact, they barely fit, three of them on the tiny platform, a hunter's blind just outside the city. But Daleina beat him to it. "Then leave," she said.

He was sorting through his healer's pack, and Ven watched him count tubs of fast-acting salve, tourniquet materials, and a scalpel. "Of course I'm not leaving. Someone has to patch you up afterward. I'm only saying I hate this. I'm not saying you shouldn't do it."

Daleina blinked. "You aren't going to talk us out of it? Say it's too bloodthirsty? Claim that Mari wouldn't want this, that it's unworthy of a candidate, that it will hurt Aratay more than it will help, that spirits are amoral, not immoral, and they can't help their instincts, and they're part of the wild beauty that is the world?"

"No."

"Good."

The two of them stared at each other, and Ven felt as if he were missing large pieces of the conversation. "Did you two just have your first lovers' quarrel?" he asked.

"I think so," Hamon said gravely.

"Huh. Much less dramatic than some I've had. Can we do this now?" He spared Hamon another pointed glance. "Without the commentary, if you please."

Daleina closed her eyes, her body still, her face blank. Ven recognized the look—she was focusing outward, feeling for spirits. He waited, patiently, somewhat patiently, not at all patiently. His fingers were itching to hold his knives, the comforting weight in his hands, but he kept them sheathed. If they were going to have any element of surprise, it was best not to look like a dangerous murderer.

She opened her eyes. "Found one."

"That was fast," Hamon said.

"What did I say about no commentary?" Ven said. "The fact that one is nearby only proves they're targeting the most powerful women in Aratay." All of the heirs and candidates were gathering in the capital, awaiting the queen's announcement of the new heir rankings. Sata had been ranked first—the older heirs would want to know if they'd moved into her position, and the younger ones would want to know where they ranked with the rest.

"It's coming," Daleina said. She added, "Told you it wouldn't be able to resist."

"How did you do it?" Ven had doubted she was strong enough to command even one of the six spirits that had overcome Sata and Mari, but she'd been insistent.

"I asked it to come kill me."

Ven stared at her.

"Told you I hated this plan." Hamon picked up a scalpel as if it were a weapon and waited. "She has alarmingly self-sacrificial instincts."

Ven scowled and leveled a finger at her nose. "We'll talk about this later." Now it was Ven's turn. He climbed higher, positioning himself between two branches, and focused, feeling his heart race and his palms sweat. He'd missed this, he realized. Just pure fight. One goal clear: eliminate the threat. He readied his bow, fit an arrow, and prepared to draw. He scanned the trees—

There.

He drew and released.

It thunked into wood. He drew and released again, tracking the slight movement in the leaves. The second one hit—

he heard the shriek. He had to finish this quickly and quietly. Sprinting over the branches, he ran toward the sound. The spirit was there, an arrow stuck in its wooden thigh. Bark— its skin—spread to enclose the arrow, solidifying around the shaft, subsuming the point.

Healing, the spirit moved fast, aiming for the platform, where Daleina waited with Hamon in a circle of firemoss light. Ven felt his lips curl into a smile that was like the wolf's snarl. He swung above the spirit and then landed down, knife stabbing into its neck.

Spirits were hard to kill—they weren't like animals with bones and blood, or at least they weren't always. They could flow into the trees or the air or the water. This one was a wood spirit. He caught it as it tried to melt into the bark, pinned it with multiple knives to the wood, the iron in his blade stopping its transformation.

It had the face of a child. Ven wished he hadn't seen that. Its face was round with baby lips and pudgy cheeks and a button nose, but eyes that were pure green with no whites and hair that was downy moss. Its limbs were long, thin sticks, and it grappled with him, trying to pin him with branches.

"Don't," it said in a reedy voice. "Please don't, don't, don't."

He hated the speaking ones. It was too easy to forget that they weren't human, to think they had emotions, to think they were capable of empathy, when they didn't, they couldn't. He continued to grip his beloved knife.

"Is that what Sata said to you when you killed her?" Daleina said—she'd climbed up beside him. "How about Mari? Did they ask you to spare them? And did you?"

"Won't, won't, won't again."

"We don't believe you," Ven said. "Do you, Daleina?"

"You came to kill me," Daleina said.

"You commanded! Answered command. Always answer command. Always, always." It blubbered, its eyes filling with green-tinged tears.

"You've defied the queen," Ven said. "This must be your fate." He drew his knife back and then stabbed it into the spirit's neck. The spirit dissolved under him, into the tree, and he knew he'd missed. "Watch out, Daleina!"

Daleina had her own knife up, ready to throw, as the spirit flew at her. Leaping up onto the branch, Hamon sliced with his scalpel. Thorns grew out of the spirit's body, think and sharp as knives. Ven leaped toward the spirit, slicing at the thorns. He sheared off several and then Hamon drove his scalpel through the spirit's eye.

"Know me," Ven said as he drove knife after knife into the spirit's body, "for I am death to all oath breakers, promise renders, and betrayers. Know me, for I am the last sunset, the night without dawn, the winter without spring. I am pain to your pleasure, silence to your shout, stillness to your speed. I hunt death." At last, the spirit trembled and lay still, limp across the branch.

He heard Daleina suck in a ragged breath. He expected her to break down. Killing a spirit wasn't easy. "That was poetic," she said.

"I have my moments," he said, and then: "This is the part where we run."

It started with the bark around the body: it grayed, turned brittle, and then crumbled, and then it spread, across the bark of the branch, blackening as if burnt.

"Come. Quickly. Bring the light."

"Let me look at her wounds first," Hamon said, pulling out his medicine kit.

"Live first, heal later," Ven said. He hauled Daleina onto her feet. She was clutching her side. "Are you going to bleed out, or can you jump?"

"Jump," she said.

Taking the lantern of firemoss, Hamon grabbed her hand, and together they followed Ven, leaping onto the next tree as the decay spread down the trunk and up to the branches. They ran along the branches as the dead wood spread to the nearby trees. Behind them, Ven heard a creak and then a thunderous crash—the tree collapsing. Other trees began to crumble around them.

It took an hour until they were far enough away that Ven felt comfortable stopping. There were still a few more hours until daylight. Time enough to kill a couple more spirits. He waited while Hamon checked both of them thoroughly, bound their wounds, and made them drink an unpleasant concoction of herbs that was supposed to ward off infection.

The next two spirits were easy to kill, in comparison. Daleina lured them to their little circle of light, and Ven fought them from the shadows. He didn't give them a chance or warning or mercy. In the aftermath, the forest crumbled around them, and they moved on, evading the forest guards, choosing only uninhabited trees.

"One more before daybreak?" Ven checked the sliver of matte-gray sky above. It wouldn't be long until sunrise now, though it would take longer for the light to filter down to the forest floor. They'd been lucky tonight was a full moon, or all the shadows would have been impenetrable. As it was, the forest was woven from grays.

"She needs to rest," Hamon said.

"*She* needs to be able to talk for herself," Daleina said.

Ignoring them, Ven said, "So far, the spirits haven't talked to each other. In another day, it will be harder to lure the last three—warnings will have spread, and they might be smart enough to guess we're hunting them. Plus the forest guards will be looking for spirit killers. Best to do as many as we can quickly." Also, the queen had said the strongest spirit in the capital would be distracted tonight, giving them a window of opportunity. He wondered how she knew, then dismissed the question. Of course a woman as powerful and intelligent as Fara studied the habits of her enemies. "We've already cut their strength in half. One more tonight."

Daleina nodded. She pressed her lips together.

Ven admired that she didn't complain. He knew it wasn't easy, what he was asking of her. Sata had once described the feeling of reaching out to spirits as scooping out your own innards with a spoon, and Daleina was less powerful than Sata had been. But Daleina was motivated, and she was issuing a command no spirit could resist.

This time the spirit came quickly, as if it had been waiting precisely for a summons like this. Ven readied his bow, but the spirit dodged between the trees. *Dammit, it knows.* It must have heard about the spirit deaths. It clearly knew, or suspected, this was a trap.

"Be on guard," he ordered Daleina.

"Told you it was secret," the spirit hissed, keeping out of range of Ven's arrow. *Oh, great, it's a clever one,* Ven thought. "For you, only you. Told you our secret. But you told, so very sad. Told our secret. She said not to tell, but we told and you told."

Daleina held up her hand toward Ven. "Wait, not yet. Who said not to tell?"

He hesitated, then cursed himself. He shouldn't have listened to her. He'd lost the element of surprise, if he ever had it. This spirit seemed brighter than the others. He kept his knife ready, his arm tensed.

"Always obey," the spirit said. "Happy to obey this. You ask, and we oblige." The spirit landed on the ground and plants erupted from the soil. They wrapped around Daleina's ankles. Branches pinned Hamon to the ground. He sliced with his knife. Ven judged the distance between him and the spirit, and then leaped, pinning the spirit down. It thrashed beneath him, but Ven sliced its arm, distracting it.

"Wait!" Daleina cried again.

About to strike its heart, Ven stopped.

"Did someone order you to kill me? To kill Sata and Mari?"

"Secret," the spirit hissed. "Never tell."

"It's trying to trick you," Hamon said. "Don't trust it."

Ven drew his knife back again.

"Halt!" a voice cut across the forest. "Do not move. Do not harm that spirit. I have an arrow trained on your heart and on the heart of your companion, and I *will* shoot."

Ven froze. Conversationally, he said, "You must have an impressive bow, to aim at two hearts at once." He eyed the spirit. It squirmed backward and squatted on a branch, regarding them with too-intelligent eyes. This spirit was child-size, with a bark-coated body and moss for hair. Its mouth was filled with thorns instead of teeth, and its feet were rooted into the branch, as if it had planted itself. It giggled, a sound like twigs breaking, and he wondered if he could stab it and deflect an arrow at the same time. It depended on whether their assailant had an arrow trained on him or on Daleina, or, improbably, both.

"Ordinary bow," the woman said, "impressive archer. Don't test me, or I'll skewer you. It is forbidden to kill spirits. Am I correct in assuming you are responsible for the slaughter of three other spirits this night?"

"Say nothing," Ven said softly to Daleina and Hamon. "She has no proof."

The woman had moved—her voice came from beside them now. He shifted his weight toward her, ready to shield Daleina, if necessary. "You realize that, in and of itself, is a damn suspicious thing to say."

"She has a point," Hamon said, also softly.

"Show yourself!" Daleina called. "Who are you?"

"Lieutenant Alet of the Palace Guard," the woman said. "I've been tracking you. You've been having a busy night, Champion Ven. Care to tell me why you decided to squander the queen's goodwill, as well as abandon your duty to the great forests of Aratay, and slaughter spirits?"

He heard Hamon swallow hard before whispering, "She's a guard. What do we do?"

Briefly, Ven was surprised she was palace guard, not forest guard, this far from the heart of the capital, but he had more important matters to worry about than who had jurisdiction. Ven's eyes didn't leave the spirit. His fingers itched on the handle of the knife. So quick and it would be over. Except this wasn't the last spirit. Six killed Sata and tried to kill Daleina. He flashed to a memory of Sata's funeral, the palace guard crowded into Heroes Grove, carrying her body in, and took a risk. "I'm hunting the spirits who murdered the Heir Sata."

"Ven!" Daleina hissed.

He forced himself to look away from the spirit and fix his eyes on the branch where he suspected the palace guard lurked. He wondered if she was alone. Most likely not, which was a plausible explanation for how two arrows could be targeted on them at once. "Sata worked with the palace guard. Did you know her?"

There was silence for a moment. "Release the spirit. I believe we need to talk."

He was taking a risk, he knew, but the palace guard had mourned her. "Daleina, tell it to leave." They could capture it again, if necessary. It would be wary, but if Ven was wrong about the sympathies of this lieutenant, then it was best for her not to directly witness them killing the spirit. She couldn't report what she hadn't seen, and so far all she had were suspicions.

The spirit's feet broke from the branch, and flowers burst from its toes and fingertips. Running along the branch on all fours, it glanced back to make sure they weren't following. Ven spared it a glance and hoped he was making the right decision. It galled him to let revenge slip through his fingers.

But he waited, outwardly calm, until the guard emerged along the branch, holding a bow with two arrows fitted. As she came closer, she repositioned the arrows, angling them inward. At this distance, he realized, she hadn't been exaggerating—she could have hit both of them. He hadn't realized she was so close, or so skilled. If he hadn't been so focused on the spirit . . .

She was young, about Daleina's age or possibly even younger, with black hair that sported a skunklike white streak down the center and black eyes that glittered as she came closer to the firemoss lanterns. Jumping onto their branch, she lowered her bow and straightened. "Heir Sata was like the big sister I never had. When my unit received word of the first spirit killed tonight . . . I left my unit to look for you."

No partner, then. He felt his shoulders unbunch and his rib cage loosen. Plus she was sympathetic, to the point of disobedience. He'd guessed correctly.

"Then why did you make us let the spirit go?" Daleina asked.

"Because the spirits are not the enemy," the lieutenant said, then she shook her head. "You have no reason to trust me, but you must. I began searching for you as soon as I heard—I knew you were the ones who needed to see."

Ven didn't move. "See what?"

"See who killed Heir Sata."

VEN TRUSTED LIEUTENANT ALET, UP TO A POINT. SHE was still a stranger—just because she looked like she could be one of Daleina's friends, that did not mean she was trustworthy. Plus she was being tight-lipped about who or what exactly she expected to them to see. They wouldn't believe her if she told them, she claimed. He pulled Hamon aside. "Go to Headmistress Hanna and tell her everything. Swear her to secrecy, but tell her the queen has given permission for these spirits to be hunted. Others can do it our stead, if necessary." Or rescue them from jail, if necessary.

"I'm not leaving Daleina or you," Hamon said.

Ven was certain the "or you" was an afterthought. He wondered if allowing their relationship to progress had been a mistake. It was one thing for Hamon to put Daleina above orders, but what if Daleina prioritized Hamon's safety over that of Aratay? *She wouldn't,* he thought. He knew her well enough to be certain of that. If it came to a choice, Hamon was in for heartbreak. *Just like I've had,* Ven thought ruefully. "You want to convince her not to come? Be my guest. But if you insist on coming with us, she won't have any backup if it turns out this is a trap." And it very well could be. One young guard couldn't hope to bring in a fully trained champion and candidate, but if she could get them into the palace, they could be subdued. It would be a clever move, and one that would win her a promotion. She seemed an enterprising young woman. "Come with us, and you can't help. Stay safe, and you might."

Hamon opened his mouth, then shut it and nodded. Sensible boy.

To Lieutenant Alet, Ven said, "He's a healer with duties at the academy. You'll let him go if Daleina and I accompany you."

"Of course," she agreed. "Provided he does not plan to harm any spirit on his own."

Hamon furrowed his eyebrows for a brief second, as if insulted, but then smoothed his face into his usual pleasant expression. He bowed briefly to Lieutenant Alet and then let his eyes linger on Daleina longer than was appropriate for mere travel companions. Then he clambered over the branches toward the academy, as instructed. To the palace guard, Ven said, "Lead on."

"I can't guarantee you'll hear what needs to be heard, but it's a full moon, plus the night before the heir announcements, so it's likely." She hesitated. "I must also ask you to protect the secret of the path we are about to take. It is known only to the palace guards."

Despite his suspicions, he was intrigued. He'd worked with the guards on palace defense, and he'd never been privy to any knowledge about secret paths.

"Also, apologies in advance for any discomfort." She struck out across a branch, creeping like a cat, with eyes darting in every direction.

"That's ominous," Daleina muttered, but followed nearly as nimbly across the branch. Ven joined her, and they traveled in silence until they reached a nondescript tree that held several derelict houses, their roofs caved in, and ladders with rotted rungs.

"This way," the guard whispered. "We keep these houses abandoned for security reasons. Hurry." She pushed aside one of the roofs to reveal a hole in the branch. She disappeared inside. Ven held Daleina's arm and dropped in first. *Clever,* he thought—it was a tunnel within the branch. He heard Daleina land behind him.

He hadn't planned on doing anything but hunt spirits tonight, but maybe this was better: he was hunting answers.

Together, they crawled behind the guard. Soon, it was darkness. Ven kept trying to see shadows in the black, to force it into shapes, but the dark wriggled away from his eyes. After a few turns, he lost his sense of direction. He felt as if the wood were pressing around him, and he pictured the weight of the houses above them. He'd never thought of himself as claustrophobic, but he felt as if he were inside a sausage grinder that would squeeze him into paste. He wanted to punch his way out of the wood. He thought of Sata—she must have felt so much fear within the wood sphere—and he thought of how Daleina had insisted on training even when she couldn't see. That kind of determination couldn't be taught. Someday she'd make a great queen . . . assuming this wasn't some kind of trap or trick. The air felt thin, and he was sweating within his armor. Spots danced across his eyes, through the darkness. "This may have been a bad idea. . . ."

"Sending Hamon was a good idea," Daleina said. "He'd hate this."

"Should I be asking questions about your relationship?" As her champion, he was supposed to look out for her emotional and mental well-being, as well as her magical and physical wellness. As himself, he had no interest in a conversation with her about that. Sata had managed her love life just fine without him, even marrying a man whom Ven didn't hate, which was more than he could have even asked. He thought of Sata's husband, how difficult this must be for him. If Ven didn't kill all six spirits, could he ever look him in the eye again, knowing how close he'd come to avenging Sata?

"Please don't," Daleina said. "Unless you want to hear about how he kisses, or how skilled a healer's hands are at—"

"Let's just crawl quietly."

Daleina laughed, and he marveled at the fact that she could laugh, in the darkness, within the wood. He felt much more like strangling someone, or pounding at the wood with every bit of strength in his muscles. But he sucked in air, and it tasted like wet wood pulp. The wood beneath his hands was soft and wet as well, and he felt it fill under his fingernails and coat the skin of his palms. If Daleina hadn't been with him, he might have lost it.

"Down," the guard said.

"Where—" he began, and then the wood wasn't there beneath his hand as he reached forward and he fell, crashing against the side and then sliding and tumbling down. He heard Daleina shriek behind him as she slid after him. He reached his hands out and spread his legs, trying to slow his fall, and then the passageway twisted, and he crashed against it, slowing, until he skidded to a stop in a heap. Daleina crashed into him.

"Sorry!" she cried.

"Shh!" the guard whispered.

Silently, they disentangled, and then they felt their way forward. The feel of the wood changed, became less spongy, more like dirt. He saw a sliver of light ahead. He crawled toward it and emerged from between the roots of a tree, within the palace treasure pavilion.

The guard beckoned them forward.

He knew Fara the moment she walked into the pavilion. She faced away from him, but he knew the set of her shoulders, the fall of her hair, the shape of her arm, the force of her walk. She strode directly to the chalice of Chell and lifted it in her bejeweled hands. Chalice in her hands, she turned, and he glimpsed her face.

"So much beauty," Fara said.

Soft, in his ear, Daleina whispered, "Is that the queen?"

He didn't move, didn't speak, just stared at Fara and tried not to think about why the guard had brought them here, to watch her.

Another voice spoke. "Not as beautiful as you, my queen." It was a thin, reedy voice that could have been female or not. Ven tried to see its source.

"The things we make say more about us than our words." She twisted the chalice. Candlelight flickered on its surface, bending the amber light around its curves. "In that way, we are alike, your kind and mine. We are both makers."

"You are pensive tonight." The speaker shifted—there, a shadow, between the pillars. "Tell me what you wish of me and mine."

"Tell me the reports from the border," Fara said.

"The new queen tests us. She prods, pokes, and then retreats."

"Keep it guarded."

"As you wish."

"Anything else?" the queen asked.

The speaker stepped out of the shadows, and Ven heard Daleina suck in a hiss of air, for it was clear that the other wasn't human. She—it—was as tall as the queen, with a woman's body dressed in translucent green silk that shifted around her body as she moved, but her head was that of an owl, with a curved beak, black eyes, and feathers that trailed down her neck into wings that lay on her back like a cape. "You must have felt the deaths."

"I did."

"And will you punish the perpetrators?"

"Of course."

Ven stiffened. She had to be lying. Unless he'd been naïve again, unless he was her scapegoat again. But no, of course she had to lie to the spirit.

Queen Fara added, "*If* they are caught. My guards have found no clues as of yet, but I will instruct them to remain vigilant." His shoulders relaxed—she was protecting him. This must be the spirit she'd spoken of, the strongest in the capital. She was distracting the spirit for his sake. *Thank you, my queen,* he thought. He silently apologized for the hideous doubts that had crept into his mind ever since the guard led them here. "But perhaps there is still an opportunity here. . . ." She laid the chalice back on its pedestal, then swept across the pavilion and halted in one of the archways, silhouetted in the candlelight as she looked out across the gardens. "Tomorrow is the heir announcement. I will call on yours to show my will—all eyes will be on the palace, and I want to create beauty they will not soon forget. They must remember I am still queen. This position is not open to them."

Ven shifted, peering into the shadows. Beside him, he heard Daleina breathing, quietly, shallowly. She hadn't moved. The guard was silent and still, her breathing slow and steady—she wasn't surprised by this.

"You will heal the broken spaces their deaths left behind. Regrow the forest. Strengthen the roots and the limbs."

"Ahh, and this will be a sufficient miracle to impress your new heirs, my queen. A reminder of your power, your specialness, your strength."

"Precisely," Queen Fara said.

The owl woman folded her hands together, her long fingers crossing over one another, as if in prayer. "This is not easy work, this miracle. It will cost. One village."

Ven felt as if the air had soured. His chest hurt, his ribs felt tighter, and he refused to examine the thoughts that swirled through his mind. She couldn't . . . wouldn't . . . Not Queen Fara. Not his Fara.

Fara held up a slender finger. "Three families, no more than twelve deaths, and you must wait until a full day after the heir announcement. No heirs this time. I will not have the miracle undermined. Understood?"

"It is agreed." Gliding across the pavilion, the owl woman held her hand over the chalice. She dragged the point of her fingernail over the flesh of her palm. Three drops of saplike blood fell into the chalice with a soft ping. She then carried the chalice back to Queen Fara, who lifted it to her lips and drank.

It took all of Ven's self-control not to burst out from their hiding place, rip the chalice from her lovely hands, and shatter it on the floor.

CHAPTER 25

Headmistress Hanna served the tea herself, in porcelain cups marked with the academy's seal. Her hands shook, and the liquid splashed onto the saucer. She set the teapot down, stirred in sugar, and forgave herself for not being calm while contemplating regicide. "You know she will not abdicate. You know her too well to think otherwise."

Ven looked as if he'd aged a decade in one night. He stood by the wide window and watched dawn rise through the branches of the trees. Overhead, the sky was the bluest blue, a beautiful day to hold such ugly thoughts. Hanna wished there was something she could say to make this easier for him, for all of them. She wished that the guardswoman hadn't dumped the matter into their laps, but in truth, she was grateful. At least they knew for certain now. The guardswoman, Lieutenant Alet, had confirmed everything Ven and Daleina had said, plus reported on other meetings she'd observed on other full-moon nights, before returning to her post at the palace. It was a chilling tale. Hence the need for tea.

"I had a cousin," Daleina said. "Her name was Rosasi." She was curled on a chair, knees to her chin, as if she were still a child, or as if she wanted to be a child, innocent again. "She used to tell wonderful stories about queens of the past, how they'd save whole villages. Never one single story about a queen destroying a village." The healer Hamon laid his hand on Daleina's shoulder, but Daleina seemed not to feel it. "The queen killed her, as sure as if she'd put a knife to her throat." Her eyes had that faraway look of a person seeing a vivid memory. So did Ven's. Hanna didn't doubt he was picturing the villages, the lives he'd tried to save, the ones he'd been too late to save.

"She sent the notes," Ven said. "There's good in her."

"Or guilt," Hamon said.

"Good enough to feel guilt."

"But not good enough to stop." Daleina lifted her head, and her expression was fierce. "All those messages she sent you . . . She *chose* for that to happen. For Rosasi, for . . ." She sucked in air as if she were trying to keep control of herself.

Hanna had suspected the messages were to assuage the queen's guilt, but she'd thought it was guilt about hiding her loss of control. But the truth was that Fara had never lost control, and she wasn't hunting traitors, as she'd once told Ven. She was trading innocent lives for power.

Slumping into a chair, Ven said, "She told me once she wasn't losing control. I hadn't believed her then. And later, she let me think . . . I am a fool."

"I knew her too, and I never suspected." Hanna tried to make her voice gentle, to reassure, to be calm, even though she wanted to rage until every shred of glass shattered.

Ven dropped his face into his hands. "Sata."

"And Mari," Daleina said.

"She also nearly killed Daleina," Hamon said. "I can't forgive that."

No—forgiveness was certainly not in the cards anymore. Headmistress Hanna could see only one solution. Queen Fara was violating the very core of what it meant to be queen. She was betraying every Renthian who had ever lived, who had ever feared the spirits, who had ever hoped for salvation. She could not be allowed to continue, and now that they knew she wasn't losing control, there was no hope that the spirits would stop her. Hanna saw the only solution clearly—and hated it.

"I remember when she first came to the academy," the headmistress said. "She was top in everything. So much promise." She remembered the fierceness in Fara's face as she passed the trials, the dedication to every class, the way she conquered every test as if her life depended on it. "So much fear."

"Fear?" Ven snorted. "Her?"

"Oh, yes. So very afraid of death, especially at the hands of spirits. So very afraid of failing. And so she never did. She was top in every class, first in every test, chosen as a candidate before all her classmates, ranked first heir. Perhaps that is where this all went wrong." Hanna sat at her desk and made herself sip her tea. It was important that she look calm. The others had not yet drawn the conclusion she had. She was going to have to lead them there. "She will never abdicate, and yet she cannot continue as queen. Otherwise, there will be more deaths of innocents, and when will it stop? She will become older, weaker, and her fear will grow. It will become worse, not better. It already has. She not only slaughters innocents, but she kills heirs, our future protectors."

"She's afraid of the wrong things," Daleina said. "Afraid the people will think she's weak if she doesn't keep supplying miracles. Afraid the heirs want to replace her. Not afraid of the spirits." Hanna nodded. The girl showed insight. It was entirely possible that Fara had targeted Sata because she was the best heir and Mari because she was the best candidate, fearing that they'd replace her.

And Daleina . . . She'd grown the spires in North Garat. Fara must have seen her as a threat too. Perhaps she saw the same things Ven had seen in the girl. Determination. Intelligence. Resourcefulness.

"She told me Greytree was destroyed because she suspected traitors," Ven said. "It is possible her paranoia started long ago, and I did not see it. Did not want to see it." His voice sounded a lot smaller than she could ever remember it. "Maybe I still don't want to see it."

"None of us do," Hanna said soothingly. "None of us did." But she was just saying words now for the sake of saying something. She did not wish to say it, the thing that *needed* saying. She wanted Ven to draw his own conclusion. She wanted Daleina to understand. And Hamon not to condemn. There was only one solution, and yet she couldn't find it in herself to voice it.

"Poison," Hamon said.

All of them looked at him.

"It can be quick, painless, and impossible to detect. Perhaps nightend berries."

Ven turned from the window. In a low, steady voice, he asked, "What are you saying?" A dangerous voice. Hanna kept her hands folded on her desk, around her tea.

Hamon didn't flinch. "She must ingest it, though."

Hanna knew of nightend berries. Rare, deadly. They'd been one of the poisons tried against the spirits, before the link between spirit and land was proven. No effect on them, but on humans . . . Usually the plants were rooted out as soon as they were found, to minimize the risk to inexperienced woodsmen and children out scavenging. Even the meat of animals who had eaten the berries was poisonous to humans. A few healers used the berries to help ease the suffering of the dying, but even they rarely carried it. A poison so powerful was not handled lightly. "The queen has her food and drink tested, always. She has never even taken tea from me. Fear of death, as I said, combined with the fear of betrayal."

"You are speaking of killing the queen," Ven said, his voice ground out.

"I am speaking of killing a murderer before she kills again. Before she destroys another village. Before she kills Daleina. She has tried once. She will try again. Do you doubt it?"

Ven was silent.

"Surely there's another way," Daleina said. "If we appeal to her—"

"Yes, we can try," the headmistress said. "But if that fails?" *When* it fails. Of that, Hanna had no doubt. "She sends you messages. She *knows* what she does is wrong, yet she doesn't stop."

"Maybe she feels she has no alternative," Daleina said.

"I will confront her," Ven said. "I will tell her she *must* abdicate."

"And if she refuses?" Hanna pressed.

"I will inform the council of champions, before she meets with the owl spirit again," Ven said. "The wood spirit said she meets with her every full moon. I'll talk to them, and the council will have a month to decide how to act."

"And then what?" She rose. "At best, they will not believe you. You are the disgraced champion. They will not see you as reliable, given the severity of the charges you will level. At worst, though . . . at worst, they will believe you, and they will act against the queen. What will she do if her champions turn against her? Be honest, Ven, what will she do?"

He looked hollow. "She will fight. She will call the spirits and defend herself. She will brand them all traitors and destroy them."

"She has become a queen of blood," Hanna said gently. "Death will fill her reign. She must be stopped. At least this way, we can preserve her legacy. She will be remembered kindly in the minds of her people. Expose her for what she truly is . . . there is no good that can come of that. It could plunge us into civil war, human against human, while the spirits are free to hunt us down. We must make the choice that will preserve the most lives."

"She's the *queen*," Ven said, pleading.

"Precisely," Hanna said. And then she waited, silent, for him to work through his thoughts. He was a logical man as well as a noble one. He had seen firsthand the damage that Fara could do, had already done. It would only get worse.

"I must talk to her first." Ven stalked to the door.

"Wait!" Hamon jumped to his feet. "What are you going to tell her? She'll come for us—for Daleina, especially—if she knows we know."

He stopped. "I will protect Daleina with every breath in my body. You can count on that." Turning to Daleina, he handed her his best knife, in its leather sheath. He didn't give her time to object or question. "Keep this, in case I don't return."

And then he walked out the door. Hanna could have stopped him. Called him back. Tried to force him to see that it would be pointless. She knew Fara well enough to know that she'd never abdicate, and she wasn't going to stop. She'd been doing this for years, even though she knew it was wrong. Squaring her shoulders, she looked at Hamon. He was fidgeting beside her desk—she noticed he'd found the string that opened the office door. "How do you suggest we force the queen to eat the berries? The queen has significant defenses at her disposal. Additionally, it would not benefit Aratay for any of us to be caught in this act."

It was Daleina who answered. "She drinks the owl spirit's blood, after she bargains. Three drops. If the poison were in the spirit's blood . . ." She swallowed, as if the words she was saying tasted foul. "Humans have been poisoned by tasting tainted meat. Wouldn't ingesting blood work?"

Hamon nodded.

There was beauty in this proposal. "It would give Ven

a chance to convince her and us a chance to safeguard our people against the aftermath of her death—the guards-woman said the queen meets the owl-faced spirit only on the full moon, so we will have a month to prepare," Hanna said. "If the queen never makes another bargain, she won't be harmed. But if she chooses to kill again . . . then she will be stopped."

THE PLAN WAS BEAUTIFUL IN ITS SIMPLICITY: SUMMON the owl-faced spirit, dose her, release her. Hamon had assured them the poison would linger in her blood for at least a month—he'd been studying nightend berries and had professed confidence in its properties. Daleina was tasked with drawing the owl spirit to the academy. Predictably, Hamon hated her part of the plan. "I don't see why you need to be bait again."

"Because it works," Daleina said, trying to stay patient, at least while he was handling the poison. They were in the headmistress's office, and he was straining the nightend juice. He'd instructed her to stay against the wall, opposite him, until every drop was in the vial. "We know she plans to kill people. She'll be happy to have a volunteer."

" 'It.' It's not a person. And it will kill you, given half the chance." He poured the juice into another vial, his hands steady, his eyes fixed on the glass tube.

"My friends won't let it kill me." That was the other half of the plan: the other candidates would put the owl woman to sleep. Beauty in its simplicity.

"I hate seeing you risk yourself again and again." He screwed the top onto the vial of poison, laid it gently on a cloth, and began prepping the syringe.

"You have to stop trying to protect me. I am choosing to risk myself. It's what I do. If you can't handle it, then maybe you should stop caring about me."

He froze, and she both wanted to breathe the words back

in and shout them louder. She couldn't carry the weight of his worry on top of her own. It was bad enough to even be contemplating what they were doing. As they stared at each other, she told herself it wasn't truly murder. It would be Queen Fara's actions that condemned her. If the queen did not make another bargain with the owl spirit, she wouldn't be harmed. If she tried to condemn more innocents, then she would be killed. Her own actions—

No. This was murder. Regicide. No matter how justified it was, she would not lie to herself about what it was she was choosing. She was going to live with this guilt and not try to rationalize it away. She was crossing a line she could never uncross. It was both the right thing and the wrong thing at the same time, but she was doing it anyway. For Greytree. To prevent another Greytree, because that was why she had done all of this—apprenticed herself to the hedgewitch, entered the academy, trained with Champion Ven, given up a normal life and a safe future—all so that what happened to her village would never happen again. This was the way to prevent it. And if it made her a murderer instead of queen, so be it.

She looked at Hamon, her resolve settled. *I will do what needs to be done, with or without you.*

"Daleina . . . I love you."

She flinched. "Let's see this through, and when it's over . . . we will see if we're still the same people we were. You don't do what we're going to do and not change."

He tucked the vial of poison into his pocket and then stepped into a closet beside one of the headmistress's bookshelves. "What I feel for you will never change."

"Don't make promises you can't keep," she said as he closed the door. She stared at the closet for a long moment, wanting to fling it open, kiss Hamon, and take back her trying-so-hard-to-be-brave-and-wise words. He loved her. Surely he was right and that would survive this act.

Surely such love wasn't just for the stories.

Crossing to the headmistress's door, Daleina knocked once. Leaning against it, she listened—Headmistress Hanna was on the opposite side, at the top of the stairs. Her friends should be arrayed on the stairs beneath her.

At her signal, the headmistress began speaking, "My students . . . not my students for much longer. Today you will be named heirs, to serve for peace and prosperity in Aratay. It is a vast responsibility, as well as an honor, but I know you are all ready. You have worked hard, and I could not be prouder."

Daleina wondered what the others thought of the fact she wasn't with them. Were they worried about her? Did they think she'd quit? Should she? What she was doing wasn't an act of a loyal heir. *I'm loyal to Aratay,* she told herself. The queen wasn't Aratay. She felt her throat clog.

"There is one more task that remains ahead of you. Word has come to me that a spirit plans to disrupt the announcement ceremony. It is an old, powerful spirit—"

Daleina heard murmurs but not the actual words. Surprise? Concern?

"It will be drawn here, into my office, and then you must use your collective strength to put the spirit to sleep. It must sleep through the announcement, then wake unharmed, none the wiser. Remember the words: *Do no harm.*" The murmurs of agreement grew louder. "Will you join together for this one last task, as my students?"

From the stairs, from her friends, Daleina heard cries of yes as well as cheers. And she knew it was time. They'd command the spirit from the safety of the stairs. The headmistress had sworn to leave the door shut. No matter what happened, her friends would be fine. Hamon, fine. Ven, far away and fine. Daleina drew in a breath, concentrated, and sent her thoughts flitting out for the owl spirit. She knew she'd recognize it—and she did.

It was here, in the capital.

Of course it was.

And it was older, smarter, and more wild than any she'd felt before. Daleina crafted a single thought and sent it to her. *Kill me.*

She felt the owl spirit respond, like a purr: *Gladly.*

Daleina stood in the center of the office, in the pool of sunlight. She faced the window and tried to keep her mind clear and her thoughts focused. If this didn't work . . . if the others couldn't control the owl woman . . . if the spirit were stronger than their combined strength . . .

But she couldn't have those thoughts. Not here. Not now. She drew a breath and thought of Arin. She was doing this for her, so she would always be safe. She imagined Arin's bakery, imagined her laughing, imagined her someday marrying the baker's boy, imagined her parents beaming with happiness.

The owl spirit crashed through the window. Shards of glass flew across the room, and Daleina ducked, her arms in front of her face. "So, you are the one who wishes to die?" the spirit said, and Daleina felt shivers up and down her back.

Now!

And she added her mind to the command: *Sleep.* A single command, from seven soon-to-be heirs at once, plus the headmistress.

Sleep.

The owl spirit hesitated, swayed, shook her head, and then stalked forward, toward Daleina. *Why isn't it asleep?* Daleina backed up, bumping into a chair, and then maneuvering around it until she was against a bookshelf.

"So very curious: I seldom am asked for death. Tell me why."

Truth? A lie? Daleina felt as if her tongue were thick.

"Ah, have you reconsidered, now that you face your

death? So very human of you. I can taste your fear, thick in the air. It's as sweet as your sweat. Do you think you can change your mind so easily and that I will simply curl up and sleep, like a tame kitten? Oh no, my sweet, you asked me to kill you, and I have come."

She had to delay, give her friends more time. "Before you kill me . . . I'd like to ask a question, if you please. Why do you kill humans? All of you. Why kill us?"

"Because you do not belong here." The owl woman snapped her beak together. "A child's question, and you are no child. You are Daleina of Greytree, candidate soon to be heir. I know you. You do not wish to die. Why did you call me?"

"You kill innocents. You don't have to. We could all live together, in peace."

"There can be no peace with humans. You mar the peace. There can only be peace when you and all of your kind are gone from Renthia." She sounded so reasonable, as if she weren't calling for their extinction.

"Then why"—she licked her lips and hoped that the others couldn't hear her through the door; surely, it was thick enough, for the headmistress's privacy—"bargain with the queen? If we're all your enemies, why offer her miracles? That proves you're willing to compromise. I believe you must want peace too—"

The owl woman laughed, a horrible shrieking sound. "You believe we compromise with her? How very entertaining. There have been others who have thought as you. Others who thought we could be tempted by other things. But no, there is only one thing we wish: your eradication."

"That's not your only wish, though. You want to build! Grow things. Shape them. I know that." Everything she'd learned in the academy, everything she'd seen in the forest, supported that. The spirits wanted to both kill and build— and the queen was supposed to resolve the contradiction between those two desires, to keep their land in balance.

"Indeed. And you stand in our way of that."

"We could work together." Daleina wondered what Hamon was thinking of this conversation. He could hear every word. "What if we didn't control your kind? No more coercion. You build, as you wish, without our commands, and in exchange, you do no harm."

"Idealistic child. It is the 'harm' bit that is nonnegotiable. We *must* harm. It is who we are, and what we do. Just as it is who you are to resist your inevitable death, to reach for life, to try to bargain with the embodiment of your death." The owl woman crossed to her, and Daleina tried frantically to focus. *Sleep, sleep, sleep.* The owl woman stroked her cheek with a fingernail. "It would be delightfully fun to watch all your illusions shattered, but you did issue a command that pleases me more."

"I withdraw the command."

"But I choose to fulfill it. You see, that is the secret that so few of your queens understand. It is always our choice, deep down. It may hurt us to refuse, even destroy what we are, but it can be done."

Daleina swallowed. This was going to fail. She was going to die, right now, with all her friends just outside the door.

Out of the corner of her eye, she saw Hamon step out of the closet. She wanted to yell at him no, their plan would fail if the owl woman saw him—if she knew she'd been injected, she'd warn the queen. But Hamon didn't move toward the spirit. Instead, he slipped behind the headmistress's desk and pulled the string before ducking out of sight.

The office door swung open, and the headmistress and all of Daleina's friends burst into the room. "Sleep," they commanded. As one, they marched toward the owl woman. *Sleep, sleep, sleep!*

The power of the combined command—strengthened by proximity—caught the spirit by surprise. Daleina felt her surprise like a ripple in the air. The owl woman's eyelids fluttered, and her hand dipped down. "Betrayal," she murmured, and then she crumpled to the floor.

So much for her choice, Daleina thought, and then shuddered. That had been close. Much too close.

Daleina's friends surrounded a shaking Daleina. Chattering, their words fell over each other, talking about how difficult it was, how they'd needed the proximity, how powerful they'd felt when their commands at last united. They'd never felt a spirit resist like that, hadn't known it was possible. If Daleina hadn't opened the door . . .

The headmistress shooed them out. "Don't wake her now. I'll summon a healer to keep an eye on her. Now you must all attend the announcement ceremony." Daleina met her eyes, and then she was swept down the spiral stairs, ensconced among her friends.

It was done.

DRUMS SPREAD WORD, CALLING ALL CANDIDATES TO the heir announcement. As Daleina and the others descended from the headmistress's office, all her friends began buzzing between their rooms and the bathroom, preparing for the announcement. Feeling as if she were floating through a nightmare, she joined them, dressing in the white robes that the caretakers provided. Caretaker Undu was there, overseeing it all, ensuring that everyone looked presentable, hair neatly pinned, faces clean, bruises hidden. If she was missing Mari on this day, it did not show on her face. She was only efficient action. Daleina let it all swirl around her as she prepared.

Considering what they'd just done, it seemed surreal.

She joined the others as they filed out of the academy, again toward the palace. This time there was no restraining the citizens. They had dressed for a party and were handing out drinks and food as they watched the candidates parade past them. She craned her neck as she went, looking for her family in the sea of people, but she didn't see them. Perhaps they'd been able to make the journey. Perhaps they hadn't.

Revi gripped Daleina's hand. "I'm so nervous I could wet myself."

Linna wrinkled her nose. "Please, try to refrain."

"I don't trust myself. I feel like any moment, my grip on appropriate behavior is going to slip and I'll start clucking like a chicken. That's how unreal this is. Chicken unreal."

"You'll be fine," Daleina told her. "Our part is over. All we have to do is hear the news." And look on the face of Queen Fara, the woman who had destroyed Greytree. *I shouldn't have come,* Daleina thought. She should have stayed behind at the academy. Helped Hamon. Waited with the headmistress. Made sure the spirit woke and left without hurting anyone.

She wondered if Ven was in the palace, if he'd been able to have his audience with the queen.

If she'd listened.

If she'd killed him.

The crowd swirling around them, they progressed through the capital to the palace. She felt, oddly, vulnerable, as if her secrets were written on her skin, and the queen would read them instantly. She slid herself behind Revi and Linna. Her hands were sweating, and she clasped them together. Nerves were normal, she told herself. No one would guess what she knew. No one had guessed anything—and that was part of the problem. Queen Fara had hidden her secrets well. No one suspected she was sacrificing the innocent. No one knew the cost in blood of all the new schools and libraries and bridges and homes.

Throngs of people had gathered, filling the trees around the palace. Vendors hawked food and drink to the spectators, and musicians riled the crowd, mixing dancing reels with battle hymns until it was a cacophony of melodies and shouts. Acrobats, the Juma, performed in the trees. Their

faces were painted blue, red, and green, and their bodies
were in a riot of colors. In duos, they flipped their bodies from branch to branch, and the crowd cheered as they
landed, ribbons trailing behind them. As a woman swirled
another ribbon around a branch, a man leapt, grabbed it,
and swung, and then another followed, until they were all
sailing from branch to branch. Catching one another, they
posed in a pyramid—feet on knees, arms stretched to their
utmost. The crowd exploded in applause, and the drums beat
out another rhythm as the acrobats split apart, swinging and
spinning from the ribbons, twisting them around their bodies. Daleina found herself staring at them, unable to look
away, as they contorted their bodies above the crowd.

And yet there was so much more to see.

Across, on a nearby platform, other performers had
seized their chance before the audience. One man stood on
a roof, loudly reciting poetry. Another, a girl, tossed balls
in the air, flipped in a somersault, and then caught them.
Three men with stringed instruments strummed so fast their
fingers were blurred, and a woman danced on top of a crate,
flicking her skirts back and forth in rhythm, bells jangling
on her ankles and wrists.

All music ceased when the ornate door blew open. Air
spirits carried the queen's throne outside, lifting her high
into the air. Cheers then erupted, complete with bells and
trumpets, until Queen Fara held up both hands. "The first
heir is . . ."

Fire spirits wrote names in the sky as she called out the
names, ranked by order of their strength. Cheers exploded
with each name, and the candidates were pushed forward to
kneel in front of the queen. She laid a thin circlet of silver on
each of their brows.

Daleina cheered with the others as each name was said—
names she didn't recognize, of heirs who had already proven
themselves, and of other candidates from other academies,

as well as her friends: Revi, Linna, Iondra, Zie, Evvlyn, Airria . . . She heard the absence of Mari's name from the list. And she waited to hear her own name. And waited, as more names were called.

Her stomach began to clench, and then she forced herself to breathe. The queen had finally seen what others had seen Daleina's entire life: she wasn't worthy to be an heir. She wasn't powerful enough. *You knew that,* she told herself. Hadn't she seen that herself during the trials? Hadn't she already decided she wasn't worthy? Faced with this moment, though, she realized she still hadn't let go of her old dream. She knew she wasn't going to be queen—she'd accepted that—but she had still wanted to be an heir.

Maybe it was for the best. One of her friends would become queen. At least no one could say she was committing regicide out of ambition.

Still, it hurt. She had worked hard. She had given up countless other futures. She had defined herself by this goal. It was time to finally accept that this wasn't her future.

"Daleina of Greytree."

The fire spirits wrote her name in the sky.

She felt a shudder shake through her. She was an heir. The last heir. She was ranked last, dead last out of all fifty heirs, but she'd been named. She knew she should feel like cheering. She'd worked so very hard for this, defied so many expectations, but she felt as if her smile were painted on her face.

Pushed forward, she was suddenly in front of the queen, who smiled at her, tight-lipped, and then laid a circle, cool metal, on her brow, and all Daleina could think was, *Murderer.*

Her friends hugged her, and they were all hugging and crying. But inside she felt cold, as cold as the circle of silver she wore.

So very young, Fara thought.

As the queen looked out over the faces of her heirs, she noted the unclouded brightness in their eyes, the innocent joy in their smiles, the relaxed happiness in their arms and shoulders as they absorbed the fact that they had succeeded and were chosen, fulfilling their hopes and dreams, not to mention their families' hopes and dreams. Each of them, on the cusp of spreading their wings, with only one barrier between them and their destiny: her life. And she was supposed to feel joy and congratulate them on their accomplishments. So very innocent, so very foolish, so very pathetic. She wanted to tell them their hopes and dreams were stupid. Find a nice shop somewhere, sell charms, marry and have kids . . . or not. Travel or pick a small village and never leave. Tend a garden and a one-room house. Listen to the canopy singers at dawn. Gather berries between the roots in the autumn . . . or not. Just don't do *this,* tossing your life away in pursuit of something that only brings pain, regret, and guilt.

Of course she said none of this. She spread her arms wide, knowing she looked like the heroic savior from some ballad, knowing that a half-dozen poets were scribbling painful metaphors to capture the moment and that later she'd have to listen to another half-dozen ballads in deep, serious voices. "You are the hope, the security, the future of Aratay—a heavy burden, I know, but take comfort in the fact that the burden is not and may never be yours. Your country is whole, and your queen is strong."

She swept forward, knowing her people would follow. Some, from curiosity. Others were herded along the paths by her guards, in a friendly fashion, of course. At her signal, ribbons were tossed from the higher boughs. Like colorful rain they fell, and the people reached their hands up, catching them, and danced with the ribbons between them. Musicians struck up a suitably inspiring march, full of horns and drumbeats that sliced through the cacophony of voices behind her and pulled them inexorably in her wake.

It would have been simpler to put the population on leashes and drag them where she wanted them to go, but this way, they at least maintained the illusion of choosing to follow her. *Sheep,* she thought. She'd been right to dread this day. It only reminded her that all her sacrifices were to improve the lives of ungrateful, fickle idiots, who would tear her down without remorse and then worship the next queen just as blindly as they'd adored her.

The dead patch of forest was ahead, with husks of houses, crumbled trees, and dead branches. No birds settled on the stumps. No animals lived in the fallen homes. Even the wind didn't blow here. Behind her, the music silenced, and the people fell quiet, watching. She didn't have to look behind her to know they'd spread out to see, none of them crossing from the living city to the dead.

She inhaled.

She'd never attempted this. To her knowledge, no one had. Dead patches were left alone until the spirits reclaimed them, and then they were tamed. It was a process that took years, and she wanted it done in a few minutes, to show them, to show herself—she could work miracles. She wasn't just *a* queen; she was the queen they needed. Spreading her hands wide, she expanded her consciousness, touching the spirits around her.

True to the owl woman's word, the spirits waited for her, at the edges of her consciousness. She called them in: first, fire. She sent it blazing over the dead patch, scorching what remained until it crumbled to ash. Rich, fertile ash. The fire roared in front of her, and the brilliant orange-red filled her eyes. Heat warmed her skin. She didn't move, keeping her hands out, controlling the fire, forcing the spirits to keep it contained to only the dead patch. The spirits wanted to struggle against her—they wanted to spread the fire to the capital, to dance on the roofs of the houses, to consume the bridges, to fill the air with smoke—but they didn't. They obeyed. And when the remains of the grove were ash below, Fara dispersed the fire spirits and called for the earth spirits. Reclaim the soil. Make it fertile again. Prepare it.

Air spirits carried the seeds to her, the acorns to grow the trees and the brambles to grow the bushes. They dropped them on the ground, and the earth spirits swallowed them. Next, water. Rain fell only on the blackened land. Then wood spirits—*grow*. Higher, faster, stronger, and the trees burst out of the soil.

Behind her, she heard gasps, and she permitted herself a small smile. Yes, the heirs could summon all six spirits. They could bring fire and rain. They could encourage trees to grow and fruit to ripen. But not on the scale that she could. Not with the spirits working *with* her, instead of against her, for that was what her bargain with the owl woman achieved: Fara didn't have to fight them; she merely had to use them.

And use them she did. When she finished with this dead patch, she moved to the next, and then the next, until she had repaired all the damage that the spirits' deaths had caused. Through it, her people followed her. She heard the word "miracle" echoing about and let it sink into the bones of her people.

Yes, it was a miracle. *And it's because of me, because of my strength, because of my choices, that it's possible.* She was the queen they needed. She was indispensable. She was also bone-deep tired, but she did not let that show.

Summoning two air spirits, she let them lift her into the air. She sat regally, as if on the throne, and waved to her people as they carried her to the palace. Below, her people cheered so loudly that their voices filled every inch of the air. She instructed the spirits to carry her up, high along the palace wall, until they reached her balcony. They set her down, and she turned once more to wave at her people, to see the worshipful adoration in their eyes. It was better than food.

Allowing her skirts to swirl around her, she swept off the balcony and into her bedroom. Curtains fell behind her. Then, and only then, did she allow herself to sag. Fara sank into a cushioned chair. She dropped her face into her hands and let the trembling that had been building inside her shake through her body.

"You work miracles, my queen," a voice said.

She jerked upright, and then she relaxed. "Ven. You're a welcome sight."

He stood by the door to her bedchamber, dressed in his formal green armor. She noticed there were circles beneath his eyes, as if he hadn't been sleeping well. He worked himself hard, too hard, but that was one of the things that she'd always admired about him: his drive. He took his duty so very seriously. "You told your guards I was welcome here."

She laughed—she knew he would discover that soon, that she'd granted him full access. "I keep no secrets from my guards." The palace courtiers had known she'd taken him to her bed, and she saw no reason to hide it. She'd instructed her guards to allow him in whenever he requested it, the same way she used to, before everything had become more complicated. It was one thing she could do to begin to erase the years of his disgrace. She wondered if he'd truly forgiven her for that or not.

"No secrets? My queen, I know that is not true."

Uncoiling from the chair, she crossed to him. She still felt tired, but he could make her forget that. Yes, this was exactly what she needed. Stopping in front of him, she ran her hand up his armored chest. "So strong and so stern. Come, it's a celebratory day, is it not? You can hear them outside. Parties will stretch late into the night. There's no more duty today."

He caught her hand in his. "Fara, you must break your bargain with the spirits."

She froze and then withdrew her hand. "You know I hate it when you tell me what to do." She kept her voice light, as if this were still a bedroom game. *What did he know?*

As if he read the question in her mind, he said, "You met with a spirit with a woman's body and an owl's head. I saw you. I heard you."

She felt as if everything inside her had turned to stone. "Tell me what you heard."

"You, allowing death, in exchange for miracles." There was pain in his eyes. She could see it. He thought she'd betrayed him, his trust, her promises. She'd known he'd see it this way. He wouldn't understand.

Fara turned abruptly from him and walked across the room, toward the curtain that covered the balcony. She didn't open it. Outside, she could hear the shouts, laughter, and music. It drifted on the air. "They celebrate the possibility of my death."

"They celebrate their lives, which they believe they have because of you. They don't know you've been bargaining away those very lives that you're sworn to protect."

"Always so righteous. Always so certain you're right. Right and wrong, so very clear. Good and evil. Night and day. But there are shadows you refuse to see. Choices that aren't right or wrong, but simply better or worse."

"Don't try to justify it, Fara. You know what you're doing is wrong."

Fara touched the curtain, widening it to see the people outside, figures in the trees. She let it fall back down. "I was chosen, out of all the heirs at the coronation ceremony. Yes, I was ranked first, but the spirits don't have to listen to that. They alone choose who they deem the strongest, the one they believe can keep them from destroying what they have wrought. They make their own choice, to gift one heir with their trust, a precious trust. I believe they chose me because they knew I could make the difficult decisions. I could make the sacrifices. They knew I'd work with them toward a better Aratay, for both humans and spirits." She squared her shoulders and faced Ven. "And they were right: Aratay has flourished in my reign. More schools, hospitals, and libraries have been built in the past five years than in the prior fifty. On the whole, people are living safer, longer lives. Happier lives, because of me, because I am not willing to settle for my limitations, because I am willing to reach for more, on their behalf. When I die, I will be remembered as one of the great queens of Renthia, the greatest queen Aratay has ever known. I will leave a legacy of beauty and knowledge and prosperity, all the things that a people need and want. And yes, there was a cost. But I am a great queen because I have paid that cost, and you have no right to judge me based on unrealistic ideals. Without the safety I promise, how many more would die? How many would live in fear and ignorance, huddled in their huts? I sacrifice a few for the benefit of the many. How is this different from the generals who lead their soldiers to war? Or the parent who gives up his own happiness for his child's well-being?" Her voice had risen, as if she were making a speech. She lowered it. "That was not a rhetorical question."

He stood, unmoving, implacable, and she wanted to shake him.

"Always you, who sees me at my weakest," Fara said with a laugh that burned in her throat. "I begin to think it's fate. Except that I don't believe in fate . . . just as I know you don't. I believe it is we who must shape the world to be the way we wish it. My words still hold true, whether it is you who hears them or another. Judge me as you will, but I have acted in the best interests of Aratay."

"Always."

"There weren't traitors in Greytree, were there?" His voice felt rough, as if he hadn't used it in a long time. "Or any of the other villages?"

"No."

He swallowed, loudly enough that it made her own throat feel dry. "I thought you were losing control."

"I told you once I never lose control."

"All those villages . . . all those people . . ."

"For the glory of Aratay."

"Innocents."

"I know. And I know you think me deplorable. It is remarkable how you have held on to your idealism for so very long. Ven, do you truly think magic comes without a price?"

"You're sworn to protect the people."

"And I have. Ask any person you pass, Are they safer than they once were? Are their lives better? Do they have more food? Can their children go safely to school? Do they have art, music, literature, dance, laughter, life? Yes to all of that. Because of me."

"Because of the people you've killed."

"Because of the sacrifices that I've made."

"You didn't make any sacrifices," he said. "You sacrificed people you didn't know, strangers you've never seen, for your own glory. For your legacy. So that you can be the greatest queen Aratay has ever known."

"Is it wrong to want more for my people?"

"Yes!" He toned down his voice, which had also risen. "Yes, Fara. Can't you see that? You've crossed a line. Queens must protect their people, not allow them to be killed. Especially not when you're only doing it for the glory of yourself! You've violated your basic promise to this world." He sucked in air. "You cannot continue to do this."

"I cannot stop." Her smile was sad. Poor, sweet Ven, so certain he could save everyone, if only he flexed his muscles virtuously enough. "The spirits guard the border for me, for all of us. The mountains of Semo have a new, ambitious queen. If I stop, the border falls. If I stop, who will make the new homes, guard the new orchards, build all the bridges this country needs? This country has needs, Ven, and this is the only way to meet them all. We are growing, and there are growth pains. With the cooperation of the spirits—"

"But they aren't cooperating with you. They're *using* you! It started small, didn't it? A harmless bargain? They offered you a prize you couldn't resist at a price that seemed like very little. What was it at first, Fara? Who did you sacrifice? An old man, in his final days? A sickly child, unlikely to ever be healthy? A stranger with a pitiful life?"

It was a criminal at first, a man who had hurt a child, a man who felt no remorse, a man who was so consumed with hate that he deserved . . . That one had been easy. Easy too when she granted the spirits freedom within a jail, full of those who deserved punishment. But that hadn't satisfied the owl spirit or her followers for long. "I have put the needs of the many over the needs of the few. It is a choice that queens have had to make again and again in every generation."

"Not like this."

"Not like this," she agreed. "I am the first who dared

see beyond tradition, to see the potential for what we can achieve, human and spirit working together!"

"If you think you are working with that spirit, you are delusional. It wants your death. It wants all our deaths. Spirits don't believe in compromise."

"She wants peace! And the only way to achieve that is by satisfying those of her kind who thirst only for blood. Once they're sated—"

"They'll never be sated. You know that." He stepped toward her, and she instinctively took a step back, then stopped and stood unmoving as he crossed to her and put his hands on her shoulders. "Fara, you have to end this, before it becomes worse. Can't you see? This path only leads to more and more death."

"I know. But it's the path I've taken, and there is no way off it."

"Of course there is. There's always a way. I can help you. Others can. Fara, beautiful Fara, you are not alone. You think you shoulder the weight of the country—"

"I *do,* Ven. And I am alone. That's what it means to be queen." She wished she could command him to understand, control him the way she could a fire spirit. She wanted him to wrap his arms around her and quit looking at her as if she murdered babies with her own bare hands. "Everything I do, I do for Renthia. You were my only indulgence, and I sent you away—for Renthia. I gave up everything I am and everything I will be and became what Renthia needs: a strong queen in the forests of Aratay."

"You *are* strong, though, and you can be strong without these bargains."

"Not strong enough."

"Then abdicate. Give the crown to someone else. Let them be strong for a while, and let yourself be happy! You've given enough of yourself to Aratay."

Fara pulled away. "Is this about your candidate? You want her to be queen?"

"It's about you! Fara, don't you see? You cannot keep bargaining with killers."

"If I abdicate, I lose the power of the crown. Lose that power . . . and the spirits *will* kill me. I have controlled too many, angered too many, earned too much hatred. I wouldn't last the day."

"Then stay queen, but stop being the miracle queen. You don't need to do more than every queen that's come before. Spirits know, you've already done that anyway. But you have crossed the line from making things better to making things worse. You have to see that." His eyes softened, pleading.

"Can't you see that?"

"I don't know how to stop."

"Say no. Next time the owl spirit offers you a bargain, say no. Call the guards. Call me. Surround yourself with champions. We will kill this spirit for you, if you wish it."

"If not this spirit, there would be another, and another. Ven . . . If I say no and the miracles stop, people will wonder why. They'll doubt me. They'll fear."

"Fara, I discovered your secret. Others may too. And when they do, it won't be just doubt and fear they feel. It will be hate."

"That's why it must stay secret." She'd known that from the beginning. If her secret were ever learned, the people would kill her. Her own champions . . . Only Ven would give her a chance like this, and she was failing to persuade him. She felt an ache, deep in her chest.

"If you swear to never make another bargain with that creature, then your secret will be safe with me, and I will defend you against any who seek to hurt you. I will be your personal guard. I will be by your side for as long as you want me. Every night, every day. I will be with you, protecting you.

"Loving you."

Fara laughed, and it was close to a cry. "You're black-mailing me with talk of love?"

"I don't want to lose you, not again. But if you keep on this path, I know I will."

"You know I won't let you destroy me. If you will not keep my secret—"

"Pledge to me: no more bargains, and I will keep your secret. I will keep you, and you me. Together. Fara, let me help you. Use me as your strength. Let me keep you safe." He raised her fingers to his lips and kissed them, and she let him. "Tell the owl spirit that the bargain is off. Refuse to give it the lives you promised, and do not give it any more."

"I cannot tell if you're trying to threaten me, or make love to me."

"Please." He turned one hand over and kissed her palm, then kissed her wrist and up the inside of her arm to the crook of her elbow. He then stepped closer and kissed her neck, then her ear. "Please. No more death. Tell them, all of them, do no harm. Be the queen you're meant to be. Don't be afraid."

Softly, she said, "I am afraid."

"Tell me how to help you, and I will. Your champions, tell them what you need—let them defend you from the spirits. Your heirs, send them to the border—let them watch this other queen. You are not alone. You don't need to act as if you were. Use us. Let us serve you. I want only to serve you." He pressed his lips against hers and kissed her as if she were lost and he wanted to find her.

She clutched the back of his neck, tangled her fingers in his hair, and pulled him closer, her lips tasting his. She arched as he kissed her neck.

"Please, my queen, do not let more die."

"I will not," she promised.

HE LEFT HER BED LATER, HER SKIN SOFT WITH KISSES, and she watched him dress in his green armor and listened to him address the guards as he left. He had to see to her safety, he said. He would be assuming control of her guard as the first step in his promise to always be beside her, and there were several people he had to speak to in order to ensure her safety.

Wrapping a blanket around herself, Fara slipped out of bed. She crossed to the balcony and opened the shade, only a few inches, to look out on the revelry. There was still music, so many different kinds of music, each piling on top of the next until it blurred into sheer joyous noise. She let the curtain fall shut, and she dressed in a red gown, one that made her feel like old-fashioned royalty. She twisted her hair into braids and coiled it on top of her head, and then she added jewels—priceless necklaces clasped around her throat, and earrings. She then laid her crown on top of her head.

When she felt every inch a queen, she glided out of her chamber. She nodded to her guards and climbed the stairs to the Queen's Tower.

She hadn't been to the top of this spire in nearly a year, but the palace caretakers kept even the stairs so clean that they glimmered. One of her predecessors had created this tower, a single spire so high it overlooked all of Aratay, or at least it felt that way. The top cleared the canopy. As she climbed, she looked out the window at the branches that thinned as she went higher and then at the tops of the trees. From above, the green looked like a sea, undulating. Sunlight spread across it, trying to pierce the canopy and, in places, failing.

The tower was a tiny room, a circle with nothing in it except murals painted on the walls around the many windows. Above, the ceiling was glass to see the stars at night.

Come. Fara sent the command spiraling.

Leaning on one of the windowsills, she let the wind blow on her face. Ven didn't understand that it wasn't about glory. It was about the needs of Aratay. Her people needed both growth and protection, the kind only she could provide. Ven didn't understand the danger posed by other lands as well. His concerns were purely insular, but she had to be aware of what was going on beyond her borders. Of the upstart in the mountains. Of the forays into Aratay.

Of the incredibly ambitious Queen Merecot of Semo.

But the girl's ambition was nothing to Fara's. Her own ambition to keep her people safe would always trump all else. If necessary, Fara would make more sacrifices, and she wouldn't hesitate.

I'll do whatever it takes to keep my land and my people safe.

If that meant making a bargain, she'd do it. And if it meant *breaking* a bargain . . . well, she'd do that too.

Ven was right in one thing: the bargains were escalating. She couldn't allow that to continue. The owl spirit had to be reminded who was queen. Fara controlled her, all of them, and the spirit could not be allowed to continue dictating terms. Breaking this bargain would serve two purposes: asserting her dominance and appeasing Ven.

Because the other choice was killing Ven, and she did not want to do that. Selfishness, perhaps, but she wanted him beside her.

The sun was above the horizon of green, near the mountains. It rimmed the mountains in gold, as if their snow-capped peaks were halos. Birds flew above and filled the air with their cries and calls, a music that was echoed, dimly, by the drums below. The celebration would go on into the evening and then the night, petering out with the dawn. Her people did like to celebrate. *Let them,* she thought. They were celebrating hope.

That was the miraculous thing about Champion Ven. He made her feel hope. He made her believe she still had choices.

She saw the owl spirit flying over the canopy. Her toes ruffled the tops of the leaves. Her head was low, and her wings out wide. Steeling herself, Queen Fara straightened.

The owl woman landed inside the tower and folded her wings. Before Fara could deliver her demands, the spirit spoke. "You have been betrayed."

The words felt like a chill wind, scattering her carefully planned speech. "Tell me."

"Your lover's protégée lured me to the academy of your old teachers who profess to love you. I was attacked by the heirs, working together, working against you. I only escaped after waking to lax captors. My queen, they wanted my confession to use against you. They know of our bargains. They seek to use that knowledge against you, to destroy you, to take your throne for themselves."

"I don't believe you." But it made an awful kind of sense. Ven had told his student. She had told others. He had broken his promise before ever making it. She thought of how he'd left. Perhaps he went to speak to them, to tell them he'd successfully blackmailed her, that they now controlled her, that she would dance to their tune. He might not even realize what he had done, that he'd placed her under the control of everyone who knew, of the heirs who sooner or later would think they would make a better queen than she.

"About this, I would not lie."

Fara looked out over the trees. Ven would try to protect her, she believed. He was a lousy liar, too caught up in honor and integrity to do what truly had to be done, but the heirs . . . She thought of Daleina, his heir. *She* would do what she thought needed to be done, and Ven's protection would mean nothing. He wouldn't be able to keep Fara safe against the heirs, especially one he'd trained himself, espccially if they were united against her. No, as before, as always, Fara was alone, and she had to protect herself. She'd been naïve to think, even for a moment, that she could do otherwise.

With a heavy heart, she let go of her plan to cancel the bargain, let go of her belief in Ven, and let go of the hope that things could be different. "I would like to propose a new bargain."

The owl spirit hissed. "You must not let them live."

Fara nodded. "You will protect me. You and your spirits must swear to keep me alive. I must remain queen. And in exchange, you may kill them."

"Them?"

"Aratay must be kept safe. I must live. I must be queen."

Her owl eyes were bright, as if she'd spotted prey on the forest floor. "You said 'them.' How many of your heirs may we kill?"

"All, of course. Swear it."

The owl woman sliced the palm of her hand. "I swear it."

Cradling the spirit's hand, Queen Fara drank her blood.

The owl woman watched the queen die.

She felt her hunger roar inside her: free, free, free! She wanted to rend flesh, taste blood, tear apart the humans who marred her perfect world. Rid them from the world like the scourge that they were. They did not belong. They must be removed.

But even as she felt her bloodlust rise, beautifully unfettered, she wanted to stop it. All her plans! All the years! All the promises! She'd found the perfect vessel. She'd groomed her. Coaxed her. Cajoled her. Trained her to suit their needs. The owl woman played the long game—and this death was not a move that fit her plan.

She felt rage rise up to meet her hunger, and she fell on the body of the queen. Her fingernails clawed the queen's motionless flesh. Her sharp beak rent her throat. She sliced her until her red dress was stained with blood. And then she flew from the window with a shriek that echoed over the forests, a shriek that drowned the screams from below.

DALEINA HEARD A SCREAM. DROPPING THE TEACUP, she jumped to her feet, and the porcelain shattered on the floor. Another scream, and the office shook as if the tree itself shuddered. Headmistress Hanna crossed to the window and clasped her hands behind her back. "So, it begins."

No! It's too soon! They were supposed to have time, to plan how to protect people, to prepare without alarming anyone. To reach their families. "You mean—"

"Go. Join the others and make them understand: the queen is dead."

Daleina ran. She burst out of the headmistress's office and halted at the top of the stairs. Below, a hundred spirits whipped in a spiral, a tornado of shimmering bodies, tearing torches from the walls, ripping apart the stairs. She couldn't go down, not into that maelstrom. Instead, she ran up toward the bells.

She passed the bell ringer, a caretaker boy no more than twelve. Dead.

Grabbing the rope that was tucked against the spire, she shimmied up it to the bells. She'd never been this close to them: two dozen silver bells. She climbed to the bell ringer's hammer and gripped it. Below, the howls, cries, and screams rose up the funnel, and she felt as if she'd been plunged back into her ten-year-old body, hearing everyone around her die.

Not this time, she thought, and swung the hammer at the largest bell.

Three tolls.

Everyone knew that ring, the three deepest tolls. She waited, and then hit them again. Once, twice, three times. From across the forest, she heard three drumbeats. Low, rolling, thrumming across the trees, cutting through the screams.

Every heir.

Every candidate.

Every student.

Every hedgewitch.

Every woman with power was needed.

Now.

Wedging herself between branches, Daleina drew in a breath. She focused on everything she'd learned in order to shut out the world, the screams, the pain, the death, the destruction that the spirits were spreading . . . and then she reached out from inside, touching those spirits. She felt their rage wash over her. Rage and joy. She shuddered away from it, and then forced herself back into the swirling darkness, and felt her mind swept inside it.

Choose.

She heard the word echoed, as if from a dozen other voices. She joined her mind to those voices. *Choose.* A hundred voices. *Choose.* A thousand. *Choose!*

And then . . .

Everything stopped.

She felt stillness. And silence.

Climbing down from the bells, Daleina descended the stairs as far as she could before the steps ended—large chunks had been knocked from the wall. The bell ringer's body was gone, vanished with the missing steps. Automatically, she reached out to the spirits, and it was like brushing her hand against moss. They were there, soft against her mental touch, but they didn't move or respond. They wouldn't, until it was time for them to choose.

She found her own way down, climbing the academy as if it were a tree without ladders, until she reached the practice ring. There, the circle had been set up as a makeshift hospital. Hamon was overseeing everything, triaging the students, teachers, and caretakers based on the severity of their wounds. A few had sheets pulled over their faces. Caretaker Undu was lying on a pallet, her face pale and blood running down one arm. Linna knelt beside her, wrapping a bandage around the wound. Daleina's eyes sought out her friends: Revi, Zie . . . there was Iondra, helping one of the younger caretakers, a girl in tears.

Daleina joined the others, moving among the injured,

helping with bandages, distributing herbs, rubbing on healing ointment. Again and again. There were few who had escaped with no wounds. Only when everyone had been tended to did she cross to the bodies covered in blankets.

Caretaker Undu was seated beside them.

"Who?" Daleina asked.

The caretaker nodded at one. "Rubi. She was a first-year student, from midforest. She had a soft voice and liked to dance. Cook often said she ate her weight in potatoes but wouldn't touch other vegetables." She turned to another. "Sarir, ten years old, an orphan. He was our bell ringer. So shy but beginning to smile." And the third. "A caretaker named Andare. He'd been here since he was a child, in the beginning as shy as Sarir had been. Thrown away by his parents as if he were trash, because they didn't want another mouth to feed. He'd been found by a traveling tinker and, as much as we could ever glean, used as a shield to protect the tinker from spirits. We found him with his heart nearly cut out—the tinker had wanted to make a charm from it, the darker side of hedgewitchery. He'd had a hard childhood, but he'd made a good life for himself here."

Daleina put her hand over her heart, remembering the boy with the scar by his heart, the one with the sweet smile and sweeter kisses. "He was kind."

"Yes, he was." Her voice was empty, and Daleina knew she was holding another grief inside her, the kind that would never leave, the kind that irrevocably changes you and your life. There were no words to fill that kind of emptiness. Daleina didn't try. She placed her hand on Caretaker Undu's shoulder and hoped she knew that Daleina was thinking of Mari too. Mari and the boy with sweet kisses and her cousin with the wonderful stories and her little friends who never had a chance to grow up. She thought of her family and prayed they'd stayed safe, that they'd hidden in their house, filled the crevices with charms, and stayed silent.

There should have been time to warn them!

She crossed to Hamon, who was packing up the extra bandages and salves. "I'm going to head into the capital," he said. "Offer my help."

Daleina nodded. "My family . . ."

He nodded. "I know. You have to be sure they're safe." He wasn't meeting her eyes, didn't look up from the bandages.

She touched his shoulder lightly. "Hamon?"

"Please, Daleina . . . I . . . Something terrible happened today."

She heard the words he didn't say: *We did something terrible today.* "Keep moving," she advised. "It helps if you're busy."

He nodded and resumed packing. She watched him for a moment, knowing that she'd been right—everything had changed, and for a moment she mourned that too.

Together, they'd killed a queen.

And, in turn, had caused the deaths of how many more?

Daleina left him to his task and his thoughts. She drifted from cot to cot, checking on the injured, trying to help, but in the end she drifted to the broken spiral stairs to join her friends. The heirs clumped together in silence.

"It feels so empty," Linna said, and hugged her arms.

Zie scuffed at a broken stair with her foot. "I tried to call one. Felt like grabbing mist. They're still there, but they're . . . not, also."

"I don't miss them," Revi declared. "It's like a holiday without them."

All of them looked at her.

"Except for the death," she amended.

"Oh, Daleina . . . I heard about Andare!" Zie hugged her suddenly. "I'm so sorry. I know you weren't still . . . but I know you . . ."

Daleina hugged her back. She felt the weight of his death on her. If she hadn't killed the queen, the spirits wouldn't have been free to harm. He wouldn't have died. His death was on her, as well as the girl and everyone who had been killed across all of Aratay.

No, she told herself fiercely. *I'm not the enemy. The spirits are.* They were the ones who killed. She and the others had stopped them.

"I wish we didn't have to have the coronation. No queen, no spirits," Revi said. "Imagine a life without them, without fear."

All of them were silent.

"I need to visit my family," Daleina said. "If Champion Ven returns . . ."

Iondra clasped Daleina's hand. "We'll tell him where you are. Go to them. In seven days, we shall all meet again." The coronation ceremony, by tradition, would happen in seven days, to give the people time to mourn and to give the heirs time to gather. Daleina embraced each of them and then jogged out of the academy.

She whistled, not certain if Bayn would be nearby or even if he would want to come. A few seconds later, though, the wolf trotted out from the trees. Kneeling, Daleina wrapped her arms around the wolf's neck. She buried her face in his fur and inhaled the musky scent. She wanted to cry but couldn't—the tears wouldn't flow. So she stood and headed away from the academy, away from the capital, with her wolf at her side.

SHE SAW MORE DEATH ON HER JOURNEY TO HER FAMily's village: mourners burying lost family members in the soft earth between the tree roots, people weeping openly as they sat by their houses. It felt as if a soft fog of sadness lay through the forest. People went through the motions of life: hurrying to gather food before it died on the vine, to hunt animals before the woodland creatures starved, to preserve what they had but couldn't cook. Without spirits, nothing would grow, no rain would fall, and no fires would light. Until coronation, the only food was what hadn't yet spoiled, and the only warmth was through clothes, blankets, and bodies. It was luck that it was summer. Daleina realized they hadn't considered the season when they'd planned their regicide.

She felt as though a fist were in her stomach, as if the world had tilted, the sun dimmed, as if her skin itched all over her body, as if nothing were right, not even the air. She hadn't expected to feel this way. It had seemed like the only choice, the right choice. As Headmistress Hanna had said once to Merecot, a bad queen can be as dangerous as no queen. Queen Fara had been abusing her power and breaking her trust with her people. *So why do I feel as though I broke something precious?*

She kept walking in the darkness, Bayn by her side. No wind blew, and the only sound was her footsteps on the fallen leaves and the rumble of her stomach as the night stretched on. The pack she'd taken from the academy had a few travelers' crackers, as well as a water canteen. At dawn, she filled the canteen at a stream and dropped Hamon's purifying herbs into it. She saw dead fish float by and scooped them out, cleaned them, and strung them on a stretch of fishing line that she attached to her pack. She couldn't cook them, but she could bring them to her family to salt and preserve. As she traveled, she also gathered nuts and berries. It was strange, seeing the bushes, knowing they were, in essence, lifeless without the spirits—they wouldn't create more leaves, their berries wouldn't ripen. Left alone, they'd wither. Eventually, without the coronation, they'd die.

Bayn hunted, and Daleina couldn't tell if he was bringing down game easier or not—the wolf had never had problems hunting, and nothing should be hungry yet. But the birds seemed to be flying less than usual. Their songs seemed sadder. Everything felt stiller. Or maybe it was only Daleina's mood, which she couldn't seem to shake.

Throughout the forest, she saw evidence of the spirits' wildness, the damage they'd done in the moments without a queen. Rocks had been split by overzealous water spirits who had cracked the land to make new springs and streams. She encountered a new lake full of half-drowned trees. Other trees had grown in twisted puzzles, curling in on themselves and wrapping together. Still other trees bore the scorch marks of lightning, but the patterns were strange, as if stray lightning had streaked horizontally through the forest. One bridge had been ripped apart. Another was coated in moss and flowers. She had to be careful of deep chasms that gaped like fresh wounds between the roots.

At last, she reached her family's village and, after explaining to Bayn where she'd be, she climbed the ladder up to the bridge that led to the center platform. The triple trees still stood, but the market had been destroyed, and no attempt had been made to fix it. Red and blue awnings hung, torn, from poles. Crates were upended and broken. All the produce was gone, and as she peered in the bakery window, she saw it was empty. Everyone had stored up everything that the village had, and now it was eerily empty. Daleina poked her head inside the hedgewitch's shop. "Mistress Baria?" It was dark inside.

Going in, Daleina pushed open the shades so that the pale light could filter through the dirty windows. She sucked in air as she surveyed the disaster—every bin, every barrel, every basket had been torn apart. Charms were strewn on the floor. Herbs had been spilled. Jars broken.

She went farther inside. "Mistress Baria?"

From the doorway, she heard a voice. "She's dead, miss."

Daleina turned to see a man she didn't recognize, a woodsman with a rough beard. "You're certain?"

He nodded. "Spirits came for her right away. Didn't like her charms. It was quick, if that helps. Did you know her?"

Daleina nodded. "My family—Eaden, Ingara, my sister Arin. Do you know them? Are they all right?" She felt her legs moving, out of the shop. She knew she should mourn her old teacher, but right now her thoughts were only for her family.

The man moved aside. He was holding his hat, twisting it in his hand. "The spirits came quick. No warning. And now . . . Do you come from the capital? Is it true? Is Queen Fara . . ."

"Yes." It was the only word she could manage.

He began to cry like a child, snot from his nose, shoulders heaving, great sobs as if the world had ended. She walked away from him and then ran toward her family's house. She noted each broken shop, each smashed window or door, each torn ladder. She ran faster down the bridge until she saw their house: the garish green house.

The pottery shingles on the roof were shattered, and the flowers in the window box had wilted. The wall had dents, as if a fist had rammed into it. "Mother? Daddy?" Daleina ran for the door, and the door was flung open. "Arin!"

Her mother ran out, followed by her father.

They threw their arms around her, surrounding her, embracing her, holding her. She held them tightly. "Arin? Where's Arin? Is she all right?" She pictured her sister, her leg still injured. If she'd been outside when the spirits struck . . . she wouldn't have been able to escape. She'd have been run down. She—

Her sister appeared in the doorway, hobbling forward on crutches. A half cry, half shout burbled up from Daleina's throat, and she stumbled forward, pulling her parents with her, and then pulled her sister into her embrace. "I could have lost you," Daleina whispered. And the truth of it hit her. "I could have lost you all." She'd done nothing to keep them safe. When the spirits attacked, she hadn't been here. She'd thought she'd have time! A month, before the queen met with the owl spirit again. "You survived. How did you survive?"

Arin pulled away and disappeared back into the house.

"Not everyone did," Mother said gently. "She lost Josei." Her voice was quiet so that it wouldn't carry into the house.

Daleina knew she shouldn't have to ask—the way Mother said the name, it was someone important to Arin. Her voice had dropped on the name. Yet, as softly as she could, Daleina asked, "Who's Josei?"

"The baker's boy."

Oh. Daleina felt her heart lurch. "Is Arin . . ." She trailed off. Of course Arin wasn't all right.

Mother put her arm around Daleina. "We were inside when it happened. The charms kept us safe. But anyone who wasn't, like Josei . . . Many died."

Inside, Arin was huddled in the corner by the unlit hearth. The shutters were still closed tight, and the house was filled with shadows. A pile of broken pots had been swept to one corner. At least they'd begun to clean up. Shedding her pack, Daleina crossed to Arin and crouched beside her. "Arin, I . . ." Like with Caretaker Undu, she had no words. She laid her hand on Arin's shoulder. "I am sorry for your loss." The words felt stilted and insufficient.

"You weren't here." Her face buried in her arms, her voice was muffled.

Daleina's throat felt clogged. "I know."

"It was all right when you left, because you were doing it for us, to protect us, you said. It was all right that you weren't here for the everyday things—breakfast together, gathering wood, making charms, falling asleep. It was all right that I couldn't stay up late talking to you, that I couldn't tell you about my first kiss, that I didn't have you to walk me to school. It was all right that you missed the impor- tant moments—birthdays, when Mother was sick, my leg.

It was all right that every time you came home you were more and more a stranger, that you know nothing about me or my life, that you didn't even know Josei's name! Because you were doing it for us. But that was a lie, wasn't it? It was for you. Because *you* were afraid. Because you wanted to be the hero. Because it matched how you saw yourself. It was your dream, your goal, your . . ." She sucked in air. Arin was shaking, and Daleina wanted to reach out to her, but every word felt like a knife strike. "You weren't here when we needed you!"

"I . . ." She'd done it for them, hadn't she? "I thought about you every day." The words sounded weak in her ears. How often had she come back? And when she was here, how much had she tried to learn about Arin and her world? On her visits, her parents had fluttered over her. Made her favorite soup. Listened to her stories about the academy. Arin too had pestered her for more and more stories. But she'd never really asked about them. Not really.

"I'm sorry."

"Go back to the academy, Daleina," Arin said. "You're home too late."

Daleina retreated and would have gone straight for the door, but her parents blocked the way. Side by side, they filled the kitchen. She noticed for the first time that there was a scrape down her father's neck and that her mother's left wrist was bandaged.

"Can't you stay?" Daddy asked. "There are still a few days until the coronation ceremony. Spend them here, with us."

"But Arin doesn't want . . ."

"She's hurting," Mother said. "She needs her sister around, whether she admits it or not." All of them looked at Arin, who was curled motionless. "Stay, please."

Daleina stayed.

E verything felt so quiet as everyone picked up the broken pieces of their lives and began the process of sticking them back together. Word spread of the queen's funeral: in Heroes Grove, the champions each took turns digging her a grave by hand. There were no spirits to swallow her into the soil. There was only a shovel, a simple shovel, very old, that was used for this one purpose: burying the queen. Daleina heard the singing—all of the canopy singers sang the same song at the same time, and it spread like a birdcall through the forest. She climbed to the top of her family's village to listen to it.

In the stillness of the forest, there was a kind of beautiful simplicity. You could be alone without fear, and so Daleina was. She seized excuses to be out in the forest, gathering the last of the berries and nuts for her family, walking the forest paths with Bayn, climbing up to the canopy. Arin spent her days inside the house, sometimes asleep, sometimes awake and crying, sometimes just sitting by the cold hearth. Mother cajoled her into eating, but she didn't eat much. She wouldn't talk to or even look at Daleina. But Daleina didn't leave, not for more than an hour or farther than a few miles. She spent time with Bayn, running between the trees, not for any real reason but just because it felt right to run. And she spent time on the roof of the house, with her father, repairing the broken shingles. He'd had to teach her how, but once she had the trick of it, she worked in silence beside him as the sun shed dappled light onto their village trees.

She was becoming used to the eerie serenity of a forest without wind. No leaves rustled. No breeze carried the scent of ripening berries or pine needles.

"Out of nails," her father said.

"I'll get more," Daleina offered. She began to climb down.

"No, you stay. I should check on your mother and Arin." He climbed off the roof, grunting as he did. She wondered when he'd gotten older. He winced sometimes when he stood up, she'd noticed. She'd noticed many things about her family that she'd never taken the time to see: her mother's habit of humming while she whittled new spoons to sell, her sister's snore that sounded like a cat purr, her father's habit of smiling whenever he was uncomfortable with the conversation, the way they all converged on the kitchen at breakfast time as if it were a choreographed dance. Her parents were trying so hard. Hammering in the last nail, Daleina leaned back on the tiles in a patch of sunlight and closed her eyes.

She felt the roof tremble—her father was back—but she didn't sit up yet. This patch of sun was nice. She couldn't remember the last time she just sat. She wondered if this was what ordinary people did: little tasks to keep their lives moving forward, filling the day with words and silences that were sometimes louder than words, tiptoeing around emotions.

"You didn't come to the funeral."

Her eyes shot open. Not her father. Champion Ven. Daleina sat up. "You're here!" For the first day, she had expected him to come—she'd left word. But when he hadn't, she had stopped thinking about him, about the academy, about being an heir. She had tried to think about as little as possible.

He sat on the roof beside her. "It was a lovely funeral. She would have liked it. She was immortalized in song, the way she would have liked, all her miracles listed out. None of her flaws."

"None of the singers really knew her."

Daleina studied his face, trying to read him. "Hamon told you? About what we did."

"Headmistress Hanna told me. Hamon has been in the capital. He joined the medical crew in the city. Hasn't stopped working since her death. He didn't come to the funeral either. There was a child who needed a healer . . . He's been trying to save as many as he can." He spread his hands and studied them, flexing his fingers. "I chose the wrong profession for saving people."

Daleina thought of Josei, the baker's boy, and of Andare. "Why are you here? I don't need training anymore, and there's nothing to protect me from." She wondered if he was angry at her. He sounded more tired than angry, but it was difficult to read his expression.

"I came to escort you to the coronation ceremony. My duties haven't ended. Not until a queen walks out of the glade, crowned."

Daleina lay back on the roof, the tiles digging into her back. "It won't be me. I won't be there." Staring up at the sliver of sky, she realized as she said the words that it was true. It felt right. She let the decision settle around her, sink into her bones.

"Don't be foolish. This isn't time for emotions."

"It's time for choices. Years ago, I made the choice to protect my family by leaving it. Now I'm making the choice to protect them by staying. This village lost its hedgewitch. I'll be its new one."

"Like hell you will. You're an heir!"

"Ranked last. I won't be chosen. You know that. And if I were to go . . . it would cheapen what we did. I didn't do it for the crown. I did it for Aratay. To go to the coronation ceremony . . . I can't do it, Ven. I won't."

"Aratay still needs you. You can't run and hide now."

"My family needs me. My sister . . . I didn't see it. All those years. I didn't know what I missed, what I wasn't choosing when I was choosing my path. I simply walked forward without looking back, and now . . . I don't want to keep making the same mistake anymore."

"It wasn't a mistake. You have the affinity. You have the skill. You have the determination." His hands were curled into fists, and she could hear the near shout in his voice. He was controlling it, but only barely.

"Others have more. Let one of them be queen. They deserve it."

"No one *deserves* it. It's a burden. Fara knew that better than anyone." His voice broke when he said her name, but he gained control again.

"It's a burden I don't want. Not anymore." Sitting up, she pulled his sheathed knife out of her waistband. "This is yours. I don't think it's appropriate for me to have."

He refused to touch it. "It's a gift. And I'm still your champion. You're my heir."

She didn't want to hear that word anymore. She was pretty sure she didn't want to hear any more of his words. Tucking the knife back in her waistband, Daleina climbed down from the roof. "My father should be back with the nails. Come and have dinner with us. It's not much, without fire, but there's enough to share."

He followed her off the roof and into the house. Slowly, they'd been fixing it, repairing everything that had broken in the moments after the queen's death. But not everything could be repaired. Arin stood beside the sink, her crutches leaning against the table. She held a broken cup in her hands, and tears were streaming down her cheeks. Daddy was standing beside her, arm around her shoulders, whispering into her hair. When Daleina and Ven appeared in the doorway, Mother crossed to them. To Daleina's surprise, Mother embraced Ven. She pulled him in. "Thank you for taking care of our little girl." She shepherded him to the table and began pulling out bowls and plates and food to offer him. "I'm afraid we don't have any baked bread to offer you. Or anything warm. But we have fresh water, and we have greens and nuts, as well as salted fish. Come, let us feed you."

"You've very kind, but I cannot stay long." His eyes slid to Daleina. "The coronation ceremony will be taking place soon, and I've come to escort Daleina."

Her mother nodded as if yes, of course, this was expected, which Daleina supposed it was. "It has been a treat to have our Daleina back, even if it was just for a little while. Made us feel like a full family again."

Daleina met Arin's eyes. Arin's lips pressed into a line, but she said nothing. She was clutching the broken cup so hard that a line of blood had appeared on her hand where the shard had cut her. Daleina crossed the kitchen and gently took the shards out of her hands. She placed them in the sink, ran water over her sister's hand, and then wrapped it in a clean white dish towel. Arin let her, and there was silence in the kitchen while all watched the two sisters.

"You come, and you leave," Arin said.

"Not this time. I told Champion Ven: this time, I'm staying here."

"You can't," Mother said. "The ceremony—"

"Will happen without me," Daleina said. "Someone more deserving will be queen—"

Immediately, both her mother and father protested, saying at the same time that of course she was deserving! Of course she was powerful and good and strong and would be a wonderful queen! Softly, Arin said, "I wish we didn't need a queen."

"Me too," Daleina said, just as softly.

"It's been nice"—Arin stumbled over the word—"without the fear. I don't mind only eating berries and nuts. It won't get cold, without the ice spirits. I wish it could be like this, peaceful, always."

Daleina felt a tear prick the corner of her eye.

"You know it can't," Mother said briskly. "When the plants die and no more grow, when no berries ripen, when the animals starve, when our homes crumble and no more can be made, what will become of us? The forest needs the spirits. Be practical, Arin. And Daleina, don't talk nonsense. You've trained for this. You've devoted your life to preparing for this moment. It's your moment! Seize it!"

That was exactly it: she'd devoted her life to becoming queen, and she knew now that it wasn't hers to seize. She wasn't powerful enough, and she wasn't good enough, in every sense of the word. "I'm ranked last. I won't be chosen." The spirits would choose that heir who was so good with air spirits, the one named Berra. Or Linna, who had manipulated the fire spirits so beautifully at Greytree. Or Zie or Evvlyn. Or one of the older heirs. There were many to choose from.

"The odds were always against you," Ven said. "I've seen your records. You shouldn't have made it through the entrance exam, but you did. You shouldn't have passed your classes, but you did. You shouldn't have made it through the trials, but you did. You are constantly underestimated, Daleina. You can't begin underestimating yourself."

"He's right, you know," Arin said, as if the words hurt her throat. "If someone has to be queen, it should be you. You're a good person."

She wasn't. She'd let Josei die. She'd killed the queen.

She wondered if Queen Fara had once been a good

person. She must have been, for the headmistress to have admired her, for Ven to have . . . Daleina looked at Ven. She hadn't thought about how he must feel, his former lover. When his eyes locked on hers, she had to look away. Her stomach twisted, and she sucked in air to steady it.

"Are you all right, Daleina?" Arin asked. "You look like you're going to faint."

"Sit!" Mother commanded. She scooted Daleina into a seat. Daleina sank into it. "Are you sick?" She felt Daleina's forehead and then her neck, squeezing. "Not warm. Not swollen."

Daleina waved her hand. "Only need a minute. I'm . . ." She didn't have a word to describe what she was. She felt a hand on her shoulder and looked up—it was Arin. Daleina covered her sister's hand with her own. "I want to stay here, with you." She felt tears rolling down her cheeks. They were matched by Arin's.

Ven pushed back roughly from the table, stood, and slapped his hands down. "No. You are an heir. You have a duty to Aratay."

"I did my duty to Aratay, and people died."

He froze. A muscle in his cheek twitched.

"Have some food, rest, and then we'll talk more," Mother said. She scurried around the kitchen, preparing food. Daddy poured water for each of them. They ate, Ven barely touching his food and Daleina barely tasting hers. She felt as if she were in the practice ring, facing a spirit. Her hands were sweating and her heart thumping. She could do this, stay here, build a life with her family. She tried to picture her future, and it was nice.

"Daleina . . ." Arin's voice was gentle and sad. "You know you can't stay."

The world felt as if it slowed. Voices faded, and colors dimmed. "Arin . . ."

"Aratay needs you."

"It doesn't."

"After all you've given up, all *we* have given up . . . You have to go to the coronation ceremony, or else it was for nothing," Arin said, her hand a warm weight on Daleina's shoulder. "You, not being here. Me, growing up without you. Josei . . . You have to at least try."

Standing, Daleina faced Arin and clasped her hands. "I'll come back. After it's over, I'll come back to stay, and we'll grow old together here. We'll be those cranky old sisters that criticize everyone's loud kids, climb to watch the sunrise even though everyone tells us not to, and I'll be overprotective and you'll boss me around and . . ."

Arin smiled, though tears filled her eyes. "Sounds wonderful."

ESCORTED BY VEN, DALEINA WENT STRAIGHT TO THE palace and knew she had made a mistake. She shouldn't be here, where Queen Fara had lived, ruled, and died.

The guards welcomed both her and Ven, and she was separated from him and escorted to a set of baths, deep in the roots of the palace tree. Between the roots, there were natural pools of blue-green water, with steam rising from them. Many of the other heirs were soaking in the waters. Others were being dressed in ceremonial clothes. Daleina scanned the pools and spotted the heirs from Northeast Academy: Revi, Linna, Zie, Iondra, Evvlyn, and Airria. She headed directly for them.

Joining them, she had nothing to say. All of them were focused inward, absorbed in their thoughts, preparing themselves for the moment when they would command the spirits as tradition demanded. *Choose me,* they'd say, and the spirits would choose a queen. *Not me,* Daleina thought. And for the first time, that thought felt right. She felt an odd sort of peace settle over her.

"You were missed," Linna told her.

"Were you home this whole time?" Revi asked.

Daleina nodded. "You?"

"Some of us went back; some stayed."

After that, they bathed without talking. Other pools held heirs from other academies. Some were older, experienced heirs, who had been through a coronation ceremony before. Others were new, like they were. All of them, Daleina knew, were more qualified and more deserving than she was. And that was okay. She'd played her role, for better or worse, and that was it.

"You missed the queen's funeral," Evvlyn said, climbing out of the bath and drying herself. She had new scars, crisscrossing her bird tattoos so that two of the birds looked as though their wings were clipped. They still flew, though. "And all of the others."

"There were many," Airria said, her sweet voice soft.

"I lost a brother," Iondra said.

"Master Bei. She was one of my favorites," Zie said.

Daleina felt jolted—she hadn't known Master Bei had died as well. Poor Bayn. She wondered if that was why the wolf had been so willing to follow her and to stay with her, even though Daleina hadn't planned to leave her home village.

They all went on, naming more people who had been lost, in the capital and beyond.

"Once the coronation ceremony is over, life will go on," Iondra declared. "We will learn to live while mourning them. All will again be as it should be. Sadness will end, or at least be replaced by the business of living."

"I'm going to be a hedgewitch in my family's village," Daleina told them. "It's the best way I can serve Aratay." She'd replace Mistress Baria. It was a respectable choice. She could do good locally. It had been foolish to ever dream bigger.

"Or you will be queen," Zie said. "You don't know."

"I do know," Daleina said. "Queen Fara knew. You are all more powerful than I am. It's why I am ranked last." She took a breath, knowing they wouldn't understand what she was about to say. "And why I will not be joining you in the grove."

"You have to!" Revi said.

"You know you're meant for this," Iondra said.

"We started this together; we finish it together," Revi said.

Daleina got out of the bathing pool and wrapped a towel around herself. "I promised my family and Ven that I'd come with you to the ceremony, but that's as far as I'll go." It was a fair compromise: she'd see this to the end, but at a distance. They argued with her more, saying she couldn't know who the spirits would choose, but she stood firm, never saying her true reason: that the queen's killer did not deserve her power.

She allowed the palace caretakers to dress her in a white gown with beaded pearls, and when she looked at herself in the mirror—her red-and-gold hair piled on her head and secured with jewels, her neck and arms painted with images of leaves, waves, flames, snowflakes, mountains, and clouds—she looked like an heir, and for an instant, her resolve wavered.

This was who she was.

This was who she was meant to be.

But something had changed inside her. Digging through her old clothes, she pulled out Ven's sheathed knife. She strung the sheath onto her jeweled belt. Now she felt more like herself.

"You're Heir Daleina, from Northeast Academy?" a voice said behind her. She turned to see a woman, a few years older than her, another heir. She stuck out a hand and clasped Daleina's. "My name is Chidra. I heard you decided not to enter the grove?"

"You heard correctly," Daleina said.

"You're an heir," Chidra said flatly. "You come."

Daleina lifted her chin and thought of Queen Fara, as she had looked as she stood in the entrance arch to the palace, and replied in just as flat a tone, "I will do what I think is best for Aratay."

"Yes, you will," Chidra said, and Daleina noticed that other heirs had joined her, fanning out in a semicircle. It hadn't occurred to her that others would care. "We must all do our duty."

"She'll come," Revi said. Linna nodded and repeated it, "Yes, she'll come." Zie: "She's coming." "There is no question," Iondra said. "Daleina comes. She's one of us."

Unable to explain why they were wrong, Daleina could only shake her head. Her eyes felt hot with tears she knew she didn't deserve to shed. She didn't deserve their faith in her, but then, this wasn't about her and what she felt.

"For the sake of those who have fallen," Iondra said.

"For Mari," Linna said. "We'll do this for Mari." She took Daleina's hands, and Daleina felt her resolve falter. She looked around, and saw the heirs of Aratay staring back at her.

Maybe they were right. Maybe her role wasn't over yet. Like Ven, she wasn't done until one of the heirs was crowned. Finally, after a deep breath, Daleina nodded. "For Mari," she repeated. And for Sata. And Andare. And Josei. And even Queen Fara.

As the gibbous moon bathed the forests in silvery light, the heirs filed out of the palace, through the quiet city, to the Queen's Grove, a sacred place just beyond the borders of the capital. People watched them from windows, from bridges, from branches. Daleina watched Ven out of the corner of her eye, marching with the other champions on either side of the heirs.

Around them, spirits flowed toward the grove. Silent, they were like a stream of clouds, flowing through the air, sweeping along the forest floor, seeping between the trees. None of them looked at the heirs. It was as if they inhabited separate worlds that didn't yet intersect, but they were all being pulled to the same place.

This was the effect of the "choose" command—the suspension-like state and the pull to the grove where they'd make their choice. Her teachers had said it was a deep, base instinct, ingrained like bird migration or procreation, a compulsion that was part of their essential makeup. The spirits needed a queen to keep them from tearing their creation asunder, as they did in the untamed lands, where they created and destroyed with wild abandon, ripping the earth to shreds. Some people believed it was a magic of the land itself, wanting to grow again, wanting balance, forcing them to *need* a queen.

As for why *here*, her history classes held the answer for that: this was the place where the first queen of Aratay claimed power and created the forest land. Each of the five lands had a place like this, a sacred place where the spirits were first bound to obey. It was what made the tamed lands different from the untamed wilderness beyond the borders. None of the heirs had ever seen the grove. You didn't go to the First Place on a whim. It was too sacred.

It felt that way to Daleina, as if she still wasn't worthy to enter, even only as an observer.

Outside, the grove was surrounded by a thick knot of trees that wove together into a wall of branches, leaves, vines, and thorns. The heirs, the champions, and all who followed halted when they saw it. Only the heirs would cross within, and the grove would seal shut once they were inside—the choosing was an inviolable sacrament, their most holy and beautiful ritual. Heirs had said it felt like touching the beginning of time or seeing the heart of creation. Daleina knew she didn't deserve to see such beauty or feel such peace. She also knew her friends wouldn't allow her to refuse. She loved them for that, for their faith in her.

On either side of her, Linna and Revi clasped Daleina's hands. "We started together," Revi said again. "We finish together."

"Your family will understand," Linna said.

They would, Daleina thought. And she couldn't explain why that made her sad.

She looked back over her shoulder and met Ven's eyes. He nodded once at Daleina. Beside him, Bayn whined like an abandoned dog. Ven laid a hand on the wolf's back.

Hamon stood on the other side of Ven. He met Daleina's eyes, and Daleina saw sadness there, the same weight that was inside her, and she was glad that he hadn't come to speak to her. There were no words that she wanted to say.

Together, the heirs walked forward.

She half expected the trees to part for them, but no, there was no magic in Aratay, not until the ceremony began. They walked a path between the trees, one that no one had walked in a long time, not since Queen Fara was crowned. Brambles had grown between the trees, as well as ferns, and the heirs had to climb over and between them until they reached the grove in the center. Twelve of them carried torches, which they set into twelve iron sconces around the grove, scaring back the shadows. The grove glowed with amber torchlight. Above, the sky was thick with spirits, as were the trees. They crawled over the ground and whispered between the leaves, burrowed through the soil, and swarmed in clusters through the air. Daleina reached out to touch them and it felt like brushing her hand against raindrops. "So many," Zie murmured.

Hundreds—thousands—of all shapes, kinds, and sizes filled the grove, and as the last heir crossed through the trees, the spirits pressed closer to one another, crawling and clawing over one another, weaving their bodies until they felt like one writhing creature above, below, and all around them. The women formed a circle, side by side, facing outward.

Daleina heard a whisper to her left: "Choose me."

And then more:

"Choose me."

"Choose me."

"Choose me."

She did not join them. Standing in the grove, she kept her mind silent. She would not be chosen; she would not allow herself to be. Her duty was to make sure one of these others became queen. Stepping into the grove was her last act as an heir.

Around them, the spirits writhed faster. The trees knit together, their bark fusing into a solid wall to keep out the non-heirs, blocking both sight and sound—the ceremony had begun, and their power had returned. Soon, the spirits would make their choice, crown the queen, and the grove would open again. A new era would begin, a better one, with a queen who valued her people's lives and who would bring peace to Aratay. One that would allow them to rebuild and move on from all the deaths and tragedy. She'd watch it happen, from her new village home, with her parents and Arin beside her.

"Choose me!"

"Choose me!"

"Choose me!"

And then, finally, an answer.

"No."

The voices faltered.

The owl woman landed in the center of the grove. Several of the heirs turned to face her, and then more, until all the heirs had pivoted to face the spirit with the woman's body and owl's head. Daleina felt a shiver creep up her spine as the spirit rotated slowly to see all the heirs. She seemed to linger on Daleina's face, but perhaps that was Daleina's imagination. "You wish us to choose? We choose no one. No human will control us."

Impossible, Daleina thought.

"You need a queen," Zie said. "You crave one. The land itself wants you to choose.

Iondra spoke. "Without a queen, you'll destroy everything, through both wanton destruction and unfettered creation."

"You can't resist," Revi said. "We're stronger than you. You must obey our command. Choose one of us. Crown your queen."

In a calm, kind voice—like a mother as she soothes her

child—the owl spirit said, "We already have a command to obey, a blood oath we cannot break."

Daleina was again aware of how many spirits there were, covering the trees so completely that she couldn't see a shred of bark, filling the sky so entirely that they blocked the moon, saturating the earth beneath their feet.

"There's only one command here," Iondra said, just as calm, her singer's voice resonating through the glade. "You must choose."

"And so we shall."

The owl woman snapped her beak open and shut.

"We choose your death."

Daleina leaped backward as the ground exploded at her feet. Earth spirits clawed out of the ground like hundreds of spiders being born. Skittering everywhere, they scrambled on many legs toward the heirs, snagging the hems of their gowns, climbing up, digging their pincers into any flesh they found. Grabbing Revi's arm, Daleina yanked her back as a hand made of mud and scales punched through the soil. Other hands burst through, pushing back the earth and heaving their bulbous bodies out of the ground. They roared, their mouths slick with greasy mud.

Several of the earth spirits charged at Revi and Daleina and then recoiled back, as Revi commanded them, forcing them to veer away. Other heirs were issuing commands as well, forcing the spirits away and down, back into the earth, but more rose up, spilling from new holes, oozing out and spreading across the grove, making the ground roll and pitch beneath them. Daleina thrust her senses outward, searching for a safe patch of earth—and felt the air spirits launch their attack. "Above!" she shouted. Others cried out at the same time.

And the sky fell.

The air spirits thickened into a dark, swirling mass, and descended fast, slamming into the heirs with the force of their wind, knocking Daleina away from Revi and the others. It threw them backward against the trees.

All the trees were alive, moving. Vines shot out, pinning the heirs down, wrapping around their legs, arms, necks. Daleina dropped to the ground, ripping away from the vines, rolling across a clump of tiny earth spirits. They attached to her skin, plunging their teeth and claws into her flesh. She saw another heir beside her, fire spirits burrowing through her ceremonial gown, writhing within her hair, and the heir fought back—the fire spirits flew backward as if thrown and hit the nearest tree. The tree spirits shrieked as they burned.

Smart, she thought. *Use the spirits against one another.*

With the earth spirits clinging to her, Daleina rolled again, toward the fire spirits, and they flew at her. *Burn,* she ordered, and the fire spirits bore into the earth spirits. The earth spirits screamed as the flames touched them, releasing their grip. Jumping up, she ran from both of them.

But there was nowhere to run.

Don't trust the fire, for it will burn you.
Don't trust the ice, for it will freeze you.
Don't trust the water, for it will drown you.
Don't trust the air, for it will choke you.
Don't trust the earth, for it will bury you.
Don't trust the trees, for they will rip you, rend you,
tear you, kill you dead.

All around her, the fire spirits raged, their flames leaping from heir to heir. Daleina called to the water spirits. *Flood them.* She pointed to the burning heirs. Cackling with glee, the water spirits funneled water toward the heirs, enough to douse the flames, but also too much, choking the heirs. *Freeze!* Daleina called to the ice spirits, and an ice spirit, shaped like an icicle with claws darted toward the water, pierced it, stabbing into the arm of the nearest heir but also freezing the water. The heir then seized control of the ice spirit, sending it against the water spirits, much faster than Daleina had done it. Following Daleina's lead, the other heirs turned their powers on the spirits, bearing their will to bend them, forcing them to defend the humans and attack the other spirits. The spirits in turn joined together to batter the heirs.

Everywhere, there was chaos. The air spirits converged on one heir, tossed her into the air, and grabbed her by the feet and hands and pulled. Others whipped in circles, creating whirlwinds that tossed heirs against the trees—she saw Revi scooped up and slammed against a trunk. Bark began to seal around her, encasing her wrists and up her arms toward her neck.

"Revi!" Daleina shouted. "Burn it!"

She wasn't sure if Revi heard, but the fire spirits swarmed her, blackening the tree, until it released her. Revi fell forward onto her knees. Her arms were raw, the skin peeled back where the bark had held her.

Across the grove, Airria was fighting other tree spirits, using air spirits to pluck them off branches and hurl them into the air. She caught several in a whirlwind that she forced to slam against a tree trunk. The spirits burrowed into the bark.

Zie called, "Daleina, watch out!"

A vine shot out like a whip. Other branches stabbed out, hurling spearlike sticks, and Daleina lunged to the side—the spears shot across the grove. She saw one hit another heir, a woman with bright-red hair and a green stone necklace. The shard of wood embedded in her shoulder, and the heir staggered backward into the waiting arms of an earth spirit. The earth spirit pulled her down, fast, and the dirt closed over her before Daleina could even react.

Daleina realized suddenly that she wasn't being attacked, not directly. The spirits were concentrating their attacks on the heirs with the most power, the ones who were raising whirlwinds and controlling walls of fire. She was so weak they didn't see her as a threat—and so she was being over-looked while the spirits attacked her friends.

Looking for her friends, Daleina spun to see Iondra strid-ing toward a tree. Arrowlike sticks protruded from her arms and thighs, but they didn't slow her. She held flames in her hands, two fire spirits coiled on her palms, and she shoved forward with her arms—sending the fire spirits shooting toward the tree. They landed on the bark, burning the tree spirits.

The spirits screamed.

Yes! Daleina wanted to shout. Calling the two fire spirits back to her now-black hands, Iondra turned. She snarled, a tower of magnificent rage, ready to hurl the fire spirits at her next target—and a tree spirit, tiny with stick arms and legs, leapt off a branch and bit into Iondra's throat. Daleina felt herself screaming, heard other screaming, as the spirit tore the flesh from Iondra's neck.

Iondra fell. Knees first, then body.

The fire spirits abandoned her, aiming for other targets. Stumbling, Daleina ran over the roiling ground toward Ion-dra's side. A fire spirit whipped past her, singeing her cheek. Smoke was beginning to cloud the grove. Its thick taste soured in her mouth.

Beyond Iondra's body, another heir fell. Roots wound around her body, and vines poured down her throat. *No! Stop!* But the spirits were too wild to hear Daleina's plea. She tried to redirect them, to picture a tower, a spire, a pal-ace! But they wanted death.

Only death.

All around her, heirs were fighting their own battles—Zie had raised an earth spirit with many arms to batter at a tree spirit. Linna was guiding a waterspout to flush out a pack of earth spirits. Another heir was forcing fire spirits to burn into the heart of a tree. But there were so many. For every spirit they deflected, twenty more flew at them.

Leaving Iondra's body, Daleina scrambled for a tree. She had to get up where she could see. There had to be a way they could work together, use their united power against the spirits. The spirits weren't united in anything but desire—most were no smarter than animals. She climbed a tree, and one of the spirits sent a vine toward her, lengthening it. *Longer,* she told it, and it happily obliged, extending the vine longer and longer, losing track of why it had wanted the vine to grow, subsumed in her will. She grabbed the vine and threw it down toward an heir who was waist-deep in the soil and sinking fast. The heir grabbed on, and Daleina leaned back, holding the rope steady as the heir climbed out of the muck.

She knew her powers weren't strong enough to help the others fight in any significant way, but that was also a blessing: because she was weak, the spirits weren't targeting her. She had the chance to look out over the grove and see the full battle. She began to shout out directions:

"Zie, send a water spout to your left. Catch the earth spirits! Chidra, the fire! Use it against the ice spirits. Drive them down. Melt them. You!"—she pointed to another heir—"Watch the ground! Send the branches into it, make it solid with the wood."

One of the heirs aimed a fire spirit at a tree spirit, forcing the flame-coated spirit to embrace the little body made of twigs. The tree spirit, howling, exploded into fire. *We can't kill them,* Daleina realized. Killing the spirits would destroy Aratay. "Contain them!" she shouted. "Catch them in their own traps! You, use the bark to cage them!"

Another heir guided tree spirits to enclose a large air spirit. Bark sealed around it. Earth spirits pulled fire spirits beneath the soil. Vines wrapped around smaller air spirits, pinning them. "Yes, that's it!" Daleina called. "Revi, use ice!"

Calling to an ice spirit, Revi ordered it to slice through the fire that licked the branches that flailed like whips, freezing both the branches and the flames.

"Linna, make a wave!" Daleina yelled.

Linna drew three water spirits to them and caused a wave to rear up and crash across the grove, washing out the tiny earth spirits. Sputtering, they scrambled onto the writhing roots.

Nearby, Zie caught three fire spirits in a whirlwind and sent them in a fiery tunnel up into the air. They arched over the grove. And Daleina had a horrible thought: they couldn't kill the spirits *and* they couldn't let them leave the grove. Not without a queen. Not without the do-no-harm command in effect. They had to keep the spirits here, focused on the heirs, or it would again be like the moments after Queen Fara died.

No, it would be worse, because everyone who could defend the people was here, either within or just outside the grove. The spirits would run rampant across Aratay.

"Keep them in the grove!" Grabbing Ven's knife out of its sheath, she stabbed at a tree spirit that had latched onto her leg like a bark-coated leech. It left bark adhered to her skin as she flicked it off. As she yanked away the bark, a water spirit slammed into her. Flailing, she tried to hit it with her knife, but it dissolved into water and collapsed around her. It coalesced again, its fishtail in the mud, and Daleina leaped to the next root as it swiped at her.

The spirits were noticing her now.

She couldn't spare any more attention on the other heirs. Every bit of energy she had was spent trying to stay ahead of the spirits, to keep in motion. She ran, leaping from root to writhing root, over the earth spirits. As tree spirits woke the roots and tried to catch her ankles, she thought at the air spirits, *Fly? Play?*

A winged ermine spirit—the same one, or a new one? she didn't know; there wasn't time to care—swooped low, and she leaped and grabbed its legs. It lifted her up, higher than the earth spirits, above the bulk of the fighting. Other air spirits dove for them, and the ermine twisted and turned. Branches hit against Daleina's legs as vines reached up, trying to grab her. Two air spirits landed hard on the back of the ermine, forcing it down. She looked up and caught a glimpse of the owl woman, sinking the talons on her human hands into the ermine spirit. Dangling from ermine, Daleina reached out her legs, felt for a tree branch, and then released, as the ermine spirit was torn away and tossed against a tree. She lost sight of the owl spirit.

Crouching on a branch, Daleina caught her breath and looked down on the grove. It had felt, from within, as if they were winning. Up here, it was clear. They weren't. She felt as if her vision was swimming, and she saw Greytree again, the torn bodies of her friends and neighbors, but this time, the bodies were the heirs.

She counted: twelve left standing.

The others—torn and twisted. One was half-caught within a tree, her face frozen in a scream. Another, body blue-tinged and covered in white flowerlike ice crystals. Another, facedown in the mud.

Her friends . . . she looked at the faces of the twelve. Linna, Revi, Zie . . . Where was Zie? She scanned the grove . . . There. Twisted across a root, a dozen arrowlike branches in her chest. Her eyes were open, staring sightless up at the sky. Beyond her, Evvlyn, her body sliced in half, one arm and one leg gone. "No," Daleina whispered.

She had to tear her gaze away and force her body to climb down the tree. Tree spirits chittered at her, hurling their bodies at her, and she called to an ice spirit, who froze her arm as well as the tree spirits, and then to a fire spirit, who melted the ice and burned her arm. She then plunged Ven's knife into the fire spirit. Flames leaped onto her hand, but the spirit fled. She thrust her hand into the muddy ground, dousing the flames. "Revi! Linna!" she called. They had to fight together, stick close, defend one another.

She waded toward them, trying not to see the bodies of the fallen heirs. They *had* to win here. It had nothing to do with surviving themselves but ensuring that Aratay survived. To ensure that the spirits didn't escape, and kill and kill until the forest ran with streams of blood.

"There are too many," Linna gasped.

"We need a plan, Daleina," Revi said. "Give us a plan."

"Can't let them escape. Can't let them die. Can't let us die. That's as much as I have." Beneath her feet, Daleina felt the soil roll again, and she sent her awareness down to touch tentacles beneath the soil, afraid of what she'd find down there. Knowing exactly what it was.

The earth kraken.

A part of her had been waiting for it. It was a miracle it hadn't struck yet, but perhaps it was prevented by all the spirits above it—the earth was full of them.

"They have to choose a queen," Linna said. The three friends shifted until they stood back to back. Controlling water spirits, Linna created a wall of water around and above them. The fire spirits couldn't penetrate it. The earth spirits were washed away. But the tree spirits walked freely through—Revi dealt with them, forcing them to turn around as soon as they crossed the water barrier.

"I can't keep this up forever," Revi said.

They wouldn't choose, not until their prior command was fulfilled, the blood oath satisfied . . . Daleina thought of Queen Fara, drinking the owl spirit's blood. "We have to take out the owl spirit. She's the one who made the blood oath. She's their leader. Without her . . ."

"On it," Revi said. "Part the water, Linna."

Linna complied, and the water split apart. Revi strode through the break—and with a shriek, the air spirits dove for her. She deflected them, forcing them to spiral away, scooping earth spirits out of the ground. Running, Revi jumped onto the back of an earth spirit with a body of rocks—one twice her size. She held on to it as it clomped over the muddy ground, and she seized control of a fire spirit, forcing it to lengthen itself into a fire bolt.

"You'll need help," Daleina called after her.

"Distract the other spirits," Revi said, jumping from the earth spirit onto an air spirit. She held the fire bolt aloft. "I'll go for the kill."

"On three, I'll drop the water," Linna said. "Ready?"

Reaching with her mind into the bedrock, Daleina touched the earth kraken. It wanted to stretch, to swallow, to eat, to kill . . . but something held it in check. "As soon as you drop the water, get off the ground. I have an idea."

"One, two, three!" Linna released the water spirits. Daleina broke for the roots, running over earth spirits and around air spirits that battered her. As she did, she reached with her mind into the bedrock.

Stretch, she told it. *Swallow. Eat.*

Whatever had been holding it in check dissolved. It obeyed because it wished to. Tentacles flexed, causing the trees to shudder, and the earth spirits toppled. Tree spirits lost their grip. Linna leaped onto the back of an air spirit. Daleina climbed up the trunk of the nearest tree, digging her toes and hands into the bark. A tree spirit entwined itself in her hair. She cut it away with Ven's knife. Climbing onto a branch, she twisted to see Revi, rising up on the back of an air spirit. She stood on the spirit's back, straight and proud, as it flew toward the owl spirit.

The owl spirit hovered in the air, and for a moment Daleina was certain that Revi had her—but then the owl spirit twisted, and . . . Daleina couldn't see! Fire whipped across the grove, and when it cleared, she saw Revi falling, plummeting.

From elsewhere, Linna screamed.

Catch her! Daleina called out. She saw the ermine spirit twist in the air, flying beneath Revi. She landed soft on the ermine's back, and the ermine angled past where Daleina perched.

Revi's throat was torn.

And the owl spirit spoke. "See what you have wrought, murderer? See what your cleverness has done? Can you see, or do you lie amongst the dead already? Soon, you will. Soon, you will all die, and then we will rid these forests of the human pestilence once and for all. The world will be as it was meant to be."

"You were meant to choose a queen!" Daleina shouted. "The world was meant to be balanced. We're meant to have peace!"

"I will be all the queen that my kind needs," the owl spirit said. "You have lost, humans. And now . . . you will all lose your lives." She turned to face the few other remaining heirs, scattered around the grove, blood-covered but still fighting. Still losing.

Daleina felt her own body crumple on the branch, her muscles refusing to listen to her brain. Revi. Zie. Iondra. Eyes filling, she saw the grove. She felt the spirits. So few left against so many. But she couldn't let the owl spirit win. Her friends' deaths would not be for nothing.

As the ermine spirit sailed past her, Daleina rolled off the branch and onto the ermine's back. Eyes burning with tears, she pushed Revi's body off and heard it hit the ground, soft in the muck. *Play,* she told the spirit. *Trick.* She lay in the same position as Revi had, strewn across the blood-coated white fur. With one hand, she smeared blood on her throat and tried to block out thoughts of whose blood it was. She couldn't afford to think or feel. So few left. She breathed shallow, let her eyes unfocus, forced her muscles to lay limp. *Play with her.*

She felt the ermine twist in the air. It trilled as it flew, and she lay limp, unseeing, reaching with her mind for the feel of the owl spirit . . . One hand she kept tucked in the fur, fingers clenched around the hilt of Ven's knife.

Closer.

Closer.

And . . .

Now!

Twisting, she shoved herself up and threw the knife, straight toward where she had sensed the owl spirit. It flew true and fast.

Straight into the owl woman's throat.

The knife embedded up to the hilt. For a moment, the owl woman only stared at Daleina. Her hands touched the knife, and then her wings hung limp. She spiraled down.

Reaching for the earth kraken, Daleina said, *Eat.*

Eagerly, it stretched its tentacle skyward. Grabbing the falling body, it pulled the owl woman down toward the writhing earth. Between the roots, the earth convulsed, and dirt sprayed up as more tentacles pierced the surface. They surrounded her, almost tenderly—until they began pulling her apart. Her feathers were plucked, her arms torn from her body. Dirt flowed into her open mouth, and her owl eyes stared upward, sightless, frozen in a look of surprise, until she was pulled beneath the earth.

Swallowed by the kraken.

The earth convulsed once more, as all the tentacles retreated.

With her disappearance came quiet, as silence then spread through the grove beneath her. It was as if their leader's death had robbed the spirits of their voices. Daleina heard only the flap of the ermine spirit's wings as it spi-

raled down. But the reprieve was only temporary. She felt
the earth spirit stretch again, deep beneath. The spirit hadn't
satiated its hunger in the slightest. It would swallow them,
the roots, the trees, the grove—it would swallow Aratay, if
it could, if she let it.

The problem was, she didn't think she could possibly
stop it.

Someone had to take control, now, before another rose
to take the owl spirit's place. They craved a leader. They
needed . . . a queen. Landing, Daleina looked for Linna or
any of the other heirs . . .

Stillness.

Silence.

Death.

No one spoke. No one moved. No one breathed. Except
the spirits. Hundreds of spirits, hungry, leaderless.

She wanted to cry. She wanted to scream. But she knew
those weren't options for her, no more than she had the
option to go home to her village. She was an heir, and that
duty didn't come with choice. At least not for her. For the
spirits, though . . .

"Choose me," Daleina whispered.

There was no one else.

Choose me.

And the spirits did.

S he felt as if a wave were crashing into her. She'd been reaching out to sense the spirits, but now she felt as if she'd been plunged into them, as if she were inside their bodies, thousands of bodies, and then torn apart and split like an ax hitting a piece of wood. She splintered, and a thousand voices cried into her head.

Daleina felt herself scream but couldn't hear it. She could hear nothing but the roaring of wind, the rush of the fire, the crackle of the ice, the cry of a tree bursting through the soil . . . And in that moment, she was the air, the fire, the ice, the life within the trees, the warmth within the earth. Water was her blood. Soil was her skin. Fire was her heart. Power flooded into her, filling her, then hollowing her.

She felt a sudden, sharp pain in her wrist.

Teeth.

The soft-hard head of a wolf bumped against her, and she was back in her own body. Bayn! The wolf had jolted her back. *Do no harm.* She forced the thought out as fast and far as she could, into every bit of water, of fire, of life. *You will do no harm.*

She felt their will shift, bending to her words, as her command sunk into every spirit she touched. She was strong—so very, very strong now. Her hand still on the wolf, she buried her fingers deeper into his fur, letting the feel and smell of the wolf ground her back in her body. She was herself again, but more. She felt the spirits all around her.

And she forced herself to look around her, at the grove. It took a moment, but her eyes at last told her mind what they saw. Spirits, dead, many of them. And the other forty-nine heirs, all of them, strewn over the roots and rocks, lying in the wet earth.

"No," she whispered.

She stumbled forward, toward where Zie lay, her eyes open, her body twisted at an impossible angle. "No," Daleina whispered again. Standing, she ran from one to the next to the next. Evvlyn, her hands clutched to her torn chest. Revi, her body slashed, red streaking her white gown. Linna, on the root, hands still clinging, mouth open as if she were about to speak, eyes sightless. Iondra. Heirs she'd recently met, Chidra and Berra. Others, whose names she didn't know. All of them.

All of them.

In the center of the grove, Queen Daleina fell to her knees in the blood of her friends as the spirits wove a crown of wood and flowers and placed it gently, reverently, on her head.

Not a crown, she thought. *A wreath, to memorialize this grave.*

OUTSIDE THE GROVE, VEN WAITED. HE HATED WAIT-ing. Stupid tradition, that the champions weren't allowed to accompany their heirs. It was a private ceremony, Fara had explained once, a beautiful moment of harmony and joy that belonged only to spirits and heirs. He should have been there, though. Whether Daleina saw it or not, she was meant to be queen. She had to be. Fara couldn't have died merely to be succeeded by someone who was inferior. Only Daleina had the strength of character . . .

The trees of the grove shifted, their roots moving aside as if they were a curtain parting, and the wolf Bayn charged through. No one else moved. They waited, at a polite distance, ready to proclaim the new queen. It felt as if they were all holding their breaths at once, as still as the air around them.

The wind, slowly, began to blow.

He heard whispers before he saw her. A ripple of words too indistinct for him to decipher. He felt Hamon grip his arm, tight.

The wolf trotted first, his muzzle red, his fur matted. Behind him, Daleina in blood-spattered white walked forward.

Blood? There was never blood at a coronation.

One of the other champions—Piriandra—rushed past Ven. Without slowing, the champion ran past the new queen and into the grove. Daleina halted, not moving, her expression as unreadable as Fara's had been.

"They're dead," Hamon gasped beside him. A guess, but he said it with certainty.

The words did not make sense inside Ven's head. This wasn't how it happened. For hundreds of years . . . this was not how it happened! The heirs walked into the grove and then walked out again, one of them crowned queen. It was a peaceful, beautiful, gentle ceremony. All the songs about it—they sang of its majesty and beauty, the most solemn and sacred moment, when all of the spirits united together to reclaim their power . . .

The other champion, Champion Piriandra, walked slowly out of the grove. Her cheeks pale, her eyes haunted. Ven saw the blood on her boots before he heard her words:

"All hail Queen Daleina! Long live the queen!"

CHAPTER 31

S he buried them there, in the grove, and she allowed the mighty earth spirit to swallow their bodies while the wood spirits blanketed the turned soil with tiny white blossoms, so many that it looked like snow. She then went to Heroes Grove and blanketed the hand-dug grave of Queen Fara in the same blossoms. Only then did Queen Daleina claim her throne, with her champion at her side.

The people called it the Coronation Massacre, and Daleina knew there were songs written about it and about her, the Queen of Blood, who'd been crowned in loss and sorrow. She refused to hear them. Postponing her coronation celebration, she announced that she would speak to the families of the heirs and left the palace nearly as soon as she entered it, to travel the forest to *them*. Her champion, a healer, and a wolf went with her, or so the tales said.

Tales are sometimes true.

She started with the families in the capital, Zie's parents and siblings, Revi's cousins and mothers, Linna's courtier parents . . . She took the wire paths to the border to sit with Evvlyn's border-guard parents, and she climbed to the canopy to visit Iondra's. She learned the names and families of the other heirs who had died in the grove, and she visited them all. She saw the barren places that now marred the once-perfect green of Aratay—the dead places where nothing grew and no rain fell, the places that had died when spirits died—and she mourned them as well, the lost forest. And then she returned to her own family, in their garish green house nestled in a tiny village.

Arin greeted her at the door. Wordlessly, she brought Daleina inside as Ven assumed a guard position outside. The wolf Bayn prowled below, and Hamon climbed onto the roof to check the charms. They took no chances with the new queen's safety.

Daleina looked at her sister. The crutches were gone, and her sister's arms were coated in flour up to her elbows. Her hair was tied back in braids, and she wore a stained apron. She had a smudge of flour on one cheek. "I'd hug you, but you would end up looking like a frosted cookie—" Arin began.

Without a word, Daleina hugged her anyway.

"Your gown!" But Daleina only held her tighter, until Arin folded her arms around her sister. "Was it as bad as they say it was?"

"I didn't mean to become queen," Daleina said, muffled, into her little sister's shoulder.

"Yes, you did." Arin patted her back. "You just didn't mean for it to happen this way." Pulling away, Arin guided Daleina to a chair, and Daleina let her. "Mother and Daddy will be thrilled to see you. They're at the market. It's being rebuilt, not sure if you saw. Everyone's been working together, with only a little of the usual arguments and typical small-town melodrama."

"How are you?"

Arin seemed startled that she'd asked. "Better." She wiggled her leg. "See?"

"Wonderful. But how are you?" Daleina studied her sister. She didn't have dark circles under her eyes, and her cheeks were their usual plumpness. She'd been sleeping and eating, which was good. The flour on her arms showed she was back to baking—a pie, she judged from the pile of peeled apples on the counter.

"I miss him, every second of every day. And everyone tells me that it will get easier with time, and I hate that they say that. I don't want it easier. I don't want to forget him."

Daleina nodded. She'd memorized every tidbit that the heirs' families had told her, and she'd told them as many stories about their lost loved ones as she knew. With every visit, she wished she had more to tell, wished she knew more moments, wished she didn't remember so imperfectly. But it was all she had to give them.

"Are you done now, seeing the families?"

"For now." She'd promised a few she'd return. For some, she was the only link to the memories of their daughter. Others had borne her presence but never wanted to see her again. She didn't blame them. She'd have loved to get far away from the person she'd become and the memories she carried, if that were possible.

"What are you going to do next, now that you're queen? Live in the palace, I know. The old hedgewitch's shop wouldn't be appropriate." Arin gave a little laugh, tight and forced.

"I suppose not," Daleina agreed. "You could come with me. Mother and Daddy too. Live in the palace." She clasped Arin's hands, dry with flour. Her hands had grown, thin and long, like their mother's hands.

"You can ask them, but no. This is our home. Besides, what would we do in the capital? You have bakers enough. And Daddy's a woodsman. He wouldn't like the city. We'll visit." Arin attempted a smile. "You can send me pretty sparkly things from the treasury, if you want."

Trying and failing to smile back, Daleina nodded. She hadn't truly expected more than that. She released Arin's hands. They sat in silence for a few minutes more, and then Arin stood again and bustled over to the stove. "Tea?"

"Yes, please." She didn't like tea. It didn't matter.

Her sister poured blackberry tea for both of them, and they sat and drank it together. Outside, a few scattered tree spirits watched the house from the nearby branches, and a trio of air spirits spiraled up to the sky. As Daleina listened to her sister talk, she also flew between the clouds. As she laughed with her sister, she also burrowed into the earth. And as they cried together, she bloomed with the tiny white flowers that now covered the graves of the hedgewitch and the baker's boy and the other villagers who had died.

Later, when her parents returned, she cried with them as well. And then, when the moon was fat and full, Queen Daleina left her parents and sister and journeyed through the forest, with Ven and Hamon and the wolf, to the palace, her home, and climbed the stairs to her chambers.

Lieutenant Alet—now Captain Alet—stood guard by her door, as Daleina had requested. She'd wanted a guard she could trust. Daleina nodded to her before going inside, and Alet returned the nod. "Welcome home, Your Majesty." Daleina walked out onto the balcony. She thought she'd be alone, alone with her thoughts and the night and the moon and the forest, but the branches around the palace were filled with people. Her people. Men, women, and children from all across Aratay had come, drawn to the palace, to be here when her journey ended. She saw woodsmen and city dwellers, shopkeepers and schoolteachers, children and babies, old men and women, healers and soldiers . . . Each of them held a lantern of firemoss, so it looked as if the trees were filled with caught starlight.

And when they saw her on the balcony of the palace, they cheered so loudly that she thought the forest was shaking. Drums beat, and they sang—every throat, loud, for her.

She saw a hint of movement out of the corner of her eye. Ven. Stepping onto the balcony, he stood beside her. "You will be a great queen, Daleina."

"You still believe that? After . . ." She didn't speak Queen Fara's name.

"Yes." He placed his hand on her shoulder.

On the other side of her, Hamon stepped forward and took her hand, cradling it. "We all believe in you."

She didn't know what to say. Out in the trees, the men, women, and children were dancing and embracing one another and laughing and singing and waving to her.

"Look at them, Daleina. Listen to them." Ven squeezed her shoulder. "Because of you, all these people are still alive."

"I won't fail them."

"I know," he said. "That's why I chose you."

But it wasn't about his choice. And it wasn't about her choice. It was about the people below her . . . and the spirits. They all chose to live, and that meant someone had to wear this crown.

I wanted it, and then I didn't, and now I truly don't. But it's mine, and I will make sure that if I'm the Queen of Blood, that blood will have meant something.

As the singing and laughing and cheering rose up toward the night sky, she covered Ven's hand with one of hers and held Hamon's hand with her other, as she looked out on the people of Aratay, and allowed herself to feel hope.

Acknowledgments

I was ten years old when I started creating worlds. I used to collect all the pieces of scrap paper I could find, tape them together with masking tape, and draw massive room-size maps of imaginary lands. I also kept a box of index cards, and on each card I wrote a made-up name, plus a list of his or her magical powers and talking animal friends. In school, I doodled pictures of fantastical creatures in the margins of my notebooks. And I wrote stories, lots of stories, about wizards and warriors and magic.

I think Renthia was born on those maps and in those index cards.

So I'd like to thank my parents for all the scrap paper. And for all the books that made me dream of filling that paper with other worlds: the Belgariad by David Eddings, *Arrows of the Queen* by Mercedes Lackey, *The Sword of Shannara* by Terry Brooks, *Alanna* by Tamora Pierce, *Dragonsinger* by Anne McCaffrey, *The Blue Sword* by Robin McKinley . . .

I'd like to thank my fantastic agent Andrea Somberg, who said, "Yes, let's do it!" when I sent her my idea for the Queens of Renthia. And I'd like to thank my wonderful editor David Pomerico, who looked at what I'd written and said, "What if this is book two and you make Daleina's story book one?" Without them, this book would not exist. I am extremely grateful for their belief in me, as well as their overall awesomeness. Huge thanks as well to all the amazing people at HarperCollins for everything they did to bring this book to life.

And thank you with all my heart to my family and friends, who willingly walk with me into magical worlds, and to my husband and children, who make this world magical every day. I love you all so much.

Sarah Beth Durst's stunning
Queens of Renthia trilogy continues with

THE
RELUCTANT
QUEEN

Coming July 2017 from Harper Voyager

Read on for a sneak peek!

Everything has a spirit: the willow tree with leaves that kiss the pond, the stream that feeds the river, the wind that exhales fresh snow . . .

And those spirits want to kill you.

It's the first lesson that every Renthian learns.

At age five, Daleina saw her uncle torn apart by a tree spirit for plucking an apple from his own orchard. At age ten, she witnessed the destruction of her home village by rogue spirits. At age fifteen, she entered the renowned Northeast Academy, and at age nineteen, she was chosen by a champion to train as his candidate. She became heir that same year and was crowned shortly after, Queen Daleina of the Forests of Aratay, the sole survivor of the Coronation Massacre. She'd heard at least a half dozen songs about her history, each more earsplitting than the last. She particularly hated the shrill ballads about her coronation, a day she wished she could forget. Instead she had it hammered into her skull by a soprano with overly enthusiastic lungs.

Six months after her coronation, now that the funerals—and so many of her friends' graves—weren't so fresh, all of Aratay wanted to celebrate their new queen, and she was swept along with them. For her part, she planned to demonstrate her sovereignty by healing one of the barren patches created during the massacre and replacing it with a new village tree.

It is, she thought, *one of the worst ideas I've had in weeks.*

At dawn, Daleina lay awake in bed and wished she'd chosen to celebrate with a parade instead. Parades were nice. Everybody liked parades. Or she could have simply declared today a holiday and sent everyone back to bed. *But no, I had to be dramatic and queenly.*

She wrapped her silk robe around her bare shoulders and walked toward the balcony. She'd chosen chambers within the branches of one of the eastern trees, rather than occupying the former queen's rooms. It felt wrong to sleep in a bed owned by the woman she'd helped kill.

Leaning against the smooth wood of the archway, she peeked out. Her loose hair, with its streaks of red, gold, orange, and brown, fell into her face, and she shoved it back. Outside, the lemon-yellow sunlight poked between the leaves, and the bark glowed warm where the light touched it. She saw hints of sky, pale morning blue, but only when the wind blew hard enough to disturb the canopy of leaves overhead. The trees were thick in this part of the forest, with branches that curled around one another and leaves that blocked most of the sky above and all of the earth below. People were already perched in the branches, camped out early for the best view. Of *her.* Sighing, she retreated. *You knew you'd have an audience,* she told herself. *Stop acting so surprised.*

An amused voice behind her said, "They're no longer calling you the Queen of Blood. Now they call you Queen Daleina the Fearless."

Daleina snorted. "The only fearless people I've ever met were frightfully stupid."

Turning, she faced Captain Alet, her devoted guard and friend. Alet always seemed to have an unnatural sense of when Daleina was awake. She'd entered soundlessly and now stood in front of the ornate door. She wore her leather armor and had knives strapped to her arms and legs. Her thick black hair with the white stripe was wound up and pinned in place, and she'd tucked at least two more knives into her curls.

"It's supposed to be a compliment, milady, but if you'd like me to discourage it, I could always stab a few of the worst offenders."

"You're too kind. Bloodthirsty, but kind." Squaring her shoulders, Daleina crossed to her wardrobe. She opened the doors to reveal her celebration dress, a confection of lace that shimmered in the morning light. She touched the fabric lightly. Seventeen seamstresses had worked on it, painstakingly adding hundreds of glass beads so she would look as if she'd been sprayed with sparkling dew. The dress would catch the light even in near darkness. It was far and away the loveliest—and most impractical—thing she'd ever seen.

"You'll have many more songs written about you after today," Alet said.

"Especially if I die."

"Especially then," Alet agreed.

Daleina arched her eyebrows. "You're supposed to say that of course I will succeed. That I'm the finest queen that Aratay has ever seen, the best of the best, the jewel of the forest, the scourge of the spirits that spill our blood, and so forth." All the courtiers were fond of those phrases, and Daleina was certain they were recycling them from when they'd used them for her predecessor, Queen Fara. Daleina knew full well she'd never been the best of the best.

She'd merely been the only one left.

Alet was silent, and then she said, "You can still call it off." Her expression was blank, hiding her thoughts expertly. Daleina had practiced that expression in the mirror, but it never quite worked for her. A twitch of her lips or her eyebrows always gave her away.

"You know I can't."

"You *can*," Alet corrected. "You *won't*."

Daleina studied her friend. Alet had a fresh scar above her eyebrow. It was puckered and red, but whoever had struck her had missed her eye. She'd chosen to wear her war armor today, instead of ceremonial. The leather still had the royal crest, but it was painted gold and green, rather than encrusted with ornaments that could snag on a branch or a weapon. *Why had she—*

Suddenly, Daleina understood. "You can't follow me. I must do this alone. That's what's upsetting you."

Alet made a face. "You'll be vulnerable to arrows, spears, any kind of thrown implement. This isn't like the trials, where you're separated from the populace. You'll be exposed to everyone and, while all your people love you deeply, a few of them also want to kill you."

"Human enemies don't concern me," Daleina said. "The spirits will protect me."

"You know you can't trust them."

"In this, I can."

Alet shook her head. The knives in her hair did not move. One stray curl slipped out of its pins to touch her forehead, though. Daleina was surprised Alet allowed even that much out of her control. "The spirits want you dead," Alet said flatly.

"They want to kill me. Slight difference. If they allow a human archer to pierce my heart with his or her arrow, then they're denied the pleasure of skinning me alive." Daleina lifted the beautiful dress out of the wardrobe and carried it to her bed. "Help me change?"

Sighing, Alet left her post by the door and crossed to the bed.

"You should call one of the palace caretakers to assist you. This ridiculous dress has at least a thousand buttons."

Daleina slid her robe off her shoulders, and it fell into a puddle of silk at her feet. "It has thirty-seven buttons, and I don't want any caretakers with me today. I want my friend."

She saw a muscle in Alet's cheek twitch, nearly a smile, and Daleina smiled back. She held up her arms, and Alet dropped the dress over Daleina's head. She felt as if she were wrapped in a cloud. The layers of skirts fluttered around her. Presenting her back to Alet, she faced the mirror while Alet buttoned her. She'd need a touch of powder under her eyes to hide the signs of sleeplessness. She couldn't let anyone suspect that she was at less than her full strength. In that, Queen Fara had been correct: the people didn't want to think they had a weak queen. Perhaps add a bit of pink to her cheeks. She looked pale, sheathed in the shimmering white and gold. "Regal or sickly?" Daleina asked.

Stepping back, Alet surveyed her. "You look ethereal." Daleina rolled her eyes. She'd never been described as "ethereal" in her life. "Just tell me if I need paint or powder."

"Neither. You're lovely, and the people should see your loveliness."

"You're in the oddest mood today, Alet." Daleina faced the mirror again and frowned. The sight of the queen on her first celebratory appearance should comfort the people and set the correct tone for the rest of the celebration. She shouldn't have allowed the dressmakers to add so many layers of skirt or to leave her arms bare. She felt both exposed and confined. Spinning in a slow circle, she watched herself in the mirror.

Quietly, Alet asked, "Have you blacked out again, Your Majesty, since the last time?"

She halted. Yes, she had, alone in her bath last night. "Not once," she lied. "It must have been a fluke. But Master Hamon will find answers. He has my complete confidence— and six vials of my blood, which should be more than enough to run every test he can think of."

"You could postpone this until—"

"Enough, Alet. If you're trying to shake my confidence, you're doing a very good job of it." Leaving the mirror,

Daleina crossed to her jewelry box. She selected a simple necklace, delicate leaves carved out of wood and strung on a ribbon of silk. It had been a gift from her family, after she'd been crowned. Her mother had whittled the leaves, and her sister had woven the ribbon. Coming behind her, Alet took the necklace.

Holding her hair up, Daleina let Alet clasp it around her throat. Alet then took a brush and brushed Daleina's hair until it cascaded smoothly over her shoulders and back. Neither of them spoke, until a bell chimed outside.

"Be strong, milady," Alet said. "Half your chancellors think you're foolish to interact with spirits without an heir ready. But then again, half your chancellors are too afraid to venture beyond their chambers."

"And the other half?"

"Already in the trees, ready to cheer your victory."

Daleina turned to face Alet. "And where will you be?"

Alet's expression didn't alter. "Right here, waiting for you to return."

Embracing her, Daleina pressed her cheek to Alet's cheek. The hilt of one of Alet's knives dug into her ribs, but Daleina ignored it. It felt good to have a friend again, as if the friends she'd lost—Linna, Revi, Mari, Zie, Iondra—were all still with her somehow, carried on by Alet. "If I were sentimental, I'd say you were sent to comfort me."

"If you were sentimental, I wouldn't like you half as much."

Releasing her, Daleina laughed.

"Go," Alet said. "Show them all what it truly means to be queen."

QUEEN DALEINA OF ARATAY SWEPT ONTO THE BALCONY. Hidden in her hair were pins to help keep her crown firmly on her head, and hidden in her bodice was Champion Ven's knife to help keep her head firmly on her neck. As she emerged, she heard the cheers from her people, who filled every available branch in all directions. Their voices blended into the wind and blew into her. She felt as if she were breathing in their love, or at least their enthusiasm. Raising one hand, she smiled at them, and they cheered louder.

Very nice, she thought. *Now, go away.*

Carefully and deliberately, she blocked them out—the sight of them, the sound of them—and she breathed, filling her lungs and then emptying them completely. She narrowed her focus to only that, her breath. Swallowing the wind, she tasted the air, sharp with pine. And then she walked forward, three steps to the lip of the balcony.

Collectively, the crowd fell silent. She felt their silence as a change in the wind, a shift of breath. Grown from the tree itself, the balcony jutted out far above the forest floor. It had no rail, only a delicate braid of living vines to decorate the edge.

Catch me. She sent the order flying like an arrow out of her mind and into the world. The moment the words left her, she flinched, even though she'd braced herself. It felt as if a strip of skin had been ripped from her body. Before the coronation, she hadn't had the power to issue a command that broad and expect to be obeyed. She'd had to trick, redirect, and coax the spirits as if they were uncooperative toddlers, but now she was expected to use the power the spirits had given her. She didn't like it, but she wasn't about to let anyone see that.

She stepped onto the air.

The wind shrieked in her ears as she plummeted. She closed her eyes, stretched her arms wide, and focused on the feel of the air slapping her. *Catch me!* She put all the force of her mind into the command, devoid of doubt, of fear, of any emotion. She would be obeyed. *Now!*

Shrieking like the wind, the air spirits whipped around her. Opening her eyes, she saw their faces, translucent with empty eye sockets and pointed teeth. They reached for her with pale multi-jointed fingers, and they caught her dress, each layer spread out until she looked like a glittering cloud.

Lift me, she ordered.

She felt their hands on her back, rotating her until she stood upright on the backs of one of them. Rising up, she tilted her face toward the canopy of leaves above and did not think about how close to the forest floor she'd come. The people in the branches were cheering again, and the air spirits snarled and swiped at them.

Do not hurt them.

Hissing, the spirits retracted their claws. A few dug their claws into the fabric of her dress, and she felt the tips on her flesh, but they did not pierce her hard enough to bleed.

Higher.

The spirits drove her upward, through the branches. Leaves slapped her face. Tiny branches stung her arms. The white lace dress wore flecks of blood between the glass beads, but it still sparkled as she burst through the canopy of leaves into the sky above the forest.

Daleina filled her lungs with the air from above. It tasted as clean and sharp as water from a mountain stream. Few ever breathed this air. Below her lay the forests of Aratay, a vast sea of green that stretched from the true sea in the south to the mountains in the north and to the untamed lands in the west. Soaring, she stretched her hands out and felt the leaves brush against her palms. She felt like a bird, riding free on the wind, until one of the spirits leered at her, its teeth bared and its tongue darting in and out. Glancing down, she checked to be certain she was high enough, and then she changed from a command to a question: *Play?* She sent the question spiraling out across the clouds—and she felt it answered.

Undulating through the clouds, an air spirit flew toward her. It had the sinewy body of an ermine and the wings of a bat. Flying beneath her, it lifted her higher in the sky. *Race?*

she asked it. She pictured a map in her head, of the forests from above, and, with her mind, pinpointed the place she wanted to go.

The ermine spirit trilled a challenge to the others. They bugled and chirped their answers, and then the race was on. Daleina wrapped her arms around the spirit's neck, squeezed with her thighs, and held on as it shot forward into the clouds. Droplets pelted her face, and then she burst out above the clouds into the sunlight. Other spirits zoomed alongside them, dipping and soaring between one another.

Slowing, the spirits dove toward an opening in the canopy. She heard their chittering laughter, like the sound of breaking glass, and she suppressed a shudder. Several feet from the bare ground, they halted and released her. She landed in a crouch and then stood.

Out of the corner of her eye, she saw they weren't alone. Seven men and women stood shoulder to shoulder in a semicircle on the edge of the barren patch, but Daleina didn't acknowledge them yet. Instead, she bowed to the air spirits. "You have honored me with the beauty of your world. I thank you."

Momentarily, the air spirits quit snarling. One of them placed its hands together, its long fingers touching one another. She saw specks of red at the tips of its nails and wondered if that was her blood or another's. The spirit bowed to her, and then all the air spirits spiraled together up and up into the circle of blue sky above the grove. She wondered what the masters at the academy would think of her approach and then decided she didn't care, not today.

Straightening, Daleina turned to face the representatives of the local village. There were four women and three men, all dressed in ceremonial robes. In unison, they bowed low to her. She bit back a shout at them to go home. She didn't want or need an audience for this. The spirits were capricious, and she'd need to summon many for this task. But these women and men knew that and had come anyway. *Spare me from curious fools*, she thought but didn't say. It would be unqueenly behavior to insult the very people she'd come to help. *And I'm the queen.*

She had to keep reminding herself of that.

The eldest hobbled toward her. Her face was sunken in so many wrinkles that her eyes were barely visible. Her lips were cracked and pale, and she licked them before she spoke. "On behalf of all, we thank you."

Thank me when it's done, she wanted to say, but again bit her tongue. A queen didn't show doubt or weakness, and this ritual was as much about appearance as it was about results. In a formal voice that carried across the grove, she asked, "Do you have the seed?"

Trembling, the woman held out her hand, fingers curled shut. Daleina waited while the woman turned her fist over and then opened her fingers. An acorn lay on the palm of her hand.

Daleina cupped her own hands, and the woman poured the acorn onto them. "Thank you for this gift." The words of this ritual were simple, even if the action that followed was not. Dropping the formal tone, she pleaded, "Please, would you return to your village? For your own safety." *Go, you trusting fools.*

The woman shook her head. "We will stay, Your Majesty. You will keep us safe."

Daleina tried again. "I can't promise that. You should leave."

But the woman only smiled. "We trust your power. And we trust you." Behind her, all of them bobbed their heads. "You ended the Coronation Massacre."

She wanted to argue more, but she couldn't spare the time or the energy, and she most certainly didn't wish to talk about Coronation Day, a day that had gone from beautiful ritual to nightmare fodder when, rather than choosing

whom to crown queen, the spirits had killed all the other heirs—her friends—and nearly killed her. She closed her eyes briefly to blink away that memory, and opened them up to look at the elders.

Pure trust shone from the villagers' eyes, the way babies gaze at their mothers. Telling herself to let their faith fuel her, Daleina knelt, laid the acorn on her lap, and dug her fingers into the soft earth. *Come to me*, she called. She felt the earth shift and rumble, as if it trembled from an earthquake. *Gently, softly, come to me.*

The earth buckled under her, and she saw the men and women topple to their knees. *Idiots*, she thought, and then she didn't spare them another thought. This required all her concentration. *Gently, softly, come to me*, she repeated.

A mud-covered hand burst out of the ground. Moss peeled away as if it were the peel of an orange, and a small manlike creature pulled himself halfway out of the ground. His voice was the crunch of rock, but she didn't understand the words. She guessed he was insulting her. She showed him the acorn. *Prepare the earth*, she told him.

His face stretched into a toothless smile. Several tongues flicked out. She followed his gaze and saw he was ogling the villagers. This was the most critical time: after a spirit was summoned, when its hatred of humans was freshest.

Again, she pushed her will firmly at him: *Dig, now.*

With a scowl, he dove back into the earth. She stood, knees braced, as the ground rolled beneath her like the sea. He and his kin would soften it beneath, prepare it for the roots that would come. Next, she needed tree spirits. Lots of them. *Come*, she called to the trees, the bushes, the grasses, the thorns, the flowers. Stepping back, she dropped the acorn into the hole that the earth spirit had left behind. *Make it grow, tall and strong.*

Laughing, the tree spirits separated themselves from the shadows of the forest. Tall, lithe, and translucent green, they

danced through the grove. Flowers flowed from their hair. Moss flourished in their footprints. Daleina spread her arms wide, welcoming them. She pushed her mind toward them, sharing an image of the acorn, sprouting. The spirits flowed to her, pressed close, and then swirled around the hole.

Yes! That's right!

Her vision split, and she saw through their eyes as they poured their energy into the acorn. The nut split open, and a tendril of green burst from its brown shell. It unfurled. Still laughing, the tree spirits danced faster, a whirl around her. She felt the sprout thicken and grow. More leaves poked out of it, and she felt as if the leaves were poking out of her flesh. Below, the earth spirit softened the soil, and the acorn's roots shot through the ground, thickening and hardening. The tree shot toward the sky, higher and higher, growing thicker and thicker. Branches stabbed out from it.

Shape it, she ordered the spirits. She pictured the trunk opening wide to form houses within. The branches were to be stairs, rooms were to be formed and shaped as if carved out of the soft inner wood. She pressed this image out toward the spirits, and they howled—they wanted the tree to be wild and free; she wanted it to be a new home for the villagers who lived on the forest floor, a safe home above the dangers of the wolves and bears and countless creatures who hunted at night.

She pressed harder and harder, bearing down on the spirits, filling their minds, and they in turn forced the tree to grow in the shape she pictured. *Grow higher, wider, like this* . . . She added more rooms and more. This tree would house many. Above, the branches spread into a canopy, blotting out the sun.

And then, without warning, her mind went dark.

Sightless, she heard the spirits shrieking and then heard the men and women screaming—for her, for themselves— as she toppled onto the churned dirt.